Holy Comfort

*For Margaret –
Find comfort in
mystery!
C.R. Compton*

C. R. Compton

HILLIARD HARRIS

HILLIARD HARRIS

P.O. Box 275
Boonsboro, Maryland 21713-0275

This novel is a work of fiction. Names, characters, places and incidents either are the product of the author's imagination or are used fictitiously. Any resemblance to actual persons, living or dead, events, or locales is entirely coincidental.

Holy Comfort Copyright © 2006 by C.R. Compton

All rights reserved. No part of this book may be reproduced or transmitted in any form or by any means, electronic or mechanical, including photocopying, recording, or by any information storage and retrieval system, without the written permission of the Publisher, except where permitted by law.

First Edition-June 2006
ISBN 1-59133-172-2

Book Design: S. A. Reilly
Cover Illustration © S. A. Reilly
Manufactured/Printed in the United States of America
2006

For my mother

Chapter One

THE CROWS MEANT nothing to Page Hawthorne. There were always crows in Rockville, and the trio this morning picking apart her carefully bagged garbage was annoying, no more. No, it was just a day like any other, unfolding on schedule. Her sons, Walter and Tal, inhaled their breakfasts according to routine, scooped up their brown-bag lunches and backpacks and headed for the car. They tumbled and rolled and vaulted out of the kitchen, bickering non-stop until she dropped them off at their school amid a flurry of hugs and kisses and restated pledges of love. As soon as Page was alone she threw a word of thanksgiving to God and entreated Him to fill her sons with faith, virtue, knowledge, temperance, patience, and godliness. Just the usual. She smiled and turned her aging Volvo toward work.

As always Page avoided the highway, taking the slow but steady route, the path that curved gently eastward past an industrial, commercial stream of storefronts and restaurants and auto repair shops, until it gradually gave way to the broad lawns and impressive homes of Middle Essex. The twenty-minute trip forced her to slow down after her always frantic mornings and to gather her thoughts before the work day began. This morning she sang along with Ralph Stanley and the Clinch Mountain Boys, lending them her best high lonesome sound, then paused before parking her car to help Dwight Yoakam and Ralph put a good scald on "I Just Got Wise." When she opened her eyes at the end of the song she smiled at the dignified stone edifice of the Church of the Holy Comforter with a possessive pride typical of the entire parish membership. It was beautiful. She felt a great wave of love rise within her, but the feeling was transitory. Her eyes drifted down the street and she noted the cars parked by the church. A Rolls Royce, a Mercedes, a Lincoln, two BMWs, and a Land Rover waited decorously at the curb as their owners attended the seven thirty Morning Prayer service. *Oh, you cows of Bashan,* she thought...and, *God help me, I am one.*

Page was early. She had forgotten about Morning Prayer and its increasing popularity—the street was clogged with cars and she had to park a block away. Normally she arrived long after the morning service was over, when those who had attended had scattered like blown leaves, skittering to their cars, nodding to each other and calling words of mutual acknowledgement. She had heard about this surge in attendance at staff meetings and had seen the Reverend Miles Costello, associate priest at Holy Comforter, bow his head and nod modestly as his friends gleefully attributed it to his popularity and charisma. She would have been blind not to notice the coterie of mature women he was gathering around him, all of them social leaders with money and self-confidence to spare. Dangerous, she had thought, but a well-known pattern in priests of a certain type. Miles Costello was the type. He owned a renovated condo, had taken a four-week trip to Ireland last summer, and it was rumored that he would soon be entering an expensive postgraduate program at the university. It did give one pause. She paused long enough to remind herself once again that it was none of her business.

Page hoisted her over-stuffed canvas briefcase and a plastic crate loaded with folders out of her Volvo and, balancing the crate on one hip, closed the back of the wagon. She transferred the briefcase and her purse into the crate and carried it, straight-armed, to the huge wooden doors of the church. Turning, she hooked one elbow skillfully through the handle and pulled the door open, backing through the doors, muttering cheerfully that there was never anyone around when you needed help.

As she entered the building, she felt suddenly and with a strange shiver the change from the brisk, clear air outside to the heavier, warmer air of the dark narthex. She stepped lightly past the open doors to the nave, glancing down the long center aisle to the marble altar, still placed, despite the bishop's disapproval, against the wall. Change came slowly to Holy Comforter, if at all. She murmured along with the worshippers *For thou only art holy, thou only art the Lord*...and crossed the polished stone floor into the carpeted hallway. Down the stairs, still struggling, she paused at the fire doors. What was that smell? This time she had to put her crate down in order to open the heavy glass doors. She wrinkled her nose again. *What?* Then realization, like torn fabric, ripped open her mind.

Smoke. Down the hall. Coming out of Miles' office. Run. Go. She lurched around the corner and stumbled down the hall, coming to an abrupt halt, her arms spread wide, at the door. Her hands gripped the door trim. Oh Jesus. Jesus. *Miles.* Oh God. She turned and ran down to the fire doors and tore the alarm out, and as it shrieked forth, she turned back and staggered into the laundry room across from Miles' office, barely reaching the sink before a spume of vomit projected out of her. Leaning over the sink she retched violently and gagged till she felt turned inside out, sinking finally, shaking and weak, to her knees. She folded, then, like a rejected rag doll against the metal legs of the sink.

She could not stay there, however. No way. She struggled to her knees and looked around until her eyes settled on a bucket, a metal one used for cleaning. She crawled over to the bucket and, bracing herself on it, stood up. She filled it as best she could with water, then, carrying it with both hands, stumbled into Miles' office. *Be bold, Little Sister.* She stood over his

Holy Comfort

inert body and proceeded to pour the water carefully on his head. Steam erupted where the water met the smoking coals. Page turned away.

She wanted to run and never look back, but, steeling herself...*Be bold, Little Sister*...Page knelt at his side and looked for signs of life. She could not bring herself to touch him. He must be dead, she thought. *He must be dead.* It was a grotesque sight. His eyes stared unseeing. He did not see her. He would never see her again. Oh Miles. With all our heart and with all our mind, let us pray to the Lord, saying, "Lord, have mercy."

It looked, she thought numbly, as if Miles Costello had been stabbed in the back. After he had fallen to the floor, burning coals had evidently been poured on his head. Another bucket, similar to the one Page had filled with water, was turned on its side under a blue chair. For the salvation of our souls, let us pray to the Lord, *Lord have mercy.*

She knew not to touch. She had seen enough TV shows and read enough mysteries to know that the police would want the scene to be untouched. *Don't touch.* She looked up and saw the crow on the bookshelf. Its beak was open. She screamed. She screamed again. That we may end our lives in faith and hope, without suffering and without reproach, let us pray to the Lord, *Lord have mercy.*

THE RECTOR, HAVING uttered familiar words of comfort from the Book of Common Prayer, gazed down at the half glasses folded in his hands. He seemed to be having trouble gathering his thoughts. Page Hawthorne likewise looked down at her own hands, fixing her eyes on the rings on her right hand, which she fiddled with nervously. She knew what was coming; most of the other twenty or so people in the room did not. She could not blame her boss, therefore, for a certain degree of abstractedness in his manner. His associate has just been found horribly murdered in the building, *in the church.* Not that they were particularly friendly. In fact, some people thought they didn't get along at all, that they hated each other, that Miles had delusions about becoming the rector himself. If the rector had been found dead instead of Miles, Page might even have suspected Miles. But that wasn't what had happened. As it was, she could never imagine Charles Pinkney, their rector of five years, indulging in violence, much less murder. He was too soft-hearted (some thought weak), too adept at turning the other cheek. Now, as he raised his head to address his staff, his brown eyes burdened by the weight of their lids and glassy with unshed tears, Page's own eyes stung as she imagined what trials he would be put through.

"My heart is sick," the rector said and sighed. He looked around the room slowly and, Page thought, beseechingly at the faces circling the table. They stared blankly back at him, waiting. He straightened his shoulders. "Miles Costello is dead."

The group seemed to suck in air en masse. At least one person started to sob.

"He was scheduled to read Morning Prayer, but when he did not show up, parishioner Tom Ward read the service. Nobody thought much of it, apparently. Not enough to look for him anyway. His body was discovered at seven forty-five this morning by Page Hawthorne. The police arrived on the scene shortly thereafter. Detectives Roy Merton and Leona Vesba will head the investigation." He nodded in the direction of the two strangers in the room. "Detectives, perhaps one of you would like to say something now," the rector said hopefully, indicating the tall, dark man who had heretofore been leaning against the wall in the corner, his arms crossed in front of his chest, and the red-haired woman next to him, whom Page could not help notice had alarmingly fat legs. All eyes left the rector and moved to the detectives.

"Hello," Detective Merton said, stepping forward. "I'm very sorry for your loss." He paused then, surveying the room. His gaze settled on Page who sat to the left of the rector between the Reverend Colin Whitefish and Sophie Carl, the clergy secretary. "Ms. Hawthorne handled a difficult situation admirably. Thank you." He nodded. Page smiled weakly and looked down at her hands. Usually she liked to be singled out and praised, but today, under these unlikely and shocking circumstances, she wished she could disappear. Her heart raced.

"At this point we know very little. Miles Costello was killed early this morning, not long before Ms. Hawthorne discovered the body. He had been stabbed once with a black-handled kitchen knife, which was still lodged in his back. Burning coals—actually barbeque briquettes—had been piled on his head. We don't know yet if he was dead from the stab wound when this occurred."

A group gasp was uttered at these last words, and Sophie Carl laid her head on the table with an audible thud, which made the already jumpy assemblage turn and look at her. Midge McIntyre, the Director of Outreach Ministries, began to cry softly.

Merton cleared his throat and reached out his hand to the rector who passed him his Book of Common Prayer. "Mr. Pinkney tells me that the designated psalm for October ninth, today, is one forty. Please bear with me while I read verses 8-10."

"Do we have a choice?" muttered Gracie Griggs, the Newcomer Coordinator. "God, I need a cigarette."

"Amen to that," nodded Diana Dunwoody, the church Registrar.

Merton stared at the two of them for an entire ten seconds. Gracie Griggs met his gaze as she slumped in her chair. Diana Dunwoody, underweight and nervous, looked away down the table. Merton once again cleared his throat and began: *"Do not grant the desires of the wicked, O Lord, nor let their evil plans prosper. Let not those who surround me lift up their heads; let the evil of their lips overwhelm them. Let hot burning coals fall upon them; let them be cast into the mire, never to rise up again."*

"So the murderer," drawled choirmaster Baylor Valentine, "was a religious person, most assuredly an Episcopalian."

"What a relief!" sniffed Gracie Griggs. "Thank God it wasn't an outsider."

Holy Comfort

Heads swiveled back and forth around the table like spectators at a tennis match. Several mouths hung open stupidly, including the one belonging to Sophie Carl, who slapped the table and whined, "How can you joke about this? I can't believe you can joke at a time like this."

"Who's joking?" deadpanned Gracie, staring at Merton as Diana Dunwoody sputtered beside her. "No, I'm serious," she said. "Isn't that the detective's point? It had to have been an inside job, someone who knew the lay of the land, the service schedule, who knew Miles for God's sake. So I guess they can round up the usual suspects and we can get on with our lives."

Everyone stared at Gracie. *It's too early for her to have started drinking*, thought Page, glancing at her watch.

"The Usual Suspects?" asked Merton.

Gracie looked at the puzzled detective squarely in the eye, pausing for effect. "Yes, Detective. The cinematic allusion aside I meant, A: those people Miles was counseling at present and B: those people Miles was screwing at present." She paused again. "You might want to start with your capable Ms. Hawthorne," she concluded with a toss of her hand in Page's direction.

"Oh good lord, Grace, please," interrupted the rector. "We musn't make a bad situation worse by atttacking each other. I expect the detectives will want to speak with each of us individually. Am I correct in assuming that, Detectives?"

"Yes, sir. We'll begin right after the meeting," said Merton whose gaze had once again settled on Page, sitting startled and pale and silent.

"Excuse me?" said Page, who had felt unusually cold throughout the meeting but now felt unusually warm. She also realized suddenly that she was in serious danger of being sick again. She quickly gathered her day-timer and keys and unceremoniously rose from her chair and headed for the door, muttering another "excuse me" as she passed behind the rector. Merton, his eyebrows raised, opened the door for her and followed her out.

The rector, his eyes still aimed doggedly at his hands on the table, said, "Well, I suppose we'll close for now so that the detectives can get on with their investigation. I just want to say that Colin and I will, of course, be available to all of you...if you want to talk.... I'll get in touch with the diocesan office. They'll have people who can help. I know you'll want to talk about this...terrible thing...So please, do feel free..."

"However," said Colin Whitefish leaning forward beside him. "I'm sure we don't need to tell you not to talk to the press at all. The rector will handle all outside interviews."

"Yes," nodded Pinkney. "Of course." He paused, gathering his stray thoughts. "Oh, by the way, is everyone here? Are we missing anyone?"

"Charlotte Pentecost," volunteered Diana Dunwoody. "I haven't seen her yet this morning."

"She called in about eight forty-five. Said she was having car trouble," explained Tammy Spivy, the church receptionist. "I told her what had happened. I hope that was okay."

"Yes, of course," said the rector distractedly. "I'll call her after the meeting. Anyone else? No...then, as our savior Christ hath taught us we are bold to say, *Our Father who art in heaven...*"

Everyone around the table, responding to the familiar words, stood and clasped hands with his or her neighbor, except for Baylor Valentine who stepped back and folded his arms. Det. Vesba, taken off-guard, joined hands with Tammy Spivy and Midge McIntyre and continued on with the rest, "*hallowed be thy name. Thy kingdom come, thy will be done...*"

PAGE HURRIED THROUGH the Great Hall and out a side door that led to the small, enclosed Latham Garden. She steadied herself on the arm of a black iron patio chair, then lowered herself into it as if she were fragile and might break. Merton, who had followed her through the Great Hall, stopping to pour a glass of ice water, entered the Garden and looked around. He offered her the glass of ice water in his hand. "Thanks," Page said, taking it and sipping. "I really thought I was going to be sick again."

Merton took the seat across from her under a spreading leafless dogwood tree. He said nothing, but gazed at Page sympathetically. Her dark blond hair hung in smooth sheets to her shoulders and her almond-shaped hazel eyes caught the sun and looked amber. She wore jeans and a simple white t-shirt. She was thin, almost skinny, and nervous. One mocassin-clad foot swung up and down mechanically as if some unseen hand had turned a key, winding it up. "You know," she stammered, after taking another sip of water, "I don't usually dress this way for work, but I wasn't planning to...meet with the public today. I thought I was going to spend the day sequestered in my office putting together the Holy Comforter newsletter on the computer. That's why I came in early. Funny how things turn out. Anyway, it was so embarrassing having to go to a staff meeting like that."

"Embarrassing?"

"Well, I don't know...not embarrassing. I just felt powerless, like a little girl or something. Like going onstage without the right costume. This whole day just started off all wrong...and I'm freezing," she said, standing up. She began to walk, rubbing her arms as she paced. "I wore a sweater, but, of course, it's like a sauna in my office. Now I can't get warm."

"Here," said Merton, standing up. "Would you like my jacket?"

Page looked over at the detective, as if noticing him for the first time. "No," she answered, an expression of shock spreading over her face. "Don't be silly. Of course, not...I'm fine."

"But you said..."

"I know what I said," she interrupted, her teeth beginning to chatter. She sat down and made a motion with her hands, signifying that there would be no more discussion of his coat. She spilled some water and put the glass down on an iron table. "Just forget it. I'm okay...I just keep picturing *Miles*...and remembering that *smell*...and then that woman, that Gracie Griggs...I haven't the slightest idea what she was talking about, by the way...I can't imagine," she said, her voice trailing off as she stared at the glass of water on the table. "Episcopalians do not cry in church," she said. "Everyone knows that."

"If you say so."

"No," she said picking up the glass of water. "I don't say so. That was my husband who told me that. Episcopalians wear linen dresses and starched cotton shirts. They do not stain their clothes with tears. They do not respond to the music and the words and the ceremony emotionally, but intellectually. It is the denomination for thinking people. That's what Chester always said, anyway." She turned to him, her eyes wide and bright. "And that's the way they think around here. Perhaps you would be wise to keep that in mind."

The detective nodded and put his hands in his pockets. Then the door swung open and the rector stepped out. "Page, are you all right?" he asked, concern creasing his brow.

"I'm fine," she said putting down the glass of water. She stood up to meet him as he crossed the brick floor and embraced her. The detective looked on, his face expressionless. He sat down. Page covered her mouth with both hands as she began to cry, great choking sobs. "I'm sorry." Her shoulders shook.

The rector patted her back and handed her his handkerchief. "Page, you're shivering."

"I'm sorry," she said inanely. "I'm freezing. I can't get warm..."

"Here. Take my jacket," the rector said calmly, taking it off as he spoke and wrapping it around her small shoulders. "Better?"

"Thank you. Yes, I feel better."

"Let's go to my office, Page. I have a few minutes."

"All right," she said, turning to go, still leaning against him. The ice water sat forgotten on the table, as invisible apparently as the detective under the dogwood tree.

Chapter Two

MERTON FOUND HIS way through the Great Hall to the reception desk and asked Tammy Spivy for directions back to Miles Costello's office. He made a few wrong turns, but accomodating staff members set him straight. Standing in the doorway, he surveyed the room. Two uniformed policemen worked separately, moving around the body of Miles Costello, which still lay where it had fallen on the floor. Detective Vesba, who had been kneeling by the body, rose precariously, both knees cracking, and handed her partner a plastic bag full of paper telephone messages. "These were on top of the body," she explained. "I've made a list of who called. Do you think anyone could have been pissed enough that this priest didn't return a call that they killed him for it?"

"You never know," he said mildly, handing her back the bag as he turned away from the body. The smell of scorched hair and flesh was strong in the room. "I doubt, though, if he would have been stupid enough to leave a message with his own name on it on top of the body."

Vesba shrugged. "So what gives?" she said. "Has Page Hawthorne recovered from her fainting spell?"

"I don't know," said Merton quietly. "She went with the rector to his office."

She pulled back one side of her mouth. "I suppose he'll administer some smelling salts or perhaps a little laying on of hands is called for." She cackled.

Merton made no effort to contradict or agree with her.

Vesba grumbled, then slashed the air horizontally with her hand. "Can you believe this office? It couldn't have been cleaned in months! There's dust everywhere and probably a million different fingerprints. There's rotting food on the windowsill for God's sake. We even unearthed a whole box of a dozen grapefruits—the rector's Christmas present from *last* year—under a pile of books and papers over on that chair. He never even took them home. It'll take ages to get through everything in here."

"What's the stuffed crow over there?" Roy asked, pointing to a large black bird perched on a top shelf of the built-in bookcases which covered one wall. "Was he a fan of Poe or what?"

"Who?" said Vesba, cocking her head.

Holy Comfort

"Never mind...I'll ask around." Merton shifted his attention to the books filling the shelves. The titles revealed no pattern of interest but rather a scattered focus. There were Bible commentaries and books on the Episcopal Church and its history, its liturgy, its sacraments, its divisions. There were novels by Flannery O'Connor and Hal Lindsey and books on spiritual warfare and cults, the New Age and Mormons, books on counseling and recovery, Darwinism and ethics. Books on death and abortion, weight loss and healing, leadership and computers. There were several *Chicken Soup* books and a smattering of titles that had obviously been gifts. None of them looked read.

Merton walked around to the alcove that formed an "L" at the back of his office. Looking at the robes which hung from a bar stretching horizontally along the length of one side of the alcove, he decided this must have been where the priest dressed before services. There was a mirror on the wall. There were several pairs of large shoes on the floor. A man in a navy blue CSU jacket squatted by the wall chipping something into a small plastic bag. "Anything interesting, Wally?" asked Merton.

The man did not look up. "Might be. We'll let you know."

Roy turned around. There were stacks of folders and books everywhere. The desk was piled high with unopened mail, old issues of *Episcopal Life* and various literary and religious periodicals. There were several dirty coffee mugs, a crumb-covered plate, a box of Kleenex, a Rubik's Cube, a Slinky, and a green Beanie Baby bear. There were notebooks in a pile on his chair with a laptop computer on top.

The office struck the detective as belonging to someone who wanted to give the impression of being an intellectual with a great deal of work to do, but it didn't look real or even lived in. It was a place to dump things, unwanted things. There were no pictures on the walls except for a framed map of Ireland, probably another gift, that hung on a hook which had already been stuck there by some former occupant.

Roy put his hands in his pockets and looked around for his partner. "Hey, Leona," he said, locating her in the alcove. "Did you find a calendar or a date book around here? Anything that would tell us where he was last night?"

"Yeah. This," she answered, handing him an expensive-looking, brown leather notebook with his initials stamped on the front in gold leaf.

"Nice," he said looking it over.

"Unfortunately, there's not one thing written in it." She crossed her arms. "Which doesn't surprise me, since our boy doesn't seem to have been a big one for organization."

He smiled. "Well, we better get that laptop to the lab and start someone looking for something in it."

"Marty here says the hard drive has been removed."

Merton snorted and glanced around the room once more. "We might as well get on with our interviews. Maybe we can find something out about that crow."

Vesba bent at the waist and then whipped her head back, causing her teased hair to stand up for a moment before floating back to semi-respectibility around her shoulders. "I hate places like this, full of rich bastards who don't give a shit about the truth." She sighed. "But we might as well start next door with Miss Hawthorne like that Griggs character advised. Hopefully she's over her case of nerves. We can catch the rector later."

"I'll take her," said Merton, directing his partner out the door and in the opposite direction. "You start with the secretary down the hall."

Vesba rolled her eyes. "Oh, sure. Why didn't I think of that?"

"HELLO," MERTON SAID as he tentatively stuck his head into Page Hawthorne's tiny office.

"Come on in," she said. "I was sort of expecting you."

The detective slid around the door and sat down in the only other chair in the office. Page was already sitting down at her desk, a built-in corner wall unit, and she did not get up. He noticed that her face was swollen a bit from crying and that her amber eyes were luminous. "This is cozy," he said, smiling. He handed her the day-timer and keys she had left in the garden. "I thought you might need these."

She nodded.

"Cozy," he repeated.

"This office is stuffy, that's what it is. It's the smallest office you've ever seen. Go ahead and say it—you won't hurt my feelings. Everybody knows it's the worst office in the building, but at least I don't have to share it. After a year with Gracie Griggs, believe me, I would have moved my stuff to a closet." She flung her pen down on her work and laughed. "I guess I did move to a closet, come to think of it." She giggled again. She hoped that her laughter did not suggest a repressed hysteria. She folded her hands, gathering herself, and said calmly, "So, where's your partner, Ms. Vesba?"

"She's talking to the clergy secretary. We probably wouldn't all fit in here anyway." The detective paused as if to suggest that the pleasantries were over. He smiled. "So what did Ms. Griggs mean when she suggested I start the investigation with you?"

Page looked away. "I suppose she was just trying to be provocative. People react differently in a…crisis." Merton did not respond, so Page shrugged. "I honestly don't know why she said that. I was *not* being counseled by Miles, and I was certainly not sleeping with him. In fact, Miles Costello, though his office was right next door to mine, had not spoken to me in a long, long time. He had, in fact, shrouded me."

"Shrouded you?"

"Yes. Miles was an expert in passive-aggressive behavior. When he couldn't, for some reason, deal with you, he shrouded you." The detective still looked puzzled. "By that I mean he never spoke, had contact or even acknowledged my presence in any way. He tried not to look at me. If he had to communicate with me, he e-mailed me…from next door."

Holy Comfort

"Why couldn't he deal with you?"

"I'm not a psychiatrist," she said, growing tired of the conversation.

"Any guesses?"

She sighed, looking up at the ceiling. "I guess I figured that he couldn't deal with strong women, women with opinions, women who actually did their jobs. The plain sad truth is that Miles Costello just wasn't very good at his job. Oh, he had a lot of people fooled, but he knew there were plenty of others who were on to him."

"And you were one of them?"

"Yes," she said, looking him straight in the eye for the first time. "Not at first maybe. He fooled me, too. In fact, when I was going through my divorce Miles was very nice to me. But he was like that. He thrived on weakness and dysfunction. So when he perceived me as needy, he turned on the charm. It didn't last."

"Why not?"

"I got better. Stronger. I started to notice things about him."

"Like what?"

She paused, thinking. She looked at her hands. "We both liked movies, so we'd be talking about movies, only I'd be talking about *The Quiet Man* and he'd start telling me about some movie with Jeremy Irons playing a professor who seduces some student in his office on his desk. And he'd keep looking at his desk. Stuff like that. Then, just like that, he cut me off."

"Did you resent the way he treated you?"

"I can't say I liked his treating me like I wasn't there, but I mostly just turned to my work and did it. I don't have a lot of patience with hurt feelings."

"Interesting," the detective mumbled.

"Well, that's just my opinion," she said.

He stared at his notebook. Page waited for him to continue and while she waited, she studied him. He was probably in his mid-thirties, she thought, somewhere around her own age. He wore jeans, a white unstarched button-down shirt, a striped tie, a rumpled tweed jacket with a pen in the chest pocket, and cowboy boots. He had short-cropped dark hair. His eyes were gray, deep set in his tanned face. They gave away very little. His mouth at the moment was set straight, the lips slack, but she had seen him smile. He had a nice smile. He smelled vaguely of shaving cream and his presence in her tiny office was unsettling. Although they tried to avoid it, their knees had bumped several times, and each time she had felt a blush come washing into her face.

"So, you're divorced?" he asked.

"Yes?" She cleared her throat. "For nearly two years."

"How long have you worked here at Holy Comforter?"

"About four and a half years. I've been a member for almost my whole life. I was married here. The boys were baptized here."

Another pause in questioning followed and Page wondered if this was some sort of technique. She noticed that Detective Merton held a pen and a pad of paper, but that he hardly wrote anything down. She must not have said anything very pertinent.

"So you have boys?" he asked suddenly. He shifted his legs and leaned to one side.

"Two," she said, indicating with her finger a picture of two dark-haired, brown-eyed boys on a large bulletin board. "That's Walter and Tal. They're nine and six."

"They look like you."

"Thank you. I think so, too."

"Where were your boys this morning?"

"Pardon me?"

"If you came in early, where were your boys?"

"I dropped them off in Before-Care at their school. I hate to do that, I hardly ever do, but I needed an extra hour to…" She stopped.

Merton had been writing on his pad, but he looked up from under raised eyebrows now to meet Page's shocked stare. "An extra hour to what, Ms. Hawthorne?"

"*To work*…I dropped them off at seven fifteen—you can check—and arrived at the church, as I told the police officer earlier, around seven forty, after Morning Prayer had started. I didn't leave my children in Before-Care so I could come in early to murder Miles Costello!"

"No?" he asked gravely, as his eyes darted playfully once in her direction. "Did you happen to see anyone leaving when you arrived? Any cars driving away?"

"No, I did not…the street was as still and quiet as…"

"What?"

"The hallway down here…when I came down…" She bit her lip and looked away.

Merton leaned forward. "Look, Ms. Hawthorne. Don't be insulted when we check out what you've said. We'll have to call your children's school—the Before-Care people—and verify what you've told me. It's how we do our job. Check the details."

"I understand."

The detective stood up, rather abruptly she thought, as if to go, but he paused at her huge bulletin board and began to study the photographs, the postcards, the typed quotations, the bulletin covers, and children's artwork that covered it. "Where did you get this?" he asked suddenly, grinning as he pointed to a scrap of paper with the typed words, 'It was a blonde. A blonde to make a bishop kick a hole in a stained glass window.'

"Oh…my Raymond Chandler quote. Someone stuck it on my door. I think it was the man who used to be the junior choir director. It was just a joke."

Merton turned back to the bulletin board. He spent several minutes longer in front of it before turning to go. "John Wayne?"

"Uh huh."

"I wouldn't have guessed John Wayne."

Holy Comfort

"Well, you would have been wrong," she said shrugging. "I didn't think a detective would jump to conclusions like that."

"Forgive me," he said, bending to shake her hand. He made eye contact with Page as he held her hand and his gray eyes lingering a moment longer than necessary. She pulled her hand back. "I have one more question," he said. "Do you know anything about that stuffed crow in Rev. Costello's office?"

She shrugged. "Not really. I think maybe it was a gift from Charlotte Pentecost. She's got the office next to his on the other side. They were good friends. But people were always giving Miles presents. It might have been someone else."

He nodded. "Thank you for your time," he said. "I'll see you later."

Chapter Three

"Hello, Detectives," the rector said, ushering them to two chairs by the large window overlooking the Gresham Garden. "I hope you don't mind, but I've asked my associate, Colin Whitefish, to sit in."

"No, of course not," said Merton, nodding to the other man who sat by the window. Whitefish, who like the rector wore a dark suit and a clerical collar, was a large, sandy-haired man with a ruddy complexion. He smiled at the detectives as he leaned forward to shake their hands. He appeared to be calm and at ease, as if being interviewed by detectives was an everyday occurrence.

"Have a seat please," said the rector.

Merton noted that the rector wore a striped shirt under his bib and collar. It was oddly unsettling. He picked up the rector's suit coat which had been carefully folded over his chair and handed it to him. "I don't want to wrinkle it."

"Of course not. Thank you." The rector took the coat and put it on. He pulled over his desk chair and sat down. He crossed his knees and relaxed. "How are things going downstairs?"

"Fine," said Vesba, trying to get comfortable in the narrow chair and failing.

"I should have come down, I know, but it's been a steady stream of people through here this morning," said Pinkney. "Not to mention the phone calls."

"There's nothing you could have done—you'd just have been in the way," said Vesba. "No offense."

"None taken," he said waving away her suggestion with his hand.

"It's a major league mess down there, Father," she continued. "Costello must not have actually spent much time there…" She waited, but the rector made no comment. "We'll head over to his condo as soon as we can. Have you been there?"

"We weren't friends, Detective, not socially. I never went inside his condo. He moved there about a year ago, I believe."

"Well, sir, could you give us some background on Costello?" said the other detective.

Holy Comfort

The rector handed Merton a piece of paper. "Here's his resume. I think most of it's factual," he said and turned a face full of pain to his pastoral associate.

"He was a blue-collar kid from Chicago," said Whitefish, "who went to a third-rate college. But he managed to get into Yale Divinity School and from there it was a short hop to Holy Comforter."

The detectives glanced at each other and Merton passed the resume to his partner.

"This is a terrible thing that has happened," said the rector. "A terrible thing." He paused, his eyes darting to Colin Whitefish, and then from Merton to Vesba. "But I should come right out and say...Miles Costello and I did not get along. Even that is a euphemism."

"Go on," said Merton.

"Well, I just want to get that out in the open." He stood up and stepped over to the window, his back to the detectives. "We had nothing in common but our place of employment."

"Did you hire Costello?" asked Merton.

"Oh no," said the rector, turning. "No. He was one of my predecessor's, Clyde Cullen's, discoveries. He hired him. I could have let him resign when I came—that's the standard procedure—but I was convinced that the transition would be less traumatic if he stayed. Cullen had just gone off to be a bishop and the congregation was devastated. I thought Miles could be a stabilizing factor, but I couldn't have been more mistaken and I've regretted that decision for a long time."

"Why?" asked Vesba.

"Miles fooled me. I thought he was a team player, but he played on no one's team except his own. In the last five years he's broken every rule. He lied. He cheated. He harrassed women. By the time I figured it out, he had built himself such a powerful following that I couldn't have fired him without placing my own job in jeopardy. I *am* a weak administrator, not for the reasons my detractors say, but because I let a man like Miles Costello get the better of me. It's funny, last week I actually went to the bishop to talk about Miles."

"And now someone has taken care of the problem for you, Charles," said Whitefish without smiling.

"Yes," said the rector. "I have no idea who."

"Could that have been someone's motive?" asked Vesba. "Taking care of your problem?"

The rector looked stunned and shook his head. "Why...no. No." He continued to shake his head slowly.

"How can you be sure?" she said, leaning forward. "I bet you've quite a following of your own, don't you?"

The rector looked puzzled; he touched his forehead.

"Excuse me, sir," said Merton suddenly. "I counted somewhere around twenty people at our meeting this morning. That seems like a lot. I mean, for a church staff."

"We have twenty-two lay staff people," said the rector turning to Merton. "Holy Comforter has around three thousand members and is one of the ten largest Episcopal churches in the country. Relatively speaking, that may not be much, compared to some of those mega-churches you read about, but it does mean programs."

"It takes staff to run programs," said Whitefish who began to count on his fingers for emphasis. "Lay ministry, adult education, youth ministries, outreach, newcomer assimilation, communications. We even have our own printing department with its own press. We have four sextons, a groundskeeper and a business manager to manage it all."

"I had no idea," said Merton.

"It's a small business really," said Whitefish.

"And yet it *isn't*," said the rector. "Of course, many people are of the opinion that it should be run like a small business."

"Our senior warden, Richardson Bell, and our junior warden, George Fontaine, to name two," said Whitefish. "Bell is like the chairman of the board, you might say, the vestry being the board."

"What about you?" Vesba asked the rector. "You don't see it that way?"

"I wish I didn't have to, but that would be naïve," he said, sighing.

"What did Costello think?" asked Merton.

"Miles wanted to get his MBA," said the rector.

"The better to run a church?" said Merton.

"The better to run *this* church," said Whitefish.

The detectives looked at one another and then at the rector who was gazing distractedly out the window at some staff members who had gathered in the garden. Then they looked again at Whitefish who continued to speak. "Miles Costello was a great manipulator. He could manipulate people, data, those personality tests. The Myers-Briggs, for instance—he just decided what kind of person he wanted to be before taking the test and then answered the questions to fit the type, the executive type. He'd point to the test result and say to one of his patrons, 'This is what I should be doing.' And the next thing you know he's in an MBA program! He was smart—sly like a fox—and dishonest. I think, deep down inside, he wanted to reinvent himself."

The rector nodded in agreement. "In a way, you could hardly blame him. I gather he had a nasty childhood, a viscious mother, abuse, the whole thing."

"If you could *believe* him," said the other priest. "For all we know he might have made that part up, too. He certainly paraded his past around like a badge of honor. I sometimes even doubted his faith—I mean, was he called to ministry or was it just a career option that guaranteed social advancement?"

The rector frowned. "Of course, this is all terrible to say. We're merely thinking out loud, trying to make sense of it all." He plunged his hands into his pockets and made noise playing with the change inside. He turned to Vesba. "And who am I to say you're wrong, Detective? It is possible, I suppose, that someone thought that by killing Miles, they'd be doing me a favor, but that person would be *crazy*...and I don't think any of my parishioners are that." He crossed his arms. "I have to believe there was good in Miles—somewhere deep down, there was good in him. Because God loved him, I tried to love him, too."

Vesba fidgeted in her chair and heaved a sigh, signalling her partner that the interview, in her opinion, was going nowhere. Her partner ignored her, keeping his eyes on the rector.

"We're all broken in our own way," continued Pinkney. "Christ is building his kingdom with the broken things of the earth...but Miles used his brokenness as an excuse and ultimately as a weapon. I believe it got him killed."

"A weapon?" asked Merton. "A weapon against whom?"

"A weapon against the world," the rector said.

"But against women mostly," cut in Whitefish.

"Now we're getting somewhere," said Vesba as she sat up straight.

"Miles had a special way with women," said Whitefish, averting his eyes. "That can lead to serious problems for a priest."

"But we don't have any proof," said the rector with a wave of his hand. "That's what the bishop told us."

"Yes," agreed Whitefish. "No proof beyond a brand new condo, lavish trips and enrollment in an expensive postgraduate program!" The red-faced priest took a deep breath and settled back in his chair. "But I've also heard some troubling rumors about a group—a 'small group' we call them—that Miles was in. His particular group consisted of men—all Yale men as a matter of fact, all his handpicked friends." The rector made a noise reflecting disgust and his colleague nodded. "Small groups are intended to be bible study groups that are lay led—no clergy—which is done on purpose and for good reason. It troubled me that Miles was engaged in a group this way. He had a very difficult time detaching from the parish."

"What do you mean, 'detaching from the parish'?" asked Merton.

"By that I mean he made friends with parishioners, courted them, really. He wanted to be their equal. But that isn't possible."

"Why not?"

"Because a priest is no more than a spiritual repairman or a plumber, really—someone you call in to fix a leak. He has to be detached, separate in order to be of any use, to be objective."

The rector nodded. "Miles was headed for trouble. We knew that. But we thought we had *time*. We were wrong."

"Yes," agreed Whitefish. "We were wrong. We thought he'd sink himself, be hoist, so to speak, on his own petard, but..."

"Miles went too far," said the rector making fists. "He must have pushed someone over the edge."

"One of your parishioners?" said Vesba. "One of your good *Christians*?" She said the last word so snidely that all three men turned to look at her.

"Yes, Detective," said Pinkney calmly. "Even, as you say, a 'good Christian' can abandon his principles for God's or for his neighbor's sake."

"Even you?" she said.

The rector blinked. "Even me." He straightened his shoulders. "There are many fine people in this parish, the salt of the earth...but we must always remember that the devil loves a playground like ours."

"And the old fart's been having a field day," said Vesba sarcastically.

"Our sins will all be exposed now, I suppose," said Whitefish ruefully.

"And maybe that's a good thing," said the rector, holding up his hands. "I don't know...confusion now has made his masterpiece. Most sacrilegious murder hath broke ope the Lord's anointed temple, and stole thence the life o' the building."

Merton followed the rector's gaze to the women in the garden. "So I guess," he mused, "what you're saying is...we keep our eyes open for someone with a hand-washing disorder."

The two clergymen turned together to stare at Merton. "Touche," drawled Colin Whitefish, grinning.

The rector's eyebrows shot up and the corners of his mouth pulled back as he faced the detective. "Very good, Detective. You surprise me."

"Why?" Merton met the clergyman's cheery amazement with blank eyes. "Because I read?"

"Well, no...I..."

"Or because I read Shakespeare?"

The two men considered each other. Vesba, left out of the exchange, fidgeted, picking lint off her blouse.

"Yes," said the rector cooly. "I apologize for jumping to a conclusion. A bad lapse in manners."

Merton smiled. "I'm not normally so touchy, but I've already been called on the carpet myself by Ms. Hawthorne this morning for doing the same thing. It was just my turn to object."

Now it was the rector's turn to smile and he did, although it looked as if it hurt him to do so. "Oh? We forget so easily, don't we, that grace is everywhere."

"Hello," she said tentatively, turning from the large pot of flowers from which she picked dead blooms. "May I help you?"

Merton stepped forward and she saw that his eyes were a startling gray, the color of old pewter. "Yes, ma'am," he answered as he extended his hand. "I'm Roy Merton. Detective Roy Merton."

"Oh, how do you do, Detective?" she replied, grasping his hand. "I'm Adair Pinkney."

Holy Comfort

"The rector's wife," he said, smiling. "This is my partner, Leona Vesba." He indicated the other detective who was pushing through the glass door. "The receptionist said we might find you out here." He looked around at the brick-paved and brick-walled Gresham garden.

"Yes. I love the columbarium. It's a comforting spot, don't you think? All these prominent folk, so quiet and peaceful at last."

Merton nodded, although he wasn't sure why. Leona grunted and walked to the wall.

"I've heard," said Adair, "that some generous parishioner has already stepped forward and offered a niche for Miles Costello's last remains to rest in. Wasn't that just a fine gesture?" They sat down together. Adair crossed long beautiful legs and adjusted her skirt. "You'll find that people at Holy Comforter enjoy making fine gestures."

"Somebody made one hell of a fine gesture this morning," said Vesba. "Final and to the point."

"Yes," said Adair. "Ghastly, really, and shocking. May I ask how your investigation is progressing on this terrible morning?"

"Investigations are usually slow-going at the beginning," said Merton. "We don't want to overlook anything or anyone."

"I suppose not. But wouldn't it be nice to find a note made with words clipped from a newspaper or with a typewriter with a bad 'M'?"

Roy chuckled. "We'll see what the crime lab turns up, but right now we're gathering information from the people Reverend Costello worked with."

"Mostly hearsay and opinion," interjected Vesba.

"Surely that's what most cases are built upon," said Adair.

Vesba smiled with her mouth only. "What was your opinion of the deceased?"

Adair glanced sideways at the detective. She sighed and folded her hands. "At first I liked Miles. He was, I think, a master at first impressions. That's a real gift, especially in my husband's line of work. But it didn't take long for me to catch on. I'm pretty good at sizing up people...especially men. Miles was a phoney, pure and simple. I came to despise him for what he was doing to my husband."

"And what was he doing to your husband?" asked Vesba.

"He was trying to get his job."

"He wanted to be rector of Holy Comforter?"

"Oh, yes. Definitely. He had a whole campaign mapped out. He and some of his supporters were preparing to send him to a very expensive MBA program at the University—the kind where you can still hold down a job supposedly and go to school on the weekend, if you have twenty thousand dollars to spare. Of course, the whole idea was totally preposterous—the idea of Miles Costello running this great, big church. He couldn't even clean up his office or make it to a meeting on time! I suppose his friends would have run the show and that was probably the plan anyway."

"What did the rector think?" asked Merton.

"For three years, I warned Chick to watch out. But he's a trusting soul, a loving soul. He couldn't believe that if he loved Miles, Miles wouldn't love him back." Merton looked confused and his partner snorted beside him. "You have to understand," Adair continued. "Chick loves everyone, because that's what we're supposed to do. As Christians, I mean. We're called to love one another. Chick is one of the few Christians I know who actually does."

"That must be hard on you," said Vesba narrowing her eyes.

"Why?" asked Adair, her eyes wide.

"Well, I mean, he must get spread pretty thin."

Adair arched a perfect eyebrow at the female detective and paused before answering. She was not sure if the detective was implying anything by her statement. Choosing to ignore any possible innuendo, she smiled. "He's a busy man. People who think he has it easy have no idea of the complexity of his job and the demands put on him by his congregation. But I'm the one he eventually comes home to."

Merton smiled. "The rector says you were home together this morning."

"Yes...Since he didn't have to be at church for Morning Prayer, we were having coffee together at home. We don't have many mornings together. We enjoy them when we do."

"Well...did the rector finally catch on then, to Miles and his plot?" asked Merton.

"I think so. It helped having Colin Whitefish come on the staff. Then there were two people seeing Miles for what he was. The numbers grew, believe me."

"What others?"

"On the staff? Well, Page Hawthorne for one and Linda Kirstein in the Church School. Anyone with anything on the ball caught on. I'm sure this couldn't be the first time you've heard this side of the story."

"No. It isn't," said Vesba sucking in her cheeks.

"Good. It's the true side. The side where the light shines...I guess you've heard the wild tales from the dark side as well," she said, waving her hand as if dispersing knats.

"I've heard opinions that differ from yours," said Merton.

"Oh. I see," she said brushing non-existent dust off her skirt. "You've not been here long enough to know that there truly is a dark side to this place. Well, you're a bright young man. You'll catch on, I have no doubt." She stood up and held out her hand. "It's been a pleasure to talk to you, Detective Merton." She turned to Detective Vesba who was adjusting her tight skirt. "And you, too, Detective. I love your earrings, by the way. They're wonderful."

Vesba's hand flew to her ear. "Thank you," she mumbled as she felt the oversized hoops pulling down her ear lobes.

Holy Comfort

"Mrs. Pinkney," said Merton, capturing the attention of the rector's wife once again. "May I ask you what you mean, ma'am, by 'the dark side' to this place? That isn't the first time I've heard that said, either."

She leveled her grave blue eyes at him. "An old friend once told me that to any church where the light shines brightly, the devil will come. And he'll sit right in the front pew at every service. He's here, Detective. He's here right now."

Chapter Four

LEONA VESBA SAT, her ample behind ensconced and settled in a tattered, slip-covered chair, in the apartment of Baylor Valentine. She touched her hair lightly, as if by touching herself she would verify her existence, and looked around the square room located two stories above the narthex in the tower. There were many framed photographs and portraits. One, on the mantle, she supposed was a picture of Valentine around the time he graduated from the University of Richmond. The pose reminded her of John Barrymore, dramatic, narcissistic, his nose held high. Then again, perhaps it *was* John Barrymore. Perhaps he had been a patron or even a member of Holy Comforter. Her mind wandered.

The furniture was all old and worn, much of it actually chewed. She cast her gaze into the corner where two small Boston terriers nestled together on a gold tasseled, velvet cushion. It had taken the mutts a good fifteen minutes to calm down after she had entered the maestro's inner sanctum. Vesba hated dogs, especially dogs with the bad luck to be named Snooky Doll and Trixie.

She felt oddly light-headed and she struggled to concentrate as Valentine recalled for her the good old days when Clyde Cullen had been rector and his wife, Beatrice Cullen, had sung in the choir. Yes, she had been a veritable angel, gracing his tower apartment with her presence and him with her friendship and patronage. Yes, that had been a golden age when fundraising had been facile and young male choir assistants plentiful. His reputation had reached its zenith. He was a choir god and Holy Comforter a choir mecca. One soprano under his tutelage had even gone on to sing at the Metropolitan Opera. (They still listed her, *emeritus,* in the choir roster.) Yes, the choir had reigned supreme as the Holy Comforter crown jewel. His word had been unquestioned. He believed he could do anything. But, ah, how things had changed! It was tragic, indeed, how everything in life had to change. Sure, it was true, that the church membership had grown, but only at the cost of letting *anyone* in. It was sad, really. Who *were* all these people anyway?

And now the ultimate indignity—to have the name of Holy Comforter sullied by a *murder*. How pedestrian! How low-down and plebian!

Holy Comfort

Nothing like this had ever occurred when Clyde Cullen was rector. There had to be some connection between the murder, *la scandale*, and all these new people. It was the only thing that made any sense.

Vesba rolled her eyes and wondered if Valentine was really such a great sack of shit as he appeared to be. She wondered what Roy was doing at the moment. She considered excusing herself and going to find him—he had to be somewhere in this rabbit warren, but instead she picked up her pad and pencil and re-crossed her fat thighs. "All this background info is wonderful," she said. "But I'd like to ask you some questions if you don't mind, sir."

He aimed his nose heavenward and exhaled.

She took that as an affirmative. "Where were you this morning around seven?"

"I was walking the pups." He pointed to the window. "Once up Dozier to College and back down Crown."

"How long does that take?"

"It depends. This morning I ran into Martha Van Patton outside her lovely home on Dozier Avenue. She was on her way to Morning Prayer wearing a new lavender tweed suit. I had to stop and gape. She..."

"And how long did you shoot the breeze with her?" said Vesba, nudging Valentine forward.

"Oh, let me see. Ten minutes, I guess. She had to rush off to Morning Prayer and the pups were misbehaving." He sent visual daggers hurling at the dogs in the corner. One of them lifted its head and growled.

Vesba restrained the growl rising in her own throat and cleared it instead. "So did you see anything when you got back to the church?" she asked sweetly.

"No, nothing, I'm afraid. We came in on the north side and slipped upstairs without disturbing anyone. The narthex was empty."

"Of course," said Vesba sighing as she made a note on her pad. She looked up and smiled toothily at Valentine. "Well, tell me Dr. Valentine—it is, *Dr.* Valentine?"

"Yes. An honorary degree," he replied, straightening his shoulders.

"You've been here so long, you must know everyone." He nodded. "So who do you think is capable of murder here at Holy Comforter?" she asked bluntly.

Valentine leaned back in his shredded upholstered chair and cleared his throat. "Well, everyone's *capable* of murder, surely. Don't you think? In the heat of *passion*...but..." He stopped abruptly. He swallowed. "But such a cold, calculated murder had to have taken some planning."

"Yes, that's true. The murderer was very careful," Vesba conceded amiably.

"The person who murdered Miles was intelligent. She was organized and planned it all out carefully. She wore gloves, I assume, and covered her tracks. She left no clues, am I right?"

"Not that we've turned up so far." Vesba smiled again. "But why do you keep referring to the murderer as *she*, Dr. V? Are you so sure it's a woman?"

"Well, good lord, yes. It's got to be a revenge thing, a love-hate thing, a *sex* thing..." He stopped abruptly again. She nodded encouragingly. "Miles was *not* homosexual," he said.

Vesba raised an eyebrow, but decided not to press him. She re-crossed her legs. "So who *do* you think Miles Costello was involved with sexually?"

"I wouldn't know," he said swallowing. "I try to mind my own business."

"Oh, come now, Doctor. I bet you know better than anyone what goes on in this building, living here in this tower as you do. I bet you even know who was here late on Thursday night, maybe even after Demetrius Barton locked up and left, don't you?"

"I know who comes and goes. Believe me, I wish I didn't, but I'm vulnerable here, living alone in this apartment. I can't sleep unless I know that the place is locked up good and tight."

"*Oh really*," her expression said.

"You can smile if you want," he said. "But this is a big place with a hundred ways to get in and out and a thousand places to hide if you want to."

"All right...I guess you're right...but you didn't answer me. Do you know who was here late on Thursday night? After Barton locked up?"

"I didn't say, because you hadn't asked me a direct question," he said. "But I *don't* know. I just know I checked the door below at ten o'clock and it was locked so I went to bed."

Vesba, unsmiling, stood up and adjusted her impossibly tight skirt and moved to the window. She leaned against the window frame and gazed out, her hand resting casually on her hip. Dr. Valentine coughed.

"You've got a great view from up here, don't you? You can see both ways up Dozier—all the cars—and, look at that, you can see right into the rectory, right into the rector's bedroom. Does *he* know that?"

The choirmaster rolled his eyes.

Vesba swung around. "C'mon, Dr. Valentine," said Vesba. "What was Costello's game? What was he up to? Did he get in over his head with too many old women? Or maybe he started horning in on someone else's territory? Someone who'd been here a lot longer, who'd established his patrons long ago when Clyde Cullen was kingfish and..."

"Wait a minute!" said Valentine, turning from the window. He placed his hands delicately on his chest. "I had nothing to do with this! I was walking my pups as I've said and Martha can corroborate every word. I have an alibi. I know nothing—just that..." He jammed his hands into his old corduroy pants. Then he raised one hand to his head as if it were about to fly off his shoulders and closed his eyes. "Miles was a good man, a good man who didn't deserve to be murdered, no matter what he was doing."

Holy Comfort

"If you feel that way," said Vesba calmly, "you should want to help. If you know something, tell me."

"None of us is perfect...I know Miles was taking money—a lot of money, more than...well, a lot. There may have been some competition there among his patrons, some jealousy." He was thoughtful before raising his eyes to Vesba. "And I wouldn't count out some of them because of their age. Old women have feelings, too."

Chapter Five

By three p.m., most of the staff of Holy Comforter had already left. Tired of speculating and exhausted by tension, they had scattered shortly after lunch. The secretaries lingered out of necessity, and Tammy Spivy still manned the phones, which had rung continuously. The clergy had gathered to pray in the rector's office.

Page stretched and surveyed her office. She had made some progress since the detective's departure earlier in the morning, but the macabre events of the day had never been far from her thoughts. All morning and into the afternoon, various members of the police department had worked in Miles' office. Although her door was closed, Page could hear them come and go in the hallway and through the wall she heard murmuring snippets of conversations. She heard when Miles' body was wheeled out into the hallway and through the fire doors and up the stairs on its way to the morgue. *Into paradise may the angels lead thee*, Miles, she thought, hoping for the best.

Oh, who, she pondered, could have done such a thing? A member of the staff? A parishioner? There must be a lot of people who had hated him or come to hate him. Those numerous women, so easily infatuated with any kindly member of the clergy, with whom he was rumored to have had affairs. She remembered those required staff seminars on sexual harassment where Miles had resentfully played games on his laptop computer. The frustrated lay ministry leaders he had ignored. Those other people he had shrouded. Perhaps one of those rich old ladies had finally seen through him and caught on to his wicked ways. At any rate, it was quite a scheme that had tripped him up, thoughtfully planned and executed, right down to the details from the lectionary. Who was the murderer trying to impress? Well, there would surely be no shortage of people for the detectives to interview. She wondered what Roy Merton had meant by "I'll see you later."

She listened to Dolly Parton and Alison Krauss and Patty Loveless wail in succession, their pure, old-timey voices, broken-hearted and fragile. From time to time Page sang along. The music was louder than she usually played it, but the hallway was empty except for Sophie Carl at the other end. There was no one, Page figured, to be bothered. Certainly not Miles who

Holy Comfort

had always hated her taste in music. He had pretended to love jazz. She was only a little embarrassed when Demetrius Barton, the sexton, poked his head into her office to see what was going on.

"I thought there was a party in here," he said seriously.

"No, Dee. Just me trying to block out what's been going on next door."

"Oh, I see," he said sitting down. "How you doin', Page? I've been meaning to ask. Pretty tough day?"

She swiveled in her chair. "It didn't start off too well, that's for sure. I'm okay, though." She smiled.

"That's good," said Demetrius. He rubbed at a stain on the knee of his chinos. "I talked to one of those detectives. Answered all his questions, you know, and he had plenty. Wanted to know about last night...and this morning."

Page nodded. "What was going on last night?"

"Just the usual Thursday night. It was hoppin'. Had the Phoenix Group and an Adult Ed Board meetin' and the choir up in the Commons. Lots of activity."

"And what about this morning? Did you see anything suspicious?"

"Me? No. I was in the kitchen mostly getting the coffee things ready for the women's bible study group. He asked about you. I said you came and went pretty much as you pleased. Didn't ask permission from me too often."

Page smiled. Then, in the quiet that followed the end of a song, they became aware that someone was talking in Miles' office. Page turned down the music and listened unashamedly, her ear against the wall.

"I don't give a rat's ass who hears me," came the strident voice of Leona Vesba, loud and clear through the wall. "This crew is a freakin' freak show of strange ducks, all looking down their collective beaks at you and me and our investigation. Don't you get the feeling they'd rather we just went away quietly and forgot about their old pal Miles? Murder is too declasse."

"Not all of them feel that way," replied Merton. His voice was much lower and harder to hear.

"Well, that's not my impression. That Valentine guy, the queen who lives in the belfry—he definitely got the point across that since we aren't Episcopalians—*cradle* Episcopalians—we aren't really appropriate choices for this investigation. How could we possibly understand the complexities of this kiss-my-ass denomination, blah, blah, effin' blah." She paused to see if her partner would chuckle. When he did, she continued. "And that old scarecrow Dunwoody! 'He was a Cubs fan—maybe it was someone from Chicago!' Jesus Christ, what a dolt!"

Merton said something Page couldn't hear, but his partner shrieked in response and started coughing. "Well, I think that Tammy girl," Vesba continued, "the receptionist, hit the nail square on the head when she said she thought we've got a shitload of suspects out there. Good luck, she said. Amen."

"Amen," said Merton.

27

"And that Gracie Griggs! Man, she was full of crap...'all that was his private business and I don't particularly care what he did behind closed doors as long as he did his job.' *Jesus*, women can be such idiots!" Vesba laughed at her own insight.

Page turned back to the sexton, shushing him with a finger at her lips, as they both stifled laughter. She turned up Patty Loveless to cover their giggling. Suddenly the partially closed door swung open and Vesba, her hands planted firmly on her extravagant hips, cried out, "Jesus Christ! *You're* the one listening to this hillbilly crap?"

Page, momentarily paralyzed, stared at her and noted the smiling presence of Roy Merton behind her. "Yes?" she eventually asked, still wide-eyed with surprise.

"We could hardly hear ourselves think next door, honey," said Vesba. "Do you mind turning that down?"

"As a matter of fact, I'll turn it off. I was just getting ready to leave," replied Page politely as she stepped back. The overwhelming concreteness of the detective was assaulting her limited space, and she felt somehow less herself. Her desire to flee escalated.

"Well, we don't mean to run you out, honey."

Page took another step backwards and tripped over a pile of folders and books, causing her to lose her balance and crash into her desk chair. She immediately put her hands up to ward off Vesba who had stepped forward to assist the obviously helpless woman before her. Demetrius Barton took advantage of the confusion and slid out of the office. Merton intelligently remained in the background.

"Whoa," hooted Vesba. "I didn't mean to..."

"I'm fine," interrupted Page as she collected herself and crossed her knees modestly. "I guess I'm just a little jumpy." She turned off the CD player and looked inquiringly at the detective.

"Thanks. I'll get out of your face now," said Vesba as she turned to leave. "C'mon, Roy, let's go."

"In a minute," he said, stepping forward into the vacated doorway, both hands on the frame. Vesba ducked her head under his arm and went out into the hall, casting him a look of eye-rolling exasperation. "Sorry for the interruption," he said to Page, the ghost of a smile on his lips. "Are you okay?"

"Oh, this...please."

"No. I mean, how are you doing as you wind up...today?" he corrected her. He looked concerned.

"I'm all right." His eyes were relentless and she evaded them by nervously gathering her things to leave. "It's certainly not every day that a priest gets murdered. Someone I know...I suppose that's why everyone took off early. They're shook up—they want to be home, somewhere they feel safe."

"You didn't."

"Didn't what?" She stopped and looked up at him filling her doorway.

"Leave early."

"No...but I was just getting ready to leave," she said, watching silently as he readjusted the other chair, moving it so he had his back to the closed door. He sat down stretching out his long legs in front of him.

"Please, if you don't mind, would you move your chair back the way it was?" she asked cautiously. "Miles used to do that. It always made me nervous."

"Nervous?"

"I can't get out when you're blocking the door like that. I feel trapped. Miles was tall too—that was his excuse, but..."

"You didn't trust him," he said. "Why not?"

She paused before answering. "I think I told you how he used to talk in a suggestive way. Very subtle. Most of the time it was nothing, really, but I didn't like it."

"Did he ever try anything...physical?"

"Once," she said, checking her watch again. "I have to watch the time as I said, and, um, will you please move your chair back?"

"Yes, of course. Sorry," he said, replacing the chair where it had been. "You were saying?"

"Well, you see when a person went to Miles for advice or counseling, his answer was always a variation on 'do what makes you feel good.' If you were upset and you loved movies, he'd say watch a movie you love. If you were overweight, oh, just have an ice cream sundae. I think it was his way of making a person feel good about herself. But it's very dangerous. No hard questions. No call to prayer, which is what the rector would do. Charles never gives easy answers, and that's what Miles was all about, easy answers."

"But how does this relate to..."

"Well, one time, after my divorce, I was talking to him and he suggested the movie therapy idea. And then he came up behind me and put his arms around me, pressing against me, and he had his hands...and I could feel his..."

"Yes?" urged the detective, his face blank.

"And he said, 'I know what I could do to make you feel better.'"

"Did you tell anyone?" Merton asked, his voice controlled and level.

"No. He let go of me when I told him to. And I figured the rector didn't need to deal with it. He had enough problems." Page looked away, her eyes settling on her desk.

The detective leaned forward, challenging her to face him. "The rector said he had his suspicions, but no proof. If you had told him, maybe Miles would have been forced to get some help, maybe..."

"This wouldn't have happened? Don't you think I've thought of that?" she interrupted. "But you want to put it behind you and forget it...I wanted to take care of it myself. I don't run to Charles about everything...I never had any more trouble with him. He was disgusting, but it's not as if he raped me." She turned finally and faced him.

He leaned back in his chair, pausing before saying, "It sounds to me like you were damn lucky, and I think you know that. Maybe somebody else wasn't quite so lucky."

As she looked at him, she thought she detected compassion in his eyes. This was not her fault. She shook her head slowly. "This is not my fault."

The detective waited. It was quiet in the hall. In the distance a door closed, a phone rang.

She exhaled. "My boys get out of school at three forty and they walk home. I like to be there when they arrive around four o'clock, so I've got to get going now," she said. She stood up, scooping her purse and a pile of folders from her desk.

"I'll walk you to your car," he said, standing up and stepping to the door. She heard it as a statement, not as an offer or a request. She felt oddly aroused. She made an effort not to touch him as she brushed by on her way out the door.

"So you're a Patty Loveless fan?" he asked as they trotted up the stairs. "I'd imagine that bordered on sacrilegious around here."

"On the contrary. Patty is a very spiritual lady."

"You know what I mean."

Page stopped abruptly at the top of the stairs. When she turned she found herself eye-to-eye with the detective who had paused two stairs down from her. "I know what you mean," she said. "You're doing it again."

"Doing what again?"

"Jumping to a conclusion...You've already put this place in that big pigeon-hole marked *Frozen Chosen*. Please give me some credit for not belonging in it alongside Baylor Valentine."

"Yes, ma'am," he said, following her into the narthex. "I thought I was."

"You must have talked to quite a few staff members today. They weren't all listening to Bach and reading George Herbert were they?" she asked as they passed the rector's office. His assistant waved and smirked. Page chose not to read anything into it.

"No. I get your point."

"Not that I have anything against Bach or George Herbert. I like them both. I like them a lot."

Merton pushed the heavy oak door and held it for Page. The sunlight was dazzling and she squinted, breathing deeply. The detective watched as she stood savoring the warmth of the sun on her upturned face. He noted the way the hair around her forehead, coming together in a widow's peak, was blonder than the rest. It was fine and shone in the sunlight.

Holy Comfort

"Even on a day like this, the sun's still shining. It's a gorgeous day. Amazing, isn't it?" she asked, opening her eyes and facing him.

He had looked away in time so she did not catch him staring. "Is he a good friend of yours?" he asked.

"Who?"

"The sexton," he said, looking past her to the lawn. "Demetrius Barton."

"He's a friend. Why do you ask?"

"He was in your office just now."

"He stopped by to see how I was doing."

"Nice," he said, focusing on her face again. He looked away and touched her lightly on the arm, ushering her through the door.

As they headed up the street toward her Volvo, she said, "This really isn't the sort of place where people..."

"Get murdered?" he said.

"No," she said. "It isn't. People cheat on their wives, they cut corners at work, they get desperate and occasionally rob a bank. But murder? I can't imagine who could have done this. It makes no sense."

"Murder is never the sensible thing to do," he said. They stopped at her car and Page slid into the front seat. He held the open door and peered in. "Be careful, okay?"

"You bet." He closed the door and as she turned the ignition, he stepped back so she could pull out. When she glanced up, she saw that he was looking down the street, past Demetrius Barton raking leaves in front of the church to the Channel Five van that was parking.

Chapter Six

Page had to tell the boys about the murder when she got home. As soon as they saw her they knew something was wrong. So, as honestly as she could without sharing too many of the details, she told them that the Reverend Miles Costello had been murdered in his office that morning and that she had found his body. Somehow they knew better than to ask too many questions.

"I never liked him," said Walter after some thought. "He was mean. Once when I went up to take communion, he pulled my hands up and said, 'Hold your hands like this' in this hissing voice. He said, 'Do you *think* you can *do* that?' I nodded, but he said, 'Say *yes*, sir.'"

"You never told me about that, Walter," said Page.

"No…but I didn't go up to communion for a long time, either."

"I remember," she said vaguely. She looked at Tal who sat still for once, listening. He gazed at his mother and asked, "Will Mr. Costello go to heaven, even though he was mean to Walter?"

"I suppose he'll have to answer for quite a few things…but that's between him and God."

"He told me once he thought you were real pretty and that I was a lucky boy," said Tal. "But I was a real little kid then."

Walter snorted loudly. "And what are you *now*?"

The conversation had summarily ended then as Tal grabbed his brother's lacrosse stick and chased him screaming out of the kitchen and down to the basement. Page did not respond to the crash.

Chapter Seven

THE OFFICE OF the mayor of Middle Essex was unpretentious and pleasant with a sweeping view of the courtyard and parking lot beyond. The current mayor, Willis McHugh, hated it, preferring his own private office on the top floor of the twenty-two story building he owned downtown. He felt small behind this large mahogany desk with his back to the window and its paltry view. He waited grudgingly for the two detectives to sit down.

"Thanks for coming," he said tersely. He looked behind the detectives at the opposite wall. "So what do you think—is this a first for Middle Essex?"

"More like a fourth or a fifth," said Leona Vesba.

"Right," said the mayor who hated to be corrected. "What I meant, of course, is that murder has no place in Middle Essex. This isn't the inner city, after all. This isn't the suburban sprawl of West County. We're different. They may have busted a crack house in Quincy Groves the other day, but not here. Nothing unseemly ever happens in Middle Essex."

"You mean, no one gets caught doing anything 'unseemly,'" said Vesba.

Willis McHugh leaned forward and hit the desk with his fist. "Well, this son of a bitch will be caught and in short order, too," he said angrily. "Do you understand?"

Vesba stopped chewing her gum. "We'll do our best, sir," she said. Merton lowered his chin.

The mayor nodded. His brown eyes shone like chocolate chips in his doughy face. "You guys from the Major Case Squad think you know it all and you've seen it all. Well, in Middle Essex things are different. I mean Holy Comforter is *my* church for god's sake. The McHughs are a founding family—members since 1913. My father was a senior warden and his father before him..."

"Did you know the victim?" asked Vesba, changing the subject.

If he noticed her impatience, he didn't show it. He smiled and his smile was more unsettling than his anger. "Miles? I knew him. I was in his small group for god's sake. We met every Wednesday morning at seven in his office. There were ten of us, counting Miles, all Yale men as a matter of fact. Miles went to Yale Divinity. He went to some rinky-dink undergraduate school, but he heard about Yale somewhere. We studied the Bible in our group. We were reading *Daniel*, which was new to most of us. We shared our spiritual journeys. It was all confidential. No one was supposed to talk about the stuff outside the group."

"What kind of *stuff* did Costello share?" asked Merton.

The mayor looked at the detective from under his eyebrows and thought for several seconds. "He used to complain in our group about how badly he was treated by the rector and that clod, Whitefish. It was really sad to see how it got Miles down. Some of us were planning to take some action—for the good of Holy Comforter, naturally. But besides those two, Miles never complained about anyone. He may have left a few broken hearts along the way, but you can hardly blame a guy for that."

"Who else was in the group, sir? Can you write down the names?" Merton slid his notebook across the desk.

The mayor pulled the notebook towards himself and looked at it. Then he picked up a pen. "I suppose you think this is really necessary?"

The detectives nodded.

The mayor exhaled loudly. "Everyone in the group got along great with Miles. He was a good guy. I'm sure you'll find this was some random act of violence." He started to write and then looked up. "If you ask me, it's television. People get too many ideas on TV. Jesus, you could watch a murder every night. It's like fucking night school."

Holy Comfort

Chapter Eight

THE DETECTIVES WALKED leisurely up the cement walk to the plain brick four unit apartment building on McReynolds Road. The building, part of a trio of identical structures, displayed minimal landscaping and needed to be painted. Inside the dimly lit vestibule, Vesba scanned the mailboxes and pushed the buzzer on the one marked *C.Pentecost.* Upstairs a door opened and a disembodied southern drawl floated down to them, amplified eerily by the distinctive acoustics of the enclosed hallway. "Detectives? Y'all come right up."

Vesba led the way upstairs, followed closely by her partner. In the gray hall at the top of the stairs, holding open the door to her apartment, stood Charlotte Pentecost, a tall, thin woman in her late thirties with large blue eyes, bloodshot from crying. She was conservatively dressed in gray flannel slacks, a starched striped shirt and a long blue cardigan with pockets into which her fists were thrust. "Come in. Please," she said pleasantly, gesturing with her head.

The detectives entered the living room and stopped. They both looked around for a place to sit. There was only a couch in the room, a white couch with a protective plastic cover on it. In front of the couch a glass and metal coffee table held nothing but an empty blue glass bowl. Across from the couch an old console-style television set with a nineteen inch screen was placed against the wall. There were two large botanical prints on the wall. The carpet was off-white and very clean.

"Let's sit at the dining room table," said Charlotte, acknowledging their reluctance to sit on the sofa. She motioned to the end of the room which substituted for a dining area. "Shall we? I'd offer you coffee, but I'm out," she explained. Merton noticed she had still not taken her hands out of her pockets. He glanced at his partner who was staring at the bulging pockets as well. They all sat down at the 1950s style French provincial dining table.

"Thank you for letting us come to see you," said Vesba.
"Oh no. Thank *you*," drawled Charlotte. "It was so thoughtful of you to come to my home. After the rector called me and told me what had happened to poor dear Miles, I couldn't think of going out, much less to

35

Holy Comforter. I just couldn't. He's coming over later to see me. It's so wonderful that you understand as well."

"We can understand that this is difficult for you," said Merton.

"Thoughtful *and* sensitive!" said Charlotte, bowing her head. "I know I must look a fright, but I've just been in such a state."

"Well," said Vesba. "What can you tell us about the late Reverend Miles Costello?"

"Miles was a good friend of mine," said Charlotte, sitting up primly. "He was one of the few people on the staff who could take a joke, for god's sake, and who didn't blush five shades of pink if you said 'asshole.'"

Vesba shifted her weight uneasily and glanced at Merton, who had taken out his pad and pen and was staring intently at them. Charlotte stared intently at him as she continued. "And he wasn't patronizing, either, like that Colin Whitefish. We worked really well together before Mr. Clodfish came on the scene and started wanting to know where I was every second of every day. I just can't work that way..." Her mind drifted off for a moment and she stared at the silk flower arrangement in the center of the table. She snapped back suddenly, jarring Vesba who jumped in her seat. "*They* have no idea how much time I spend working at this job when I'm home at night and on weekends. And, you know, there's some damn meeting practically every night. I'm exhausted half the time, but don't think that just because I work at a church, anyone cares. *They* don't care. So what if I compensate myself a little time-wise? It's just because there isn't any other kind of compensation offered. Now Miles understood. *Miles* could handle it. He was flexible..."

"You're saying Costello understood the comp time you took?" interrupted Merton, raising his eyes to meet Charlotte's stare. "Comp time like yesterday when you called in saying you had car trouble?"

"Yes," she said coyly.

"But you didn't have car trouble, did you?" said Merton.

"I have an old Porsche. I'm *always* having car trouble, Detective."

"Okay. Costello understood about old cars," said Vesba. "So you got along fine with Costello? You were friends?"

"Oh yes. We were friends—I mean...we had a professional relationship for six years, since before our present rector and company. We saw each other at work. He had lots of other friends outside work."

"Girl friends?"

"Yes, *girl* friends," said Charlotte, no longer coy. "But he never got too serious. Clergy have to be so careful that way. He was careful."

"So, Ms. Pentecost," asked Merton, shifting in his seat and leaning forward over the table. "Do you have any idea who would have wanted to kill Costello?" He stared at her and she stared back.

"I have no idea, I'm sure, who would want to kill Miles. He was well liked by *almost* everyone." She paused, for effect the detectives knew, and swallowed. "However, I know for a fact he didn't get along with the

Holy Comfort

rector. So by association, Colin Clodfish, the rector's toadie, didn't like him, either. They were planning something. It's no secret that Pinkney has wanted to get rid of him for some time. He's always been jealous of Miles' popularity."

"Costello was more popular than the rector?" asked Merton.

"Well, the rector isn't really one of us, of course."

"What does that mean?" asked Merton.

"His mother was *Jewish*," she whispered, like it was a big secret. Then she smiled and sat up. "Not that *I* care, but some people do. You might be surprised how many."

The detectives stared at her as she smiled blandly. Then Vesba said, "You were *saying* they were out to get Miles."

Pentecost nodded. "Yes, ma'am, they were."

"Get him?" asked Merton. "Couldn't the rector just fire him? He was his boss, after all."

"Fire Miles?" she said. She put a hand on her chest and chuckled in the back of her throat. "Oh, that would have set off quite a firestorm! Yes, indeedy. Miles had lots of friends, powerful friends, the kind who wouldn't think twice about retaliating. To fire Miles would have very likely cost Charles his job."

"So whoever offed Costello was doing Pinkney a favor," said Vesba. "Is that what you're saying?"

"They may have thought so," said Charlotte. "But that remains to be seen."

"Who would have wanted to help the rector in that way?" asked Merton.

"Oh, I'm flattered that you think I might know, Detective. But really, I'm not in the rector's inner circle and I don't know who is."

Vesba took a deep breath, preparing to interrupt.

But Charlotte, despite her denial, continued. "Of course, there's Adair Pinkney, the wife of Charles. *She* would do anything for her husband, the man, after all, who plucked her out of obscurity and made her the grande dame she thinks she is today. She's an ambitious woman, and don't let anyone tell you different. And, of course, there's Page Hawthorne..."

"Page Hawthorne?" asked Vesba, glancing at her partner and back to Charlotte who did not miss the exchange.

"Well," she said, settling back into her chair and into her subject. "You've met her, I'm sure, and I bet you thought she was such a lady, so perfect. Well, let me tell you, she was chasing Miles Costello all over the place after her divorce. She used to come on to him at work and she was always in his office, laughing it up. I know she seems like Miss Snow White, but that's all an act, believe me..."

"Was Costello interested?" asked Vesba.

"*No,* Miles was not interested. Who would be?" She expelled air noisily through her nose and crossed her arms. "You know, her ex-husband Chester actually told me he used to pass out on top of her on a regular basis—you know, from boredom!" Charlotte stopped abruptly and focused on both detectives, noting their fixed stares. She looked back and forth slowly and then, smiling innocently, shook her head and continued. "Well, anyway, Miles finally had to tell her what was what, and then, boom, she starts on the rector. Changed teams, so to speak. I have no idea how far she got with him, but they're pretty cozy. Perhaps you've noticed...I suppose she'll work her way through them all."

"To what do you attribute her behavior?" asked Vesba.

"Don't ask me," Charlotte replied brightly. "Some women are like that—a man in a collar is a real turn-on. But I'll tell you another thing—Page Hawthorne is one competitive bitch. After the Reverend Belinda McClelland left and they had no clergy person to move into her office, the business manager offered it to me. Well, Page pitched a fit—she was sharing an office with Gracie Griggs at the time—she wanted her own office, the bigger the better. She thought she *deserved* it. Please. She isn't really even ministry staff. She just runs the production department and communications. Big Deal. Well, you can see who won that fight. I had seniority, *and* my job is a lot more important. I'm really considered para-clergy, you know."

"Para-clergy?" asked Vesba.

"If all the clergy are out of the building, I'm really in charge. I mean, no one's actually said that, but it's true."

"Uh huh," mused Vesba. She was losing patience with Charlotte, but before she could bring the interview to an end, Merton posed another question.

"Ms. Pentecost, what do you know about that crow in Costello's office?"

"The crow in Miles' office? How observant of you to notice! Actually, it's a raven. I gave it to him."

"May I ask why?"

"You can ask away, Sugar," she said and waved a hand vaguely through the air. It disappeared again under the table.

"Then why a raven?"

"Well, it's a long story, but I gave it to him to remind him of St. Meinrad. Miles used to be Catholic and I thought he'd get a kick out of the raven, but I don't think he paid much attention to it...Maybe he should have..."

"Why? I'm not familiar with..." began Merton, leaning forward, urging her to continue.

"Well," Charlotte said, also leaning forward. "You see, the story of St. Meinrad—he was a hermit who lived in the ninth century—ends with his *murder* by thieves. They rob him and kill him and carry away his few possessions. But what they don't know is that Meinrad had been feeding two ravens who visited his hermitage. He'd befriended them. They were his pets. As the murderers depart, the birds follow them back through the woods and into town, cawing and darting at their heads—making a big commotion.

Holy Comfort

The villagers who witness this display decide to hold the men until they can figure out what's going on. When they find the murdered old man, they know who has done it. They burned them alive, you know."

"An interesting gift," said Merton, straightening back up.

"I guess I thought Miles could use a raven to watch over him." She stared at him and her eyelashes fluttered. "I guess you could use a raven to tell you who killed Miles."

"Why did you think Costello needed a raven to watch over him?" he asked. "You said he was careful."

"Oh, it was just a joke," she said. "And not a very good one as it turns out."

Vesba stood up then and her partner followed her lead. "Thank you for your time, Ms. Pentecost," she said, extending her hand.

"Yes, thank you, ma'am," repeated Merton. "We appreciate your talking to us."

"Is that all? No more questions?" Charlotte teased. "Why, that didn't take long at all."

"Disappointed or relieved?" asked Vesba, lowering her hand which had been ignored.

"Neither," Charlotte shot back icily. "Just surprised." Then, turning her attention to Merton, she took his hand and shook it. "It sure was a pleasure talking to *you*, Detective."

"Yes, ma'am." He smiled and winced. Her hand, although surprisingly small, was powerful. "That's quite a grip you have."

"Oh, yes," she replied merrily. "I'm very strong. I swim every morning—one hundred laps."

"Every day?" he asked. "Did you swim today?"

"How could I? My car wasn't working."

Merton smiled and Charlotte returned his smile, flashing the disquieting and overeager grin of Carol Channing. "Then you were stuck at home?"

She nodded. "Waiting patiently for the nice Amoco man to jump start my car. You can check. It was Jerry from up the street." She indicated a southwest direction with her head.

"Well, goodbye and thank you again, Ms. Pentecost," said Vesba, a note of finality and farewell clearly tolling.

"Goodbye then, Detectives," replied Charlotte shrugging. "Ta ta."

The detectives turned and scurried down the steps and out into the sunlight. Merton took long strides down the walk as his partner struggled to keep up.

"What do you think of Miss Para-clergy?" said Leona as they reached her car. She was breathing heavily and beginning to perspire. "An interesting combination of southern belle and Teamster?"

Merton swung into the front seat and pulled his long legs inside. He glanced up at the second story window of her apartment while he waited for his partner to get settled. "She's strong enough to drive a kitchen knife into a man's back, that's for sure. Do you think she was stuck at home this morning?"

"We better check with Jerry down the street," said Vesba, fitting the key into the ignition.

"Light thickens and the crow makes wing to the rooky wood."

"Don't start with that shit, Roy."

"While night's black agents to their preys do rouse."

Holy Comfort

Chapter Nine

AT THE TAIL end of the day, when the moon was high in the sky, shedding its dim light through the curtainless window, Roy Merton finally sat down in his black leather chair and lifted a bottle of Corona to his lips. He drank deeply and set the bottle down. He leaned back and closed his eyes and thought of the misnamed church and the dead body discovered there by the pretty little woman who didn't like tall men to block her door. He visualized the bulletin board in the tiny office and the pictures haphazardly tacked there. There was the nineteenth century man sitting stiffly in a chair on a raised wooden deck in a grove of trees, his head down-turned, writing. *Life is dreaming*, someone had written on the photo. Next there was a picture of a vaguely familiar girl, about four years old, with her blonde head tipped to one side, her shoulder raised to meet it. She was smiling and thinking *There's no stopping me.* There was a young Johnny Cash with soulful dark eyes singing, *because you're mine, I walk the line*, and there was John Wayne, very young and slim in a buckskin suit, with a wry, toothy smile not so unlike the smile of the others. An older Ernest Hemingway stood knee-deep in a cold stream, holding a fly rod and net, a face-splitting smile and squinting eyes reflecting his mood. Next to Hemingway was a snapshot of a young man, similarly attired and also standing in a cold stream. He held a trout, and the smile on his face was likewise youthful and spontaneous. His eyes were squinted in the glare of the sun, his hat pushed back, exposing his fine high forehead. There was a striking similarity in the two photos, the likeness of the joy of the moment shielding a troubled heart. What did these people mean to her? What exactly did she mean by the *denomination for thinking people*?

What was she thinking, embraced in the comforting arms of the rector who wore striped shirts? The rector who didn't believe there was anyone in his parish crazy enough to murder a priest, even one who had delusions of seizing his power and even his job. He thought of him and his beautiful wife, each the other's alibi, who could have worked together or separately to murder the priest, with or without the colution of the red-faced Whitefish, who was driving in from his home across the river, sixty-five miles away. He thought of the crazy quilt of church employees, most notably Gracie Griggs, pointing her fingers carelessly, denying her own culpability, and of Charlotte Pentecost, para-clergy, circling like a crow around the truth.

He pictured her again, the target of many fingers. Hers was the only firm alibi of the bunch, but still the fingers pointed. He thought of her finding the body while Demetrius Barton emptied the dishwasher and Baylor Valentine walked his dogs, stopping to chat with Martha Van Patton on her way to Morning Prayer. He thought of Miles Costello grabbing her from behind, his hands wandering over her body, his ugly words whispered in her perfect ear. He thought of her until he fell asleep and thought no more.

Holy Comfort

Chapter Ten

"I'VE NEVER BEEN inside one of these places, have you?" said Vesba as she jerked on the parking brake, making a noise like a frog being throttled. Her partner did not notice the noise or her question, so she poked him.

"What?" he said and rubbed his ribs. He continued to gaze at the list of names in his notebook.

Vesba sighed and crossed her arms under her large breasts. "How much do you think a house like this would set you back?" She whistled to underscore her question.

Merton looked up, redirecting his gaze to the house which was about the size of the govenor's mansion but made a much louder statement about the wealth of the people who lived there. Unlike the other houses in the neighborhood, it was new. It had been wedged in sideways on what was probably an old tennis court or maybe some old lot someone had sold off. It had no yard to speak of and more roof lines than a French chateau. "A million, give or take," he answered casually.

Vesba whistled again. She looked at her unresponsive partner and sighed. "Well, c'mon. How many names we got left on that list?"

Merton looked at his list again. "Three."

"Great," she said opening her door. She struggled out and stood up, planting her hands firmly on her hips, which caused her charmeuse blouse to gape where it was buttoned. "Let's hope this lady has more to offer." Together they walked up the long brick path to the door. Vesba punched the doorball several times.

In time, the great green door opened and a small, middle-aged black woman in a black dress and white apron asked if she could help them. Vesba explained who they were and the maid, dispensing with the suspicious look she had given them initially, invited them to enter. Turning, she led the way into a black and white tiled hallway into which Vesba thought she could surely fit her entire one-bedroom southtown apartment. They followed the maid into a large dark-paneled room, richly decorated in shades of blue. The blue carpet was deep and Vesba felt herself sinking.

A dark-haired woman in a silk paisley dressing gown lounged carelessly on a large damask sofa by a huge stone fireplace where a crackling fire jumped and snapped. An elaborate arrangement of fresh flowers sat on the coffee table. The woman did not rise from her recumbent position or even turn to acknowledge her visitors, but still gazing into the fire, said, "I'm afraid I can't talk long. I'm expecting my masseuse very soon."

At first glance, Merton judged the woman to be quite beautiful, but when they moved closer and were invited to sit down in matching club chairs across from her, he realized she was not beautiful, only expensively and carefully made up. She had a fake tan which he guessed covered every inch of her skin which was no doubt waxed and buffed to near-perfection. Her face had a carved look to it, as if the nose had been pared down and the skin stretched across enhanced cheekbones by a fancy plastic surgeon. Her hair was expertly colored and highlighted. She turned away from the fire to look at her guests, swinging her slippered feet to the floor.

"Thank you for letting us come," began Vesba, taking the lead. "We appreciate how busy you are."

"I appreciate your appreciation," she replied slowly, focusing her attention on Merton whom she had only just noticed.

"Your name was on a phone message found on the body. We're following up," said Vesba.

"Good for you," said Ellen Chevalier.

Merton cleared his throat and asked, "Did you see Miles Costello on Thursday night?"

"Yes. He came over about seven o'clock. He was supposed to meet me in the afternoon, but he stood me up."

"Were you angry with him?"

"No," she scoffed. "Not really. He did it on purpose. He did it all the time. It was a little game we played. He knew that I would get angry initially, incensed really, and that would make me very, very hot. He'd let me smolder for a few hours and then…we'd enjoy real passion. We'd play act a little…He'd beg for my forgiveness—on his knees. Usually I'd forgive him."

"So it was just playacting?"

She gazed at Merton. "Of course. We were simpatico. Miles understood me."

"How long did he stay?"

"About three hours. He left around ten o'clock. I remember because my husband's plane was scheduled to arive around then and so we thought…"

"You're *married*?" asked Vesba.

"Well, of course," Ellen Chevalier answered impatiently, sitting up straighter and crossing her legs. "Chevalier is my married name. I'm a Kornbelt by birth."

"No kidding? As in the beer?" said Vesba, her interest renewed. "I thought all the Kornbelts were Catholic."

"Not this Kornbelt." Ellen looked at her watch and glanced at her nails.

Holy Comfort

Merton coughed. "Didn't Reverend Costello have a problem with...seeing a married woman?"

"No. I was his patron. Why should he have a problem?"

Merton leaned back again and cast a sideways glance at his partner who snorted and folded her arms across her expansive abdomen. She recognized the look from her partner and lobbed a question to their hostess. "Well, ma'am, did anything strange happen that night? Like a phone call...or maybe Costello was distracted..."

"Distracted? I should say not," said Ellen irritably. Then she paused, reconsidering. "Miles was paged several times during...well, he finally had to respond. He didn't tell me who it was..."

"He had a pager?" asked Merton.

"Well, yes. Didn't you find one on his body? He always wore it everywhere." Her eyes were suddenly wide. "Do you think that's significant?"

"It might be," said Merton. He lowered his chin and looked up. "It might be that person wasn't as understanding as you."

"I'm sorry I can't tell you who it was," said Ellen Chevalier.

"As we mentioned, yours was one of the names on the phone messages found on his body," he said taking out his notebook again. "There were other names: Martha Van Patton, Carol Sprague, Ginny Bishop..."

"Oh please," she interrupted, waving away his suggestion. "Those are all old ladies!"

"Patrons?" he said, raising an eyebrow.

She scowled. "I wouldn't know. We didn't have club meetings."

"He never talked about anyone?"

She put her right elbow in her left hand and laid a finger on her cheek. She gazed at the ceiling as if wracking her brain. "He had a sort of harem at work, in the office. At least that's the way he made it sound—as if they were all crazy about him. He could have cared less, of course, about those pathetic old drunks with no money. They had nothing to offer him, really."

"None of them?" asked Vesba.

"Of course, there was Page Hawthorne." She paused, noting the reaction of the detectives, and leaned back on the sofa. "I went to school with her sister. Page was a few years behind me. She married Chester Hawthorne, but they were divorced a while ago. I heard she had a hard time—she got the kids, you know, but not much money. Not that she needed it. What she needed was support, a shoulder to lean on and *sex*, no doubt. So she leaned on Miles. Miles was very kind that way. He tried very hard to give people what they wanted."

"So it was a pastoral relationship?" asked Vesba.

"I couldn't really say," said Ellen. "People were talking...even Chester asked me about them once at some party. But I think, after awhile, she began to annoy him. She used to page him sometimes, a lot, he said. I couldn't say for sure whether she was the one the other night..."

"He never mentioned who..." said Vesba, stealing a sideways look at her partner.

"Oh no," she said. "It was just a mosquito buzzing in his ear."

"We've taken up enough of your time," said Merton, standing up and pulling Vesba with him.

"Thank you," said Vesba wrenching her arm back.

Merton looked down at the other woman and smiled. "Ms. Chevalier, just for the record, where were you on Friday morning around seven?"

"In bed with my husband." She put two fingers to her mouth and kissed them. "Leave your card with my maid, won't you, so I can call you if I think of anything else?" Merton bowed slightly and, touching his partner's elbow, escorted her towards the door where a large, blustering figure suddenly blocked their escape.

"Bradford!" said Ellen Chevalier in a startled manner reminiscent of high school drama class. "I'm afraid I'm running late because of these detectives." She jumped up and came to the door, passing Merton and Vesba. She put her hand on the other man's arm. He bent to kiss her.

"Detectives?" he said straightening.

"Yes," said Ellen, turning to Merton. "Bradford Cole, meet Det. Merton."

Cole stuck his hand out and grasped the detective's. "We need to talk."

Vesba, ignored, reached for Cole's hand. "I'm Det. Vesba."

"I haven't even had my massage yet, Brad," said Ellen. "You can watch if you want."

He glanced at Ellen. "I'll be back in a few minutes. Go ahead and start your massage." She pouted, but he ignored her. "I'll walk you out," he said to Merton.

In the vast checkerboard hallway, Bradford Cole stopped and eyed the detective. "What kind of progress are you making on this case?"

"We're covering all the bases. It takes time..."

"It just seems to me," Cole interrupted, "that you could spend your time more usefully than interviewing Ellen Chevalier."

"Her name was on a phone message found on the body."

"So what?" Cole said aggressively. "People called Miles all the time. People always wanted to see him. They were always making demands. He did the best he could."

"Meaning what?" asked Vesba.

Cole glanced down at Vesba who barely reached his shoulder. "Meaning he couldn't be there for everyone."

"So some people got frustrated?" asked Merton. "Anyone in particular?"

Cole narrowed his eyes. "Look, Miles was a popular guy. Everyone liked him except maybe a few of his fellow priests who were jealous of him, but he could handle them." Cole was breathing hard and now surprisingly his eyes began to fill with tears. "He was a big guy and they always called him to handle problems with the panhandlers and homeless types who come to the church for money. Those other wimps couldn't handle that shit. No, even *they* needed Miles." He wiped his face with a large hand and cleared his throat. "Look, I want to offer a reward...you know, fifty thousand, whatever. Anything to help catch the sonofabitch who did this."

"You'll have to talk to someone else about that," said Merton quietly.

Cole's shoulders began to shake and he looked away. "Miles would give you the shirt off his back if you asked for it. He was really like that. People respond to goodness like that. They loved him."

"Everyone loved him? Even those who were frustrated by his...lack of response?"

Cole turned back and looked at the detective. "There was no one in particular. Priests like Miles who are young and healthy and—they can get into some trouble now and then, but Miles was careful. He was aware of the dangers of..."

"Sexual harrassment?" asked Vesba.

"He never sexually harrassed anyone! He didn't *need* to. He had plenty of women willing and...I mean *he* was the one getting harrassed, let me tell you."

"Tell me," said Merton. "Please."

"All right," he said folding his arms in front of his chest. "Talk to Page Hawthorne. She really strung him along for a while. She could never really make up her mind if she was interested. He used to say she paged him all the time...that she was practically stalking him. I mean, I think she's basically a good kid, but she's pretty fucked up over men. Miles said she was a classic passive-aggressive type."

Chapter Eleven

CHESTER HAWTHORNE SAT at his desk and waited for the two detectives to be shown in. He scanned the room. It was a large office with large windows looking out over the downtown skyline. His mahogany-paneled office with its splendid view filled him with a great sense of well being. He was a success. Anyone could see that. He was a partner in the number two law firm in town. He was a junior member of three of the best clubs in town. He wore twelve hundred dollar suits. He still had all his hair and a thirty-four inch waist. He thought of his best friend, Tony Spitz, and his office, located on the third floor of a seedy building in the suburbs, where he practiced law alone, reduced to answering his own phone when his secretary was at lunch. Tony belonged to two of the same clubs, but he was losing his hair, and was still married, but just barely. It was just a matter of time before he too would be thrown out, lock, stock and pinstripe suit. He smiled, imagining the inevitable.

His eyes moved quickly over the detectives, evaluating—one fat and female, the other tall, lanky and male—both of no interest to him. He turned away, back to the window. "I don't have much time, Detectives. I have to be on the golf course in an hour. I only came in this morning to square up some loose ends."

"This shouldn't take long," said Merton. "We're talking to as many people as we can who knew Reverend Costello. You were in his small group."

"Yes, I was."

"Why was that?"

"He asked me to join. I knew most of the men in the group. He went to Yale. He worked with my wife."

"Your ex-wife?"

"Yes, Detective. My *ex*-wife." He turned to have a better look at Merton. He was unimpressive. Good-looking, he supposed, like a Marlboro Man or a NASCAR driver. He smiled, enjoying the analogy.

"Can you tell us about Costello? How long did you know him?"

"Not very long. I'd only just joined his group six months or so ago. My friend, Tony Spitz, encouraged me to join. I can't say I was as taken

Holy Comfort

with the group as he was. Studying the Bible was my wife's thing, not mine, but I thought I'd give it a whirl."

"We heard you were reading *Daniel*," said Merton.

"What?"

"In your small group."

"Oh. *Daniel*...something from the Old Testament. Pretty crazy stuff, children's stories, really...Miles liked *Daniel,* though. He liked all that apocolyptic jazz..."

"Did you like Costello?"

Chester Hawthorne shrugged. "Miles was a good enough guy. A bit of a climber, but I liked him well enough. He had ambitions. For a while I thought that they included my wife..."

"Your ex-wife?"

"Yes, my ex-wife," said Hawthorne impatiently. "He had a bit of a thing for Page—following our divorce, but nothing came of it."

"Didn't it bother him, having you in his group if he was interested in your ex-wife?"

"No. I think he liked that. We had a bond, you might say. He was very competitive."

Merton uncrossed his legs and leaned forward. "Did it bother you?"

"What? Costello and Page?" Hawthorne leaned back in his chair. "No, Detective. She was my ex-wife as you've pointed out. She was open game."

"We've heard from some people that *she* chased him..."

"Page?" Hawthorne said, coming very close to smiling. "No way. That's hardly her style. She's *enjoying* her celibacy, take it from me." The two men's eyes met and held for a moment until Chester glanced away.

"Why would anyone say that...about her chasing him, then?" asked Vesba.

Chester Hawthorne turned to Vesba for the first time and his mouth pulled back on one side. "People project their own desires on other people, especially people they don't understand."

The detectives glanced at each other and Vesba shifted in her client chair. "Where were you, Mr. Hawthorne, on Friday morning around seven?" she asked.

"Right here," he answered, swiveling back around to face them. "Right here. Ask my assistant, she'll verify my statement. Believe me I had nothing but regard for poor Father Costello. If he wanted to fuck my ex-wife, he was welcome to her."

Chapter Twelve

"You're so kind to come to my home, Detectives," droned Martha Van Patton. "I've been somewhat incapacitated since my most recent hip surgery. I appreciate your kindness."

She didn't look so incapacitated, thought Vesba as she gazed at the erect old woman artfully posed by the French window. She looked like she could play a hard game of tennis and then beat the pants off you in bridge. Yeah, she must have been beautiful once, back during the Punic Wars when women wore their hair in French twists and linen sheaths were all the rage.

"I've been thinking and thinking about dear Miles ever since I heard the terrible news. I believe I've been in a sort of daze since then. I couldn't think."

Vesba rolled her eyes over to Merton who sat uncomfortably in a deep club chair next to her's. He seemed to be leaning forward on his knees to prevent being swallowed up by it. He looked straight at Mrs. Van Patton while she concentrated on some spot behind his head, unburdening herself of her recollection. She spoke in a steady, unemotional tone.

"All I could think about was what a terrible loss to us all it is, what a terrible *waste* it is to the church. Miles was, you see, by far and away the most talented of the clergy, but then that made his very presence a threat to the others. *He* should have been the rector. He was so much more suited for a leadership role there." She turned from the window, her fists tightly clenched at her sides. She pressed her lips in a tight line and stared at Merton.

"Was there a possibility that Rev. Costello's role at the church might change?" he asked.

"Anything is possible," she said cooly. Then she turned back to the window, her anger flaring again. "Poor Miles. He had reached a point where he had become quite unhappy."

"Unhappy?" repeated Vesba, rousing herself.

"Yes. He was so misused, you see, so under-utilized, *banished* in effect to the church school. His gifts were not being allowed to blossom, to yield fruit." She crossed her arms. "Pinkney wanted it that way. He wanted Miles to look bad. It was a plot to get rid of Miles. I'm sure of it."

"A plot?" asked Vesba, irony creeping into her tone.

Holy Comfort

"Yes," said Mrs. Van Patton, taking note of the irony and turning. "Very definitely. I was thinking about that very thing as a matter of fact, when I remembered something else, and I called you. I remembered something Miles told me, oh, probably a year ago. Yes, a year ago, I think. It might be important to you now. He told me about a confrontation he had had with Page Hawthorne. I'm sure you've spoken to her by now. She works at the church. Quite capable, but deeply troubled, I'm afraid." She paused and her eyes moved to Merton. "Do you need to write this down?"

His hand moved inside his jacket and he pulled out a pen and a spiral notebook, which he flipped open to a blank page.

Mrs. Van Patton nodded and sat down. "Miles was very upset. He told me that they had argued and that Page had said some very hurtful things, crazy things about his leaving the ministry and his not being suited to the priesthood. She actually questioned his calling, I think."

Merton scribbled down a few words and turned his gaze again on Mrs. Van Patton. "Did he say why they argued?"

"I don't remember, exactly. But I do know that Page was pushing him. She wanted to be more than friends, if you know what I mean."

"More than friends?" repeated Vesba.

Mrs. Van Patton turned her attention indulgently to Vesba. "She wanted to be his lover and eventually she wanted to be a clergy wife."

"Really?" said Vesba.

"In my opinion, yes...and he wasn't interested in her...not in that way. But he could never be unkind to anyone—not Miles. Anyway, nothing could have hurt Miles more than to have his call questioned. He was devoted to God, to the church. I remember he sat in this very room, in that chair," she said, pointing dramatically to a Jacobean print wing chair by the fireplace. "And he wept right in front of me. He was devastated. I was shocked. I tried to console him, to tell him, of course, he was born to the priesthood. How could some silly, love-struck girl make him think otherwise? 'Listen to me,' I told him. 'I believe in you.'" Mrs. Van Patton stopped suddenly and looked at her hand, which she had begun to shake at Vesba. She cleared her throat and folded her hands in her lap as she continued. "It took some time, but he seemed to get over it and on with things. He never mentioned it again. About that time, Carol Sprague and I came up with the idea of sending him to Ireland. That cheered him up."

Mrs. Van Patton stood up and moved to the mantle where she fingered a snapshot lovingly. Her bowed head caught the reflected light of the blazing fire and her ash blond hair, carefully swept back from her face, appeared to sparkle. She looked deceptively young in the redemptive firelight. "See," she said, handing the picture to Merton. "Here we are. Miles and I...and my husband Jasper."

Merton took the picture. Miles had his arm around Mrs. Van Patton who stood between him and her husband, a wizened old man in his eighties. A chill spread through the detective as he focused on the cold, hard eyes of the smiling priest. He handed the picture back without comment and smiled.

Mrs. Van Patton replaced the photo on the mantle, leaning it against the wall fondly. "I'm not sure what was going on between Miles and Page Hawthorne. I believe it was one-sided on her part, but I can't be sure of that. She's a pretty thing...and deeply intelligent. But she's a troubled girl. I knew her mother, you know. She was a dear friend of mine. I've known Page a long time, since she was a little girl. She had everything, always. But she never fit in. She never...did what was expected. Well, she did marry Chester Hawthorne—that was a relief to her parents. I think they were nervous the entire time she was away at college, worried that she'd find someone inappropriate, unsuitable, back east. But she made her mother happy. She died before Page made a shambles of the marriage, before she walked out with those two darling boys. She never got back on track after that. Anyway, I'm not pointing fingers, but...I wonder, I just wonder...what she might be capable of..."

Vesba cleared her throat. She leaned forward and rested her elbows on her knees and held her hands about a foot apart, fingers spread. "Now let me get this straight," she said. "You're saying that Page Hawthorne wanted to be a clergy wife, Costello's wife, but he didn't want anything to do with her so he blew her off—gently, you say, because he could never hurt anyone—and she got sore and told him off and, maybe, just maybe, she killed him?"

"I never said *that*," said Martha Van Patton icily.

"I believe you suggested that," said Vesba, standing up. Mrs. Van Patton turned away. "And it's a theory, certainly, but I wonder what you think about the *other* women in Costello's life?"

"Other women?" said Mrs. Van Patton. "What are you talking about?"

"Other women such as Ellen Chevalier, another one of his patrons, who paid him to—"

"Leona," interrupted Merton. He stood up and walked over to the mantle where the old woman stood. "Mrs. Van Patton, were you aware that Reverend Costello had female patrons besides you and Mrs. Sprague?"

Mrs. Van Patton turned slowly to face him. She shrugged her shoulders and clasped her hands. "Miles Costello was a popular fellow, a fine churchman with a wonderful future ahead of him. He was certainly not promiscuous, if that's what you are implying. I told you about Page Hawthorne simply because he had confided in me...about her. And because he had seemed so urgent in his...pain."

Det. Vesba snorted. "Did he ever tell you about the *pain* Ellen Chevalier put him through? Did he ever tell you how he begged her for forgiveness on a regular basis?"

The old woman's eyes grew large and she steadied herself with a hand on the mantle. "I don't know anything about Ellen Chevalier," she said evenly. "But I think you should leave now. I'm tired."

Holy Comfort

"No problem," said Vesba. "But first, could I ask you a question?" Mrs. Van Patton nodded, but did not look at either detective. "Baylor Valentine said he saw you on Friday morning while he was walking his dogs and you were on your way to Morning Prayer. Did you see anything odd? Someone unexpected or…"

"No," said Mrs. Van Patton. "Nothing unusual on Dozier Avenue. Just the cars of my friends who were at church to attend Morning Prayer. Perhaps there was something on the *other* side of the church, on Westborough Avenue, the side more accessible to the general public. I never walk on that side." She turned away. "I believe you can find your way out," she said.

HE TURNED ON the light and looked at the small black book in his hands. It said *Holy Bible*, stamped in gold. It felt heavy in his hands, this revised standard version translated from the original tongues being the version set forth in A.D. 1611, and so forth.

He crossed the room and sat down in the black leather chair. He wondered again about the pointing fingers of Holy Comforter and their single target. Even Leona had noticed the venom-tinged comments, the bitterness with which they were said. *She's enjoying her celibacy, take it from me…She's pretty fucked-up over men…He used to pass out on top of her on a regular basis…She never got back on track…I just wonder what she might be capable of…* Is she 'deeply troubled'? Is she really? Why are these people, with their 'fine gestures' so determined to make him think so?

He opened the book and rifled the pages forward and back until he found what he was looking for on page 841. *In the third year of the reign of Jehoiakim of Judah, Nebuchadnezzar king of Babylon came to Jerusalem and besieged it.* Perhaps there is something to help here.

C.R. Compton

Chapter Thirteen

ON SUNDAY MORNING, Roy Merton walked three times around the perimeter of the Church of the Holy Comforter inspecting the pie-shaped wedge of land on which the pseudo English structure reposed. He counted six doors in and out of which a murderer could probably come and go easily enough without causing as much as a raised eyebrow during the early morning hours. Because there was no parking lot, cars were now parked all along the two roads, Westborough and Dozier, which intersected at the point of the Holy Comforter pie. It was not unusual, he could see, for highly-motivated parishioners to walk a quarter mile to get from their cars to the church. For those who couldn't, or wouldn't, make the trek from their cars, there even appeared to be a valet parking attendant.

The triumphant strains of an organ voluntary floated out over the lawn, failing to evince any emotional reaction from Merton. He almost smiled, picturing Baylor Valentine in a musical reverie, but unlike his partner, the organist failed to amuse him. He waited for the exiting throng to thin and then entered the building through the empty kitchen with the intention of revisiting the crime scene on the lower level. As he turned the corner into the hallway designated *Clergy Area* in gold leaf on the glass door, a small boy rocketed directly into him from the other direction. He took a step backward while the boy ricocheted onto the floor. Merton bent to pull him up, but another, slightly larger boy flew in between and pulled his fallen comrade roughly by the hand. "You idiot," he whispered. "Why don't you watch what you're doing?"

"I didn't mean to!" hissed the smaller boy.

"Sorry, sir," said the older boy. "Are you all right?"

"I'll live," said Merton putting his hand on the shoulder of his assailant. "You okay?"

The boy coughed and brushed off the seat of his chinos. "I'm fine," he said. "I'll live, too."

A door opened down the hall and Page Hawthorne emerged from her office. She stood with one hand on the door frame and gazed down the hallway. "What are you boys up to?" she called. Her eyes flicked once to the detective.

54

Holy Comfort

"Tal ran into this man, Mom. He's such an idiot," said Walter, shaking his head.

Merton started walking down the hall, his hand still on Tal's shoulder. Walter followed, his accusatory eyes pushing his brother forward.

"Are you all right?" she asked Merton as Tal moved to her side, embracing her.

He nodded, a glimmer of a smile on his lips, his hand rubbing his abdomen.

"You have to be more careful, Tal. You could have hurt someone."

The boys stared at the carpet. Tal giggled.

She smiled, too. "Boys," she said looking down. "This is Detective Merton." She looked up. "Detective Merton, meet my sons, Walter and Tal. I hope they've apologized."

The boys shook the detective's hand manfully, in turn, and mumbled more apologies.

"You two can go play on the playground now. Just please be more careful and try not to run anyone else down on the way."

"Okay, Mom," they shouted as they took off running.

"Walk!" she shouted after them. "And stay on the playground!" She watched for a minute and then turned into her office. "I'm sorry," she said.

"They're just boys," he said behind her.

"Unruly boys," she said.

"They're certainly well-dressed," he said, making conversation. "Blazers, khakis, loafers. I don't see many kids wearing *ties* these days."

She turned around and looked up at him. "That's just the uniform around here. They like to dress up on Sundays."

"No criticism implied," he said, meeting her questioning eyes and smiling.

She turned back to her desk. "I've got a little work to do here," she said, dismissing him.

"May I sit down?" he said, refusing to be dismissed. "Since you're here, I'd like to ask you a few questions."

"Okay," she said. "Be my guest. But like I said..."

"I'll wait," he interrupted. He sat in the second chair and left the door ajar.

While Page turned on her computer and shuffled papers purposefully, Merton studied the books that covered one whole wall of her tiny office. There was a row of Bibles, commentaries, concordances, hymnals, and prayer books. Above that were several rows of books by authors with whom Roy was mostly unacquainted: George MacDonald, Oswald Chambers, Martin Smith, Richard Foster, Evelyn Underhill, Henri Nouwen, Calvin Miller, Hannah Whithall Smith, Morton Kelsey, J.J. Packer, Dietrich Bonhoeffer, Michael Ramsay, and Peter Marshall. There was half a row devoted to someone named Frederick Buechner. A few names, such as C.S. Lewis, Martin Luther, John Updike, and Billy Graham were familiar. Then there were a few more rows with anthologies. These were mixed in with novels as varied as *The Catcher in the Rye, A River Runs Through It* and *The Wind in the Willows.* There were multi-colored post-it notes sticking out of all of them.

As he sat and contemplated the brimming shelves, he picked up *Pilgrim's Progress* by John Bunyan, opened it at random and began to read. *Pilgrim was taken to a large upper room that faced the sunrise. And the name of the room was Peace.* He looked up, then, and found Page gazing at him. He closed the book.

She smiled, obviously amused by his discomfort, and said, "Go ahead. Please, Detective, help yourself."

He quickly returned the book to its place on the shelf and re-crossed his legs.

"I don't mind if you look at them," she said.

Roy cleared his throat as his mind raced, trying to think of something intelligent to say. "What are all the post-it notes for?" he asked, clearing his throat again.

"Well, they mark a place where there's some good quote that I think I may be able to use sometime," she explained smiling broadly. "I use quotes a lot in my work. In my newsletter and in the service leaflets. It's what makes my job interesting to me."

Roy looked a little confused, so she continued, picking up a folded piece of paper. "See, here's a service leaflet from a few weeks ago. The Gospel reading for that day was Matthew 16: 21-28. That's where Jesus rebukes Peter saying, 'Get behind me, Satan! You are a stumbling block to me; you do not have in mind the things of God, but the things of men.' This comes shortly after Jesus has said he's going to give Peter the keys of the kingdom. But then Peter has said some dumb thing, demonstrating once again that he just doesn't get it yet. In effect, he's tempting Jesus and Jesus doesn't need that. So on the back of the service leaflet where there's some extra space I put this quote from Henry Van Dyke. See?" she asked, handing him the leaflet, which he took and dutifully read.

> *A vessel filled to the brim with water is apt to spill a little when it is shaken. Peter is so full of human nature that, whenever he is excited or agitated, it seems to overflow, and some word or deed comes out, which would be almost childish in its impulsiveness, if it were not for the virile force of the great strong heart behind it. The consequence of this is that he is more often in trouble, more frequently rebuked and corrected, than any other of the disciples.*

"You see?" she said looking at Roy. He nodded in reply. "It's my little way of teaching, of getting a point across to the parish. I know it's nothing, really. Such a small thing, but to me it's wonderful. That is, if anyone reads it...but it doesn't really matter. Maybe one person on that

Holy Comfort

Sunday read the quote and realized how much he or she is like Peter, how we all are like Peter—believing and faithful one minute, doubting the next, so humanly imperfect...well, you see, don't you?"

Roy nodded again at Page whose cheeks were pink with enthusiasm. "Probably more people read that back page than listen to the entire sermon," he remarked.

"I've heard that," she said. "Maybe it's true."

"You must be a very well-read person."

"Relative to some people, yes. Relative to others, no."

"Relative to me," he said, a brief smile crossing his face and brightening his eyes.

Page was silent as she took the leaflet which he held out to her. In the moments that followed, as the two of them looked at each other, he became acutely aware of her pink cheeks and that the office was, indeed, stifling.

"Charles says you know your *Macbeth*," she said.

"I read what I like," he said. "And I remember things."

"Well, that's what we all do, right? Once we finish college." She stopped abruptly, catching herself with a little intake of breath.

He smiled. "I went to college."

"But not everybody keeps reading, even what they like," she said turning back to her computer. "Excuse me, now. I just need to get some things to take home."

"Take your time," he said.

He watched her as she moved efficiently at her desk, never glancing behind, oblivious once again to his presence. He noted her short wool skirt and silk blouse, beneath which a lace-edged camisole was visible, and wondered if he would be able, sitting by her in church, to keep his mind free of impure thoughts and focused on God. He doubted it. While he was wondering, she turned and asked, "Would you like some coffee?"

"Sure," he said, wondering what he had said 'sure' about.

She stood up, smoothed her skirt, and squeezed by him. When she returned she set one styrofoam cup down on the desk and handed another to him. She sat down and picked up her coffee. "What do you want to ask me now?" she said, sipping.

He swallowed some coffee. "We've talked to so many people about Costello," he said. "We've interviewed the staff, the clergy and the wardens. We've talked to the men in his small group and the women who gave him money. We talked to everyone whose name was on a phone memo dumped on his dead body. Everyone has an opinion, but there is no one thing that everyone agrees on." He drank some more coffee and set the cup down. "That said, there seem to be two schools of thought regarding Costello. On the one side are the people who felt that he was angling for the rector's job, that he was a scoundrel who chased women and cared for no one but himself. On the other side are his friends and supporters who thought he was a great and multi-talented guy who was held down by the rector who was himself plotting to get rid of Costello."

Page sighed but said nothing.

"There's no forensic evidence yet. Just a lot of opinion."

"Are you leaning one way or the other or is that not kosher to ask?"

"I know who I'd like to believe," he said, narrowing his eyes and staring at her. "I'd like to believe you."

"Go ahead, then. Believe me," she said. "Believe Charles Pinkney."

He exhaled. "Don't take this the wrong way, Ms. Hawthorne. But there are quite a few people who really don't like you very much." He pried at her eyes with his own, but Page was looking down. Her cheeks appeared to burn. The detective continued. "The people who were Costello's closest friends and supporters all say you had a thing for Miles Costello. That you chased him, talked with him behind closed doors, paged him at all hours of the night…"

"That isn't true," she interrupted. "I never paged him…or *chased* him." The detective waited for Page to go on. "It's totally ridiculous."

"Miles Costello must have told them all something."

"But it *isn't* true. Why would he have lied about it to them?"

"Maybe he wanted it to be true."

"Why? Who are *they*?"

"Griggs and Pentecost," he stated flatly, watching for her reaction.

"Oh my goodness," she said. "How can you take those two seriously?"

"Ellen Chevalier and Brad Cole said the same things." She did not react this time and was silent, refusing to comment. Merton continued. "Why did he talk to them about you?"

She thought about the question for a minute before answering. "Maybe he was covering for someone. Someone who really did page him a lot and…"

"Maybe he wished it was you."

Page expelled a loud breath of air. "You keep saying that, but that's a crazy idea."

"Brad Cole also said you strung Costello along and then dropped him and wouldn't talk to him. He said Costello described *you* as a classic passive-aggressive type."

Page forced herself to look the detective in the eye. "Miles was the passive-aggressive, and I'm not the only person he shrouded. You must have heard about his behavior from other people…"

"Uh huh."

Page sighed and rolled her eyes. "No matter what I say, I'm going to sound defensive, and that isn't fair. I have nothing to defend!"

"Maybe he was trying to make someone jealous."

"Who? That doesn't make sense, either."

Holy Comfort

"Your ex-husband didn't agree with Cole—about you chasing Costello. He said you weren't the type, that you were enjoying your celibacy."

"Oh, that's cute," said Page, leaning back in her chair, swiveling away from the detective. "Wait a minute," she said, turning slowly. "Why did you talk to Chester? He hardly knew Miles. I don't understand."

"Chester Hawthorne was a member of Costello's small group. Didn't you know that?"

"Why would I know that? We're divorced."

"Well, he was one of the Yale men," said Merton. She looked even more confused. "Reverend Whitefish said that Costello's small group was made up of his hand-picked buddies. They all happened to be Yale alumni."

"But Chester never cared about bible study or prayer or anything spiritual for that matter. He was an Episcopalian because his parents were. He went on Christmas Eve and Easter and grumbled about that. I didn't know he even knew who Miles was, much less that they were friends." She shook her head. "What else did he say?"

"He said Costello was very competitive, that their mutual attraction to you, past or present, gave them a bond." Page rolled her eyes again. "So you see Costello might have gotten a kick out of making someone jealous."

"Not Chester."

"Well, Ellen Chevalier said he used to stand her up on purpose, to make her mad in order to heighten their sexual…"

"Oh, please. Spare me the details," said Page with distaste. "You must see how sick all this sounds, even coming from his so-called 'friends.'"

"I agree," said Roy. "He enjoyed playing with fire, and it's no stretch to see how it could have gotten him burned."

Page nodded, swiveling again in her chair. "I've been wondering about some of the people at work who were his pals. My nine year old would call them 'losers.' I might be a little kinder, but they're unstable, and it wouldn't take much to set them off."

"How so?"

"Gracie Griggs and Charlotte Pentecost are desperate creatures. They have no money, just the salaries they make here, and that's hardly enough to live on. Their futures are bleak. Charlotte, for instance, is single and doesn't want to be. I wouldn't put it past her to be working here simply because she thought she could meet rich 'eligible' men. On the other hand, Gracie is married, but to a drunk who's given up even trying to work. Their lives are desperate because they don't want to take care of themselves. They want someone else to take care of them."

"Do you think they thought Miles would?"

She nodded. "I do. At least they counted on him to protect their jobs."

"If you're right, they certainly wouldn't have a motive for killing him," said Merton.

"No, except they were deluded and if they found out they couldn't count on Miles...for anything...they might do something."

"Do you really think either of them is capable of putting together such an elaborate plan?'

Page shrugged. "I don't know."

"What about Martha Van Patton?" He leaned forward in his uncomfortable chair. "She had a theorey that concerned you as well."

Page sighed. "I really had no idea I was such a hot item of gossip. My life is really so dull. What exactly did *she* say?"

"She said you wanted to be a clergy wife and that when you were unsuccessful in your bid for Miles, you had a fight and told him he should never have become a priest, that you questioned his 'calling.'"

The color drained from Page's face completely. The detective's expression did not change as he continued. "She said he sat in her living room and cried about it. He was devastated, she said."

Then Page smiled, the left corner of her mouth quivering slightly. "He must have played it to the hilt," she said.

"Did you say that to him? About his calling?"

"Yes. I said it. You want to know when?"

He nodded. A dent appeared between his eyes.

"It was right after he tried to seduce me in his office. I believe I told you about that. Right after he grabbed my breasts and slid his hand between my legs."

The detective blinked, but otherwise his face remained unmoved. She leaned forward. "I had just broken away and told him to get his nasty hands off me. He laughed at me and said, 'Oh c'mon, baby, relax.' I told him he was a disgusting hypocrite and he called me a repressed little bitch who didn't even know what she wanted. I said how dare you—how dare you call yourself a priest. He said, 'Oh, c'mon, Baby, it's just a fucking *job*. I'm just an *actor*. I wear a fucking costume, for God's sake. Don't you get it? Don't you get it?' I said 'No, I don't get it. I'll never get it' and I sort of lunged for the door. He said, 'Run, baby, run' and he laughed."

"So he turned that scene into scorned Page questions the good priest's calling?"

"Apparently so," she said, leaning back in her chair, pushing her hair back. "I can't believe he told Martha Van Patton...and twisted it so. But he'd say *anything*. Anything."

"It got him a trip to Ireland."

"Oh," she said, her incredible almond-shaped eyes turning once again to him.

"He knew how to use things to his advantage. He may not have succeeded where you were concerned, but he made that failure work with Mrs. Van Patton."

"I underestimated Miles. I had no idea he was so debased." Page shook her sleeve and looked at her watch. "I should go. I've made the boys wait long enough. I hope this conversation has helped."

Holy Comfort

This dismissal he could not ignore. "I appreciate your letting me...your help," he said.

Page stood up then and began to gather her things to go home. Roy joined her and, taking her sweater from the back of her chair, helped her put it on. He glanced at its label, which read *ALPACA, MADE IN PERU*. It was extremely soft and fuzzy and he was tempted for a moment to run his hands down her arms, but he restrained himself, plunging his hands instead into his pockets until she was ready to go. Then he cleared his throat again and held the door for her, turned off the light, and followed her upstairs. They turned left in the narthex and went through the Great Hall where a handful of diehards still stood in groups and talked. Demetrius Barton stood at a table, clearing the coffee urns onto a cart. He nodded to Page when she waved. They exited out the south doors on the side of the church by the playground. Page waved to the boys from the top of the steps.

Their cars were parked in different directions so they parted company on the sidewalk in front of the church. They had not spoken since leaving her office. They said goodbye shyly, eyes averted. Merton took a few steps and paused. "Ms. Hawthorne," he said, stopping her. She turned. "Costello was a dangerous man."

"Dangerous?" she said. "I'm not sure dangerous is the right word..."

"Yes, it is," he said. She stared blankly in his direction. He smiled. "She feared no danger, for she knew no sin."

She turned around and hurried to her car. He watched her go for a moment. There was no swing in her narrow hips. She walked capably like an athlete with no pretense, no sexual suggestion. She threw her bag and her purse into the car as the boys scrambled inside. She got in herself without looking back. She was gone and he turned to find his own truck.

She was a funny girl, a strange girl. Strange to him, at least. But she did not strike him as "deeply troubled." No, he didn't buy that. Troubled, only perhaps because her own mother's friends and the people she grew up with thought she didn't fit in. Troubled, perhaps because she was not safe alone in a room with an ordained priest. Troubled by a detective who would not leave her alone and asked too many troubling questions.

What was she thinking about now as she drove home? Miles Costello? Martha Van Patton? What to have for dinner? Did she ever think about the troublesome detective? The one who watched her surreptitiously, who knew how the hair on the nape of her neck grew in a whorl and that there was a mole on the curling pinna of her left ear.

Chapter Fourteen

IT WAS ALMOST a relief when Page dropped the boys off at their school on Monday and headed down Montgomery Road toward work. She listened to Lyle Lovett on the CD player and ticked off the landmarks as she guided her Volvo, cruising past the Westway Cleaners, the Gas House Car Wash, the Rock Point Baptist Church with its large sign *Love your enemies—It'll drive them crazy!*, Lenny's Drive-In, St. Mary Queen of the Universe Catholic Church, two Shubert's Markets and a Dierdorf's Market, two McDonald's and a host of other fast food restaurants and bars. As she neared the church, the houses became gradually bigger, the lawns greener, until at last she turned at the Westborough Congregational Church onto Crown Avenue and the Episcopal Church of the Holy Comforter appeared, a humble picture of medieval propriety. She parked a block away and ambled slowly down the sidewalk, enjoying deep breaths of the brisk fall air, savoring them for they would have to sustain her through the morning.

She greeted Tammy Spivy, stopping to admire her flowers, and inquired if anything was new in regards to the investigation. "Not that I've heard," she replied. "Miles is still dead." Page shot her a sardonic half-smile, checked her message box and headed downstairs. After opening her office and dropping her purse and omnipresent file folders, she poured herself a cup of coffee and strolled down to Sophie Carl's office where Sophie was unpacking for the day.

"Did you have a good weekend, Sophie?" she asked as she sat down in a chair next to Sophie's fish tank.

"I ripped down all the wallpaper in my dining room. It was very therapeutic."

"I bet. Maybe I should try that."

"Yeah. Only problem is, now I have to put up the new stuff."

Page smiled. "Is that a new outfit? I like it."

"Oh, thanks," said Sophie looking down to check on her outfit. "Shopping is also very therapeutic. I got this at the mall. I just went crazy at the Fall Sale at Golden's. Charged over two hundred dollars worth of stuff! Larry didn't even care. I think he was glad for me to be out of the house, because when I was home I was either tearing something apart or crying like

Holy Comfort

a baby. We went out to eat twice. I just could not get my act together. How about you?"

"I took the boys to Hog Hollow to pick out pumpkins. That was our big adventure of the weekend. That and Walter's soccer game, which they won. Walter even scored. He was so happy."

Sophie looked fondly at her friend, thinking that it had not been a very exciting weekend for a single woman even considering Friday's events. "So what did you do for therapy?"

"I don't know. I tried to keep my mind on the boys and off of here, but that didn't work, really. I tried to remember when the last time I saw Miles was. I think it was Wednesday after the staff meeting. It was back down here. He was looking for Styrofoam cups up in the cabinet and there weren't any. I came down and needed a cup too, so I said I'd go down to the coffee machine in production and get some. When I came back he was gone and his door was shut. I put the cups down, got my coffee and went back to my office. I never saw him alive again."

"I saw him Thursday afternoon. He'd missed some appointments and we sort of had an argument. I feel bad about that..." Page murmured in agreement. Sophie smiled, remembering something. "I saw the detectives upstairs. I think they've been here since Morning Prayer, talking to the regulars."

"Vesba the Lesba and Roy the Boy Toy?" rang out the braying drawl of Charlotte Pentecost who strode into Sophie's office and threw herself into the chair next to Page.

Sophie chuckled and pretended to look for something on her uncharacteristically cluttered desk. Page ducked her head by way of a greeting.

"Oh, *what*? Have I shocked Miss Page again?" Charlotte moaned, placing a hand on Page's knee. "I'm so sorry. Mean old vulgar me has gone and forgotten we're in a church, after all, *again*."

Page moved her knees so that Charlotte's hand fell limply onto her chair.

"Have you talked to the detectives yet, Charlotte?" intervened Sophie.

"Oh, yes. The Leona and Roy Show came by to visit me late on Friday afternoon. I was an emotional wreck, of course, so they came right to my house. I told them everything I know, which is practically nothing. The rector came by after, imagine that. We prayed together. It was very special."

"I always thought you and Miles were really close, Charlotte," sighed Sophie. "But you don't seem to be taking this very hard."

"People express their grief differently," she said, giving Sophie a wintery look. "Anyway, I just came in today for the funeral. Then I'm going home."

"Don't you have a Lay Ministry Board luncheon today, Charlotte?" asked Page.

"That's right," said Sophie. "I'm sure I have that on Colin's calendar."

"Jesus. Didn't he cancel that?" said Charlotte. "Well, Colin can manage without me. I'm too upset to even *think* about going to that meeting." She fanned herself with her fingers, then turned her attention to Page. "Nice outfit, Page. Understated, charcoal gray, but shows off your legs. Great choice. And I bet you're wearing it for the benefit of the Roy Toy, aren't you? He's *just* your type—he even wears Wrangler's, for god's sake!"

"Larry wears Wranglers," said Sophie. "Is that supposed to *mean* something?"

"Page knows what I mean," said Charlotte ignoring the secretary. "I'm sure she noticed."

"How would you know if she'd noticed or not, Charlotte?" asked Sophie. "You weren't even here on Friday. Sure, he talked to Page—several times—but..."

Charlotte's eyebrows flew up. "The detectives did seem particularly interested in our Page when they talked to me on Friday. And I hear you met with *him* again on Sunday after church in your tiny office. Sipping coffee, bumping knees. I wonder what all that can mean?"

"She did find the body," said Sophie. "Of course they would be interested. It's not as if she's a *suspect*."

"Well, now," drawled Charlotte. "I suppose when it comes to that, we're all suspects. Right, Page?" She patted her knee again and waited for an answer.

"I think I'll check my mail," said Page, glancing meaningfully at Sophie. "I'll see you around." She stood up and headed out of the clergy area and down the hall toward the mailboxes without a backward glance.

"Did I say something?" Charlotte asked. "Jesus, she is so...sensitive."

"Right," Sophie said irritably. She made a show of neatening a stack of paper until she heard the door open and looked down the hall. "Look, here come your detective friends, Charlotte. Maybe they're looking for *you*," she said indicating Vesba and Merton who had just pushed through the fire doors. Merton looked into Page's office as he passed. Neither woman missed the glance.

Sophie sucked in her cheeks and looked up. "Can I help you, Detectives?" she asked, glancing at Charlotte who had thrown her shoulders back and moved to the edge of her chair.

"The funeral's at ten? Is that correct?" asked Vesba, focusing her attention on the clergy secretary.

"Yes. That's correct," replied Sophie. "We're expecting a large crowd."

"Oh, yes, indeedy, we *are*," said Charlotte, her big-eyed gaze never wavering from Merton. "Mr. Leonard of the valet parking company was just

Holy Comfort

arriving when I drove in this morning. We always have valet parking at Holy Comforter. It's just our way."

"Is that so?" snapped Vesba. "I always say that valet parking should be a priority at any church, right up there with visiting the sick and preaching the gospel."

"We just came down to see Colin Whitefish," said Merton. "Is he in? His door is closed."

"I haven't seen him this morning," said Sophie.

"Det. Merton," interrupted Charlotte. "I have to ask. Where are your cowboy boots, your jeans? Not riding the range today?" She leaned forward as she asked, gesturing extravagantly with her left hand. She touched the sleeve of his dark gray suit and looked up at him, her eyes wide and innocent. "You look positively Brooks Brotherish!"

"When in Rome..." he said, his eyes blank as they swept over Charlotte.

"You should visit Rome more often," said Charlotte, grinning.

He smiled at Charlotte, then turned to his partner. "Let's wait upstairs in the rector's office," he suggested, taking Vesba's arm. "We'll see you ladies later."

Sophie watched the two detectives head back down the hallway. She noticed that Detective Vesba appeared to be struggling to keep up with her partner who was striding purposefully, apparently in a hurry to get upstairs.

Chapter Fifteen

THE CHURCH WAS not so full as everyone had expected. About a quarter of the available seats were filled, mourners sitting along the aisle and concentrated in the middle. There was no family seated in the first rows.

As the rector walked slowly down the center aisle, he intoned the familiar words of the Anglican service, the same words spoken over the centuries for kings and paupers alike. *I am the resurrection and the life, saith the Lord; he that believeth in me, though he were dead, yet shall he live; and whosoever liveth and believeth in me shall never die.*

The service was short, beautiful, unchanging. There would be no sad words spoken by grieving family members, had there been any, or friends—only a short homily by the rector. No maudlin displays—that was the Holy Comforter way. The Lesson from the Old Testament would be read by a layperson and the choir would sing something appropriate, designated by Baylor Valentine.

There was no coffin Page noted absent-mindedly, no pall. There was no body, of course. It had gone to the morgue for an autopsy and so the police could look for clues. Fibers, hair samples, finger prints. Who really knew? Then, she supposed, when they were finished, the body of Miles Costello would be cremated and his earthly remains stowed in the columbarium of the Gresham Garden. Willis McHugh had donated the niche, the one next to his in-laws. The Reverend Miles Costello would never leave the Church of the Holy Comforter now.

I know that my Redeemer liveth, and that he shall stand at the latter day upon the earth; and though this body be destroyed, yet shall I see God; whom I shall see for myself and mine eyes shall behold, and not as a stranger.

Page remembered her mother's funeral six years earlier at Holy Comforter and her father's two years later. She had been to countless others, all beautiful, all paradoxical in their spirit of sadness and expectation. The tears one shed were always for the living, she thought, those left behind to grieve and start over. She felt no sadness today for Miles, only a growing sense of dread.

For none of us liveth to himself and no man dieth to himself. For if we live, we live unto the Lord; and if we die, we die unto the Lord. Whether we live, therefore, or die, we are the Lord's.

Holy Comfort

Page stood alone at the very back of the church on the Gospel side. Her hands gripped the back of the dark pew in front of her. Her knuckles, she noted, were white. The nausea returned. With relief she sat down along with the rest of the congregation to hear the reading of the Old Testament Lesson. Bradford Cole, Miles' close friend, read chokingly from Isaiah: *He has sent me to bind up the brokenhearted, to proclaim freedom for the captives and release from darkness for the prisoners, to proclaim the year of the Lord's favor and the day of vengeance of our God, to comfort all who mourn...*

The day of vengeance...why did Page have the feeling that Miles' death itself was an act of vengeance? Like a robot she rose for the twenty-third Psalm, which she mouthed automatically. No sound would come. Her mouth was unnaturally dry. From very far away it seemed Colin Whitefish began to read from John: *I am the good shepherd. The good shepherd lays down his life for the sheep. The hired hand is not the shepherd who owns the sheep. So when he sees the wolf coming he abandons the sheep and runs away...*

The Gospel of the Lord.
Praise be to thee, O Christ.

Page looked around. The church was dark. Even on a sunny day it was a dark church. Dark wooden pews marked its length, dark beams formed the vaulted ceiling, and low, dark stained glass windows filtered the available light to a minimum. Darkness characterized it and gave it its air of mystery, of awe. Page shivered.

She saw the four members of the production department lined up five rows ahead of her, their shoulders shaking as they sniffled and sobbed. She saw Charlotte Pentecost, tall and erect, standing with Midge McIntyre and Gracie Griggs. She saw the senior and junior wardens and members of the vestry, the Director of the Church School, visibly moved and weeping. She saw the confirmation class, standing as a unit, and the aristocratic old ladies in their fur coats. She saw a score of younger women scattered throughout, stunned and silent. She saw a group of younger men, Miles' peers, a tall blond man among them...*Chester.*

She saw them all as in a movie, removed and separate from her, and as her voice had left her earlier, so the ability to stand vanished as her legs turned to water and she collapsed on the pew. She felt pressed down as if a crushing weight had been placed on her shoulders. Where was the Holy Spirit today? *Holy Spirit?* A voice inside her seemed to whisper, *Get out, Little Sister. Get out now. If you have to crawl, go.*

Page pulled herself up with her arms and veered drunkenly out of the pew. She staggered out the back side door, pushing past Diana Dunwoody in her green altar guild smock, who whispered stupidly, "The service isn't over, Page." Page ignored her, concentrating on the impossible task of moving her feet. Once in the narthex, her eyes focused again and, choking back a sob, she stumbled out into the hallway and to the stairway which led to the basement. There she collapsed again, sitting down on the top stair and laying her head on her knees. She leaned against the plaster wall, which felt cool, and she revived a little. *Jesus Christ, Son of God, have mercy on me a sinner,* she began to repeat, mouthing the mantra which rang in her head, *Jesus Christ, Son of God, have mercy on me a sinner.* Over and over, she said it, until she felt the weight dissipate and she opened her eyes and saw, a few steps below her, Detective Merton leaning casually on the railing.

"Better?" he asked.

Her hair was damp around her face and she felt drained and weak. "You wouldn't understand," she whispered.

"Maybe I would."

"No you wouldn't. I'm not sure I do. It was just a feeling. A ghastly feeling."

"Hold on. I'll get you some ice water." He headed up the stairs and into the Great Hall where Demetrius Barton and another custodian were still setting up for the reception. In a few minutes Merton returned with a glass of ice water which he offered to Page.

"Thank you," she said trying to smile. She took the glass, which felt heavy and slippery, and put it to her lips. "You're always giving me water…I feel like the woman at the well."

"Have you been eating?" he asked, sitting down on the step next to her. "You need to eat something."

"I'm fine. The water helps," she said, struggling to get up.

"You better stay put," he said.

"No, I can't stay here," she said unreasonably.

He put his hand on her arm. "Just wait a minute or two. Be still."

Be still. She sat back down and rested her head against the wall. He did not move his hand. The glass of ice water was cold on her knee. She took a sip. She felt the weight of his hand on her arm, but she could not look at it. She felt him looking at her but she did not turn her head. She heard him breathing. She felt her heart pounding. "Help me to my office. Please," she said.

"All right," he said kindly, keeping a firm grip on her arm and leading her down the stairs.

Her door was locked, so she handed him her keys and he let her in, guiding her to the desk chair. "You need some fresh air in here. At least leave your door open."

"I'm fine. I'll be fine."

"Excuse me," he said, bending at the waist and leaning down, "but you don't look fine. You look white as a sheet."

"Your concern is…noted…but, really, I'm okay." She tried to smile. She took another sip of ice water. Her hand was shaking.

"What scared you up there?"

"Scared me?" she said. *Is a trumpet blown in a city, and the people are not afraid?* "Nothing scared me."

He took a deep breath and stood up very straight. "All right," he said.

Holy Comfort

She could tell he didn't believe her for a second. She tried to concentrate. "It was just a terrible feeling...like all the people up there, all those familiar people up there, were...*strangers.*"

The detective sat down on the edge of her desk and waited while Page took another sip of water.

"My husband was there. Chester was there."

"Your ex-husband?"

"Yes. I know you said they were friends, but he was...it was..."

"It was what?" he asked quietly.

She looked over at his thigh on her desk with the gray wool fabric stretched across it and at his folded hands. She looked up at him. Something moved in the hall. A body appeared in the dorway. "You all right, Page?" asked Demetrius Bell.

"I'm fine," she said.

Demetrius glanced at the detective who continued to stare at Page. "Well, okay," said the sexton who paused before turning back to the hall.

"I'll be all right, Detective Merton." She made a brave attempt at smiling.

"If you say so," he said, standing up. "But stay put. I'll be back."

In an instant he was gone. Page was confused. Was it really just an empty stomach that had caused her to feel like she had in the sanctuary? No, it was different. It *was* fear, she realized, real fear brought on by her awareness of what the BCP called "the spiritual forces of wickedness." She remembered that from the baptismal service. She leaned on her elbows and ran her fingers through her hair, staring ahead at her computer screen. There, where she had taped them, were the words *"Be still before the Lord and wait patiently for him; do not fret when men succeed in their wicked ways, when they carry out their wicked schemes."* She closed her eyes and repeated them. *Be still and wait...Be still and wait.*

Soon she heard the familiar sound of the fire doors opening and closing and she opened her eyes. Standing in the doorway was a man, but it was not Roy Merton. It was Harry Rose, the retired navy cook who, along with his wife Hazel, prepared food almost daily for a variety of church events. He was balancing a tray, which held a steaming bowl of soup, a half pint carton of milk, a spoon, a napkin, and a dish of crackers. "At your service, ma'am," he said smiling as he set it down.

"Oh, Harry!" she exclaimed, looking at the tray as if it held treasure. "How nice of you. You didn't have to go to all this trouble."

"No trouble...here. I also brought these cookies," he said, handing her a napkin wrapped around two fancy cookies from the reception. "But you can only have these if you eat your soup and drink all your milk." He laughed.

"Have a seat, Harry, if you have a minute, and keep me company while I partake of this feast."

"Okay," he said, obliging her. "You know, I'd like to take the credit, but it was that detective who came in and said you were feeling poorly. I *can* take credit for the soup. Made a big pot of it for the lay ministry luncheon."

"It's yummy," she said, taking a sip. It was chicken noodle soup. The sight of it made her want to gag, but she managed to say, "Thanks, Harry."

"Well, rest and be thankful," replied Harry, obviously pleased to have pleased Page. He leaned his long, lanky body back in the chair. Now in his sixties and quite bald, Page imagined that he must have been handsome in his youth. Too many unfiltered Camels and too much booze had taken their toll, however, and now he looked a bit like a worn out and slightly dissipated Dwight Eisenhower.

"I could package up some soup for you and the boys, if there's any left after lunch, and you could take it home. Save yourself some cooking. That detective said you weren't eating, and we can't have that now. I might have some cookies, too."

"Harry, you're too good to me," she said forcing herself to finish the soup.

"Naw. I ain't that. I guess all this has got you down. You discovering the body and all."

"Yes. It has."

"It's tough, but you gotta eat. You gotta keep your strength up."

"I know. I'll try to do better. Thanks again for the soup and…everything."

"Okay, well, I better get back up or Hazel will wonder what's become of me. We've got that lay ministry lunch, you know, after the reception," he said, gathering up the tray. "Stop by on your way out and I'll have that food for you."

"Okay, Harry. Thanks a million," she said mustering a big smile for him as he left.

She did feel better. The hot soup and the visit from Harry had helped a lot to lift her spirits. Now she felt as if she could tackle the work which had piled up on her desk. She put Alison Krauss in the CD player and set to work.

Holy Comfort

Chapter Sixteen

NOT TOO MANY people bothered to stay for the reception following the funeral of Miles Costello. The staff, with the notable exception of Page Hawthorne, came in for a few minutes, but most, having sampled the refreshments, took off fairly soon after they got there. Gracie Griggs and Diana Dunwoody, however, staked out a corner of the Great Hall and appeared to settle in for the rest of the morning. Charlotte Pentecost fluttered from one man to another in rapid succession, gesticulating dramatically and laughing too loudly, until Colin Whitefish caught up with her and reminded her of the luncheon coming up later that morning and of her duty to attend as the program director.

The two detectives circled the room, taking note of the familiar staff faces and the parishioners they had met. Ellen Chevalier was notably absent, but there were only a few faces they did not recognize. After awhile Merton left his partner who had been cornered by Baylor Valentine and swung into the kitchen, hot and humid despite the whirring fan, in time to hear Hazel Rose's strident voice rising in consternation. "Harry, just get out of here until I call you!"

Merton smiled, catching Harry's eye as the older man saluted his wife and turned to go out into the alley. "I'll just go have a smoke, dearest."

"Hello, ma'am," the detective said, nodding to Hazel.

"Maybe you could keep him busy for a little while?" She smiled as she patted her short gray hair lightly. "Here. Have a lemon bar."

Merton took a yellow rectangular confection from the proffered silver tray and smiled sheepishly. "I believe I will. Thank you, ma'am." Nodding again, he turned and headed for the back door just in time to see Adair Pinkney and Demetrius Barton emerge from the hallway which led to the sexton's office. Her hand rested on his arm and something about the familiarity of the gesture caused the detective to pause. Adair looked up and, catching his eye, froze for a moment. Then she smiled and said something to Barton and turned to the detective. "Well, hello, Detective Merton," she said. "We meet again."

"Yes. I've just been to the funeral."

"Indeed. Somewhat above and beyond the call of duty, I should think."

71

"We wanted to see who came."

"Ah," she said knowingly. "The murderer returns to the scene of the crime, eh? Well, it was a nice service, don't you think? Charles did an admirable job under the circumstances."

Merton nodded. He noted that the rector's wife, although erect and slim in a flattering dark suit that probably sported an expensive label inside, looked tired and older than she had just a few days ago.

"Well," she said. "If you'll excuse me, I must go back and circulate."

"Of course," said Merton. He raised the lemon bar in his hand in an awkward salute. She turned and left the kitchen. Demetrius Barton was nowhere to be seen. Merton turned once again to the back door and stepped out into the alley behind the kitchen. Turning away from the dumpsters and a chaotic jumble of discarded boxes and crates, he saw Harry Rose leaning against the wall of the building, a cigarette hanging on his lips and a halo of smoke lingering above his head. The older man smiled and, indicating the wall, said, "Join me, son."

"Let's walk a little," said the detective, motioning toward the deserted playground at the end of the alley. Both men ambled down to the wooden climbing structure. Harry found a seat on a railroad tie wall and Roy stood next to him, resting one shoe on the wall and leaning on his knee. "So, how did the soup go over?" he asked, licking the last remains of the lemon bar from his fingers.

"Oh, just fine. A big hit, I think. She ate it all. Drank her milk, too." Merton nodded. The older man was thoughtful for a while. "She works too hard, that girl. Puts a lot of herself into her job...not many people appreciate it. Some downright resent it. That's usually the way."

"What do you mean?"

"People like Page make the others look bad, or so they think." Harry finished his cigarette and flicked it away from the playground into the bushes. As he shook another out of his pack, he continued philosophically. "This place, you may have noticed, is chock full of phonies. But there's nothing phoney about Page. No sir."

"And what makes her different?"

Harry snorted. "I'll tell you something that distinguishes her from everyone else. She respects my kitchen. She comes in, she asks for something. She never takes. She says please and thank you. Most people here think because they're members, they own the kitchen. She don't. Other people, they help themselves."

"To what?"

"Anything they want. Food especially. Any food in the kitchen is there to be used for some particular event, not just to feed the hungry passing through. And dishes, same thing. People never think that someone's got to wash 'em. A lot of people here are takers. They take what they want without thinking how it affects anyone else. They're careless."

"And knives?"

Holy Comfort

"Yeah, and...hey, now what you're talking bout is downright stealing. Like I told you and your partner, those knives are a set that belongs to me and Hazel personal. Not the church. Bought and payed for by us to use on our jobs. That's why we usually keep 'em with us all the time. Whoever took that knife knew what to look for."

"Any ideas?"

"Well, I don't want to point no fingers. I like it here. Even the phonies are mostly polite. I don't pay 'em no mind. There's a few on the staff I could do without. I guess it's no secret there's no love lost between me and ol' Grace Griggs." Harry glanced at the detective whose elevated eyebrows encouraged the older man to continue. "You might say me and Hazel got the concession here on catering all the meetings, luncheons and dinners, but for awhile Grace Griggs refused to use us—she went *outside* for her newcomer dinners—we weren't good enough!" Harry flicked his cigarette away and reached for another, crumpling the empty pack. "She accused me of being drunk on the job! This from a woman who spent half of the last dinner we catered for her with her dress unzipped!"

Merton raised his eyebrows again and smiled.

"Yeah. But me and Hazel, we're still here. I know there's those that would stick up for us and have. Page Hawthorne is one. Adair Pinkney is another. Both of 'em real ladies. Not disrespectful magpies like Grace Griggs and Charlotte Pentecost." He nearly spit the second name out.

"No love lost there, either?"

Harry laughed. "She's a taker. She takes what she wants...and swears like a sailor while she's doing it. But I'm just the hired help, Detective. I ain't entitled to opinions. No, if you ain't Ministry Staff, you ain't nothing in some people's minds."

"You mean the 'para-clergy'?"

"The what?" asked Harry. "What's 'para-clergy'?"

"Oh, it was just something Charlotte Pentecost said about herself, that she was considered to be almost clergy."

"Shit," said Harry. "She does build herself up in her own mind. Sort of sad, really." He flicked his cigarette away. "The people who go to this church—they don't think much of the staff. We don't get paid enough to earn their respect. Money talks here."

"Uh huh. So there might be some resentment on the part of some staff members?"

"Could be, if you cared what those people thought."

"Harry!" yelled Hazel Rose from the kitchen door. "Harry, where are you?"

"My angel calls," he said standing up. "I must fly to her side."

"Thanks for the talk." Merton stood and extended his hand to shake.

"Anytime," said Harry gripping the detective's hand. "There's soup in a plastic container in the fridge. I'll be leaving after lunch, so maybe you could take it on down to Page before she leaves..."

C.R. Compton

The two men's eyes met and the detective smiled and looked away. "All right. I can do that."

The screen door from the kitchen banged open. "Harry! C'mon!" called Hazel.

"I'm coming! I'm coming!" he muttered as he hitched his white pants up and hustled, elbows out, back to the kitchen.

Holy Comfort

Chapter Seventeen

MERTON LOWERED HIMSELF into the ragged chair opposite the rector. It was a nice office, if a bit worn at the edges. The Oriental rug had a hole in it and all the chairs had threadbare patches. Probably the rector was uncomfortable with the congregation spending money on his office. Or maybe he never even noticed the puffs of stuffing spewing from the arms of his chair. The walls were covered with framed etchings and several pictures of church buildings, including an oil painting of Holy Comforter. There was a crucifix and an icon of some sort with a gilded picture of a big-eyed Jesus.

The detective glanced at the rector who was gazing at him, his fingers tented, his manner patiently indulgent. "Thanks for giving me a minute," Merton said. "I just wanted to ask you about the book of *Daniel*."

The rector looked mildly surprised, but said nothing.

"The small group that met with Miles Costello was reading it," said the detective, taking out a spiral notebook from his jacket pocket. "It's a pretty strange book."

"You read it?" said the rector regarding the detective from hooded eyes. "You're quite a reader."

"It passes the time."

"Oh. It's more than that I think," said the rector, bouncing his tented fingers together. "You're looking for another connection, Detective, like the Psalm."

Merton nodded. "Maybe. Could you tell me anything about the book? What's the deal with the dreams and the bizarre symbolism? Is it all camouflage?"

"Well, that's the nature of apocolyptic literature, you see. The first half of *Daniel* is rather familiar stuff to anyone who went to Sunday school—Daniel and his three friends, Meshach, Shadrach and Abednego, the Firey Furnace and the Lion's Den. Nebuchadnezzar and his dreams. The Writing on the Wall...but it's the second half of the book—filled as it is with visions and apocalyptic prophesy that interests you, am I right, Detective?"

"Yes. I guess. There was one part...I wrote it down." The detective flipped pages in his notebook and then stopped. "Here. Chapter eleven, verse twenty-one: 'In this place shall arise a contemptible person to whom royal majesty has not been given; he shall come in without warning and obtain the kingdom by flatteries...and he shall become strong with a small people. Without warning he shall come into the richest parts of the province...' Doesn't that sound like someone?"

The rector looked intently at the other man. "You're talking about Miles?" The detective nodded. The rector shook his head wearily. "These verses," he said, "have been fair game for religious eccentrics and crackpots for centuries. Napoleon, Hitler, the Pope, and many other historical figures have been detected, and wars from the English Civil War to World War II have been identified. It's tempting to contemplate, but I don't believe Miles Costello was the antichrist."

The detective looked at the rector from under his eyebrows and smiled. "It just seems strange that his group was reading that particular book..."

"But he didn't 'obtain the kingdom,' did he?" interrupted the rector, leaning forward. "Not quite."

"Who's to say what might have happened if he hadn't been murdered?"

"No one can say," replied the rector, leaning back in his chair.

"Maybe someone in the group..."

"Detective, hold on," said the rector, picking up a Bible from the table between them. He began flicking the pages, turning hurridly to *Daniel*. "I think it says somewhere here...yes, here. Listen. 'He shall seduce with flattery those who violate the covenant; but people who know their God shall stand firm...' You see. The saints of the kingdom will win..."

"Stand firm and...*what*?" The detective levelled his eyes at the other man.

The rector sought the scripture again. "Shall stand firm *and take action*..."

"My point exactly," said the detective. "What if someone decided to take action?"

"But why? From all accounts those men were his *friends*, hand-picked to be in the group."

"Maybe at first. But suppose one of them caught on to what Costello was doing?"

"But what *was* he doing? Do you really know? Colin tried to find out, but it's not as if we had any proof beyond hints of impropriety and the alleged gifts he was receiving from rich women."

"We've looked at his bank statements and at his brokerage accounts. He had nearly a quarter of a million dollars in cash and mutual funds."

"I had no idea," whispered the rector, suddenly pale.

Merton cleared his throat. "There were semen stains found on the wall in his office," he said. "Preliminary tests show they match with the deceased man's DNA. Did you have any idea that there was sexual activity going on in Costello's office?"

Holy Comfort

The rector looked stricken. He had closed his eyes at the mention of the word "semen." He opened them now as he replied, "No." He took a deep breath and asked, "On the wall? Which wall? The one back in the dressing alcove?"

"Yes. The wall which divides his office and Page Hawthorne's office."

Charles groaned and leaned his forehead down onto his hand. "I had no idea."

Merton stared fixedly at the rector. He said evenly, "Tell me, Rector, were Page Hawthorne and Costello ever involved...sexually involved?"

"No, they were not," replied the rector, looking up.

"Did you know that she was afraid of being alone with Costello in her office with the door shut?" The rector shook his head. "He was tall and he'd move the chair, blocking the door in order to stretch out his legs. She was trapped then. She didn't trust him."

"You've been very thorough, Detective."

"If she had been hit on, or even raped, would she have confided in you?"

"Yes, of course. I'm sure of it," answered the rector, taking a deep breath and exhaling. "Why do you ask?"

Merton paused and looked at his notes. "Page Hawthorne told me that Miles Costello did make sexual advances toward her in his office on at least one occasion. She said she didn't want to bother you with it, that she handled it herself."

The rector gulped for air and whispered, "Dear God."

"Do you believe Page Hawthorne was telling the truth?"

"Of course. If she said Miles...did that, I believe her. Page would never lie about such a thing. It's absurd."

"But you were sure she'd tell you if Costello had forced himself on her..."

"That's different," the rector said quickly, looking away. "I can see how she might not want to tell anyone about that."

"How can you be so sure Ms. Hawthorne and Costello never—"

"Because I know Page. She is a...Godly person."

The detective smirked.

The rector frowned. "I suppose it's the nature of your job to suspect everyone of the worst, but I don't understand this." Charles gripped the arms of his chair and glared at Merton. "Why all the questions about Page Hawthorne? You couldn't possibly have taken seriously the childish accusations of Gracie Griggs. That's all they were, you know...the childish babbling of a degenerate woman seeking attention."

"And what about you, Mr. Pinkney?" asked the detective in a cool, even tone. "Have you ever engaged in sexual activity with Page Hawthorne?"

The rector looked at Merton for a moment with a confused, inquiring expression. "You baffle me, Detective," he said. "I want to be cooperative, but this is absurd and your line of questioning is insulting. We have no right to discuss Page Hawthorne this way...what does any of this have to do with the murder?"

"Please, just answer the question."

"The answer is no. Never."

"All right. Any ideas then about who was with Costello when those stains got on the wall...female or male?"

The rector got up from his chair slowly and walked over to the window. He looked out at Gracie Griggs and Diana Dunwoody and sighed. "I never had the impression that Miles was gay, or even bisexual. He certainly had lots of male friends...I don't think those were sexual relationships...but then, what do I know? Honestly, Detective, the man disgusted me...and frustrated me. I wanted to help him. I would have...but obviously I was as repellent to him as he was to me. He must have hated me...if he ever tried anything with Page, it might have been as a weapon with which to hurt me, and that could explain why she didn't tell me about it. She was protecting me. He was always trying to draw me out, to bait me. He wanted a full scale war, a street fight—that was his style. But I retreated and I thought he had, too. I tried to ignore him, but he had an aggressive streak which wouldn't quit. If he tried something with Page and failed, he would have tried again with someone else."

"Who? Who do you think?"

The rector turned and looked imploringly at Merton. "I don't know. I can't even guess..."

"Why not? Why can't you guess?"

"Because I...because I just don't know what went on downstairs. You can see how isolated I am up here in my office, cut off from my staff. It's what the parishioners want, what they expect: the top man in the big office upstairs. I can't change that. It's just the way the plant is set up."

"Didn't you ever take a walk downstairs?"

"Occasionally, of course. But I'm not a hands-on administrator. I prefer to delegate. I have to trust my associates, Colin especially, but Miles, too..."

"So, basically, Costello had a free rein..."

The rector stared at the detective. "Yes."

"So you had no idea what was going on. You had no idea that Page Hawthorne was being victimized. You just had no clue..." Charles Pinkney stared at his hands. The detective looked at his notes. "The other day you talked about sacrificing your principles for your neighbor's sake. If you had found out about Ms Hawthorne, how might you have reacted? You got pretty hot under the collar just now."

"I see where you're going," said Pinkney. "You think I might have picked up a baseball bat and stopped him from hurting her again." He

Holy Comfort

paused, considering. "Who's to say what I might have done? The fact remains I didn't know," he concluded.

"No, but might someone *else* have been trying to protect Page Hawthorne?"

"Who would have known?"

"It's possible that other people were more aware than you—"

"Yes, I suppose," said the rector, cutting him off. He smoothed his hair. "But the baseball bat doesn't jibe with the premeditation of the burning coals."

The two men were silent for a while. Merton watched the rector who seemed quite calm now and empty of the anger which had bubbled under the surface such a short time ago. Pinkney gazed out the window at the four women who had gathered in the garden, chattering like chickadees and blowing smoke, then turned suddenly. "You know, Detective, you seem to be focused on Page Hawthorne. I wonder if it wouldn't be more appropriate to look at some of these other women, for instance, Gracie Griggs or Charlotte Pentecost or even Diana Dunwoody." He gestured again to the window. "They were, by most accounts, quite close to Miles, and yet they seem oddly less than devastated by his passing."

"Perhaps they're in denial."

"That's what Colin says, but I'm not so sure. It just seems strange."

"Mr. Pinkney," the detective said. "There is one thing that I don't understand about the Reverend Miles Costello. All the people we've talked to—they either paint him as Sir Galahad or the devil incarnate. Hardly anyone was non-commital, except maybe the senior and junior wardens."

"Politicians," said the rector dismissively.

"So where's the truth? Down some middle road?"

"No, I don't think so," replied Charles Pinkney quietly, his eyes downcast. "I think there were two Miles Costellos. The one who truly wanted to please his friends, those who could do him good. That Miles, although he was neither humble nor kind, could approximate humility and kindness. The other one didn't care about anyone or anything or about pretending or acting as if he did. The latter is the one who found it so easy to turn his back on people, to shroud them, to use sex as a tool to get what he wanted. It was a sad day when he was ordained. It gave him carte blanche to use and hurt people and call it Christian vocation."

Chapter Eighteen

THE RECTOR HAD given the two detectives permission to use Salisbury Hall, because the children's choir only rehearsed there twice a week with a volunteer director. Such work was beneath Baylor Valentine's talents. The room was large and airy with leaded glass tracery windows which overlooked the church battlements on the south side of the new building. They sat in blue stackable chairs and drank coffee which had been warming for hours.

"Do you ever feel like you should maybe be wearing armour around here?" remarked Vesba. "It would sure fit in with the general décor, and might actually come in handy when it comes to interviewing parishioners." She waited for her partner to chuckle, and when he did, she continued. "So tell me how your talk with Pinkney went. Was he more forthcoming than before?"

"He was open. A few direct questions threw him, but I believe he was truly surprised and he tried to be honest. He didn't try to hide anything."

"What surprised him?"

"Costello's DNA on the wall for one thing."

"Go on," urged Vesba, crossing her arms across her ample bosom. "Did he have any ideas about who he was with when it got there?"

"Not really. He seems to have been pretty out of the loop where his staff was concerned. Sort of made an ivory tower of his office. He says he didn't know about Page Hawthorne being assualted by Costello."

"Assaulted? That's mighty strong language," sniffed Leona. "Nothing *happened*."

"Well, he didn't know. He was shocked. He said she may have been protecting him when she kept quiet about it."

"So now *he* needed *protecting* from big bad Costello? Please."

"Some people think he might have been in danger of losing his job. Mrs. Van Patton and the mayor certainly made it sound that way. Adair Pinkney thought so, too."

Leona grumbled. "Well, what about *him* and Miss Priss? Were *they* fooling around?"

Holy Comfort

"He said no."

Vesba let loose with a snort and shook her head. "Devoted to his wife, eh?" Leona snorted again and threw up her hands. "Well, maybe *she* did it. Adair had a motive, after all. You said she thought Costello was plotting a coup. Maybe she was plotting her own coup."

"She has an alibi."

"She was with the rector. Not exactly airtight."

"It doesn't matter, anyway," said the other detective, studying his cup of coffee.

"What doesn't matter?"

"Ms. Hawthorne's sex life...she didn't kill Costello. She wasn't involved with Costello. Whoever killed him was. We need to find out who *that* was. All the rest is just...distracting us."

"Us? You mean you. She's distracting *you*."

"Maybe," Merton said calmly. He threw his empty cup into the wastepaper basket. "But Costello did talk about her, *lie* about her to other people."

"You really think he was that pathological?"

"I'm not sure I'd call it pathological, but people lie all the time, they exaggerate. I think Costello despised everyone around him—the women at work, the aged members of his fan club—he probably got a big charge out of lying to them, especially about Page Hawthorne."

"Miss Goody Two Shoes? Payback for turning him down?" Leona had been leaning on her crossed knees concentrating. Now she leaned back and rested her arms on her stomach. "The problem is it's all a guess. We are awash in hearsay. Nobody actually *knows* anything."

"Somebody knows."

"You're talking about the killer."

Roy nodded. "Whoever paged Costello Thursday night when he was with Ms. Chevalier and then lifted the pager off his dead body Friday morning."

"Oh yeah," said Leona picking up her spiral notebook. "The pager company told me their records show that Costello was paged eight times Thursday night, all after six forty-five p.m. The calls were all made from the church."

"And what activities were going on at Holy Comforter that night?"

Leona checked her notebook again. "Let's see...The Phoenix Group—that's the singles group—met at seven p.m. They had a guest who spoke on the topic of dating after fifty. They had dessert and coffee and left before nine p.m. About fourteen people attended, including Charlotte Pentecost and Colin Whitefish. There was also an A.A. meeting at seven p.m. It was held in the multipurpose room downstairs. About twelve people usually attend, mostly non-members of the church—but, then, they are supposed to be *anonymous*. The Adult Education Board met in the Library at six p.m. and was gone by seven p.m."

"Who's the staff connection with that committee?"

"The rector," said Leona. "There was also choir practice at seven p.m. in the Commons Room—that's upstairs in Valentine's tower. They all left by nine p.m."

"So who could have made those calls from the church?"

"Besides Colin Whitefish and Charlotte Pentecost, about sixty people, including Demetrius Barton, the rector who lives next door and was—allegedly—at home that night following his meeting in the arms of his wife. And Baylor Valentine, of course."

"As well as practically anyone else with a key—or even without a key since the church was open until nine p.m. or so. When was the last page?"

"Nine forty-five."

"When did Demetrius Barton lock up?"

"He says," replied Vesba, flipping pages, "nine thirty p.m."

"Did he mention whether anyone was still in the building?"

"No, not specifically. He said he locks up when he thinks everyone has left, but it would be real easy for someone to go unnoticed...and, of course, there's always Baylor Valentine in the tower. He's always around."

"I wonder if Valentine, and for that matter Barton, would cover for somebody?"

"Withhold information from us? In a minute they would," said Leona. "Everybody's dancing around, covering their Episcopalian asses."

"You're exaggerating, Leona. You're frustrated and you're exaggerating."

"Don't tell me I'm frustrated."

"You have every right to be frustrated. We're all frustrated." She stared away out the window. He folded his arms. "How's Valerie?" he asked.

Vesba sighed. Then she smiled half-heartedly and shrugged. "She's fine. I had to ground her again, for a week this time."

He nodded, picturing Vesba's fifteen-year-old daughter. Slim and pretty, bored at her school, Our Lady of Perpetual Sorrow, unchallenged by everyone but the boys she hung out with. For years she had spent too much time on her own due to Leona's job and now she was acting out, testing the limits of her mother's guilt-ridden goodwill.

"She's supposed to stay with my mother upstairs, but Mom sleeps a lot, you know, and...it's not a great situation." She sighed again. "We're coping, though."

Merton nodded again, wishing he had something constructive to say.

"My life may be fucked up, but I look around this place and I want to puke," she said suddenly. "Everybody and their freakin' opinions. 'Maybe it was someone he was counseling, one of the *newer* members. Or a *transient*, some poor jerk looking for a bus token. Certainly not a *member*.' All they care about is bad publicity and the negative effect this may have on their pledge drive."

Holy Comfort

Roy did not respond immediately, so she stood up and walked over to where he was sitting and waved a hand in front of his face. He blinked and refocused his attention on her. "So what do we have so far besides a lot of opinions?" she said. "And no evidence except some dried semen on the wall?"

Merton put his elbows on his knees and ran his fingers threw his hair. "We have two, maybe three, theories."

Vesba hoisted herself onto the side of the choir director's desk and crossed her legs. She admired the pink shoe on her small foot and said, "And those would be?"

Merton held up a finger. "Someone knew what Costello was up to and didn't like it. He killed Costello in order to protect Page Hawthorne and maybe other women who were victims."

"And who do you have in mind?"

"Demetrius Barton, Charles Pinkney, even Harry Rose."

"They all have alibis."

"Not particularly good ones," said Merton. "Except Harry, I guess. He and Hazel were cooking for the Presbyterians in Quincy Groves. And I'm beginning to think Charles Pinkney wouldn't come out of his office to hurt a fly. Besides which he maintains he knew nothing about what was going on downstairs which makes it a moot point."

"That leaves Barton. Do you really think he cares enough?"

"Haven't you noticed he's always around?"

"Always around when? And who? Page Hawthorne? When *you* are? Maybe he just doesn't like you." She laughed and slapped her knee. Merton threw down the pencil. "So what's the second theory?" she said, holding up two fingers.

"Someone found out what Costello was up to, got jealous and wanted revenge. One of his lady friends or fellow staff members who looked to him to protect their jobs. Or possibly someone who found out and took upon himself the mantle of righteous indignation and decided to rid the church of his bad influence."

"Like one of those guys in the small group? I can't see any of them caring enough."

"Pinkney didn't go for that theorey either, but it fits with the burning coals and the scripture."

Vesba sighed. "Did you say there was a third theory maybe?" She ran her hand down her leg and smoothed the stocking by her ankle. Merton continued to stare at his hands.

"Someone really did think he could help the rector."

"Again, who would care enough?" said Vesba shrilly. "Not Adair Pinkney? She was home with perfect Charles. But, hey," she said, jumping off the desk. "Do you think Costello ever tried anything with her? That would double her motive and her husband's or anyone in theory number one who maybe wanted to protect *her*."

"The mind boggles," he said looking up finally. "We can't let ourselves get carried away."

Vesba grunted. She began to count on her fingers. "Barton, Pinkney—Charles *and* Adair—Pentecost, Griggs, Valentine, Van Patton and who-knows-who-else old ladies, plus nine small group members...Jesus. We're nowhere!"

He pushed away from his desk. "I say we pack up here for tonight and head back to the station."

"Yeah, while the crow makes woo-woo through the sticky wicket."

"I'll meet you back there. I have to drop by the kitchen."

"Why?"

"I said I'd do something for Harry Rose."

Chapter Nineteen

Page never left her office after the funeral. The only person to stop by was Charlotte Pentecost. "Page," she drawled as she slid unasked into her office and dropped into a chair. "Page, where were you? *Everybody* noticed you weren't at the reception."

"Everybody?"

"Well, two or three people. Chester was there. He asked about you. I told him I supposed you were working. Always so conscientious. Must meet those deadlines..."

Page leaned back in her chair and prepared to listen to Charlotte ramble on about Chester. Her ex-husband was a favorite subject of Charlotte's.

Charlotte clasped her hands together and sighed. "Chester's looking awfully good these days, isn't he, Page? He must be working out, so fit and trim. And the tan suits him. He just got back from St. John's, you know, that's why his hair looks bleached. God, he was gorgeous—robed in a cloud with a rainbow above his head; his face was like the sun, and his legs like fiery pillars..."

"Surely, you exaggerate."

Charlotte slapped her thighs and shrieked. "Maybe so, but he looked good enough to eat! Anyway, I had a lovely visit with him."

"I was surprised to see Chester. I never knew Miles and he were friends."

"Oh *yes*, Page, they were buddies! Chester was in Miles' small group. Didn't you know that?"

"I heard that recently," Page said distractedly. She was no longer paying much attention to Charlotte. "I was surprised. That's all."

"Sure you were," said Charlotte focusing on Page's face. She blinked. "Well, I got caught by Colin Whitefish and forced to go to that goddam lay ministry luncheon. He's so insensitive with that life-must-go-on attitude. One of these days I'll make him kiss my ministry ass, but until then, I've had enough for one day. I'm out of here. I just wanted to give you the report on Chester. Ta ta!"

She was gone. Page turned back to her desk and stared at the computer screen, unseeing and heedless of the words before her. She thought about Charlotte and pictured her with Chester, laughing too loudly and touching his arm, and Chester sneering. Didn't she ever notice how people reacted to her? People could be downright rude to her and she never seemed to catch on. It almost made her want to be their friend all the more. She wondered again about Chester's membership in Miles Costello's small group. It was a crazy idea, Chester studying the Bible, Chester sharing his spiritual journey with the other members, Chester *praying*. Of course, that was assuming that this particular small group did what the other small groups did. It was none of her business, but she had sometimes wondered about that. She wondered now until a sudden movement in the doorway surprised her and she jumped in her chair.

"I'm sorry. Did I startle you?" asked Merton.

She looked at his mouth, the lips parted, hesitating on the last syllable. She bit her own lower lip and looked down at her hands in her lap lying loosely palm upwards. "No. Yes. I was just thinking."

"Deep in thought?" She nodded. He stepped into the room. "May I come in?"

"Sure." She glanced at her watch. "I should be getting set to leave, but come on in."

"Here, this is from Harry," he said, handing her a plastic container full of soup.

"Thanks. Harry's so sweet." She said nothing about the lunch, but waited while he sat down.

He settled himself, then looked at her rubbing her temple as if doing so would erase the troubling thoughts inside her head. "My husband was at the funeral today," she said after a while.

"You mentioned that."

"Did I? It was just so odd..."

Their glances intersected and held for a moment. "I wanted to tell you about one piece of forensic evidence we have," he said. "CSU found dried semen on the wall back in Costello's dressing room."

Page tapped the wall next to her with her knuckles. "This wall?"

Merton nodded. "Costello's DNA, his semen."

"Any theories?" asked Page.

"Well, this evidence seems to back up Pinkney and Whitefish's suspicions that he was..."

"Acting inappropriately?"

"To say the least," said Merton. He did not smile. "When I told the rector he was quite surprised that Costello was doing it here, and he was surprised when I told him about the incident involving you, but..."

"You told him about what Miles did to me?"

"Yes."

"Charles didn't need to know that," she said frowning. "This is all so hard on him."

Holy Comfort

"Hard on *him*?" said Merton.

"Yes," she said, heaving a large sigh. "Don't you see? He has such high expectations for everyone, and we all disappoint him."

The detective blew air through his teeth. "Did you ever think that perhaps, if he hadn't been protecting himself in that ivory tower he calls an office, he might have stopped Costello before things got to the point where someone thought they needed to kill him? To hell with his high expectations, if you ask me."

"Charles was waging his own battle in his own way," she said calmly. "Using prayer."

"You're kidding me," said Merton.

She shook her head. "No, I'm not kidding."

"If I recall correctly, even Jesus broke up the furniture. A little righteous anger wouldn't have hurt Charles Pinkney and it might have saved others some real grief."

"I don't want to argue with you, Detective," she said as she checked her watch. She dropped her hand into her lap as if the watch was too heavy to hold up for long.

He shook his head. "I'm sorry. I have a hard time understanding...him."

"I should be leaving," said Page. "This has been a very long day. I feel about a hundred years old." She stood up then, and he watched her gather her purse, folders, soup, and coat. "Do you need to use my office?" she said.

"No," he said and stood up. She turned abruptly and headed down the hall. Merton switched off the light and closed her door.

In the dark narthex upstairs, Merton watched Charles Pinkney emerge from his office. "I thought I heard someone out here," said the rector. "Are you leaving now, Page?" He did not notice the detective in the shadows. He slipped his arm around Page. "Let me walk you to your car. I need the fresh air."

As they turned together to go, Merton started to call out, reminding her to eat something for dinner, but he swallowed his words and stared mutely at the exiting couple.

THEY WALKED IN silence to Page's Volvo, and when they reached the car, the rector turned to her. "Listen, Page, I did want to ask you something. What happened during the funeral? Why did you leave?"

Page opened the back door and put her folders and soup inside. "I felt sick," she said, straightening as she closed the door.

"Is that all?" he asked, urging her by his tone to continue.

She opened the front door and rested her right arm on the top. She gazed down the street. "There was an oppressive, heavy *thing* weighing on me." Page paused, remembering. "There was *something*...something almost tangible, which choked me, sucking the air right out of me, making it impossible to take part in the service. There was a voice in my head telling me to get out, and I did. I made it to the stairs going down to my office and I sat down and rested. I remember the wall felt cool on my head. Det. Merton found me there...he helped me."

"Helped you?" asked the rector stepping closer.

"He got me a drink of water and helped me down to my office. That's all."

"Did you tell him what you told me just now?"

"No, I didn't think he'd understand. *I* didn't understand." She looked at the rector. "I told him about seeing Chester there and that I was startled."

"Yes. I gather Chester was in Miles' small group," said Charles. "When I spoke to Det. Merton today he showed some interest in that small group. He even went to the trouble of reading *Daniel,* because they were reading it in the group. He wanted to discuss it with me. I told him that while it may satisfy our curiosity to unravel apocalyptic language, we shouldn't be led astray."

Page smiled crookedly. "But he's interested in solving a murder; he's looking for clues, not salvation."

The rector sighed. "He seems to be interested in you, Page, as well. He asked a lot of questions about you and your relationship with Miles." Page raised an eyebrow. "He seems to think you figure into this somehow, that perhaps someone was trying to protect you."

Page rolled her eyes. She swung down into her seat. She opened her purse to find her keys. He bent at the waist and stared into the car. "What do you think about *him*, Page?" said the rector. "I mean the detective."

She paused. "I think he's a lot like you," she said. Charles raised an eyebrow. "What I mean is he's a practised listener. And he's not afraid to say nothing."

Charles stared down at her, unsmiling. He looked as if he wished he had never asked such a personal question. He changed the subject. "The spirit is strong in you, Page. I'm not surprised you felt it today."

"Feel what?" Page asked, not following at first. Then she remembered and shivered. *"What was it?"*

Charles continued to stare, his large intense brown eyes boring into her. "It was the presence of evil."

"In the sanctuary? I thought that the sanctuary was one place you could go to escape..."

"No," he said, his eyes softening. He smiled. "A church is made by men, for men. The devil loves churches. Paul said it best: 'For we wrestle not against flesh and blood, but against principalities, against powers, against rulers of the darkness of this world, against spiritual wickedness in high places.'"

"Against spiritual wickedness in high places..." she whispered as she gazed down the street.

"Remember, Page: '*Ye are of God* and have overcome them: because greater is he that is in you, than he that is in the world.'"

Holy Comfort

"But what do we do?" Page said looking up at Charles.

"We pray." Their eyes met. "We pray without ceasing." He smiled and his smile dismissed the darkness, brightening the dark day, inviting grace. "*I will fear no evil: for thou art with me; thy rod and staff they comfort me.*"

He watched her as she turned the corner and drove out of sight, but he did not move, remaining in the road. He was there a few minutes later, when his wife stepped out of the rectory and walked towards him. "Charles, dear, you're standing in the street," she said, putting an arm around him and ushering him as if he were a very old person back to the sidewalk. A gust of wind blew a tangle of large, dry sycamore leaves dancing around their feet and ankles. "Charles, Tammy's been trying to find you. There's a call from the bishop."

"Oh, dear," he responded absent-mindedly. "I suppose I'll have to take that, then."

"No, Chick, just call him back in a few minutes and let Tammy know where you are." She put her hand through his arm and began to guide him back to the church. When they reached the door, she released him, patting his hand and brushing his cheek with her lips. "C'mon, now. One day at a time. You'll get through this."

"I know," Charles said, brightening a bit. He gazed at his wife, admiring her, overcome with affection. "I'm fine. Really. You always see to that. I'll try to get away early. We'll have a drink."

"I'd love that, darling, but you know you have to go see Ethel Weinrich at five o'clock."

"Yes, of course...well, later then..."

"After the EMC meeting at seven."

Charles closed his eyes and breathed deeply, expelling air noisily through his nose. "I'll rub your feet..."

"And you can tell me what's up with Page."

"With Page?" he asked, his eyes clouding over.

"And the investigation," she said brightly. "Now, go. Call the bishop."

Charles disappeared into the entrance of the dark church. Adair Pinkney turned, picked up a cigarette butt from the brick pavement and headed back to the rectory through the Gresham Garden.

Chapter Twenty

Work continued at the Church of the Holy Comforter. Morning Prayer and Evening Prayer were read daily, meetings were held, rehearsals went on as scheduled, but any time two or three were gathered together, the topic of conversation always ended up being murder. The Murder.

The rumor was that the forensic reports had turned up very little; nothing, in fact, that pointed to anyone in particular. The murder weapon had been one of Harry Rose's personal knives, which he kept locked in the sexton's office off the kitchen. Everyone knew that there were literally hundreds of keys around, and anyone who wanted access to practically any office in the church could easily get it. And, anyway, Harry wasn't even positive he had locked up his knives that night. Harry and Hazel Rose themselves had no motive and ironclad alibis.

The talk was endless. The aged ladies of the Church Service League were shocked but spellbound. Nothing this interesting had happened at Holy Comforter in over fifty years. The Wednesday morning Men's Bible Class was divided as to whether they should form a prayer ring or a vigilante group. The Altar Guild busied itself with keeping fresh flowers in front of Miles' crypt in the Gresham Garden columbarium, although everyone knew Miles was not yet in it. The Choir, under the direction of Baylor Valentine, discussed the idea of having a benefit concert in Miles' memory to raise money for their upcoming tour of England which would be dedicated as well to his short but meaningful pastorate. The Every Member Canvass Committee openly discussed the unheard of idea of postponing the entire event until the following year.

Much talk was devoted to the subject of the two detectives. Although only a small percentage of the parish had actually had any direct contact with them, many had seen them and their visual impact served as a basis for universal judgment. Detective Merton, most agreed, *looked* like a good detective, and most had heard of his soft spoken approach and polite demeanor. Ellen Chevalier, however, spoke often of his "trailer park" charm, of his country manners and his obsequious language laced with "yes ma'am's." The subject of Detective Vesba, not surprisingly, gave rise to much hilarity, the women of Holy Comforter hooting en masse about her

Holy Comfort

voluptuous figure and tacky wardrobe, her flaming red hair and ribald vocabulary. It was a relief and a comfort to be able to feel so superior.

In the Gresham Garden, Gracie Griggs lit up a Pall Mall, the brand she had been smoking since she was a freshman at Agnes Scott in the early 1960s. Smoking, drinking and too much sun had aged her and sapped her energy. Inactivity had broadened her hips and ruined her posture. She slumped against the columbarium wall now and crossed her legs. "So how was the prayer meeting, Midge?" she asked sarcastically.

"Oh, it was all right I guess," answered Midge brightly. "A lot of silent prayer, you know."

"No, I don't know. That's why I asked," snapped Gracie. "And sit down, Midge, for God's sake. You're making me nervous." She indicated an empty spot on the wall, which was annoyingly crowded with flowers and plants as a result of the funeral the day before.

Midge sat down. "George Fontaine and a delegation of parishioners were praying for us in the chapel," she said less brightly.

Gracie snorted.

"Well, if they feel like they're helping in some way, I don't have a problem with it," said Midge, still smiling.

"I suppose we can use all the help we can get." Gracie inhaled slowly, savoring her cigarette, already regretting the time when she would have to go in.

Charlotte burst through the glass door, which Gracie had propped open. She carried a plastic chair in both arms and she threw them down noisily as she neared the wall. "Diana's somewhere behind me. She's bringing coffee."

"Here I am. At your service," called Diana gaily, approaching with a tray laden with china cups, a carafe of coffee and a plate of danish. "I found the pastries in the kitchen and helped myself. I hope no one minds."

All four women laughed and Diana passed the coffee around. Gracie stubbed out her cigarette on the wall and reached for the pastry. "Oh, Charlotte, you'll love this!" said Gracie chewing. "Midge says George Fontaine and some parishioners were praying for us in the chapel."

Charlotte smiled lazily with the right side of her mouth.

"Oh, yes, can you believe it?" agreed Diana.

"I *can* believe it," said Charlotte icily. "And it's the least they can do. I'm sure they felt very good about themselves by the time they headed off for the office."

Diana looked nervously around. "Well, I just wish the rector had limited our prayer meetings to the Ministry staff. I mean, let the rest of the staff have their own meeting. It's just ridiculous—a circus, really."

"Yes, yes, Diana, but we must love our neighbor and *embrace* our inferiors. We're brothers in arms, after all," suggested Charlotte reasonably. "We must, as always, follow the example of the oh-so-inclusive Charles Scudder Pinkney."

"Huh!" huffed Gracie, finishing her danish and reaching for another cigarette. "That's exactly why I am refraining from attending those...*prayer* meetings. What are you praying *for* anyway? Nothing's going to bring poor Miles back."

"Yes, Midge, what are you all praying for?" asked Charlotte sweetly.

"Healing, I suppose. Courage..."

"Courage!" said Charlotte. "That's rich. Courage for *what*?"

"The courage to go on...to persevere in the face of, you know, evil," Midge answered, meeting Charlotte's gaze bravely. Her wispy white hair danced in the breeze and her hand automatically went to her head, searching for a bobby pin. "And I guess some people might be praying for the wisdom to understand...and some might pray for aid...for the detectives to catch the killer."

"Oh, yes, of course," said Charlotte impatiently. "God's will be done and all that jazz."

"Yes," said Midge quietly, setting the half-eaten danish in her hand down on a napkin. The four women sipped their coffee and pretended not to notice the uncomfortable silence.

Finally, Charlotte said loudly, "Well, tell us how did our favorite role-model, Page Hawthorne, pray? She's always so competent at everything."

Midge and Diana exchanged worried glances. "Oh, she was pretty quiet," said Midge. "She didn't have much to say at all."

"How truly disappointing," said Charlotte. "Too shy, I suppose. Too introverted. Too uptight. Well, what did you all do then? Say the Lord's Prayer and leave?"

"Oh, no," said Diana, chuckling. "Linda Kirstein prayed a lot. She gets a lot of practice at the community Bible study she goes to. She went on and on, you know, *have pity* this and *have pity* that. And a lot about sin."

"Why am I not surprised?" asked Charlotte.

"And Colin was good, too," continued Diana, on a roll and the center of attention. "He prayed for courage, mostly."

"What a wimp!" interjected Gracie.

"Oh, please," snorted Charlotte. "I'm getting a visual. And what about our rector?"

"He prayed and he read a psalm," said Diana, somewhat deflated.

"Psalm 70," said Midge. "*But as for me, I am poor and needy; come to me speedily, O God.*"

"Oh, I like that. *Poor and needy*, you say?" said Charlotte, sucking the juice out of the words as she repeated them. "I'll have to remember that. Psalm 70."

"You surely can't beat the *Psalms* for praying," suggested Midge spritely.

"No, you surely can't," agreed Charlotte, mimicking her spriteliness exactly.

Holy Comfort

"Well, I've got to get a move on," said Midge after another unpleasant silence. She stood up and dusted off her bottom. "Thanks for the danish, Diana."

"Oh, don't thank *me*," laughed Diana. Charlotte and Gracie joined her, snorting with laughter, but made no move to leave. They waved goodbye to Midge.

Gracie and Diana lit new cigarettes and leaned back, enjoying the sun on their weathered skin. Charlotte, facing the rector's office window, seemed deep in thought. Finally she said, "Look, dears, the counselor is in," indicating the window.

The two older women turned to gaze through the window. The detectives and the rector were standing at his desk, looking down at something.

"Those two detectives are becoming regular fixtures around here," said Charlotte.

"They look busy, but they don't seem to make much progress, that's for sure," said Gracie.

"It's been five days," said Diana nodding in agreement. "I would have imagined that five days would be enough to solve one murder. I mean, with all the forensic tools they have these days, infared lights and DNA tests and all, how difficult can it be?"

Charlotte gazed at Diana with an indulgent, maternal smile on her lips. "Well," she said, "Miles is certainly no longer front page news. How sad, really."

"Yes, how sad," repeated Diana sadly.

"Now if one of our members had been murdered it would be different," said Gracie. "They'd pull out all the bells and whistles then. Willis McHugh would make sure of that."

"Well, I'm sure Detective Merton and Detective Vesba the Lesba, are doing all they can," said Charlotte. They all tittered. Then Charlotte looked at her watch. "Zut alors! I must fly," she exclaimed. "I'm ten minutes late for a meeting with Colin. C'mon, ladies, back to the trenches."

"Yes, I suppose it's time," agreed Gracie, stubbing out her cigarette and collecting the other butts.

"Back to the salt mines!" chimed Diana as she struggled to balance her tray of coffee cups.

Chapter Twenty-One

"What do you think, Detectives?" asked the rector quietly as he stood in his office gazing distractedly out his window.

"I'd say you need to buy some new shirts," quipped Vesba, prompting the rector to turn around, his eyebrows raised like semaphore flags over his startled eyes.

"Don't you think this is related to the murder?"

"It's hard to say, Mr. Pinkney," replied Merton who had been standing over the rector's desk examining the pile of starched dress shirts carefully placed there. He lifted one by its hanger and inspected more closely the slashes in the front of the shirt where it would cover the rector's heart. "We'll send these shirts over to the lab right away."

"Of course," agreed the rector. "Of course."

"Where were these shirts when you found them?" asked Vesba, rummaging for her pad and pen in her large vinyl handbag.

"They were hanging in my closet here," he answered, indicating a door and opening it. "Bessie, our laundress, washes and irons them for me every Monday and Thursday, downstairs in the laundry room."

"The laundry room where Page Hawthorne found the bucket and filled it with water..." said Vesba.

"Yes. It's in the clergy area across from hers and Miles Cosetello's offices," agreed the rector.

"So someone could have found the shirts down there, right?" asked Merton. "Do they sit down there for long after they're pressed?"

"I really don't know. Bessie brings them up. Or Demetrius." Charles sighed. "They just appear starched and ready to wear."

"Nice arrangement," remarked Vesba.

"On the other hand, someone could have gotten into your office say, at night, when you were gone, and slashed them?" said Merton.

"Yes. I suppose so," agreed the rector. "So many people have keys..."

"Do you lock this closet, sir?" asked Merton.

"Always. There are some very expensive stoles and chasubles stored in here. Not that anyone..." he broke off, lurching into the walk-in closet.

Holy Comfort

He rustled through the hanging bags until he found one in particular, unzipped it and checked its contents slowly. "Thank God," he said as he reappeared.

"No more damage?" asked Vesba.

"No. It seems our slasher only wanted to ruin my personal property. He or she didn't touch the seventeen thousand dollar Bowen chasuble." The rector sighed and turned to the detectives. "Do you think this is a warning of some kind, Detectives?"

"It's hard to tell, sir. There was no apparent *warning*, as you say…" mused Merton.

"It could be someone's just trying to get us off the track," proposed Detective Vesba." Or someone wants to get in on the fun…"

"I hardly think—" began the rector, but Vesba cut him off.

"There are plenty of wierdos around. Even here, Padre."

"Of course. You're right," the rector said. He was tired already, and it was only nine thirty in the morning. He had made his bizarre discovery when he had returned to his office following the Women's Bible Study held every Tuesday morning at eight in the lodge room. Shocked and sickened, he had contacted the detectives who had arrived at the church shortly after receiving his call.

"Has anything like this happened before…to you, sir," asked Merton, carefully watching the priest's eyes.

"No…" said the rector. "No. Just the usual letters—'letter bombs' as Page calls them. Someone or other is always writing a letter informing me what I'm doing wrong, how bad my sermons are. You know…"

"Fan mail, eh?" said Vesba.

"Hardly," said the rector, casting a look at Vesba which would have frozen a less self-aasured person. "But letters are pretty standard. Everyone gets them. Colin does. Miles did, I'm sure. Even Page Hawthorne."

"Ms. Hawthorne? Why is that?" asked Merton.

"She's the editor of the newsletter. She's a perfect target for criticism by parishioners with nothing better to do but nitpick and judge and demean. She handles it rather well."

"Which parishioners? Do you have a list?" Vesba asked, her pen poised to write.

"Is that really necessary?" asked the rector. "The people who come to mind are harmless, mostly sad cases with an ax to grind against the world in general and no power whatsoever, no control over their environment beyond the power of the pen."

"The letter bomb," said Merton seriously. "But couldn't the letter bomb give way to razors or even charcoal briquettes when the letter bomb fails to get results?"

"I see your point, Detective Merton," said the rector. "But…really I can't imagine…"

"Imagine," said Vesba flatly. "Go ahead. Imagine."

The rector looked at Vesba, confusion clouding his eyes.

"Have you received any of those kinds of letters since the murder?" asked the other detective.

"Why...yes I have."

"May I see them? Do you have them here?"

The rector moved uncertainly to his desk and opened a large file drawer. He scanned the stick-up labels and pulled out a bulging file, which he laid on the top of his desk. "Here. There are four, no five, that I've received since the ninth. Two are from the same person." He handed them to Merton.

"May I take these with me?" he asked. The rector bowed his head. "Good. Detective Vesba and I will take a look at them later and if we have any questions we'll give you a call. Try not to worry, sir."

"Do not be anxious about anything, eh? Of course, Detectives, and may the peace of God which transcends all understanding, guard *your* hearts and *your* minds in Christ Jesus."

No sooner had the detectives left, bearing the ruined shirts away in a plastic evidence bag, than his assistant buzzed the rector to say that Bradford Cole was in her office demanding to see him.

"Does he have an appointment?" asked Pinkney as he rubbed his furrowed brow with both hands. He sighed as she answered in the negative. "Show him in."

Seconds later, Bradford Cole emerged from the outer office, closely followed by his assistant who threw the rector a quizzical look from behind Cole's back, her shoulders raised in a perplexed shrug. Then she backed out, leaving the rector to face Cole, an angry bull snorting and pawing the ground.

"Have a seat, Brad, please," the rector offered, guiding Cole to a seat by the window.

"No," Cole said in a nasal whine as he made a downward motion with his hands like a referee signing 'time out.' "I'm too angry to sit down. I don't want to sit down. Not in your office. Ever."

"All right, Brad," the rector said carefully as he sat down. "What seems to be the problem?"

"What seems to be the problem? Jesus Christ. My best friend is dead and you're asking me what seems to be the problem?"

"Of course. I know that..."

"Jesus, you're an idiot. You're not half the priest Miles Costello was. And you'll never be. Holy Comforter deserves better and if it's the last thing I do, I'll see you gone from here. It would be the best thing for us and the best thing for you."

"Why are you threatening me?" asked Pinkney calmly.

"It's no threat. I'll do it," said Cole, his voice rising. "Why don't you just admit your incompetence and give us a nice, civilized divorce? The marriage just hasn't turned out."

The rector continued to sit serenely, his fingers tented before him, and contemplate the irate man. He had always thought Bradford Cole was a

Holy Comfort

blowhard, a reckless, thoughtless, spoiled adult-child. When he had served on the vestry, every meeting he had attended had been fraught with tension. He had threatened to quit and Charles had prayed that he would. He raised his voice. He cursed. Although his family's reputation was unimpeachable in this town, Charles thought that Bradford Cole seldom behaved as a gentleman ought to behave. Speaking quietly in a tone one might use to calm a hysterical child, he said, "I see a distraught and grieving man in front of me who's frustrated that justice is not being served quickly enough. We're all frustrated...and grieving. Believe me, Brad—"

"Oh shit," Cole cut in, shouting. "Yeah, you're grieving. My ass you're grieving. You're glad he's gone, you're—"

"Why on earth would you accuse me of that?" the rector asked, bewilderment shading his face. "Miles was one of God's children. He was—"

"He was the greatest guy I ever knew," interrupted Cole again as he lowered himself heavily into a chair. "I'll never have a friend like Miles again." The big man began to cry then as he buried his face in his hands and let go, his shoulders shaking with each sob.

The rector put a hand on Cole's shoulder and, leaning low so his face almost touched the other man's head, said quietly, "Pray with me, Brad. Let's pray. *Lord, you consoled Martha and Mary in their distress...draw near to us who mourn...and dry the tears of those who weep...You wept at the grave of Lazarus, Your friend...comfort us in our sorrow.*"

Chapter Twenty-Two

THE TWO DETECTIVES sat once again in Salisbury Hall, this time reading the letters entrusted to their care by the rector. Vesba took a sip from her can of Diet Coke. "Listen to this—it's from Martha Van Patton: 'I feel compelled to reiterate my disappointment with your handling of the funeral of Miles Costello. Your homily was so devoid of feeling as to be almost insulting to the memory of that great man and priest, my friend'...*blah, blah, blah*... 'Jaspar and I had been planning to increase our annual pledge for the year from $20,000 to $27,500. However, in light of your failure, once again, to rise to the occasion, we cannot in good conscience do as we planned. We will not contemplate leaving Holy Comforter, although I admit I am tempted, because Holy Comforter is, after all, our church. We will still be members long after you are gone. Please acknowledge the enclosed check for $5,000 as our gift for this calendar year. I trust you will find some use for it. Signed, Martha Bailey Van Patton.'

Vesba whistled. "Wow. Money talks again. And will you look at this? She carbon copied her letter to the bishop and to the senior warden! This lady's got a real high opinion of her opinion."

Roy glanced at her, contemplating her words.

Leona continued, "What I don't get is why is she so angry with Pinkney? Sure she's sad about Costello, but why take it out on Pinkney? What did he ever do to her? What do these people expect from their priests? What do they want for their twenty thousand dollars?"

Merton hesitated. "I think they want to feel needed, if not for themselves, then at least for their money. The more money, the more they want to feel appreciated. It's the first thing they withhold. I bet Charles Pinkney treats everyone the same, regardless of their pledge. I bet that drives them crazy."

"So when they're happy, appreciated, they give their dough?"

"I guess. They certainly showered it on Costello. Look what Mrs. Van Patton said about how when Page Hawthorne hurt his feelings, she and Carol Sprague hatched the plan to send Costello on a little dream trip to Ireland. She felt needed, like Costello needed her. She showed her appreciation with money again. Costello knew the game and how to play."

Holy Comfort

Vesba squinted. "Yeah, I have to admit there was definitely something weird going on there. I mean why did she drag us over there to tell us that story?"

He shrugged. "Why do *you* think?"

"I sensed some jealousy there," she conceded. "Like she wanted his full attention. *Look at me.* Jesus."

He drained his coffee cup and stood up, moving leisurely to the coffee maker. "What about the other letters? I've got two from the same nut in the choir who is obsessed with *Anglican Tradition* and the rector's apparent ignorance of it."

"Uh huh. Sounds like the letter I read from one of Valentine's pals. He says blatantly that Pinkney isn't up to the job and asks why don't you just leave us in peace. He hints that he hopes Costello's death will be followed by the demise of the rest of the clergy staff! Can you believe it?"

"It must be hard to get letters like that," Merton mused. "Even if they're laughable."

Vesba muttered her agreement. "Here's one more, a little note from guess who? Charlotte Pentecost! It says: 'Dear Charles...I know this must be such a difficult time for you, seeing your enemy cut down like that. The guilt you are feeling must be terrible. I know how busy you are, so I have taken the liberty of calling Father Francis, your spiritual director, and telling him what has happened. He said he'd be in touch with you soon. My thoughts and prayers are with you. Please let me know if there is anything else I can do.' Holy shit! Miss Para-clergy strikes again! *Anything else I can do*? Try minding your own business!"

"Yeah," said Merton, gathering up the letters. "I wonder how the rector responded to that."

"You can bet she didn't get what she wanted—his attention!"

"No. I suppose he was polite—always the Christian gentleman."

"That must be the hardest part of his job," said Vesba. "That and keeping a straight face."

Merton smiled. "Well, let's not worry about these until we've heard from forensics about the shirts. We've talked to Van Patton and Charlotte Pentecost. I think the others can wait."

"I agree," she said. "Those queers in the choir are all bark."

"Okay then," said Merton. "I'll talk to you after lunch." As he turned to go, he swung into his jacket and stuffed the letters into his inside pocket.

"Where are you going?" she asked, her hands planted firmly on her hips.

He paused, apparently to think. "I want to talk to Page Hawthorne again. I think I may ask her to go out."

"*What?*" said Vesba, her voice thin and shrill. "That's a *crazy* idea, Roy." She walked to his side and pointed her finger at his face. "You can't be serious."

"It's worth a try," he said stepping away towards the window. "I think she might warm up away from this place..."

"*Warm up*? Are you referring to the case or...?"

"Yes," he said, rotating his shoulders. "Yes."

"What exactly do you think Ms. Hawthorne knows?"

"She's got to know more and I think she wants to help."

"Why would she want to help?"

"She feels guilty for not telling anyone about Costello."

"And you think you can sweet-talk what she knows out of her?"

"I'm not going to sweet-talk her."

Vesba looked at her partner's back with an exaggerated expression of incredulity and said, "Bullshit." Then she crossed her arms and propelled herself to the window. She tilted her head back.

He turned and lowered his eyes to her face.

"You are deluding yourself, Roy. You just want to get her skinny little ass in bed."

Merton sighed and turned away, looking down at the carpet. "As a matter of professional courtesy, I will try to explain. I believe Ms. Hawthorne is the key to this mystery. The people who like her and the people who don't have all mentioned her name in connection with Costello. He was connected to her somehow. Their offices were next door to each other. He was fucking someone on the wall between their offices. Even if she was unaware or if she's blocking...she's got to know something was going on. She's always in that little box..."

"All right. So if you do this thing...if you ask Ms. Hawthorne out...where are you thinking of going?"

"I was thinking of taking her to the Wildhorse Saloon. She likes country music."

"Oh, Jesus...dinner, dancing, a deep meaningful discussion. I see."

"It could work."

"And you might get lucky."

"Shut up, Leona," he said, shoving his hands in his pockets. He still refused to meet her eyes. "Just back off."

"Well, what about her?" asked Vesba, who was not about to back off. "Is this fair to her? Maybe she actually likes you, and if she agrees to go out, it's because she's interested. I mean, what other reason would she have for agreeing to go out with you? It's not like you're going to say, 'Let's go talk about the case over dinner' are you? You'll be using her no matter what happens."

"No, I won't," he said turning back to her. The two partners glared across the room at each other.

Vesba sighed dramatically and threw her arms in the air. "Well, I can see you've convinced yourself. I'm not getting anywhere...so are you going to give equal time to Charlotte Pentecost?"

"What?"

Holy Comfort

She smirked, glad to have caught him. "Her name comes up almost as often as Ms. Hawthorne's and you know it," she said, resting her rear end on the edge of the window sill. "You really ought to give her equal time, Roy. But I guess she doesn't appeal to your sense of...what? Chivalry? She doesn't need little glasses of ice water and trays of soup. Nobody's tripping over themselves to put their jackets over her shoulders." She paused and inspected her nails. "Tell me, Partner, if Ms. Hawthorne looked like me, would you ask her to the Wildhorse?"

He looked her in the eye. "No, I wouldn't."

"I didn't think so." She looked at her watch. "Why don't I go nudge the crime lab," she said.

"Fine," he said. "I'll see you later."

"Not if I see you first."

Chapter Twenty-Three

MERTON WATCHED AS Page shut down her computer. When he had knocked gently she had nodded, signaling him to sit down. She had not said hello or for that matter, anything at all. She had continued to work. She was wearing a dark purple knit dress. Ecclesiastical in color but not in form, the dress was tight, showing off her small bones and her small curves. She looked especially vulnerable. She wore tiny gold hoops on her ears and no other jewelry except her diamond guard ring and ruby anniversary band on her right hand. The stones were large, the rings obviously expensive. Except for a little lipstick, Page wore no makeup that he could discern. Her beauty and lack of pretension beguiled him, just as they confused Vesba, who he knew was naturally suspicious of any woman who did not appear to spend at least two hours getting dressed in the morning. His eyes followed her as her ponytail bobbed up and down as she worked, but she seemed to be wholly unaware of his scrutiny. In fact, Page seemed to take his presence largely for granted. He was variously insulted and intrigued by this. Was he beneath her notice or was she simply comfortable with him being there?

As Page switched off her computer, signaling that she was finished for the day, she pulled the covered elastic band which held her ponytail in place out of her hair. She shook it a little and pushed it behind her ears as she turned to smile at Merton. He returned her smile and was opening his mouth to speak when suddenly a bustling noise was heard in the hall outside. Someone was laying down packages. "Knock Knock," came a distinctive sing-song voice from outside the office.

"Come in, Kitty," replied Page, immediately brightening.

The door opened and a short, round, exuberant woman of indeterminate age appeared, beaming, and entered the tiny office. "Well, two's company and three's a crowd," she laughed, acknowledging Merton who had stood up and was offering his seat. "Especially if the third person is me! No. No. You sit back down, honey, I'm not staying. I just stopped by to bring Page some flowers." She held out a round glass vase exploding with roses.

"Oh!" she exclaimed as she reached for them. "They're beautiful, Kitty. Are these from your garden?"

Holy Comfort

"Yes! Behold the last rose of summer...or fall. Whatever. They're my Mr. Lincoln roses. They've done so well this year. They seem to thrive on my ignorance and neglect!"

"Well, they're heavenly," Page insisted, setting them down and giving Kitty a big hug. "And you're so nice to bring them to me."

"Well," Kitty sighed, her face becoming still, her round blue eyes thoughtful. "I heard about what happened and how you found the body. Nobody should have to see something like that, especially not a sweet thing like you."

Page, who still had her arm around Kitty, patted her shoulder and glanced over at Roy who had continued to stand, not quite sure what to do or where to look. "Kitty," Page said, "have you met Roy Merton? He's one of the detectives working on the case."

"Well, no. I'm pleased to meet you, Detective Merton," she said, grabbing his hand and pumping it. "I'm Kitty Epstein, and I must say you're even better looking than I've heard."

Merton appeared to blush and Page said, "Aw, shucks, ma'am," which sent Kitty into paroxysms of laughter.

"Page, honey, you kill me," Kitty said between hiccups. Slowly she calmed down and her face and tone became serious. "Well, I'll leave you two. There isn't enough room in here for two thin people, let alone two thin people and a fat person. Which reminds me, we didn't see you upstairs at lunch today for Church Service League. Are you eating, Page?" she asked, stepping back and looking her up and down. Page crossed her arms across her chest and looked suspiciously at Merton who raised his eyebrows and shrugged. "You gotta eat. Now promise me you're going to go home and make yourself a good dinner. Maybe I could bring you something in tomorrow—"

"Oh, no, no. Don't go to any more trouble on my account. The roses are beautiful, but—"

"You can't *eat* roses," interrupted Kitty. "I should have thought to bring you some food. Well," she continued, looking around the office and fanning herself, "it beats me how the person who does the most work has the tiniest closet for an office and *some people* who do next to nothing but spend our pledge dollars and take long lunches have the proverbial corner office with windows! Have you noticed that about us here at Holy Comforter, Detective? Sometimes we do things just a little bit backwards."

"Well, the first shall be last and the last first, Kitty. I guess I'm in just the right spot," interjected Page.

"Yes you are, dear. I know you are." Kitty looked serious. "You know, Detective, this is a very spiritual lady. She has a real clear view of the world because she washes that spiritual window of hers every day. You should listen to her."

Merton gave Kitty his conspirator's smile, but did not comment.

"Well," said Page. She hugged her friend and thanked her again. Kitty hugged her back, shook Merton's hand and said confidentially,

"Definitely more Dick Powell than Robert Montgomery. I don't know what Evelyn Schwartz was talking about!"

After Kitty left and was safely seated in Sophie Carl's office down the hall, Merton and Page returned to their chairs. She said, "So try to fit her into your Holy Comforter pigeon hole, Detective. It can't be done."

"She's a real nice lady," he said. "Definitely an exception that proves the rule."

"Not as exceptional as you think. Actually, Kitty is one of those rare birds—a *cradle* Episcopalian."

The detective recognized the exaggerated reverential tone used by certain members of the parish when speaking of the former rector Clyde Cullen. He smiled. "So are you one of those cradle Episcopalians?"

"Hell, yes."

"And does that make you better than...the average non-cradle Episcopalian?"

"Some people think so."

"Do you think so?"

"Hell, no," said Page, leaning back in her desk chair and stretching her arms over her head. She yawned largely and apologized.

"So tell me," continued the detective with some effort. "What did she mean by you washing your spiritual window daily?"

She crossed her legs and leaned sideways, her chin on one hand. "Cleanliness is next to godliness?"

"She wants me to try to look through that window," he said, leaning forward. "Maybe I'll see something." Page regarded the detective through narrowed eyes. "I'd like to try," he said. He cleared his throat. "I have an idea."

Page nodded, her eyes half closed. She seemed to imply that he should go on.

"I was thinking that maybe you'd like to go with me to the Wildhorse Saloon tomorrow night."

Page continued to gaze at him.

Merton swallowed and continued. "You know, that's where they have the line dancing and country music...and you like country music so I thought you might like to go. With me. For dinner."

"And you propose to look through my spiritual window *there*?"

"You're probably busy."

"Well, no," she said, sitting up. "But I'd have to find a babysitter for the boys."

He sat up also. "Will you go if you can find a babysitter?" he asked doubtfully.

"It's a school night, you know."

"I'd get you home early."

"Well, then, I guess it would be okay."

"You don't sound too sure."

Holy Comfort

"Well, I'm not," she said matter-of-factly. "It's just that I haven't been out since my divorce. Not once. And I was married for nine years. I guess I'm a little out of practice."

"Out of practice?"

She rolled her eyes and smiled. "I suppose this wouldn't really be a date…"

"A shared eating experience."

"Good. Much better," she said, still smiling.

"I'm sure Kitty would approve."

Page leaned back again and narrowed her eyes at him. "I just assumed that you would have a girlfriend…or a wife."

"No, ma'am," he said with certainty.

"And you want to have dinner with me?"

"Yes. Why does that surprise you?" he asked as his eyes swept over her. "I like a blond who can make a bishop kick a hole in a stained glass window."

She looked away. "That isn't me. It was funny because it was the opposite of me."

"I don't think so." He leaned forward. "Look, no strings, ma'am. I just thought it would be nice to talk in a time increment longer than ten minutes about something other than Costello's murder."

She exhaled too loudly. "Well, if I can find a babysitter, and that shouldn't be a problem since I am blessed with the five teenage O'Malley sisters across the street, I'll go. There's just one thing."

"What's that?"

"You've got to stop calling me 'ma'am' right now." She ventured a small smile.

Merton threatened to smile himself, the corner of his mouth twitching upward. "All right. It's a deal. Do you think you can call me tonight and let me know? About the babysitter?"

"On the phone?"

"On the phone…here's my card. I'll write down my cell phone number."

"This is becoming so complicated. Your card." She giggled, taking the card. She cursed herself inwardly for giggling. What was it about this man that caused every ounce of sophistication to drain out of her?

Chapter Twenty-Four

AFTER DINNER THAT night, Page told the boys to put on sweatshirts and to go retrieve the old, rippy quilt from the back of the hall closet. Then they went out to their backyard and spread the quilt on the lawn which slanted down to one of the many creeks that crisscrossed Rockville. Even though it was October, it was still warm and the night was magically clear and crisp.

Lying on their backs, one boy on either side of their mother, the three looked up at the stars and the moon, which was a brilliant fingernail on a holy field of dark blue. They pointed out the Big and Little Dippers and Orion and his belt. They found Venus. Page felt her boys move closer to her and she knew they were dizzy with insignificance as she was, floating on their quilt under the vast and limitless sky spread out like a tent above them.

"Prince Andrei looked up at the stars and sighed. Nothing ever turns out the way you think it will," she whispered.

"Who's Prince Andy?" asked Tal.

"Prince Andrei," corrected Walter. "Prince *Andrei.*"

"He's a character in a book called *War and Peace*," said Page.

"Prince Andrei looked up at the stars," began Tal wistfully.

"...and sighed. Nothing ever turns out the way you think it will," finished Page. "That's very true, you know. Prince Andrei was kind of sad when he said it, but it doesn't have to make you sad. It's just that you're always going to be surprised by life. And I suppose that's a good thing after all. That's why I never wish for things."

"You never wish, Mommy?" asked Tal.

"No. Wishing seems like such a one-way proposition. Like buying a lottery ticket."

Walter snorted. He knew what his mother thought of the lottery.

"Jesus says, just ask. Directly. Say what you want, what you need, what you seek. You'll get an answer."

"Really?' asked Tal, still doubtful.

"But we don't always get what we pray for," interrupted Walter who had been silent except for the snort, listening.

"No, Walter, we don't," said Page, looking over at her handsome older son. "Sometimes God says 'no' and sometimes we don't understand why. Usually though, at least in my experience, I can see later why the

Holy Comfort

answer was 'no.' Anyway our prayers are always heard and our prayers are always answered."

"It's almost like the sky is a big black board," said Tal, "and the stars are writing. Like a code. Only we can't read it. God can read it."

"*Seek him that made the Pleiades and Orion,*" she quoted softly, "*and darkeneth the day into night...The Lord is his name.*"

The three were silent for awhile, intent on their stargazing and their own thoughts. Page's thoughts turned inevitably to the Church of the Holy Comforter and to Miles Costello whom she had once considered a friend, before things had changed. Now she felt remarkably little for him. She felt horror, revulsion at the crime, but for Miles himself, very little. She would not miss him.

When she had started to work at the church, she had been excited about the prospect of getting to know, perhaps befriending, the youngest priest. Like so many others, she had been initially charmed by his quiet manner and apparently humble demeanor. *Like so many others.* But working with him, she had found him to be inconsistent and unreliable and, worst of all, shallow. His advice was unoriginal and suggested memorized platitudes. His knowledge hinted at back cover summaries and quotations. His whole life seemed like a movie preview where the clips chosen revealed the best the film had to offer and made viewing the film itself unnecessary.

Roy Merton had told her that Miles was a dangerous man. *A dangerous man?* He was a boor, certainly, and a low-life, but dangerous? Was she so blind? So...naïve? What had Miles done to someone to make that person want to kill him? He had pushed her and she had said no, and he had backed off and laughed it off, making fun of her, making her feel stupid. Did he push someone else? Didn't he stop? Had he really had sex in his office? Against the wall? *Her wall? The desires of the wicked.* Her mind turned in a descending spiral and she stood once again in the doorway of Miles Costello's office, the smell of burning hair and flesh smashing into her consciousness like a bucket of cold water...*hot burning coals...fall upon him...cast into the mire...*

She sat up suddenly and turned to Walter. "Let's go inside," she whispered. "I think Tal has fallen asleep. I'll pick him up and you fold up the quilt, please." Tal was such a feather child, still barely fifty pounds at age six, that Page could easily carry him into the house and up to the boys' room where she helped him undress and climb into his bed. "Goodnight, baby," she said to him as she tucked Curious George under his arm and kissed them both.

On her way downstairs, she mustered her resolve to call Roy Merton, fingering his card in her pocket. In the kitchen she dialed the number on the wall phone as Walter watched in a detached manner, concentrating on spinning his lacrosse stick. The phone rang three times and then Merton's voice greeted her. Their conversation was short and business-like, concluding in less than a minute. When she hung up she sighed. "God," she said quietly, "I must sound like such a dork."

"You don't sound like a dork, Mom," said Walter whose presence Page had all but forgotten. "Who were you calling, anyway? Are you *going out* tomorrow night?"

"Yes. Actually, I am."

"*With who?*"

"With *whom*. I'm going to dinner with one of the detectives who's investigating the murder at church. Detective Merton. You met him on Sunday when Tal nearly knocked him over running into him."

"Oh, him." Walter thought for a moment. "So it's like a date?" he asked in a doubtful tone.

"No, not like a date. Well, sort of like a date...I don't know, Walter. We'll see how things go tomorrow. He's a nice guy."

"Where's he taking you?"

"The Wildhorse Saloon. He likes country music, too."

"Cool," said Walter who was losing interest. "Can I watch TV? My homework's done and there's bull riding."

"Okay, sure. I'll be there in a minute," she said. "Put that lacrosse stick in the garage first."

Walter rushed off to the den, and Page turned to the stove to put the water on for tea. She got out a mug and a tea bag and stood looking out the kitchen window while she waited for the water to boil. She thought about using a mug for tea. Her mother always used a cup and saucer, preferably bone china. Never a mug. Her mother would never have worn blue jeans or padded around the house in athletic socks. Page chuckled a little. Her mother would never have agreed to go out, whether it was called a 'date' or not, with a police detective. Who were his parents, anyway? Where, indeed, had he gone to high school? She could just hear her mother asking those questions. Of course, she had no answers. She knew remarkably little about him, but somehow she didn't much care. It wasn't as if she was going to marry the guy, she would have said to her mother. She wasn't looking for anyone. He had just appeared. She was quite happy being single, making decisions alone, bringing up the boys. She thought they were doing pretty well.

Sometimes she felt an ache inside, the lonely ache of the unloved, but she had felt that ache when she was still married, and that had been much worse. She wondered again why Chester had wanted to marry her. Why did anyone want to marry anyone? Why had her parents gotten married? Were they in love? She had never witnessed much evidence of mutual feeling or even concern. But then, you never knew what went on between two people. You really never knew. It was presumptuous to speculate, but human nature to do so. She had a feeling the Pinkneys had a good marriage and that they were still in love. She had walked to her car once with Charles after a meeting late at night, and she had watched him go into his house and, then, watched through the large window which stretched from the landing up to the second floor, as he bounded up the stairs. He had looked like he couldn't wait to find Adair and tell her all about the evening

Holy Comfort

and then, or perhaps first, make love to her. Chester had never bounded up the stairs to her. No one had. She had stood on the sidewalk, transfixed, watching, as she stood now, blindly staring out the kitchen window into the dark, the tears starting as the kettle shrieked.

Chapter Twenty-Five

It was barely seven a.m., but the Ballard Street Cafe was already jammed with people. Businessmen in starched white shirts, their charcoal gray suit coats hung carefully over the backs of chairs, and business women in dark dresses gathered in twos and fours to drink coffee and eat English muffins.

In a corner of the smoking section three men sat quietly waiting. They fingered their coffee cups and read the menu. One of them looked out the window and aimlessly counted the cars in the parking lot.

"I guess this is it," whined Tony Spitz. "No one else seems to be coming." He looked at his watch and shook his sleeve down. He surveyed once more the familiar room, craning his neck to see the front door. He sighed.

Chester Hawthorne stared blankly over the other man's shoulder and smoked. There were twenty-seven cars in the parking lot.

"It doesn't matter," said Willis McHugh. By his tone, the two other men could tell that it did.

"It just seems sad that just last Wednesday morning we were all together for our small group, Miles included. And now this *is it.*"

"So much for Bible study," said Hawthorne dully.

"We could keep meeting," said Spitz.

"What would be the point?" snapped McHugh, putting an end to any discussion on the subject. "Personally I'm only interested in finding out who killed Miles and locking them the hell up."

"Too close to home, Will?" asked Hawthorne.

"You might say so. Yes, goddam it." Willis looked around for the waitress, and catching her eye, waved his empty water glass.

"Do you think these detectives have a clue?" asked Hawthorne.

"I don't know," McHugh said vaguely. "They're the best we have." The waitress arrived and poured water noisily, the ice cubes boucing gaily. The mayor sneered and said, "Thanks."

After the waitress had stepped away, Hawthorne said to her back, "Uh, I'd like some more coffee...if it isn't too much trouble." He rolled his eyes at Spitz who laughed. The waitress returned and filled his cup.

Holy Comfort

"Thanks," said Hawthorne, dismissing her. He straightened up from his slouch and reached for the individual half and half packages on a saucer in the middle of the table. He selected one and tore it open, emptying it into his coffee. "So what do the best we have *have*?" he asked.

The mayor met Hawthorne's weary gaze, their identical brown eyes locking momentarily and then drifting apart. Chester Hawthorne was his cousin. He did not like him very much. He did not like most of his numerous cousins, truth be told, but that hardly mattered. They were his cousins. "Not a whole hell of a lot," he said sighing. "The crime, the murder, was extremely well planned. No stupid clues left behind, no Agatha Christie hints. The crime scene was clean. And no one's saying much that's helpful."

"They came to see me," said Hawthorne. He sipped his coffee thoughtfully. "They said it was because I was in Mile's small group..."

"They talked to *me*," interrupted Spitz. "I was vague and non-committal, just like you said..."

The two other men glanced scornfully at Tony and then back at each other.

"As I was *saying*," continued Hawthorne. "They said it was because I was a friend of the deceased, but then they asked me a lot of questions about Page. I didn't like it. I didn't like *him*. He kept correcting me whenever I'd call her my wife. '*Ex*-wife?' he'd ask. A real asshole."

"I wonder where they're going with that?" mused McHugh. "It's just possible, Ches, that they think Page knows something. Her office is right next door to his and..."

"They're just grasping at straws, inventing connections that don't exist. As if Page...I'd bet my last dollar she had no idea what Miles was into."

The men were thoughtful for a while. Hawthorne finished off his cup of coffee and leaned toward McHugh. "I'd just like to know who sent those clods barking after Page. I bet it was Brad Cole...or..." Once again the two sets of identical brown eyes met and blinked together in recognition of their common thought.

"*What*?" asked Spitz. "Are you thinking *she* told them?"

"Shut up, Tony," snapped McHugh. "*Shut up*."

"Well...what about Miles?" asked Spitz, his feelings hurt. "Did he leave anything behind, anything to incriminate...someone? Like a journal or e-mail? My God, he used his computer all the time...all those stupid dirty jokes and pictures he'd send...that must have been on his computer..."

"As far as I know, they found nothing. His laptop was clean...there was no pager found on his body."

"But, Will," said Hawthorne carefully. "I am a little worried about...what are we going to do about Brad? I talked to him at the funeral—he's a basket case. He's losing it. There's no telling what he might say now or—"

111

"I know," interrupted the mayor. "I know. But there's a way to channel his anger in a constructive way, a healthy way. We can use it to our advantage. I'll see to that."

Hawthorne stubbed out his cigarette and stood up. "I've got to get going. Life goes on."

Spitz remained in his seat, his elbows resting on the arms of his chair, his hands hanging limply over his lap. "We never even said a prayer for Miles."

"Jesus, Tone," said Hawthorne looking around at their neighbors. "Get a hold of yourself." He threw some dollar bills on the table and turned to go.

"Watch your back, buddy," called McHugh. "Watch your goddamn back."

Chapter Twenty-Six

ADAIR PINKNEY HAD been waiting for them. She hurried out of the rectory when they drove up to the church and motioned to them to come over. Vesba grumbled, but they detoured as requested.

"I don't want my husband to know you're here, Detectives," said Adair as she ushered them into her large beige living room. She was wearing beige pants and a matching cashmere sweater set and a silk scarf with horseshoes. She looked very put-together, thought Vesba, except that she was wearing glasses. Did she usually wear contacts or was she wearing the glasses because she needed them to survey the street?

"Chick has enough on his mind," said Adair as she sat down with the detectives. She perched on the edge of her beige chair and clutched a needlepoint pillow. "But I'm concerned about this latest...vandalism. I couldn't sleep last night wondering if he's in danger. What do you think? Is this the work of the same person who killed Miles?"

"We don't know for sure, ma'am," said Merton. "But the two events seem unconnected."

"Why do you say that?" asked Adair.

"Someone's playing with your husband's mind," said Vesba, ignoring her question. "Any idea who would do that?"

The rector's wife stared for a moment and then waved her hand dismissively. "Oh, who knows anymore? I looked around on Sunday at all those familiar faces in church and I couldn't help thinking, 'Was it you?' or 'Was it *you*?' And *now*! Dear lord...I can't imagine what would motivate someone to do that to Chick. I mean Miles Costello was...so different."

"You mean you can understand someone murdering *him*?" asked Vesba. "But not someone wanting to hurt your harmless husband?"

"Yes," said Adair with a new edge to her voice. "I suppose that is what I mean."

"From what we've gathered," said Vesba, crossing her legs noisily, "there are more than a few parishioners who aren't big fans of Charles Pinkney, who might enjoy playing with his mind a little, making him sweat."

"I suppose you're right," said Adair sighing. "It's not as if this was the first time. People do the strangest things. I remember when Chick found the bag of garlic hanging in the fuse box outside his office."

"Garlic?" repeated Vesba.

"Used to ward off vampires, Detective," explained Adair. Both detectives stared. "And, of course, we've had more than our share of roadkill thrown on the front steps."

"Who would have thought?" said Vesba, her jaw dropping. "Right here in Middle Essex?"

"Yes," said Adair as she stood up. "I'm sorry, Detectives. I guess I have over-reacted. I apologize for wasting your time." She tossed the pillow on to the chair and held her hand toward the front hall as the detectives stood up.

Outside, Vesba stopped on the sidewalk and grasped her partner's arm. "Give me credit, please, for not saying anything." Merton chuckled but offered no credit. He shook off her hand and started walking as she continued, "I refrained from telling her my main theorey of the shirt-slashing. That is, that someone is trying to throw us off the trail, someone like Mrs. Pinkney."

Merton stopped at the massive oak doors of the church. "C'mon, Leona."

"C'mon nothing. Haven't you wondered—maybe Adair has an idea about who knocked off Costello. Maybe the idea worries, or even scares her, a little, and she starts thinking, and her busy brain starts turning over ideas. Maybe she thinks she'll take some heat off ol' Charles by slashing his shirts." Merton folded his arms and shifted his weight. Vesba continued, "And you know lots of times perps can't stay away, they're too curious. That explains the little hand-wringing scene just now. She was wondering if her little delaying tactic was working."

"You think she thinks *Charles* murdered Costello?" said Merton.

"Just an idea," said Vesba as her pager buzzed at her belt. She picked it up. "Speak of the devil," she said, showing the screen to her partner. "The crime lab beckons. Let's say our prayers that we can maybe put ol' Adair's mind to rest."

Holy Comfort

Chapter Twenty-Seven

WELL, THIS WAS what you got when you prayed for patience: more situations in which to practice being patient. *Thank you, Lord.* Page wondered fleetingly what Roy Merton was doing as Tony Spitz sat in her office and droned on. "Just last week, after our Wednesday morning group, Miles told me to do something that really made me happy. And I said I couldn't think of a thing. And he said, well, try to remember a time when you were happy and think why you were happy and do that. And I said the last time I remember being happy was in high school. I was on top of the world. My friends and I, you know—Chester and Wallace and Mac—we were the smartest and the richest, there was nobody who could look down on us. I was headed for Yale. Life was ahead of me, the world stretched out at my feet. But things didn't quite work out, you know, like I thought they would."

"But why were you happy, Tony?" asked Page. "Because you felt superior?"

"I guess so."

"Well, what's changed then?"

"It's not the same, that's all. The world's changed."

"No it hasn't. Not your world. What's different?" she asked a bit contentiously.

"It just feels different."

"You're almost twenty years older—possibly a little wiser."

"Alice and the kids—they don't make me happy."

"Maybe you shouldn't expect other people to make you happy, Tony. It doesn't work that way. You have to like yourself—inside. All the trappings of success—your club, your school, your address—won't necessarilly make you content inside."

"I just wish I could go back."

"Maybe you should try to make Alice happy. Maybe *that* would make you happy."

Spitz groaned. "I doubt it."

Page narrowed her eyes at Spitz. "Is that why you joined Miles' small group? Were you looking for big answers to life's hard questions?"

"I joined because he asked me. I guess I was flattered. He had put together a pretty stellar group, you know. All Yale graduates, mostly members of the club, and some heavy hitters, like Willis McHugh and Brad Cole. Anyone would have been proud to be included. Chester even joined."

"I heard that," she said. "How did Chester and Miles get along?"

"Oh, they got along all right," said Spitz. "Although Chester didn't like it that Miles was trying to get into the club. He thought he was social-climbing and that it was inappropriate. He thought you should be able to go somewhere and not have your minister breathing down your neck. I used to say, but Miles isn't like other ministers, he's different. And he'd say, yeah, he's *different* all right. But he was just kidding. They did have one thing in common, though. They both hated Charles Pinkney."

Spitz blew through his lips like a winded horse.

Page smirked.

Misreading the smirk as encouragement, he blurted out, "Page, have dinner with me tonight. We'll go to the club."

"Where's Alice?"

"In Florida with her mother. She took the kids. *Come on*," he said breathlessly. "Come on, Page, come to dinner and then we...I feel bad about Miles. I don't want to be alone."

"Maybe that's what Miles had in mind," she said, no longer trying to control the irritation in her voice. "Return to your youth—get lucky on the golf course under the stars—but not with me. Go home. Call your wife. Grow up, for God's sake."

"Jesus...I was just looking for a little sympathy, Page. You could give a guy a break. But I guess that was never your style."

Page stood up and put on her sweater. "I have a meeting now, Tony," she lied. "You can sit in my office if you care to, but I have to go."

"No, I'll go." Spitz sighed wearily and stood up. "Maybe I'll see you at the Burton's Friday night."

"No," she said turning off the light. "I wasn't invited."

Spitz looked wistfully down the hall to Miles' office, noting the yellow police caution tape criss-crossing the door. "Nothing will ever be the same now," he said.

Page did not hear his remark. She had already turned the corner, passing through the fire doors. On her way upstairs she slowed down and thought to herself how glad she was to be having dinner with the detective that night and not with that vestry member.

Holy Comfort

Chapter Twenty-Eight

"Thanks for seeing me, sir," said Merton as he walked to the window and sat in the chair opposite the rector.

"Of course...what do you have for me?"

Roy held up a manila envelope, but did not hand it to the rector. He paused for a moment, searching the other man's face. He looked like a banker with his slicked back black hair and his charcoal suit which fit his trim body perfectly. His eyes, however, did not belong to a banker. They held hurt and pain, loss and remorse, but they held no fear. They were the deep brown eyes of Johnny Cash or Merle Haggard, poet's eyes. The detective laughed to himself, imagining what the rector would think of his comparison. Would he know it was a compliment?

Charles Pinkney crossed his legs and rested his manicured hands on his thigh. He cleared his mind and waited patiently for the distracted detective to begin.

Merton cleared his throat and handed the envelope to Pinkney. "The shirts were covered with fingerprints. Our slasher was careless...which says to us that he couldn't be the same person as the murderer who was obsessively careful."

The rector stared at the unopened envelope in his hand. "I suppose you've been unable to identify the fingerprints."

"Actually, yes, we were able to come up with a match." Merton stared at the other man, knowing that what he had to say would surprise him and probably hurt him. "Sir, the fingerprints belong to your organist, Baylor Valentine."

"How in the world could you know that...?" His voice trailed off. He still had not opened the envelope.

"Dr. Valentine was arrested in 1973. He was booked for soliciting a minor, a male, in the central west end. The charges were dropped. I'm guessing some fancy lawyer at the church got him off. It's hard to believe he held on to his job..."

"The things they don't tell you when you accept a position as a rector," said Pinkney. He shifted his legs and avoided the detective's eyes, which stared relentlessly at him. He sighed and smiled wanly. "Well, I'm not sure what to do now."

"You don't have to do anything right away...if you don't want to."

"Thank you. I'd like to talk to Colin Whitefish about this. Then I suppose I'll have to talk to Baylor." His hands became fists and he struck his leg once. "Why, *why* would he do such a thing?"

Merton did not venture a guess, but continued to stare at the other man. *Yes*, he thought, *why*? Why destroy this man's property? Well, at least they knew who had done it. Now, if only the murderer would slip up, leave a fingerprint or two, drop a clue.

The detective glanced at his watch: three twelve p.m. He might be able to catch Page Hawthorne before she left to go home. "Do you have any questions, sir?" he asked the rector whose thoughtful gaze angled away from him out the window.

"No," Pinkney answered. "No. I don't think so."

"Let me know what you decide to do about Valentine. I'll leave the forensic report with you. We'll need to question him about the murders again, what with this violent act toward another member of the clergy. But we can wait until tommorrow if you like."

"Thank you, Detective Merton. And thank you for keeping this...episode...under your hat. There's really no need for this to get out."

"You're welcome." The detective rose from his chair and walked to the door that led to the hallway, taking long strides. "Goodbye," he said, turning back to the rector who had remained seated and staring.

"Goodbye," the rector answered, having nearly forgotten the detective already.

"Are you sure you're all right, sir?" The sight of the distracted rector had tapped some neglected source of empathy within the detective. He wanted to comfort him, to reassure him. "Can I do anything?" he said.

"No," said the rector, rising from his chair, avoiding the detective's eyes. "I believe I'll go home for a while. Adair has been quite upset about this latest event. I need to talk to her."

When he swung into the clergy area hallway and saw that Page's door was closed, he felt something inside him move, something thud. It was disappointment and it took him unawares, ambushed him and knelt upon his chest, inhibiting his movement. He stood in the hall and contemplated the floor, the carpet, his shoes.

The sound of another voice down the hall made him look up. The voice was saying something about helping him. The voice was speaking to him.

"May I help you?" repeated Charlotte Pentecost.

"No," said the detective.

Charlotte stood by her own door, one hand poised on the frame, the other supporting her chin in a thoughtful pose. "Miss Page has left for the day—*early*, you may note. She hinted at some mysterious goings-on tonight, something to prepare for, you see. You wouldn't know anything about that, would you, Detective?"

Holy Comfort

"No," he said again. Although he could see that Charlotte was moving slowly towards him and his instinct to flee was spiking, his boots remained rooted to the floor.

"She wouldn't say, of course, but I think she's got a big date," drawled Charlotte.

"Good for her," said Merton.

"I'll say, good for her," she said. "Of course, it could just be that it's talent night at the Cozy Corners Elementary School. She's probably pouring the Kool-Aid."

She was right up next to him now. He looked down bravely into her expectant blue eyes. "And what about you, Ms. Pentecost?" he said. "I heard the Lay Ministry Board was having a special seminar on 'Hildegard of Bingen: Frustrated Middle-Aged Visionary.'"

"Oh, very funny," she said touching his arm. "Aren't you the clever detective?" She grinned, but there was no amusement in it.

"Occasionally I read something other than a car magazine."

She made a noise in her throat. "No, I *knew* that! I could tell right off that you're a very special, experienced kind of learned man. I bet we could find lots of things to talk about."

"Maybe another time," said Merton, abruptly turning. "Nice to see you again." He did not look back.

Charlotte Pentecost crossed her arms over her chest, breathed in and breathed out.

Chapter Twenty-Nine

When Merton arrived on the dot of six thirty p.m. and jumped out of his black Ford pickup, Page, who was watching out her living room window, felt a twinge of regret and something approaching terror clutch at her lower intestines. Why had she said yes? Why was she taking this risk, especially at this stressful time in her life? Her routine was simple—she liked it that way. No surprises. Now, all of a sudden, there were surprises galore, a whole grab bag full of possibilities. She took a deep breath as he sprinted up the front walk and told herself that this was, after all, no big deal. It was just dinner and maybe a dance or two. It would be an interesting place which would, no doubt, afford many topics of conversation. *Be bold, Little Sister.* No problem. The doorbell rang.

She walked slowly through the living room and approached the front door. The die was cast. She opened the front door and greeted the detective who was dressed the way she had first seen him: in jeans, white shirt, tweed jacket, and cowboy boots. He had exchanged his usual tie for a string tie with a silver bola.

He smiled.

She returned his smile. "I wasn't sure what to wear—is this okay? I could put on jeans."

"No. You look fine. You look *great*," he assured her. "I like your jacket."

She looked down at her little suede jacket. "It belonged to my mother. She bought it in Sedona in 1956." She looked up at Merton who was staring. "Let me just tell the boys goodbye." She turned and strode into the kitchen where she opened the door that led to the basement. "Walter. Tal. I'm leaving!"

Thunderous footsteps reverberated through the house as the two boys, followed by their babysitter, came running up the stairs. "Wait! Don't leave yet! I want a kiss!" called Tal.

Walter drifted into the front hall while his mother gave last minute instructions to their neighbor, Colleen O'Malley, and Tal hung from her waist in a final embrace. He held a lacrosse stick, spinning it expertly.

Holy Comfort

"Hello, Walter," said the detective, offering his hand. "Good to see you again."

"Hello," replied the solemn-eyed boy, lowering the stick and shaking the outstretched hand manfully. He faced the stranger suspiciously. "You won't be late tonight? It's a school night, you know."

"No, we won't be late."

"The boys should be in bed by eight thirty, Colleen," said Page, walking into the hallway with Tal. She turned and picked up her purse from the hall table. Her eyes met Colleen's and the babysitter mouthed, "He's a babe," causing her to blush and hurry for the door. "Bye, boys, be good!" she called. "And, Walter, put that lacrosse stick in the garage."

"Rockville's nice," he said, as he backed out of her driveway.

"I love it," she agreed as they turned onto a tree-lined and shaded street. "We moved here a little over a year ago following the divorce. I had only been here a few times, but there was just something about it. It was like I got one of those messages from God: 'Move to Rockville.' So I did. The house isn't exciting or unusual, but I love it. It's mine, you know…and you can hear the trains going by in the distance."

"Trains?"

"All the time, whistles and everything. And the boys love their school. I always went to private schools—I have no experience with public schools at all—but I honestly can't complain. It's like this great present somebody gave me. 'Surprise!' The town is just very old fashioned. Normal. You can walk downtown, to the library, the YMCA, and the donut shop and the Hallmark store…I guess I'm babbling."

Merton glanced over at her. "Please. Go on. You're not babbling."

"Well, that's all. I just feel right at home here." Page took a quick sideways look at Roy. He seemed so relaxed, so at ease. This was clearly no big deal for him, going out to dinner with someone he hardly knew. He probably did it all the time. On the other hand, she admitted inwardly, she was extremely nervous. She clasped her hands together on her lap and crossed her legs. Her palms were damp and her stomach was leaning to queasiness. To compensate, she was babbling like an idiot. He was just being polite when he denied it.

She stole another look and met his glance. He smiled as if he knew how nervous she was and it amused him. Thankfully, he knew better than to comment, or worse, to give advice, such as 'relax' or 'loosen up.' She hated it when men gave women advice on how to behave when in their company.

She knew that Roy Merton understood the impact he and his gray eyes had on women, and she had no doubt that he used it to his advantage in his work. He had probably used it with Martha Van Patton and Ellen Chevalier and Charlotte Pentecost. She supposed he had used it with her. She was not immune.

"What did you mean," he asked suddenly, "when you said you got one of those messages from God?"

"Just that. An idea. A direction. The light bulb in your head switches on. I've learned that when you receive one, it's real important to obey, and not to waste time doing it." When Merton did not respond, Page continued in a rush, "I guess that sounds crazy to you. I guess a detective would think that sounded kind of psycho—hearing voices and all that."

"No. I just don't understand. How do you *receive* the message? Do you actually hear a voice? How do you know it's from God?"

"Well, sometimes you do just hear a voice—a still, small voice—inside your head or your heart, really strong saying something. And sometimes you're reading scripture and a verse just jumps right out at you. Boom. Or a song will play on the radio at just the right moment when you were wondering about something."

"Some people would say that's just a coincidence," he interrupted.

"Yes, some people would say that. Me, I don't believe in coincidences. I believe in the unseen hand guiding me...I guess the more you practice talking to God and listening, especially listening, I guess you just get better at knowing when He's telling you something."

"Has He told you anything recently?"

"Oh yes. He said, 'Go to the Wildhorse. Have fun.'"

"No kidding?"

"Yes, I'm kidding!"

Merton glanced over. "Don't be offended."

"I'm not." Page looked out the window at the lights flashing by. Well, she thought, she would do her best to enjoy herself. She turned to him and said brightly, "So what about those Rams?"

Merton laughed and turned onto the highway, which led ultimately to the fabled Wildhorse Saloon.

As they pulled into the parking lot Page asked, "I guess you've been here before?"

"Once or twice," he answered noncommittally.

She tried to imagine what the other women...she assumed more than one...he had brought to the Wildhorse were like. Did he act as formally with them as he did with her? Or did he put his arm around them easily, pulling them to him? How would she react if he did that now?

Once parked, he hopped down out of the truck and came around to her side to open the door, but she had already opened it and was trying to maneuver out of the truck in her narrow skirt. He took hold of her elbow and helped her jump down. "Thanks," she said when she was on the ground.

"Let's go," he suggested, dropping her elbow.

The outside of the Wildhorse Saloon resembled an airplane hangar. Its design was largescale and industrial with a curving metal roof. Only the huge neon sign featuring a cowboy on a bucking bronco hinted at what was inside. When Roy Merton swung open the door and Page stepped through, she felt like Dorothy stepping out of her black-and-white Kansas farmhouse

Holy Comfort

into a Technicolor Oz. All of her senses were assaulted at once. The enormous room was discordantly noisy, tightly packed with strangers, and smelled of perspiration, sawdust, grilled food, and beer. She was glad when he took hold of her arm again and guided her to the stairs and up to the mezzanine where a costumed waitress showed them to a table overlooking the dance floor. Although still crowded upstairs, she felt separated enough from the jostling throng to begin to relax. She looked down and was amazed by what she saw.

A dance floor the size of two high school gyms was flooded with light, exposing seventy-five or so brightly attired couples two-stepping in a free-flowing circle. The couples varied in age, size and costume, but still managed to suggest a homogeneity that was startling and ultimately reassuring. Page relaxed.

There was no band tonight. A disc jockey introduced songs on a PA system and the songs were then piped throughout the building. The music was the kind of country music Page did not especially like, the kind played on the radio. She had always believed, however, that bad country music was ten times better than bad rock or pop music. So she sat back and enjoyed the persistently upbeat strains of Tracy Byrd.

They both ordered beer which was served in bottles. "You don't seem like the longneck beer type," he said, raising his bottle to tap against hers. "*Salud.*"

"When in Rome," she said. "You do seem bent on typecasting me. What type are you?"

He chuckled, but his eyes did not smile. "I guess I'm the lawman type."

"The lawman type? That would be Gary Cooper or Henry Fonda maybe?"

"Henry Fonda?" he said, making a face.

"Wyatt Earp," she said. "*My Darling Clementine.*"

"Sorry," he said. "I always think of Burt Lancaster as Wyatt Earp."

"Well, of course you would. *Gunfight at the O.K. Corral*—memorable mostly for Kirk Douglas coughing up blood as Doc Holliday and a great theme song. Burt was solid, but I prefer *Clementine*. Don't you remember Victor Mature as Doc finishing the soliloquy that the drunken travelling player can't? 'To be or not to be...'"

"I've never seen it," he said apologetically. "I'd like to."

"I've got it at home; you can borrow it."

They drank their beers slowly and ordered dinner. Page feared she was working too hard and vowed to herself that she would not worry about anything and enjoy watching the other patrons as they danced and mingled and made merry. Her laconic partner seemed content to sip his beer and watch her watching the Wildhorse spectacle. Then, without any warning, he reached across the table, took her hand and pulled her up. "C'mon. They're playing a slow one. It's Patty Loveless. C'mon," he coaxed. "Just a little two-step."

She followed him reluctantly downstairs and onto the immense shiny wood dance floor, not at all confident that she could pull off a little two-step. But when he pulled her close, she felt that rush of feeling she used to experience way down deep inside of her when, looking up in the backyard of her old house, she would see Tal or Walter, two years old and too young to be climbing so high, standing on top of the slide, hands over his head, holding onto nothing but air, crying for the sheer joy of it, "Look, Mommy!" That feeling in the pit of her as her heart clenched in her chest between horror and ecstasy.

Merton's hand at the base of her back guided her by a simple change of pressure and she felt a part of the crowd flowing around her in a great circle of happiness. When he smiled down at her, she actually felt weak in the knees. To counteract the effect, Page made herself remember how her husband had danced. Chester was very good, a technician, having learned his moves in the fraternity houses of the Ivy League, but she disliked his style which determined that he never look at her, but constantly face away. It was, no doubt, the ultimate in cool, but it seemed too aloof, and that was not, she thought, what dancing should be about. Merton tilted his head down as their hips moved together. Did she feel his lips graze her hair? Her heart pounded.

When the song ended he did not immediately let her go but leaned down and whispered, "Thank you," his cheek touching hers.

"Well, thank *you*," chirped Page, making light of the moment and regretting the words even as they left her mouth. He let go of her then and led her back to their table where dinner was waiting.

The food was not very good and Page was not very hungry, but she tried to eat to be polite and because she figured that one of Merton's motives in asking her out was to get her to eat. It seemed to be a mission with him. He ate heartily as if to set an example. All Page could think of was dancing with him again, circling that polished floor in his arms.

After she had eaten what she thought was an acceptable amount of food and pushed the rest around on her plate like a finicky child, she excused herself to go to the ladies' room, which was on the other side of the saloon. Because of the immense size of the building and the line outside the restroom, Page was gone for nearly twenty minutes. When she returned to their table, Merton was tipping back in his chair, talking to two tall blond women in tiny denim skirts, matching fringed vests, sleeveless t-shirts, and white cowboy boots. One wore a cowboy hat. Page felt a stab of resentment. She knew she must look like a child next to them, proportionately. She slid into her chair and muttered a hurried "hello."

"This is Liz and Laurianne," he said, indicating the statuesque pair. "Meet Page, ladies."

"Pleased to meet you," they chimed. There being nothing else to say, Liz, on the left, smiled and winked and said cheerfully, "Well, we were just passing by. We'll be on our way." Laurianne, on the right, raised her

Holy Comfort

hand and waved to them as she said, "See ya!" Then they both waved to Merton and moved on.

Page smiled. "I apologize for taking so long. There was a *line*."

Merton smiled at her, as if at some private joke that she was not privy to.

"What?" she asked.

"Your reaction to Liz and Laurianne. It was just pretty funny."

"I'm easily intimidated."

He shook his head. "You don't have a clue, do you?"

"A clue about what?"

"About how beautiful you are," he answered, nailing her with his gray eyes as he leaned forward.

She averted her eyes.

"And now I've embarrassed you. All right. How about another dance?" he said, reaching across the table and taking her hand. "C'mon." She did not object.

"COME IN FOR some tea?" she asked as he pulled his truck into her driveway.

As they headed toward the house, Merton knew he was moving into unknown country. His experience had always been that an invitation into a woman's apartment or house after a date meant one thing: an invitation to her bedroom. Somehow he had the feeling that Page Hawthorne did not intend to imply any such thing. She was going to make tea.

Page paid the babysitter and watched her cross the street to her house. Then she turned to him and asked, as if he had been inside her house a hundred times, "Put on the water, will you? I'm going to check on the boys."

While she was upstairs, Merton dutifully put on the kettle and then quickly checked out the first floor. The kitchen was fairly large. It contained the usual appliances and was dominated by an island with three stools. He pictured the boys eating their breakfast there while their mother made their lunches before school. At one end of the kitchen there was an office with built-in cabinets, a desk and a computer. A framed picture of John Wayne hung over the wall-phone. *The Man Who Shot Liberty Valance* he thought. Very cool. He noted his card pinned to her bulletin board; it looked impermanent, like the dental appointment reminder under it. The living room was dominated by a handsome highboy, an immense oil painting over the fireplace and two walls of built-in bookshelves filled with books. An oriental rug, slightly worn, but still warm and vibrant, covered the floor. There were more books on the coffee table. The furniture was old looking, but whether or not they were antiques, he had no idea. The walls that were not covered by books were covered with more pictures, which to the detective's untrained eye, looked old and original—no prints or framed posters. There were etchings and watercolors. In the dining room a large welsh dresser held an assortment of old-looking china. There were more pictures, including family portraits. There was a glass-covered cabinet full of old pitchers, cups and saucers, lead soldiers and plates. In the den beside the television and stereo, there were shelves of CDs, DVDs and videos. He was busily reading titles when Page came back downstairs.

"This is quite a collection you have here," he said, openly impressed.

"There are more in the basement." She smiled at his reaction. "Yes. Well, some people go to Disney World. We buy books and videos."

"They're awesome. John Wayne. Errol Flynn. Steve McQueen."

"Even Henry Fonda. There's *My Darling Clementine*. You can take it home. I trust you."

He looked up from where he squatted in front of the videos, his gray eyes sparkling. "So where's that tea you promised?"

"I'll be right back." When she returned with two steaming mugs of tea, he had put on an old Emmylou Harris CD. She handed him a mug.

He sniffed at his mug as he settled into her comfortable, well-worn couch. "You have a nice house," he said looking around. "Lots of old things."

"My pieces of history. Not everybody likes old things, but they give me a sense of continuity and remind me of my family, where I come from and who I am," she said, sipping her tea and warming her hands on the mug. "What's your place like? Where do you live?"

"I have a condo in Parkwood Forrest. I have a comfortable chair and a TV."

"A minimalist."

"I don't need much. I'm not used to having much."

"That's a good thing, an enviable thing. I've often thought I should pare back, but I don't know—I wouldn't know where to start. So I just keep adding bookcases."

He chuckled.

Encouraged, she continued, "It was so amazing to me when all of a sudden there were VCRs and you could buy movies, actually own your favorite movies. What a mind-blowing concept! I grew up waiting and waiting for particular movies to be on TV and then you were at the mercy of the television stations. It was like a miracle buying movies. I'm sure I was quite greedy about it. Now I see my boys being totally spoiled. They can see a movie over and over whenever they want and I think it almost ruins it for them. I almost have to ration some of them now."

"Do you remember John Wayne Theater and Errol Flynn Theater on Sunday afternoons, on Channel Eleven, I think. Back before the days of cable TV?" he asked. Page nodded. "We lived for those movies, my siblings and I. They were something you could count on."

"We felt that way, too. We loved Errol Flynn—he was so handsome and dashing and that voice—but he was such a rotten person in real life. That started to come through in his movies. In some of his later

Holy Comfort

movies he just seemed bored and embarrassed, but John Wayne was different. He was a rock. You could count on him. I think he was much more of a father figure to me than my own father."

"Why's that?"

"My father just wasn't around much. He traveled a lot and when he was home he stayed in his study alone. He drank. We were an annoyance to him, too loud and boisterous. He just wanted to be left alone."

"Is that why you have a picture of John Wayne in your kitchen?"

"He's my kitchen god. I have him by the phone so he can protect me against telemarketers."

Merton laughed and Page smiled at him. "It's hard to explain the way I feel about him, but I think he showed me what a man could be like. Strong, but gentle; opinionated, but fair. Consistant. People never give John Wayne enough credit as an actor, and part of that's because all he had to do was look into the camera and you know what he was feeling. All the great movie actors are like that."

"They're telling the truth."

"They hardly ever win awards, but people know. They're real. It's their inner core shining through. They *aren't* pretending. A lot of actors don't have that inner core. All the acting in the world can't overcome that." Page sipped her tea and glanced over it at Merton.

"I think I know what you mean, but...John Wayne was probably just a regular guy in real life, don't you think? He loved women and his family and being with his friends—drinking, playing cards. He was just a...simple guy. I don't know how much that would really appeal to you."

She put her mug down and when she looked at him her mouth was set in a hard, straight line. "I'm not *looking* for John Wayne, you know. I'm not *looking* for anyone," she said quickly, her voice reflecting her annoyance. He didn't get it. No one ever did.

"No?"

"No," she said, easing up. "It's just that there are people who are *different* from everybody else...like when you read something really, really great and you know that you could never write anything that wonderful in a million years, but you just feel good knowing there was ever someone who could. It makes you feel good to be a human being."

He smiled and nodded and took another drink of tea. "This is good," he said.

"Would you like some more? I'll get the pot."

"Sure," he said watching her go. His mind raced forward and he checked it, telling himself to forget about it. She was not like other women. She was no Liz, no Laurianne.

She returned in a minute, carrying a blue and white teapot. She refilled both cups and put the pot down on a magazine. "Excuse me. If you don't mind, I'm going to take off my boots," she said as she sat down. "They're killing my feet."

"Go right ahead," he said calmly, although the idea of her taking off something had given him a slight jolt.

"This is always a bit of an ordeal," she said commencing to tug her right boot off.

"Here. Let me show you the easy way," he said as he slid off the sofa and crouched in front of her. He took a boot in both hands and, after giving the inside a quick knock with the palm of his hand, wriggled it back and forth. It came off easily, exposing a big, white boot sock underneath. She laughed, and he looked up at her before moving to the next boot.

"Thanks," she said, smiling down at him when he was finished. Then she leaned over and took off her socks as well. She turned back to Merton who had taken his seat at the end of the couch again and tucked her feet underneath her. "I guess I've been talking a lot."

"I don't mind listening," he said, feeling somehow that a response was necessary. "I'm not much of a talker myself."

"I've noticed," she said, smiling. It was the kind of smile that told him not to take offense.

He did not take offense. "Tell me about Holy Comforter. How do you fit in there?"

"You don't think I fit in there?" she asked ingenuously.

"No," he said.

She shrugged. "I've lived in that community all my life. It's all about mutual envy, life for the sake of satisfying our desires, of perhaps one day throwing the perfect dinner party. It's spiritual suicide."

"Spiritual suicide? But they're such pillars, aren't they?"

"Jesus called them whitewashed walls. Church to them is really just another place to be seen, another opportunity to get dressed up and wear good jewelry, a place to make business connections…"

"All of them can't be that bad."

She had been staring into her tea as she spoke and she glanced up then to find him looking at her. She smiled faintly. "Rockville suits me fine. It's a healthy place to bring up my boys. We should go to church here, too."

"Things could change. Don't you think this murder will shake things up at Holy Comforter?"

"No, I don't. The people who were close to Miles will get over it, find someone new. It's not as if they really care about anyone. Miles was an outsider after all."

He nodded. "I can't tell you how many people told us Costello was originally a Roman Catholic, like that made a difference in his getting murdered."

"They are distancing themselves already from Miles. The worst part is they'll probably find a way to blame Charles for everything—'poor management skills, don't you know'—and they'll get rid of him. That will be the only shake-up that happens as a result of all this."

"Really? You think this will turn back on the rector?"

Holy Comfort

"Yes. I do." She did not elucidate and he did not pursue the question. Finally she asked, "Roy, may I ask you a question? Off the subject?"

"Of course."

She sipped her tea. "It was quite unusual to have someone come down to my office and just sit like you did this week. It was nice. Why did you do that?"

The question was not what he had expected and the detective's mind flickered. "Pilgrim was taken to a large upper room that faced the sunrise," he said. "And the name of the room was Peace."

She stared, but she didn't say anything.

He did not smile. "I read it in your office," he said. "It just came to mind."

"You're a very different sort of person from the people I usually meet."

"Is that why you agreed to go to dinner tonight?"

She glanced up at him. "Yes, partly, and because you noticed my bulletin board and the fact that my sons look like me. Most people miss all that."

"Paying attention is in my job description."

"It should be in everyone's. I always want to say to people, oh, *pay attention*. You already do."

He put his mug down, then picked it up again, needing to occupy his hands. He sighed. "I liked it that you just accepted that I was there in your office. You didn't seem to want anything from me."

"And what do you want from me?" she said. Moments passed. He did not answer, because he did not know how to answer. He could not admit that, so he said nothing.

Finally she gave him a break. "Someone once said, if you seek the truth, you may find comfort."

"What have you found?" he said.

"A room named Peace."

He put down his mug. "You're a very different sort of person from the people I usually meet."

"But we're not so different, are we?" She reached over and took his hand. "I want to show you something."

He followed her willingly up the stairs, although he had no idea what to expect. Was her bedroom upstairs? What did she want to show him? His mind reeled. He pulled his hand away from hers.

In the tiny hallway at the top of the stairs, she carefully opened the door of the bedroom on the right. She motioned him to look in. "You see there," she whispered, indicating two sleeping children in old-fashioned twin beds. "Those are my treasures. They're all that matter to me."

Merton looked at the boys and then down at their mother whose lustrous head remained poised by his shoulder. He could smell the shampoo she had used to wash her hair. He felt almost giddy and moved immediately away from the door toward the top of the stairs where he sat down and waited for Page who had gone into the bedroom. In a few moments she joined him there. Their shoulders touched and he willed himself not to move or to react.

"They're fine boys," he said.

"Their father never appreciated them," Page said softly, deeply aware of his shoulder against hers.

"That's hard to believe," said Merton.

"I know. I never could quite believe it myself. He mostly just ignored them." She shifted her weight towards the wall and looked sideways at Merton who stared doggedly ahead. "I suppose I shouldn't be surprised. My father mostly ignored us. I guess I married what I was used to, and I guess I could have lived with that. I never expected anything more."

"What changed?"

She took a deep breath and exhaled. "One night Chester was drunk, which was not unusual in itself, and we argued, and he hit me. He hit me twice. Walter saw him do it and he went crazy and attacked him, pummeling him with his little fists and kicking him. Chester backhanded Walter out of the way and picked up Tal, who was only about four at the time. We were upstairs in our bedroom in our old house, and he carried him over to the open window and kicked out the screen. Then he grabbed him by his little Oshkosh overall straps and held him by the open window, screaming, 'I oughta throw the little bastard out. You wanta see me do it?' I really thought he'd do it. I told Walter to run for help. I tried to remain calm for Tal. I just kept saying, 'Please, Chester, give him to me. Give him to me.' My ears were roaring and I was afraid I'd faint, but I just kept praying. You know how it is sometimes when you know you've got to be decisive, and what's more, make the *right* decision? I didn't know what to do. Should I try to wrestle Tal away from him? Or would that only make it more likely that someone would go out the window—Tal, me or possibly Chester who was straddling the windowsill? I was afraid Chester would fall out with Tal. I was a mess, paralyzed with panic. I sort of inched my way forward chanting, 'Give him to me. Give him to me.' It seemed like forever, but Charles actually came really fast."

"*Charles?*" he asked, turning finally to look at her. "Didn't Walter call 911?"

"No. He called the rector," she said. "Can you believe it? Charles and Adair were having a dinner party—I think the bishop was there—but he never hesitated. I don't think he even told them where he was going. He just ran. Got to our house in about two minutes. I think the sight of him shamed Chester into handing Tal over. He stayed upstairs with Chester for about an hour. I took the boys downstairs and just held them. We could hardly breathe, Walter and me hugging Tal like a Tal sandwich. Finally Charles came downstairs and took us back to his house. We stayed there a few days until Chester cleared out. Charles got me the best divorce attorney in town, who coincidentally happened to be the senior warden at the time."

Holy Comfort

Merton said nothing and stared down the stairs.

"I guess you see—or hear about—stuff like that every day in your job."

"No. Not every day." Standing up, he took her elbow and guided her down the stairs. At the bottom he stopped and sat down again. She sat down, too. "Are you in love with him?" he asked, looking at his hands.

"In love with whom?"

"You're in love with the rector, aren't you? Charles Pinkney?"

"No," she answered in a tone that left no doubt. "Of course not. What would make you say that?"

He said nothing and stared blindly ahead.

"No," she said again. "I admire him. He's such a good man—the best, but—"

"Is he in love with you?" he interrupted. She stared at his profile. "He came to your rescue once. Would he have done it again?"

"You don't understand. He absolutely treats everyone the same. You just have no idea how detached the man is."

"Detachment," murmured Merton. "It comes with practice." Then he cleared his throat. "I'm not so sure anymore about your boy, the rector."

"No," said Page. "I've given you the wrong idea. Charles would never harm anyone. He was kind to Chester. He never judged him. He..."

"Why did you tell me all this then?"

She sighed. "I suppose I wanted you to understand something about me. That I'm not all that complicated or different. I live a simple life and the boys give me great joy. It had nothing to do with Charles or the murder."

He turned to face her. His eyes were bleak and dark, humorless like a March wind.

"Roy, what's the matter?" she whispered and raised her hand as if to touch him.

He caught her wrist halfway to his face and squeezed it, making her wince. "I should go," he said, looking past her to the door.

"What?" she whispered. "What did I say?"

He forced himself to look down into her face, into her amber eyes. He felt a pang, a brief anguished spasm, which made him angry. "Nothing," he said. "I should go." His eyes were still hard and unreadable.

She returned his gaze and did not flinch as he stood up and pulled her roughly up with him, even when her wrists felt like twigs that might snap at any moment in his grip. For a moment his eyes were wide and wild, his breathing checked like hers, waiting. But the moment passed, and it was not the faraway, questioning call of a child asking for its mother that stopped him. She saw it in his eyes. Some pain, some question flickering across and disappearing. She could hear him breathing. Then the faraway voice called out again, questioning again, and his gaze traveled up the stairs. "Goodbye," he said as he released her and stepped to the front door. Without looking back, he opened it and walked outside. The door closed behind him and he was gone.

"Goodbye," she said softly as she slowly turned and drifted up the stairs. She opened the door to the boys' room and walked over to Tal's bed where she leaned over and kissed his forehead, smoothing back his hair. "Are you all right?" she asked.

"Mommy?"

"Yes?"

"Mommy?" He was only barely awake.

"Move over," she whispered, pulling back the covers and climbing in next to him. He turned away and she molded herself to his back and pulled the blankets up.

"Goodnight, Mommy."

"Goodnight, Baby," she said, holding him close, enfolding him. "Everything's okay."

Chapter Thirty

Roy Merton was so disconcerted that he never even noticed the car parked in the cul de sac that slowly followed him out of the lane and stayed behind him as he headed out onto Taylor Road. It stayed with him when he turned onto Montgomery Road, and still he did not notice. He drove down the empty street, his mind clouded by confusion, and then pulled into the parking lot of the Trainwreck Bar where he sat, breathing deeply, staring into the dashboard of his truck. What had happened? Why had he reacted like that? What did he care if the rector had played hero? Why did he hold her wrists like that? It had all happened so fast he hardly knew, but something like a hand had pulled him back, something like a voice had said let her go. He had insisted on leaving. He had slammed the door. Why? If he had kissed her, she wouldn't have resisted. No. She was as misunderstood by people and as much of an outsider as he was. But even he had misunderstood. He had jumped to a stupid conclusion, letting his feelings blind him. She wasn't telling him about the rector at all...*I suppose I wanted you to understand something about me.* What? Sure, her boys were her treasures...and she had been married to a monster in an expensive suit. She was unsure of herself and nervous about proceeding. *And what do you want from me?* I want you to change my life. *Teach me to hear mermaids singing.* The whole nine yards.

Chapter Thirty-One

THE TREE WAS large and its branches spread wide, providing a broad canopy which covered a huge portion of the quadrangle at Middlebury College. Under this dark awning of blue leaves, where the light from the cloudless vermillion sky did not penetrate, sat her mother.

"Mommy," she said. "Oh, Mommy."

On a bench under the tree her mother sat, as still and erect as a monument. Her hands were clasped in her lap, her knees were braced and her ankles crossed in an old-fashioned pose of ladylike propriety. Her face was composed as well in a state of profound harmony and calm. She did not smile, but considered Page, at length and from some distance, with her thoughtful brown eyes.

"See," Page said. "See who I've brought." She drew the man closer so that they stood touching, arm in arm. She looked up into his face, into his great gray eyes, stirred by his proximity. Then, remembering her mother, she turned back to her. She had not moved except to unclasp her hands which now laid palms-up, as if she expected to receive something. She regarded the gray-eyed man, clad in a fringed buckskin coat, trail-worn khaki-colored pants and a faded double-breasted shirt. She studied his clean-shaven face and long Buffalo Bill hair. She saw the gun at his hip and the Spanish boots on his feet.

"*What, Mommy?*" Page asked. "*What do you think?*"

Her mother looked forward in a blank brown stare. She said nothing. She had nothing to say.

Page plunged her face into her hands. "Shall we learn nothing together? *Nothing?*"

She was crying and disoriented when she opened her eyes. Then she knew. She sat up and looked around in the half-light of the boys' bedroom. She swung her feet down to the floor and readjusted the covers over Tal. Then she crept downstairs to her own room, took off her clothes and got into her own bed. She pulled the covers up to her chin and prayed for dreamless sleep.

Holy Comfort

At seven thirty the boys were eating cereal and Page was making lunches. The routine of the day was well underway when the phone rang. Page groaned but stopped what she was doing and beat Tal to the phone on the wall. "Hello," she said trying to sound cheery.

"Page." It was the rector.

"Yes," she said pushing a stray lock of hair behind her ear.

"Page, I want to tell you before you see this on TV and before you come in," he said. His voice was scratchy and unnatural. "There's been another murder at the church. Bradford Cole has been murdered."

After a moment Page said, "What can I do for you? Shall I call anyone?"

"No. No thanks. Colin and I are taking care of that."

"Should I come in?"

"No. Stay home for now. The place is swarming with police. Merton and Vesba...they only want to talk to staff members who were here last night and you weren't."

"All right," she said. She wondered if Merton had said specifically, "Not Page." She bit her thumbnail.

"You understand, Page. I am in the way as well." His voice broke. "Oh, Page, I am poured out like water; all my bones are out of joint."

"*My heart within my breast is melting water.* Promise me you'll tell me if there's anything I can do, Charles. And let the detectives do their work. You do yours."

"Page..." The rector paused. "I'll see you tomorrow."

"Thank you for calling, Charles," she said, hanging up. She returned to the kitchen island where she had been making sandwiches. She smiled at Walter and Tal who stared at her. "There's been another murder at the church," she said. "Bradford Cole."

"Are you going to work?" asked Walter.

"No. That was Charles on the phone. He said to stay home."

"Good, Mommy. I don't think you should ever go back to work," said Tal.

She looked at her sons, their brown eyes round with concern. "Don't worry about me. You're the one with a math test today, Walter. I think I'll sit down for a while before I take you to school. Try to finish your breakfast."

She drifted into the den, sat down on the couch and conjured an image of Bradford Cole. He was one of the city's social elite, a twice-divorced, unhappy, angry man who had been Miles' closest friend. Earlier in the week Page had wondered how Bradford was taking Miles' death. Hard, she had no doubt. He had told her once, "I don't know what I'd do without Miles." She had wondered a lot about that statement and it had fueled her conviction that Miles counseled the needy not so they would get better, but so that they would need him all the more. He encouraged dependence.

Bradford Cole had asked her out following her divorce, but she had turned him down. He was a nice man who had always heaped compliments upon her, calling her "complicated" and "mysterious," but she had felt some basic dread when he came near her and she wondered what deep secrets his former wives held in their hearts. Come to think of it, it was after her final turn-down of Bradford that Miles, previously friendly and even complimentary, had made his vulgar proposition and shrouded her.

Now they were both dead. Miles and Bradford were dead. Page picked up a prayer book from the bookshelf and checked her lesson calendar for yesterday's psalm. Had he been murdered last night or early this morning? Well, she would start with yesterday, Wednesday, Ocotber 14, after the nineteenth Sunday after Pentecost. Psalm 42: *Why are you downcast, O my soul? Why so disturbed within me...Why have you forgotten me? Why must I go about mourning, so oppressed by the enemy?* So many unanswered questions, thought Page. She turned to the lesson in Romans and then in Matthew. She shivered as she read Christ's words: *You are the salt of the earth. But if the salt loses its saltiness, how can it be made salty again. It is no longer good for anything, except to be thrown out and trampled by men.*

Page stayed home all day. According to the television news, which she watched on and off, Bradford Cole had been discovered by custodian Demetrius Barton at seven a.m. on Thursday morning. He was found in the office of the late Reverend Miles Costello. He had also been stabbed in the back. His right hand had been burned, charred black, actually. Time of death was estimated between ten and eleven p.m. Wednesday.

Detectives Merton and Vesba had been duly approached by TV reporters to shed official light on the new murder, but both had given only the shortest of statements. Roy Merton looked tired, Page thought, and his eyes were guarded. Detective Vesba was much more forthright, speaking brashly into the camera. The television stations replayed her video ad nauseum, but no more information was forthcoming. The forensic team went about its business on the same site where they had labored before and where last week's yellow police streamers lay broken and strewn about.

Now there were two murders, two victims. It was, indeed, unthinkable, just as Senior Warden Richardson Bell had said in a TV interview, that such terrible acts could take place at such a hallowed place as the Church of the Holy Comforter. It was obvious to Page, watching his strained face under the Hilton Head tan, that the stakes were now much higher. Since Bradford Cole was a member of an old, respected local family, his death would strike fear into the imaginations of his powerful social peers.

Holy Comfort

Chapter Thirty-Two

THREE MEN SAT in a room in silence. One man sat hunched behind a desk and stared out the window at nothing in particular. One man smoked and one man studied his reflection surreptitiously in the glass front of the bookcase next to him.

The man behind the desk turned suddenly and bowed his head, slapping his forehead with both hands. The noise shocked the other men back to stiff-backed attention. They turned together to look at the other man.

"Jesus Christ!" moaned Willis McHugh. "Brad Cole! I can't fucking believe it. He was the meanest son of a bitch I knew."

Chester Hawthorne stubbed out his cigarette and peered at his cousin as he resumed his relaxed slump. He blinked but made no other response.

The mayor continued. "I can't believe the idiot went to Costello's office—at night! What was he thinking?"

"You know damn well what he was thinking," drawled Hawthorne through tented fingers. "His brain was in his crotch as usual."

"Christ! I was counting on him to wear down Charles Pinkney. He was the man for that job. He told me he'd made a good start yesterday. And now he's fucking dead!"

"I've never understood your animosity toward Pinkney, Willis," said George Fontaine with distaste. "The man's a nonentity…easy to ignore at the very least."

"The man is not a nonentity, George," said McHugh. "Ask Chester here. He knows."

Hawthorne eyed both men from under his eyebrows. He paused and then said quietly, "I'd still be married if it weren't for the bastard."

"What? I don't see the connection…" asked Fontaine.

"He's got Page wrapped around his finger. He's the one who convinced her to get a divorce. Do you think she ever would have done what she did—hired Dennis Newcomb—without help from Pinkney? No way."

"Well, I wouldn't know about that…but the rector's not interested in politics. He's too detached to care who's in charge. He doesn't even know he's *not* in charge. I say leave him where he is—what harm can he do?"

"What *harm* can he do?" repeated the mayor scornfully. His short neck was bright red. "Have you even been to a service lately? I look around and I don't know half the people—and that's at the eight o'clock service! Jesus, I can only imagine what the nine fifteen and eleven fifteen are like. My wife sat next to some woman who actually wanted to pass the peace! Mimi bitched for weeks about that. Thank god she's in the Bahamas now or I'd never hear the end of these murders. 'Can't you control things, Willis?' she says. 'Can't you keep things in order? God,' she says, 'I don't go to church to be preached to. If I hear about the Body of Christ one more time, Willis, I'm going to vomit. Who are these people anyway? Where did they come from? I want to see my friends when I look around, Willis' Jesus, she can go on and on, but she's right about one thing. We've got to take back our church."

"Pinkney won't last. Not now," said Hawthorne quietly.

"I was counting on Cole to wear him down," repeated McHugh.

"Cole being dead will be more effective than Cole alive," said Hawthorne. "Pinkney will be out. The bishop will see to that."

Holy Comfort

Chapter Thirty-Three

THE BOYS WERE fed, bathed and ready for bed, eagerly awaiting the beginning of professional bull riding at eight p.m., when there was a knock at the door. Page reluctantly got up and went to see who it could possibly be so late. She peered through the window where she had pulled aside the curtain. It was Roy Merton. Her heart began to pound. She had not expected to see him again so soon. Not tonight. What was he doing here? *Oh stop,* she told herself impatiently as she opened the door, but he had seen her hesitate and had noted the question in her eyes.

He was wearing the dark gray suit she had seen him in on the televison news. His hands were in his pants pockets and his tie was loosened "I'm sorry to bother you," he said in a voice that sounded like worn-out sandpaper. "May I come in for a few minutes?"

She nodded and stood aside. He looked her up and down, noting her loose-fitting jeans and gray sweatshirt with *Williams College* across the front in faded purple and he smiled, despite himself. Then the smile froze on his lips and his eyes widened. Page turned around instinctively to see what he had seen that so surprised him, even though she knew what it was. Merton stared blankly as a man came up behind her, materializing from the kitchen and laid a hand proprietarily on her shoulder. The man was only a few inches taller than Page, but he was handsome, with startling blue eyes set in a weathered tan face and straight, wheat-colored hair. He wore chinos and a plaid shirt. The man in the picture, the man with the trout, smiled broadly and tendered his hand. "Hello," he said, "I'm Billy Custer."

Merton nodded unsmiling and struggled to control and conceal the shock which had flooded him and which he knew must be clearly evident to both Page and her guest.

"This is Detective Merton, Billy. He's investigating the murders I told you about at church," said Page.

"Uh huh," the man said. He looked at Page. "Why don't I go keep the boys company while you two talk?"

"Thanks," she said touching his arm. The man headed back to the den. "Can I get you some decaf?" she inquired, turning back to the detective.

"Well, no thanks," he said, as if the question confused him.

"You can drink coffee on duty, can't you? They certainly drink enough on those cop shows on TV, always in Styrofoam cups. I always found that oddly appealing. I don't know why." She caught him staring at her and she said, "You look exhausted."

"I'm fine."

"Mom!" called Walter from the den. "It's starting. You're going to miss Terry Don West!"

"I'll be in soon," she called back. In response to the detective's quizzical look, she explained, "Professional bull riding—our favorite spectator sport."

He crossed his arms and stared at her.

"Well, I'm getting myself some coffee anyway," she said, heading for the kitchen.

He followed her as if drawn by a magnet and watched her take down a mug, fill it with the warm, dark beverage, pour milk into it, and turn to face him.

"Let's go sit in the dining room," she said.

He followed her through the kitchen to a room with an Oriental rug and red drapes. They sat down on chairs with blue damask seats, and she waited for him to speak, warming her hands on her mug.

He sighed and folded his hands on the table. "Who's Billy Custer?"

"A friend," she said, noting the dent which had appeared between the detective's eyes.

"A friend?" he repeated.

"Billy Custer is my brother's best friend. They go way back together to fifth grade at the Bingham School—thirty-odd years ago. I've known him all my life. He's like a brother."

"And where did Billy Custer come from?"

She narrowed her eyes. "He lives in Chicago. He drops by sometimes when he's in town," she said, trying to beat down the annoyance which increased with each of his peevish questions. As he sat calmly across from her, she gave up the effort and said, "You didn't come over here to ask me that, so why?" She glanced away.

He raised his eyes. The dent was still there. He tried to focus his thoughts. "I'm not sure. I thought that perhaps you could help me. Did you know this Bradford Cole? Everyone, including a former U.S. senator, seems to have, and several have read us the riot act."

"I bet," said Page. "It was one thing when it was just some murdered priest. That was bad enough. But now—it's one of them. They're scared and they're angry."

Merton nodded. "Willis McHugh wants things cleared up and he wants it done now. He wants everything back to normal by next week. As if they ever will be normal around there. What the hell is 'normal' anyway?"

"It's how they all operate. Willis is used to having people jump. He expects results."

Holy Comfort

"We all want results," he interrupted. "*Jesus*—but it's maddening. There are no clues. No evidence. Just hearsay, innuendo, gossip—an unending, vomitous mass of opinion."

It was Page's turn to interrupt. "I don't think I can add anything besides more of the same myself."

"Maybe not, but tell me what you know about Bradford Cole and his relationship with Miles Costello."

She considered his request for a moment and as she thought, the dent in his forehead, which had been fading, disappeared. "Well," she said. "They were best friends, although Brad was quite a bit older than Miles. My impression was that he and Brad had lunch together at least once a week. I think Brad really liked having a minister for a friend. It made him feel like a better person, just by association. He was on a lot of boards, important boards, and I think he could be a real pain in the neck—you know, getting people fired. He always wanted to control things. For a while he'd stop by and come see me in my office when he was in the building to see Miles. I liked him. He called me 'Kid.' He was funny and he made me feel attractive and young and witty at a time when I needed to feel that. I think Miles encouraged him. But when Brad asked me out, I said no, because there was something under the surface with him that was...scary. It was one thing to talk in my office, another to go out alone with him. I caught him looking at me once and the look was like a combination of him hating me and wanting to eat me."

"Lust," said Merton without smiling.

She turned away. "I also didn't like the feeling *Miles* gave me."

"Which was?"

"Well..." she said, hesitating. "It was almost like he was pimping for Brad. It was weird."

The detective scowled. "So why would whoever killed Miles, kill Bradford Cole?"

"You're sure it's the same person? In Agatha Christie books the second murder is frequently unrelated."

He snorted. "It's the same M.O. The tie-in with the liturgical calendar...and all that fire and brimstone." He gazed at her from under heavy lids. "Did you read the lectionary, by the way?"

"Yes," she said. "The psalm was interesting, the why-have-you-forgotten-me questions. But the Matthew quote was scary when you think of a killer with an agenda reading it out of context."

Merton pulled a piece of paper out of his inside jacket pocket. "*It is no longer good for anything, except to be thrown out and trampled by men,*" he read. "I guess he meant Bradford Cole. What made him no good for anything anymore?"

She shook her head. "I don't know."

"What about that burned hand? What did that mean? The rector wasn't a lot of help today," he said, sighing.

"That burnt hand has to point to Archbishop Cranmer who was executed by Queen Mary."

"But why yesterday? Why Brad Cole?" he said, unable to keep a note of impatience from his voice.

"The sixteenth—tomorrow—is a special day of devotion in honor of Hugh Latimer, Nicholas Ridley and Thomas Cranmer, three martyrs of the English church who were burned at the stake. Archbishop Cranmer stuck his hand in the flames so it would burn first, because that was the hand with which he had recanted. It seems odd that the murderer didn't wait until Friday to do Brad in—if the hand is supposed to mean something."

"Maybe he's getting sloppy, impatient for some reason. Maybe he couldn't wait."

"Or it could mean," said Page, her eyes widening, "that there's going to be a third victim on Friday. Cranmer, Latimer and *Ridley*—all three were victims of 'Bloody Mary,' all three were martyrs. Maybe Costello, Cole and a third person are martyrs to some cause—"

"Bloody Mary," repeated Merton. "What exactly was her problem?"

"The queen was called 'Bloody Mary' for burning over three hundred protestant heretics at the stake—a murderer on the grand scale."

"Could our murderer somehow identify with Mary, then?"

Page nodded slowly. "She was a very unhappy, vindictive, desperate woman, obsessed with her husband, Philip of Spain. He couldn't stand her, so he lived in Spain. But Mary wanted a baby so desperately she invented a pregnancy."

The detective was thoughtful.

Page said, "Maybe Brad Cole promised the murderer something and he recanted, took it back. That would explain the burned hand. Maybe Miles Costello did, too."

"A baby?"

"It's possible, isn't it?"

"Of course." He stared across the table at Page.

"Do you think that Brad knew who killed Miles and he confronted that person?"

"It's possible, but this murder was as well planned as the first. The only person surprised was Mr. Cole. You should have seen his face."

"It still could be that the murderer was victimized by both Miles and Brad. Revenge is a very strong motive, and then that 'it's no longer good for anything' line fits in nicely."

"I think so, too. Especially with what you said about your feeling that Miles was pimping. Maybe you weren't the only one he tried to fix Brad up with."

"But *who*?" asked Page. Her mind was a blank. She had purposely not paid attention to Miles' alleged love affairs, preferring to distance herself from him in everything. "Unhappy, desperate women are bread and butter to a priest like Miles Costello."

Holy Comfort

The detective nodded.

"Perhaps you should find out if any of those women you've talked about—Ellen Chevalier, Charlotte, Gracie, Diana, Mrs. Van Patton—wanted a baby...or *something* Miles promised..."

"What do you think?" he said.

"I don't know, but...Charlotte maybe. She's the age where a woman might be thinking about her biological clock. As for the others wanting something, it's all just guessing. Of course, the whole thing with Brad Cole really confuses the issue. It seems so unlikely that both of them..." Page stopped. She was babbling again. The detective no longer appeared to be participating in the conversation, so she sipped her coffee and waited to see if Roy would continue. She tried to concentrate on enjoying the warmth of the steaming mug. But the detective was distracted and seemed to be staring at the table or something on the table. She followed the angle of vision and found her own wrist which lay inside up, the fingers of her right hand resting loosely through the handle of her mug. Her wrist revealed a large new bruise, approximately the size and shape of a thumb. She glanced up and their eyes met for an instant and then she glanced away. She kept her left hand in her lap.

"Let me see your left hand," he said roughly. Page did not look at him, but pulled up her hand and held out her wrist for his inspection. He took her hand lightly, pulling it toward him, and then set it down on the table. "Page," he said. "I'm..."

"Mom!" shrieked Tal, racing into the room. "Mom, you're missing the whole show. They're already starting the third go 'round. C'mon," he said, grabbing her hand and pulling.

"Tal," she said too harshly. "Don't be so rude. I have to finish up with Detective Merton. Now run along." She patted his small pajama-clad bottom for emphasis, and he shot Merton a derisive look as he trotted out of the dining room.

"I'm sure Walter put him up to that," she explained.

"They're good boys. I'm intruding," he said. He stood up. "I should go."

She stood up. She waited for him to say something about her wrists, but he only glared at her. "Why did you come over here tonight?" asked Page. "Certainly I haven't told you anything that couldn't wait until tomorrow."

"I had a hunch," he said. He took a step towards her. She could hear him breathing, but she didn't look up. "From the beginning it's seemed somehow that this whole thing has had something to do with you. The facts support this. You worked next door to Costello. You were friends. He made a proposition. You turned him down. You were friends with Brad Cole. You turned down his proposition as well. Now they're both dead. Who else have you turned down?"

She looked up and swallowed. "Chester?"

"Yes. Chester, Bradford, Miles—all Yale men, all in the same small group." He reached inside his pocket and took out a folded piece of paper. He unfolded it and began to read. "Augustus Tully, Tony Spitz, Willis McHugh, Amos Peacock, Alex Reardon, Gordon Kelly, Chester Hawthorne, Brad Cole, Miles Costello. Do you know any of these other men?"

She shook her head. "No," she said. "Not really."

"You weren't friends with any of them? None of *them* asked you out?"

"No," she said in a low voice. "But yesterday afternoon Tony Spitz dropped by my office to talk. He asked me to dinner...I told him to get lost. It was really nothing at all. Before that I tried to get him to talk about the small group and I asked him how Chester and Miles got along. He said all right but that they had one main thing in common." She paused. "He said they both hated Charles Pinkney."

Merton murmured something she couldn't hear. "I think we need to explore this pimping angle. Costello *could* conceivably have been pimping for his small group."

"Those are all well-respected men in the community..."

"I have no doubt, but what difference does that make? I for one trust your impression. Now the trick is going to be getting one of those well-respected men to talk. They didn't say much in our first go 'round." He smiled as if it was a very difficult thing to do and gazed through the kitchen to the door of the den. "I've taken up enough of your time."

She picked up her mug and walked into the kitchen where she put it in the sink. He followed her to the front door.

"It's over, Mom," said Walter as he rounded the corner into the front hall. "You missed everything."

"Who won?"

"You don't care," said Walter.

"Tater Porter," said Tal sleepily as he drifted into the hall.

She ruffled Tal's hair. "Both of you run along upstairs. I'll be up in a minute."

"Yeah, sure, Mom," said Walter, his voice dripping with sarcasm. As he turned to go upstairs, he threw the detective a look of such antagonism that Merton threw up his hands in surrender.

"Go," she said, pointing up the stairs.

"I'll get 'em started," said Billy Custer, entering the hallway. He paused for a moment. "Nice to meet you, Det. Merton. Good luck on your case." He smiled, winked at Page and followed Walter and Tal.

As soon as they were all upstairs, Page turned to him.

"Lucky boys," he said dreamily.

"Are you okay?" she said, clasping her hands behind her back.

"Sure," he said turning to go. "Why wouldn't I be?"

She blushed and her small nostrils flared slightly. "Well, goodnight then."

Holy Comfort

He sighed. "Look, I'm sorry about all the questions tonight." He glanced upstairs. "And I'm sorry about those bruises. I don't know what to say about that." His voice faded out. He cleared his throat. "When is Billy Custer going back to Chicago?"

"Tomorrow," she said.

"Uh huh," he mumbled. He stepped to the door and paused. "Ms. Hawthorne, I want you to promise me you'll be on your guard."

"I'll be on my guard," she said, holding her hand up like a scout.

"Fine," he said. "I'd appreciate that." He tipped an imaginary hat and left.

She watched him as he walked slowly down her brick path toward his truck in the driveway. He stopped once to look up at the stars and the moon. She wondered what he was thinking as he gazed heavenward. Was he calling to the stars to bend and comfort him as she had so many times? She knew that it had been hard for him to say he was sorry. He was the type that never apologized. But it wasn't much of an apology. Not really. She considered for a moment calling out to him—just to say goodnight again—but she stood frozen, mute and statue-like in the doorway.

When he reached his truck he allowed himself one look back, but she had already gone inside. The door was closed. It was as if he had never been there.

He noticed for the first time the old Grand Wagoneer parked back behind the garage. He had been in such a hurry before that he hadn't seen it. He had been so glad to see her and to be asked into the house, even though he had to admit he had caught the shadow of reservation in her eyes. But he had drunk her in like a tonic nonetheless, her beauty soothing his ragged nerves like a balm.

Then he had seen him. Billy Custer from Chicago. He swallowed hard, pushing down the negative feelings that were rising like bile within him. There was so much about her that he didn't know. She had a brother, a brother with an old friend. Well, he had seemed like a nice enough guy. He was no Tony Spitz or Willis McHugh, no Trip or Chip or Trey. No, Billy Custer hadn't seemed to resent the intrusion. He had left them alone without a thought to watch TV—bull riding—with the boys. He was probably a decent fellow. Why then was he so bothered by his being there? Because Billy Custer was *still* there, in fact, and *he* was driving home. Billy Custer was going home tomorrow. Billy Custer, he realized, could have sat through hours of bull riding because he knew she was just talking to a police detective who would eventually leave.

Chapter Thirty-Four

ANOTHER STAFF MEETING was called on Friday morning in order for the rector to express his deep regret concerning the latest murder and to introduce, once again, the detectives to explain what had apparently happened. This time everyone already knew what would be discussed, because they had all received a call from either the rector or from Colin Whitefish on Thursday. Most had been given the day off. Almost all of them watched the news. There were no gasps of shock this time, no tears of anguish. Practically everyone knew the deceased, but very few had had any kind of personal relationship, social or church-related, with him.

The entire staff was in attendance this time. Even Harry and Hazel Rose stepped into the Lodge Room from the kitchen and stood at the back of the room. Charlotte Pentecost sat at the opposite corner from Page where she had a good view of both her and Merton. Her gaze moved easily back and forth between them, as she noted, so did that of fat detective Vesba. What's going on, thought Charlotte. Why is she so interested? After a while her stare rested on Merton, and she suspected, he knew it. His glance flickered her way several times and she met it each time, but his attention was fleeting, always gravitating back to Page Hawthorne.

Page, Charlotte noted, was wearing a short black skirt with her ubiquitous black tights that made her spindly legs look like bird legs. Personally, Charlotte hated short skirts. She always wore trousers or occasionally an ankle-length skirt in order to hide her slightly knocked knees. It was so typical that Page's legs were perfect, even if a little on the thin side. She was also wearing a black turtleneck and one of her expensive Peruvian sweaters, imported by some college friend and sold through that catalogue. This one was a patchwork of individually knitted squares. Its buttons were silver discs, like the ones that dangled from her ears. Charlotte had always thought that dangley earrings were tacky and, really, when she thought of it, so was silver. She only wore gold jewelry herself. Page was wearing her black suede shoes from that store in New York. Charlotte snorted. She hoped Page wasn't trying to impress Merton. As if he cared. All he cared about anyway was what was underneath the clothes. She wondered if he had seen it, touched it. No. Not yet. Not enough time. Page would

Holy Comfort

never surrender so fast. No, she thought, gazing serenely at the tall detective, not even he was that good.

Charlotte's gaze strayed to Detective Vesba. Now she was something else—a great, voluptuous, cream-filled pastry of a woman. Renoir with a little Harley Davidson thrown in. She wondered if she was jealous of the attention given by her partner to Page. She bet Vesba hated Page. She wondered if she had ever done it with her partner, some hot night after locking up some felon. She pictured them together following too many congratulatory beers, sloppy and noisy. No. He probably had some code about not fraternizing with co-workers. He no doubt drank alone, too. She wondered how much that bothered Vesba. She glanced over at Baylor Valentine, the stately old Virginian, as he stared across the table at the two detectives. Did he have a thing for Vesba? He was probably picturing her now, even as he stared at her, bulging out of a sexy black leather outfit—maybe with a whip. But that was all wrong. Doctor Vee was only interested in young men, everyone knew that.

She contemplated the rector, holier than thou, as usual. She studied for a moment his perfectly shaped skull and his heavy-lidded eyes, half-closed now in prayer. She swore sometimes he looked as blissed-out as any flower-child, which, she supposed, he had probably once been. He probably had long hair then and a beard. Maybe he had even looked like his hero, Jesus. But it was not drugs that fueled him now. No. It was love for his brothers and sisters in Christ. In fact, he was probably the only one in this room who was actually thinking of old Bradford Lockwood Cole. The irony was pretty humorous. If he only knew what Brad had said about him, how he had hated and reviled him and schemed to get rid of him. He would have done anything for Miles, though. He loved Miles. And now he was dead. She thought of his skinny old-man legs, blue-veined and hairy, and of his large paunch which hung over his shorts. He had liked to play with trains; they were his passion. She wondered if Page knew about his passion. No. She had turned him down so she would not have had the pleasure of seeing his train room.

Well, look, she thought, Gracie Griggs was going on the nod. It was early in the day for her to be so far gone already. At least she wouldn't be making any infantile, provocative remarks, which would only serve to send those brain-dead detectives scurrying in Page Hawthorne's direction. Better by far to be unconscious. But to be honest, Gracie wasn't solely to blame; old Roy had caught the scent early. He was already on the trail. She should have been there at that first meeting. She had only herself to blame. She was here now. *And I'll be around to pick up the pieces. As soon as they fall. You'll see, Detective. She'll turn you down flat, if she hasn't already. Look my way. I dare you.*

Page stood up absent-mindedly and grasped the hands of Colin Whitefish to her right and Sophie Carl to her left. She murmured the Lord's Prayer along with the rest of the staff and hardly knew how they had gotten there when they all uttered the Amen at its conclusion.

She had chosen the sweater she was wearing because of its too-long sleeves, which she hoped would conceal the twin bruises on her wrists. She glanced down to check. She smiled with relief and blushed. She had managed to keep her eyes averted from the detectives, from Merton in particular, throughout the meeting, trying not to show that she knew more than anyone else there, that she had talked to the tall detective about the case, that he had confided in her, that he had asked for her help. She had to admit that it was exciting, but she felt disconnected from the rest of the staff and wondered if anyone noticed. Then she caught Charlotte Pentecost staring at her from across the table. Someone had noticed. She glanced away and jumped as fingers touched her elbow. "Sorry, Page," said the rector, pulling his hand away like a person who has touched something hot. "But I need to talk to you."

"Sure," she said, smiling. She set down her day-timer and keys and lowered herself back into the chair. Charles sat down next to her.

"Rich Bell wants to send a letter to the parish," he began. "It'll be from both of us. I'll write it, then he'll spin it."

Page nodded. "If you can get it to me in an hour, we can print it this morning and mail it this afternoon. First class, I assume."

"Yes. All right. I'll write it now and fax it to Rich. I'll explain the time frame."

"Okay. It'll be a push, but we can't wait until Monday. I'll tell my staff and we'll be ready. We printed envelopes last week, so there shouldn't be a problem."

"You're the greatest," he said patting her hand.

Page looked down at the rector's hand, which still rested on hers. He removed it and stood up.

"Call me when it's ready," she said, rising. She did not envy him that job.

The staff had cleared out of the room quickly and when she entered the Great Hall she was vaguely grateful that it too was empty. When she passed Tammy Spivy's desk, the receptionist, who was engaged on the phone, gave her a thumbs up sign and pointed to the bouquet of flowers sitting on her desk. She smiled and mouthed 'thank you' to Page who returned the smile and headed for the stairs. It was just an arrangement from the grocery store, but she knew today would be a terrible one for Tammy and she had thought the flowers might brighten it for her somewhat. Tammy was crazy about flowers.

Holy Comfort

Chapter Thirty-Five

"MY GOD," DRAWLED Charlotte Pentecost, lifting her cup of coffee. "Things are getting pretty exciting around here."

"Murder, mayhem, more murder," chimed in Gracie Griggs.

"And *sex*," shrilled Diana Dunwoody. "Don't forget *sex!*"

The three women sat knee to knee in Gracie's office with the door closed. It was a large room full of office equipment long ago abandoned by Gracie who refused to use a typewriter, much less a computer. She was, as she was fond of telling people, *not* a secretary. She wrote her reports out by hand, preferring to have someone in the production department type them up and enter newcomer data on the computer. The equipment gathered dust, and lately, it had been noted, so did Gracie. She had started falling asleep at her desk, slumping over when the afternoon grew too long. She was glad, therefore, to have a diversion. Maybe Charlotte and Diana could keep her awake.

"Believe me, I've all but forgotten what sex is," mused Gracie. "But let's not get into that. What sex are we talking about anyway?"

"Sex with regards to Page Hawthorne and Detective Merton," said Diana confidentially. "Charlotte says they're hot and heavy."

"Oh, not Miss Perfect! I don't believe it," Gracie said, shock striking her almost dumb. "Not for a minute!"

"Well, you're to blame, Grace dear," chortled Charlotte. "With your 'You should start with Ms. Hawthorne' at that first meeting! I mean I wasn't there, but I heard all about it. According to Midge, the good detective followed her out of the room like a setter on point."

"Well, I don't even know why I said it. I certainly wasn't serious. Everybody knew that. There was never anything between Page and Miles. He thought she was pathetic—a scared, little, uptight, sexless princess. We all know that..." she trailed off, losing her train of thought. Then suddenly she laughed sharply. "Ha! You mean the detective *believed* me and thought she and Miles were a hot number?"

"And now Detective Merton and Page are the hot number!" crowed Diana.

"Well, not quite," interjected Charlotte. "We shouldn't get carried away now."

"But you said..." began Diana.

"*What* did I say, Diana?" said Charlotte icily. She sat up and straightened her shoulders. "I never said anything. Nothing really. I said they went out. Once. We all know Page would never hop into bed with anyone on the first date. She'd have to confer with our fearless leader and get his approval, and then she'd have to *pray* about it..."

"Oh God, though," interrupted Gracie. "This is too rich. You mean to tell me she's been having sex with that hillbilly cop—the one in cowboy boots? Now, that's a little out of character, I have to say."

"No, Grace dear. That's *not* what we've been saying. That's the rumor that's circulating, but it's just a rumor. Our long-legged, well-hung detective friend is not interested in Miss Page. He can tell a cold fish when he sees one."

Diana and Gracie hooted appreciatively. Gracie spilled her coffee and, choking, began mopping it up.

"No," continued Charlotte. "He bailed out early and headed back to Jefferson County where he rustled up some trailer trash more to his liking."

The three women shrieked again gleefully. "I hear," Charlotte went on, "that the detectives think Page has 'a thing' for clergy. That she's fucked 'em all. One at a time, I assume."

"Oh God, no," groaned Gracie, on the verge of hysteria. "All because I said that about asking Page first? I don't even remember saying it, and now they imagine she's some sex-starved, clergy-obsessed nympho?"

"Pretty amazing, isn't it, ladies?" asked Charlotte calmly. "It really makes you stop and wonder about the police department."

"So where's Page now?" Gracie asked, wiping her eyes, trying to settle down. "She's not in her office."

"She's working," said Diana. "And making darn sure somehow that we all know it. They're putting together some all-parish letter down in production. I think they actually think *we* should help. I told them straight-out I was too busy to stuff envelopes."

"It's not in *my* job description..." sighed Gracie, looking at her watch. "Hey, it's time for lunch. I've got to get home." She started opening file cabinet drawers in search of her purse.

"Righto," said Charlotte laconically, her blue eyes hooded and vague. "You go, girl." She stood up and moved out into the hall with Diana, her arm slung casually around the older woman's skinny shoulder. She looked down fondly, noting Diana's twenty-year old lime green wrap skirt and pink and white print golf shirt, her matching tortoise-shell barrettes which pulled back her graying hair from her leathery, aging face. She considered how the woman had not changed her mode of dress—you could hardly call it style—in twenty-five years. She had probably not unlocked those knees either, not since the second of her two children had been successfully produced. She was interested in only one thing, and Charlotte knew it was neither reading—*could* she read?—nor music, nor art, not even

Holy Comfort

cooking. No, she was interested only in talking to her friends, her circle of friends, known since birth and added to only slightly over the years from the ranks of the Junior League and the church. To have some new morsel of gossip to share, some tidbit was, for Diana, to experience power.

Charlotte patted her now, squeezing her shoulder conspiratorially. "Now, Diana, what I said was confidential. No matter what we think of Page, we always have to think of Holy Comforter first. We can't spread tales. Why, the next thing you know, this story could be in Morey Nieman's column! We don't want our dirty linen aired there!"

"Oh, God save us from that!" Diana laughed gaily, breaking into her smoker's hack.

Charlotte removed her arm and said, "Have a nice lunch," to the air around her and slunk into her office across the hall. The door closed behind her.

Chapter Thirty-Six

THE HALLWAY WAS deserted. Even Sophie, who had helped with the mailing for a few hours, was absent from her office. The yellow police tape still eerily cordoned off the door to Miles Costello's office where, unbelievably, people had left bouquets of flowers and even Teddy bears by the door. She remembered overhearing Baylor Valentine murmuring about tacky new members and their sentimental clutter. He had even harangued the rector about cleaning up the 'rotting pottage' at a ministry meeting earlier in the week. Page had seen Charles set his jaw and knew he would be resolute in his determination to do the exact opposite. Resolution aside, sometimes Page couldn't help wishing that Charles would just for once put his foot down and tell Baylor to shut up and sit down.

There was someone in her office. The door was open and the light was turned on. A cloying, sweet aroma wafted into the hall. "To what do I owe the pleasure of this visit?" asked Page as she turned into her open doorway. She did not mean to sound sarcastic, but it had been a long day, and the last person she expected to find waiting in her office when she returned from the Production Department late in the afternoon was Leona Vesba.

"So it's my turn to burn up in your little cubby hole, what of it? I've just heard so much about it," she said, fanning herself as she attempted to cross her legs. "Jesus, it must be ninety degrees in here."

"It is warm. I'm sorry," she said. "Do you want to talk to me about Brad Cole?"

"No. We know you couldn't have killed him. You were out dancing with Merton, which I have to admit is a very good alibi as alibis go."

"Yes. I guess so," said Page crossing her arms. "So what *can* I do for you?"

"Nothing, honey. I just wanted to tell you something," said the detective, re-crossing her knees and adjusting her tight skirt. She fixed her pale blue eyes on Page's forehead. "Sometimes my partner's methods are different from mine and sometimes I have to admit that unconventional

Holy Comfort

works. Sometimes it backfires. I told him from the beginning that I thought it was a shitty plan, but he insisted..."

"What plan?"

"His plan to get to know you better. He figured if he turned on some of his country boy charm he might wind up with some information we could use—"

"What kind of information?" Page interrupted again.

"For one thing, he wanted to find out whether that Griggs character was right about you sleeping with Costello."

"Sleeping with Miles? You actually took her seriously?"

"Everyone is a suspect. We were duty-bound to check it out. Roy thought she was probably right, especially when he saw you with Pinkney—all hugs and kisses. He figured you were sleeping with him, too. That you had a thing for priests or something." Vesba let her last comment sink in. "That's what the Wildhorse was all about."

"And what did he find out? Anything relevant?"

Vesba sighed. "He found out you're the vestal virgin I told him you were."

"If only he'd listened to you in the first place," said Page cooly. "Is that what this is all about? Him not listening to you?" She stared at the detective for several long moments.

Vesba's bottom lip drooped and her eyes reflected emptiness.

Finally Page said, "Did you have a point to make when you came in here?"

Vesba sucked in her lower lip, vaccuming a bit of drool, and narrowed her eyes. "The point is this case isn't solved yet, and so he's still here and so are you. I don't give a rat's ass about you personally, but Merton's my partner and he's got to do his job." Page did not respond. Vesba smiled. "Don't get me wrong, honey. He thinks you're pretty cute and I don't doubt that you're going to hold a place of honor on his belt, as far as notches go."

Page smiled back, although she hardly felt like it. She un-crossed her arms and held out her hands. "So which is it, Detective? I'm confused. Am I a vestal virgin or a notch?"

Vesba murmured something and shifted her gaze. "I don't think Roy told you anything and that's what's bothering you," said Page. She stood up, and as if on cue, someone knocked on the door.

"Come in," shrieked Vesba, as the door swung open knocking into her chair. "Jesus. Get me out of this Polly Pocket office."

Merton stepped into the room, smiling. He acknowledged his partner's presence in the room and turned to face Page, his smile instantly fading. "What's the matter?" he asked cautiously.

"Ask your partner," Page replied as she reached under her desk for her purse.

He looked at Vesba who was critiquing her nails. "What's going on? What are you doing in here?"

"Girl talk," explained Vesba, her countenance benign, her pale eyes blank. "Just girl talk."

"What are you up to?" he said with a little more force.

Vesba sighed and opened her hands in an exasperated gesture. "I just told her that she needs to let you do your job."

He looked at her stupified for several seconds before turning back to meet Page's eyes. "Page, I…"

"Don't, please," said Page putting up a hand.

"No, I…" he began, but she interrupted him. Standing on her toes, she slipped her hands behind his head and pulled his mouth down to hers and pressed hard for several seconds.

She released him and stepped back. He blocked the doorway. "Let me pass, Brutus," she said as she tipped her head and her hair fell across one eye. "I'm way behind schedule working my way through the clergy staff."

"What?" he said putting a hand on her arm.

She took the hand and dropped it. "Talk to your partner." He moved aside. She walked past him and looked back over her shoulder. She paused. "And don't worry, Detective. That kiss won't leave a scar."

Merton watched her retreat down the hall, his face reflecting a strange combination of conflicting emotions. "What the hell was she talking about?" he said, his voice a hoarse whisper. "Talk to my partner about what?"

"Nothing," snapped Vesba, placing a chubby hand on her partner's broad back. "We've got work to do."

He looked into the empty office. He looked down at her desk and saw a videocassette box with a black and white photo of a young Henry Fonda. He picked it up.

"What's that?" asked Vesba.

"None of your goddam business," he said. He turned back to the hall and caught the eye of Demetrius Barton standing in the doorway of the laundry room, his arms crossed in front of his chest, smirking.

"Hello," said Colin from behind his large mahogany desk. "Come right in."

"Sorry about not knocking," said Page. "I needed to escape from something in the hall."

"Dragons?"

"No. Just detectives."

Colin raised an eyebrow and held out a hand. "Have a seat, please."

She sat down and crossed her knees. She glared at the wall. Colin said nothing, but his still raised eyebrows asked for further explanation. Instead she posed a question. "Why is it," she said, "that when you think you've finally gotten your life in order…"

"You said it was detectives."

"Well, isn't that enough? I just played a scene that was…"

Holy Comfort

"Was what?" asked Colin.

"So B-movie." She looked up. "It was kind of fun."

Colin's eyebrows jumped again. "Well, Page, it's true there are policemen everywhere you turn around here and yellow police tape...and flowers and bad poetry."

She nodded. "Life seems so...*disrupted*."

"Yes, and it is disturbing," said Colin. "However, disruption isn't always negative. It can be quite cathartic, depending on what you—"

"But it's not just the disruption," interrupted Page. "I can't help thinking about what happened to Miles and now Bradford Cole, right here in our own hallway. They're dead. Someone we know may be a murderer." She tapped the arm of the chair with her finger.

Colin sighed wearily and relaxed back into his chair. "And it's okay to be upset about it. You've experienced a frightening event and terrible loss. You're doing the best you can just coming to work, which is more than I can say for most of my team."

"How are they coping? They don't seem to be troubled much, but I suppose that's unfair."

He rolled his eyes. "How can anyone tell? Gracie missed most of the week and Diana comes in just to get updates so she can call her friends. Charlotte's been giving me the run around and won't sit down long enough to talk. They're all in serious denial."

"Maybe we all are," she said. "I didn't even like Miles. I just want to move on."

"He was our co-worker, like it or not, Page, our companion on the way. We saw him several times a week, and now he's gone. We'll never see him again. No goodbyes, no apologies, no chance to make things right. That's a hard change to deal with under the best of circumstances, and, good grief, you found him! You have that mental image to deal with that none of the rest of us do. Don't beat yourself up about this, Page. We all need time."

She nodded. "I think I'm just tired."

"Of course, you are," said Colin. "We all are, but we'll get through this and be stronger for it."

She looked up and knew he was right. He would be stronger. But she wondered about the rest of the staff. Where would they all be in six months?

"We'll have lunch real soon," he said. "I'll take you to lunch at that new place out on Montgomery, that Thai place. We can talk about how it feels to be knocked out of one's rut by disrupting circumstances and where one goes from there."

Page chuckled. "You've been in charge of Adult Ed too long I think, Colin."

He chuckled in agreement. Then Sophie Carl buzzed him, apologizing, and asking if Page was still in his office. "Tell her Walter is on line three for her."

"I forgot the time! The boys are home," she said, grabbing the phone from Colin's oustretched hand. "Walter?" she said calmly. "Yes, dear, everything's okay. I just got tied up here at work. Your key worked? You're inside? Good. I'm leaving right now, so don't worry. I'll be home in twenty minutes. You boys watch TV—stay inside until I get home. Okay. Goodbye, honey." She hung up the phone and looked at Colin who was reading through his pile of messages.

"If you want to talk some more, Page, just let me know," he said, standing up and moving around the desk. "And don't be so hard on yourself. You're a great girl, our shining star here on the staff."

"Thanks, Colin, for letting me cry on your shoulder."

"That's what it's for," he said, meaning it.

Page left Colin's office, waved to Sophie, saying a hasty "Thanks," and headed to her office where she gathered up her things. The scent of Detective Vesba's White Shoulders perfume still hung in the air, reminding her of their embarrassingly public exchange. She hurried upstairs.

Page paused at the doors and looked outside. It was dark and overcast. The clouds held rain—she could tell by the smell of the air and its weight—she could feel it. She breathed deeply, filling her lungs and hoped the rain would hold off until she got home.

"Page!" shouted a voice behind her.

She jumped and half turned back into the dark narthex. Before her eyes could readjust, a plump hand reached out and slid along her back until it rested on her shoulder.

"Page! We missed you *again* at lunch. Where have you been keeping yourself?"

"Oh, Kitty," Page said, her eyes rolling back. "We've been working all day to get an all-parish letter in the mail—over thirteen hundred units. The courier just picked it up."

"Oh, really? Another letter?"

"From the rector and the senior warden. It's about the two murders, of course."

"Of course. I can't imagine there's a person around who hasn't heard. I don't suppose there's any new information in the letter…"

"No, not really. It's more of a plea *for* information…and patience and prayers."

"Well, I'll look for it in the mail," said Kitty, focusing intently on Page. "How are *you* doing? Eating any better? I bet you skipped lunch today."

"I'm fine," Page said, pushing open the door and moving outside, away from the honest, but relentlessly penetrating, blue eyes. "Which way are you parked?"

Kitty, following closely behind her, motioned eastward.

"I'm parked the other way," said Page, stopping. "It was nice to run into you, Kitty. I'm still enjoying my roses."

"And what about the company of that good-looking detective?"

Holy Comfort

Page said nothing, but stared back at Kitty.

"I suppose you're wondering how I know that. Well, I'll tell you. I heard it at the Helen Sweetwater Guild luncheon today. Diana Dunwoody was holding forth like a child with a new toy—something to show and tell. I tried, Page, to cut her off, but you know how it is with her and her friends—it's like a feeding frenzy. There was blood in the water. Yours, I'm afraid."

"Well, it isn't the first time," said Page, trying to smile. "I'll live."

"Yes, but you might want to lie low for a while. The conversation concerning you was rather colorful. Stay home. Read a Jan Karon book."

Page laughed. "I might consider it, but tomorrow's the funeral and I should come in for that."

"Why should you? Bradford Cole won't notice...who cares what people think, Page? In the long run, one missed funeral won't matter."

"I hate to give them the satisfaction of thinking I care about their gossip."

"Well, it's up to you, dear. You can take my grandmotherly advice or leave it, I'll still love you."

Page embraced Kitty, her arms wide, hugging her tightly. "Thank you, Kitty."

"Hang in there, sweetie," Kitty said as Page turned to head down the street toward her car.

When Page rounded the corner where Crown ran into Dozier Avenue she saw him right away, lounging against her car, his arms folded across his chest and his cowboy boots crossed at the ankles. She slowed her pace and tried to walk casually down the sidewalk. He looked up as she approached. He did not smile. "Excuse me," she said as she reached the car, but he did not move away. "I'm in a hurry," she said with more urgency. "I'm late. The boys are already home."

He stood up straight and moved away from the door. She put her hand on the door handle, but he took her elbow and turned her so she was forced to face him. "I apologize for any stupid things my partner may have said."

"Forget it," she said indifferently.

He gazed passed her head. "I won't forget it."

Her eyes flicked up and she felt herself blushing, remembering the other thing. "There's no need to apologize," she said. "Your partner was just...she feels left out, I guess, like she doesn't know what's going on." She looked down. He still held her arm. "I've got to go now," she said.

He relinquished her arm. "Will you be home tonight?"

"I have plans," she said as she unlocked her car and slid inside. She looked up. "And, Detective, that kiss was just me doing Lauren Bacall to make a point to your partner. She said some pretty rude things about me and the clergy staff."

He crossed his arms again and stepped back into the street. "You were very convincing."

She chuckled, but he was not smiling. She looked up at him. "Did you ever really think that I...that I slept with Miles? That I had an affair with Charles?"

"I wondered. It's my job to wonder," he said. "I was wrong."

"Did you tell your partner that?"

"Yes. She was skeptical."

Page nodded. The engine turned over. She pulled into the road and glanced back. His arms were still folded, but he was looking at the sky.

Holy Comfort

Chapter Thirty-Seven

THE RECTOR STOOD and watched the great orange ball make its final descent behind the rooftops of Crown Avenue. A sailor's delight. Tomorrow would be another spectacular day. He prayed in his head. Father. *Father.* He waited for his friend to arrive, for Colin to arrive. He needed his strength, his support. He needed him to be there with him. What was taking him so long?

He realized that he was struggling, like a swimmer caught in an undertow, to keep his head up. All week he had listened and listened and held hands and proffered tissues. He had prayed and prayed till his knees and back ached. He had run at night through the park, because his days had been too busy, because he had no time to exercise during the day. He had no time for himself. At night he had run farther than usual, hardly aware of the street beneath his feet, streaking through the dark, night after night. But there was no abatement, no blunting of the feelings he could not even identify. Horror...shock...guilt. *My eyes fail looking for my God.* Oh Lord, scorn has broken my heart, do not let it leave me helpless. O God, who gives endurance and encouragement, give it to me, to me. Give it to me.

Now where was Colin? He felt himself becoming annoyed. He, who hardly ever lost his balance, was irritated that his friend had not arrived yet when he needed him. Colin was his rock. Where was he? Colin!

"Charles, I'm here." Colin stood in the doorway leaning forward tentatively. He had waited a few moments before speaking, afraid of disturbing the rector, but Charles had not turned around, completely oblivious. "I came over as soon as I could. There were a few fences to mend. There always are."

Charles turned around now, slightly dazed. "Nothing serious, I hope." He gestured to a chair and they sat down.

"No. Nothing much. Something with Page Hawthorne. I gather it had to do with an argument with the detectives."

"What about?" Charles cushioned his head in his hand.

"I don't really know, but I'm sure she'll work it out. She can take care of herself."

"I wish I could be so sure." The rector stared at his associate with half-open eyes, holding him with the pain that momentarily blurred his focus. "I've been concerned for Page ever since...she found Miles' body. I worry that..."

"*She did it?*"

"Colin," the rector said, exasperated by his colleague's words and the urgency with which he said them. "Are you out of your mind?"

"I don't know. It's just a thought...and not such a far-fetched thought. It must have occurred to you as well. She's smart enough to have pulled it off. And the quotes from scripture are just up her alley. She had a motive."

"She had no motive! No more motive that you or I..."

"The way people are talking, that's more than enough."

Charles turned to Colin, his eyes like smoldering coals. "Get behind me, Satan," he mumbled.

Colin began to chuckle, but was suddenly silenced in his heart's core. "I'm sorry," he said.

"I shouldn't have to remind you of all people that this is no laughing matter," said the rector. "I am appalled by what I hear whispered in this place, the jokes and the constant speculation..."

"It's wrong, of course, but it's impossible not to wonder. I apologize." He folded his hands and waited for the rector to speak.

Charles turned again to the window and swept the contempt from his mind, visualizing a large hand removing with a single movement the emotional detritus of the previous conversation. Once his mind was clear, he could love his friend as if they had never spoken.

"My shirts," said the rector finally, turning back to face Colin. "I forgot all about them in the midst of yesterday's new development. The forensic report came back. My shirts were covered with finger prints. The person who did it was careless, sloppy, so the police are quite convinced that there is no connection with the murders. No direct connection."

"Whose prints?" asked Colin. "Do they know?"

"They know. It was Baylor Valentine."

"Valentine! *No...*"

"Yes." The rector watched Colin as the big man's bulk seemed to melt into his chair.

"How in God's name did they match the prints?"

"He was arrested in the Central West End, back in the '70s, something to do with a male prostitute. His prints came up on the computer."

"Oh Lord...did you know anything about *that?*" Charles shook his head. "The bastards! No wonder Bay is so devoted to Clyde Cullen. He must have saved his job...and his reputation."

The rector said nothing, but nodded distractedly.

"But why would Bay...w*hat was he thinking*?" asked Colin.

"I couldn't say. No one's spoken to him yet. I wanted to talk to you first and maybe Rich Bell."

"I wouldn't tell Rich," said Colin.

Holy Comfort

"Baylor will have to retire now. I may need Bell's support when Baylor's fan club inevitably turns this into a conspiracy against him and..."

"But surely he'll cooperate now."

"One would hope so, but..."

"But why attack you? You've always supported him and honored him. What's he suddenly got against *you*?"

The rector shook his head slowly. "It makes no sense to me, either."

"Unless...unless he's trying to—I don't know—distract the detectives or, what do they call that? Throw in a red herring?"

Charles shook his head again. "They shall be driven away by the wind."

"Who?" asked Colin, distracted by his own thoughts and visions.

"The *wicked*, Colin. The wicked."

"Oh," he laughed. "I wonder."

The two men sat in silence for some time engrossed in their own separate thoughts. Charles' mind flickered erratically from Baylor Valentine to Page Hawthorne to the vestry meeting less than an hour away. Whatever was going on with Page, he had to face the problem of his organist first. He had to prioritize. That was his job. For now there was Valentine. He was a snobbish, pompous old curmudgeon, opinionated and bigoted, but still, despite his age, one of the finest organists in the city. His choir was well recognized for its ability, although lately it had shown signs of weakness and dissent. The rector sighed, realizing that he would have to confront him and soon. There was no putting it off, no hoping the problem would disappear, no expectation of someone else dealing with it. He studied Colin, whose eyes were closed in thought. Colin would be able to handle the situation undramatically, unemotionally. He might make some enemies, but he wouldn't care. Charles cared, wanting always to be all things to all people, to be liked as well as respected. It was a failing, he knew, a serious failing. Caring, he knew, would be his undoing.

Suddenly Colin opened his guileless blue eyes and said, "Say, Charles, how about something to eat? I'll never make it through the vestry meeting if I don't eat something."

"Of course," Charles said distractedly. "Let's see what Adair has in the kitchen. I'll admit, eating was the last thing on my mind." He stood and gestured in the direction of the kitchen, allowing the larger, hungrier man to lead the way.

In the kitchen, Adair Pinkney was slicing cheese with a black-handled kitchen knife and arranging it on a platter with fruit and crusty French bread. "Hungry, boys?" she asked as they entered.

"You mind-reader, you!" Colin said as he reached for a piece of cheese.

"Have something to eat, dear." Adair addressed her husband who hung back, still thoughtful and distressed.

"All right," he said, choosing a small piece of Gouda. He stood with it poised halfway to his mouth, apparently having forgotten why he was holding it.

"Colin, would you like a glass of wine?" asked Adair.

"I'd love one...but I'd better stick to water."

"Okay," she said smiling. "How about you, dear?"

"What?" asked Charles, noting the cheese in his hand.

"Something to drink, dear?"

"Oh, no, nothing. I'm fine."

"Come, then, let's bring the tray and sit down." Colin grabbed the platter and Adair followed with his glass of water and her own glass of wine. Charles drifted behind, still distracted and self-absorbed. From the doorway he said, "Would you mind terribly if I went upstairs and tried to unwind before this vestry meeting? I'm really not hungry." Without waiting for an answer, he turned and left.

Adair followed him into the hall. "Darling, what's the matter?"

"Oh. It's this thing with Bay Valentine, and now Colin has told me something else. I've just got to sort it out."

"What *else*?"

"Oh nothing, really. I'll tell you later after the meeting." He was edging away from her, heading for the stairs.

"All right," she said, understanding almost at once that she was wasting precious moments. "I'll see you later."

Holy Comfort

Chapter Thirty-Eight

"Well, lookee here. The handsome Detective Merton!" cried Charlotte, recognizing the detective as he came through the door at Lenny's Diner. "Come here and sit by me, darling. I've been saving you a spot," she said, patting the stool next to her in a manner that she somehow managed to make suggestive.

Merton caught her eye and realized there was no avoiding doing what she asked. "Hello," he said, trying to smile.

"I don't believe I've ever seen you here, boy, and, believe me, I'd remember."

"I stop by when I'm in a hurry. I live around the corner."

"Oh really? Let me make a note of that."

He laughed. "Can I buy you a burger?"

"I've already ordered my usual—two cheeseburgers and a rootbeer. And anyway, I don't allow a man to pay for dinner on the first date."

"When did this become a date?" he asked, looking at her sideways.

"Only in my vivid imagination, Detective," she said, patting his hand which rested on the counter. He withdrew it immediately. "It's only fair, don't you think, seeing as how you've already taken out Ms. Hawthorne."

"How did you know that?" he asked too quickly.

She blinked. "Are you kidding? Everyone knew about Page's big date. Sorry to hear you didn't get lucky."

"You have quite a mouth, don't you?" he retorted, no longer pretending to be amused. Since Lenny's was only about ten feet by ten feet and the food was cooked in between two parallel counters, all of the five other people in the place had heard their exchange.

"So sorry. Did I hit a sore spot? *Mea culpa.*"

He turned to the cook behind the counter. "Give me a double burger with fries and a Coke, please. And I'd like that to go."

"Sure, pal," the cook replied, adding in a lower voice, "and don't let Charlotte get to you. She doesn't mean any harm."

Merton met the man's smile but did not return it. "Keep the change," he said handing him a five-dollar bill. He stared straight ahead, apparently fascinated by the grill.

Charlotte was silent also, resting her chin in her hand and gazing out the window opposite her stool. "We always seem to get off on the wrong foot, don't we, Detective?" asked Charlotte quietly. "It's too bad. We could be such good friends."

"What makes you think I need a friend?"

She shrugged. "I don't know. I do know you're barking up the wrong tree with Miss Ice...with Page."

The detective paused and took a long, deep breath. "What the hell did she ever do to you?"

"Nothing," she said evenly. "She never gave little ol' me the time of day. You see, she doesn't need friends, not so long as she's got the ear—and God knows what else—of the rector."

"Jealous, Ms. Pentecost?"

"Are you?"

He held his eyes on hers, although he desperately wanted to look away. "Does it bother you that the rector pays more attention to her? Especially since you're para-clergy and have the more important job? But there you are reporting to the number two man, Whitefish, while she's got the rector himself. And he thinks she's so smart, so well-read, so spiritual. Why doesn't he notice that you're pretty smart yourself, that you're well-read. Why, you knew all about that old saint with his crows, didn't you? Too bad Miles didn't appreciate that present. He wasn't the type, though. He probably wouldn't have appreciated the lectionary tie-in with the coals and the burned hand, either. Who were you trying to impress, Charlotte? Charles Pinkney?"

She turned to stare at him, her mouth ajar. "*Me*? What are you talking about, Detective?"

The man behind the counter pushed a dinner plate in front of Charlotte and handed Roy his food in a brown paper sack with a cup of Coke. Roy immediately stood up and grabbed it. "Take it easy, Ms. Pentecost," he said on his way out the door. He made a mental note never to return.

"Sure thing," she replied brightly to the room.

ROY STEPPED ON the gas and tore out of the tiny parking lot, headed home. He would barely have enough time to eat his dinner, shower and shave for the second time that day, before he had to head back to that pretentious pile of stones, ludicrously named Holy Comforter, for a special meeting of the vestry. He and Vesba had been summoned to appear at seven fifteen p.m. by the senior warden. There was no getting out of it.

He slowed down when he realized he was driving forty-five miles an hour in a school zone. *Calm down*, he told himself, but he felt completely out of joint. He still wasn't sure what had happened in her office that afternoon or why he cared. Why couldn't he blow it off? Where was his professional detachment? There was too much to do to allow himself to become distracted. He swallowed hard and proceeded slowly.

He looked in his rearview mirror. Someone was following him, someone in an old black Porsche. He slowed down again and then pulled into a driveway. The black Porsche sped by. *Jesus Christ.* He grabbed the steering wheel. He closed his eyes to clear his mind and steady his breathing. A picture of Page sitting demurely at her desk, her small frame securely encased in wool and cashmere and black tights, came uninvited to his mind. She threw back her head and laughed, raising her arms as she leaned back, running her long fingers through her dark, golden hair. Life was absurd, wasn't it, Detective Merton? So absurd. *I'm way behind schedule.* She tipped her head to one side and laughed again.

He took a deep breath and opened his eyes, casting the vision into oblivion. It was already six thirty. He checked his rearview mirror to make sure the Porsche was nowhere in sight and then slowly backed out into the road.

Chapter Thirty-Nine

AT SEVEN FOURTEEN p.m., Detective Merton, wearing his gray suit once again, raced up the stairs at the south entrance of the church. He had spent so much time at the place, he was actually beginning to know his way around. This was no mean accomplishment. The doors to the Lodge Room were closed. Roy checked his watch. He was not late. Should he knock or wait? While he was deciding what to do, Leona appeared around the corner, apparently having parked on the opposite side of the church. "Let's wait in the library," she said by way of a greeting. The door was unlocked and they went in. Leona sat down at one of the round tables. She had not changed her clothes, but commented to Roy, "You look—what? 'Positively Brooks Brotherish' tonight, Detective."

He turned away and pretended to look at the books in front of him.

"I see you're still mad at me," she said. "Why don't you try growing up, Merton? Life would be so much more pleasant."

"I gave up expecting life to be pleasant when I grew up."

"Life's a bitch and so am I," she said. "Get over it."

He cracked a smile.

She sighed heavily. "So I'm in a crappy mood," she said and paused. "Valerie got herself suspended."

"For doing what?"

"For mouthing off to the sisters."

"Good for her," he said twisting his head to face her. "When are you going to take her out of that school anyway?"

"I live in the city. Where else is she going to go?"

"Move."

"You know I can't afford it."

"I'd help you," he said, sighing because he understood the futility of this conversation. "You know I would."

"I couldn't leave my mother."

"Get a bigger place. Move her with you."

"She's lived in that flat for fifty years."

Merton threw up his hands. "Then don't complain when Valerie screws up."

Holy Comfort

"She's got two years plus good behavior 'til she graduates. She'll live. I did."

He rolled his eyes. Out in the hall a door opened and within moments the senior warden, Richardson Bell, appeared at the door. He looked, thought Roy, like a movie star playing the part of a senior warden. "Detective Vesba, Detective Merton, would you join us now, please?"

Leona stood up and Roy followed her out the door and across the hall to the Lodge Room. Richardson Bell indicated that they should sit in the two empty seats to the right of his chair which was placed at the head of a large rectangle of tables surrounded by twenty or more chairs in which members of the vestry sat. The rector sat to the left of the senior warden. It was easy to discern who was in charge.

Roy looked around the dark-paneled, inadequately lighted room. He saw a few familiar faces including those of Colin Whitefish, who seemed to be staring at him, and George Fontaine, the junior warden. Along the walls sat eight or ten other people, including Martha Van Patton. These were non-vestry members of the parish who had come to the meeting as spectators, he assumed, out of curiosity. The vestry members around the table included seven or eight men in suits who appeared to have come to the meeting directly from work and two or three women who looked to have done the same. A few younger women and several older men in varying degrees of casual attire rounded out the group.

When called upon, Roy gave a short summary of the two murders and their ongoing investigations. Then he looked sideways at his partner, signaling her to field any questions. He was vaguely aware of some verbal lobbing, wherein Vesba was forced to repeat herself beyond a point she found reasonable. She began to sweat. The rector coughed a lot and at one point he excused himself and exited the room, heading for the kitchen, coughing dramatically all the way. Roy was only partially conscious, and was relieved when Vesba pinched his arm, signaling him to get up and retreat. As they closed the door behind them, everyone started talking at once, and Roy heard Richardson Bell beat on the table with his fist.

"Walk me to my car, Merton," Leona chuckled, halting him with a bejewelled hand on his arm.

"I'm parked on the other side."

"I don't give a rat's ass where you're parked. Walk me to my goddamn car."

"Maybe you can intimidate the vestry, Leona, but it doesn't work with me," he replied evenly. "I'm going home. We've got a full day ahead of us and I'm tired."

"Oh yeah," she said, opening her hand. "That reminds me. The rector passed me this note." She handed her partner a folded piece of fine bond paper.

> *I am meeting with Baylor Valentine at the rectory tomorrow morning at seven thirty a.m. Colin Whitefish will be there. I would*

appreciate it if both you and Detective Merton could be there as well. Thank you. Charles Pinkney +.

He read it and handed it back. "I'll be there."

"Do you want me to pick you up?"

"I'll meet you at the station at seven fifteen. We can come in together if you want."

She looked him in the eye and swallowed. "Look. I'm sorry about what I said to Miss Tightass—Miss Hawthorne—but I didn't say anything that wasn't true."

"The hell you didn't," he shot back, surprising himself with his sudden anger. "I'm way behind schedule working my way through the clergy staff? What was that all about?"

"I may have exaggerated. I just wanted her to realize that we're in the middle of an ongoing investigation and she's getting in the way."

"If she's in the way, I put her there, Leona." He glared at her. "And for a very good reason, which I have tried to explain to you."

"She's the common denominator," said Vesba contemptuously. "I heard you. I'm just not sure I agree."

Roy gazed toward the doors. He fiddled with the change in his pockets. He did not respond.

"But don't get me wrong, Roy," she said. "You can common denominate her all you want. It's nothing to me. I just don't think you should kid yourself. She's not even your type."

He turned slowly and gazed at his partner. "How the hell do you know who my type is?"

She chuckled. "I've been watching you operate for nearly six years, partner."

He chuckled, too. "You may have been watching, but you didn't see much." He raised his eyes to meet her bland blue stare.

She flushed. He turned and headed for the door. "Go home, Leona," he said.

"Go fuck yourself," she screamed to his back.

Roy waved to her without turning around and wondered what on earth the vestry made of her screeching imperative, hurled at him with such magnitude. There was no way they could have missed hearing it. No way.

Chapter Forty

ROY DID NOT stop to turn on the light but walked through the living room straight to the kitchen where he opened the refrigerator and took out a bottle of Corona. He opened it and walked back to the living room. He dropped into the black leather recliner and picked up the remote control. He took a long drink of beer and set the bottle down half empty on the floor. He placed the remote next to it and laid his head back, closing his eyes. It had been a long day, one hell of a long miserable day at the end of a long week.

He slumped down in the chair, his hands resting on his widespread thighs. They had wasted most of the day going through Cole's condo. It was a typical bachelor's residence, not so different from his own, actually. Cole's had been decorated at some point by a professional and his closets were full of expensive clothes, but it had the same empty feeling, like someone was just passing through. He looked around in the dark. He had more books, more CDs, and there was no elaborate train set-up. Cole, the big rich kid, still looking for laughs with the likes of Ellen Chevalier and spiritual guidance from Miles Costello. Poor bastard. She had said no to him and no to Costello. She had said yes to him. Why? *That kiss won't leave a scar.* He tried to remember the kiss, but he had been so surprised he had felt nothing, his eyes staring as she tilted her head back. Then a memory of the Wildhorse rose up within him so physical that he nearly moaned. He could have crushed every one of her ribs when he embraced her on the dance floor. He could have held her all night like that, but he had bruised her wrists and left. *That kiss won't leave a scar.* Chandler? Or Faulkner trying to sound like Chandler? He understood nothing and Leona understood even less.

And what about Charlotte Pentecost? Where did she fit in? What did she know? *Me?* she had asked. *What do you mean?* Why had she followed him in her car? She had stared at him relentlessly this morning at the staff meeting, her eyes moving away from him only to glance at Page. What was Page to her? Did she know how he felt? No, she only thought he wanted to sleep with her. He *did* want to sleep with her. They all wanted to sleep with her. *Sorry to hear you didn't get lucky.* Just like the rest of them. *I have plans.* Plans that don't include you.

He finished off his beer. *Light thickens, and the crow makes wing to the rooky wood.* He had another long day ahead of him with Baylor Valentine to be confronted and Bradford Cole to be buried. He would probably see her at the funeral. He remembered her at Costello's, huddled against the wall, perspiration on her forehead, shivering. He had put his hand on her arm and felt her tremble. It was no act. He had wondered, but he knew, even as he wondered, that she was scared to death. What did she fear? What was she afraid of?

He sighed. At least there had been no third execution today, the special day of devotion for Latimer, Ridley and Cranmer. No third martyr to a madman's cause. But what about tomorrow? He leaned over and picked up the black book from the orange crate next to his chair and the lesson calendar he had borrowed from Pinkney's secretary. Psalm 116. *The cords of death entangled me, the anguish of the grave came upon me; I was overcome by trouble and sorrow.* Jesus. There was no rest in sight, no rest for the stupid, the careless, the hopeless.

Jesus.

Holy Comfort

Chapter Forty-One

THE RED SKY the night before had been deceiving. The temperature had dropped overnight and the sky now was overcast, so the rector, Colin Whitefish and Baylor Valentine walked quickly without talking.

In the living room of the rectory, Detectives Vesba and Merton sat waiting with Adair Pinkney. As they entered and Baylor Valentine saw who was there, he grunted and froze, placing a hand dramatically over his heart.

"Are you all right, Bay?" asked the rector, taking his elbow and leading him to the couch.

The organist mumbled and allowed himself to be placed in a seat. He sat down, but did not lean back. "What's going on?" he whispered. "I thought we were meeting to discuss the final plans for Cole's funeral. Why are *they* here?"

The detectives exchanged sidelong glances but remained silent observers. Adair Pinkney excused herself and left the room.

"They need to hear what we say," said Charles.

"Why? *Why*? I don't understand," said Valentine, exhibiting total bewilderment at the situation.

The rector ignored the question and said, "Richardson Bell would be here, but he had to fly to Chicago. He'll be back in time for the funeral. There's no point, I suppose, in beating around the bush, Bay. You're here because we know you destroyed my shirts with a razor blade. Your finger prints were all over them. We'd like to know why." The rector looked calmly into Valentine's eyes.

The organist looked around the room at the assembled people, contempt suddenly and luridly evident in his face, a sneer on his lips. "You people," he drawled and made a scornful clucking sound with his tongue.

"Talk to us, Bay. Tell us why. I deserve that much," said Charles.

"*Deserve*? Oh, kid me not, *Charles*," he hissed. "I owe you nothing."

Charles and Colin exchanged glances and Charles, shrugging, said, "Then I suppose we have no recourse but to let the detectives arrest you."

"*Arrest me!* You wouldn't *dare*! After all my years of service which have amounted to no less than slave labor for this church...my only home for forty-five years!"

"Yes." Charles stated flatly. "I'm afraid so."

"Don't you *care*? Don't you care what happens to Holy Comforter? Don't you care what a circus the media will make of it, of *me*?"

"You should have thought of that before you slashed my shirts."

"Oh, you bastard."

"Calm down, Bay. You're beside yourself," said Colin Whitefish who looked uncharacteristically pale.

Vesba shifted her weight from one side of the chair to the other, recrossing her voluptuous thighs. Merton's eyes held fast to the rector who sat, never moving, accepting the verbal assault with utter calm.

"You're bluffing," said Valentine. "You don't have the balls to file charges."

No one argued with him. There was no need to argue. The time for argument was past and he knew it. Baylor Valentine was the one who was bluffing and quietly, his energies spent, he quit, his massive frame visibly shrinking into the couch on which he sat. He began to cry. His shoulders shook and his chin sank into his chest as a great eruption of tears flowed unchecked down his cheeks onto his maroon Shetland sweater. The rector handed him a handkerchief, which he petulantly refused to accept. Vesba, groaning, lifted herself out of her chair and moments later returned with a box of Kleenex, which she tossed onto the couch. Valentine seized a handful of tissues and began, between sobs, to vent.

"Oh, you...*you* would never understand in a million years. Never. You *think* you serve God, but you don't know the true glory of serving God with someone who *really* knows how. *I do*. I could never explain to you what it means to me, and how you've corrupted this place ever since you and that woman moved into Clyde and Bea's gracious home, bringing your *modern* art and your monotone furniture and tearing up the carpeting for your stenciled floors just like you tore out the life's blood of this church. You think by keeping Rite I you'll assuage our pain, that we'll ignore your small groups and your spiritual directors and your foot washing and incense—"

"You're ranting, Bay, for God's sake, pull yourself together," said Colin harshly, stealing a look at Charles who stared straight ahead as if mesmerized by the organist's caricature of outrage. "Enough is enough. Tell the detectives what they want to know and you can walk away with your reputation intact. But make no mistake, *this time* walk away you will."

Valentine raised his bleak eyes to the detectives, to Vesba in particular, a pathetic expression of supplication, reminding her of portraits of Emmett Kelly or Saint Sebastian with the arrows sticking through him, spreading over his face. They all waited while he made up his mind. It didn't take long.

"Where shall I start?" he asked. "What do you want to know?" He directed his questions to the detectives, having finished with the priests. This was not for them, he seemed to say. Nothing was for them.

"Tell us, Dr. Valentine," said Vesba. "Tell us who was here late on the Thursday night before Miles Costello was killed."

Holy Comfort

"No one out of the ordinary. I swear. Demetrius Barton was here until ten o'clock or so. He locked up when he thought the place was empty like always." He leaned forward. "But you couldn't possibly think *Demetrius*...just because he's *black* doesn't make him a killer!"

"Dr. Valentine," interrupted Merton. "Tell us whose car you saw parked out in front after everyone else had left."

The organist sighed deeply and looked from Vesba to Merton and back to Vesba before heaving another cavernous sigh. "I saw a dark blue Taurus wagon—Gracie Griggs' car."

"You're sure?"

"Yes. There's a dent in the back that she never got fixed."

"What about Wednesday night?"

Valentine lifted his head and dropped his chin down on his chest, exhaling loudly.

"Is that a yes?" asked Vesba.

"Yes," he said primly. "As you no doubt are aware, all evening events scheduled this week were cancelled. There was no one around, but the car was here."

The detectives exchanged glances and Vesba asked, "Why did you slash the rector's shirts?"

"Why?" he repeated wearily. "I don't know...After you and I talked, I got to thinking...I thought maybe you were getting close...and I thought about what you said about whose cars were here Thursday night, and that that must be important...and I remembered Gracie's station wagon, and the pieces started to fit together and I thought, oh my god, *Gracie*? Not Gracie Griggs. No! But then I know she was close to Miles and very jealous of his friendship...and that she's angry and unhappy and drinks too much. Who knows? Gracie's a fine woman, a fine woman, but she's fallen on hard times and can't seem to right herself. It's possible, I thought, maybe she needed something from Miles and he wouldn't give it to her. He could be like that."

"So why the shirts?"

"Something just snapped."

"But why the rector?"

"*Because it's all his fault*...can't you see? If it weren't for him, Miles wouldn't be dead and Gracie wouldn't...he puts too much pressure on everyone. He expects too much from people like Gracie who have problems, who are weak—"

"Oh, come now, Bay," said Colin. "We've tried and tried to help Gracie, but she doesn't seem to want to help herself. We've sent her to counselors and to the diocesan employee assistance people. I've talked to her ad nauseum. We've suggested A.A. We've threatened. She's resisted everything. She just doesn't care."

"So you'll get rid of her along with Charlotte, no doubt, and *me*," said Valentine. "We've all felt the blade hanging over our heads. Midge McIntyre can't be far behind."

"You committed a crime—that's why you're going," said Merton. "You committed felony breaking and entering and misdemeanor vandalism, sir."

"I committed no *felony*. I have a *key* for God's sake. How is it breaking and entering?"

"You're lucky we don't drag you in right now for questioning," said Merton, displaying finally the impatience he had been holding in. "You've demonstrated violent intent. You live at the church, two floors above where the murders took place. You have no real alibi. If it weren't for Mr. Pinkney's—"

The rector stood up abruptly, ending the discussion. "Bay, we'll discuss your severance package when Richardson Bell gets back and we'll set a date for your *retirement*. You will mention this to no one. If the word gets out, we'll know it came from you and you will vacate the tower immediately. It's up to you. I'll see you this afternoon in my office before the funeral."

"The *funeral*," gasped Valentine. "Everyone will be there—the Bishop, Senator Putnam. I hope I can—"

"Shall I call Wamble at the Cathedral?" cut in Whitefish impatiently. "It's short notice, but I'm sure he could step in."

"No," said Valentine with all the dowager dignity he could muster. "The show must go on."

"Good," said the rector. "And now, if you'll all excuse me..." He bowed slightly. Then he left the room and disappeared.

Colin Whitefish turned to the organist. "You better listen to him, Bay. Not a word to anyone. Not to Sonny, not to the choir, no one. Do you understand?"

"I'm not a child."

"No? Then start acting like an adult. Wipe your nose and go back to your tower and start collecting your things."

The organist looked at the priest with what he hoped was a look of utter contempt, but he knew it would not have the hoped-for effect. There was no hurting a self-serving, insensitive oaf like Colin Whitefish. He was not an artist. He had no idea how an artist suffered. "Well," he said, waving his hand like a handkerchief, "if I'm excused, I shall depart. I'm going to call Clyde Cullen right away."

"Don't do that, Bay," said Colin Whitefish, his face flushed bright red. "God forbid you should make a move on your own. You heard what the rector said. We'll UPS your crap to the YMCA, because that's where you'll be living if you tell anyone about this."

The organist threw his chin up and left.

"Good God, I hope for once he can keep his big mouth shut," said Whitefish with some vehemence.

"Do you think maybe we were too hard on him?" asked Vesba, surprising even herself. "He's just a pathetic old man."

Holy Comfort

Colin laughed. Ignoring her question, he posed another. "Is that information about Gracie Griggs at all helpful? As her supervisor, I find it extremely difficult to see her planning two such elaborate crimes and carrying them out."

The detectives nodded and Merton said, "Yes. It is hard to imagine. And it doesn't make much sense what with the second murder. Do you think the rector is all right?"

"He'll be okay. Charles loves Bay, sin and all. It broke his heart to do what he did."

"I don't understand that kind of love."

"Charles tried to explain it to me once when I complained about a particularly vitriolic parishioner, the kind who never hesitates to criticize my character, ancestry, talent or faith. He said that he always tried to remember that in each of these people he was seeing the Face of God—sometimes in deep disguise." Colin chuckled. "I suppose I've had glimpses of that Face, but Charles is way ahead of me on his spiritual journey."

"I guess I'm not even on the road."

"Oh, you're on the road, Detective. We're all on the road. It's the same road, after all."

Chapter Forty-Two

It was Roy who broke the silence finally as they sped down Westborough Boulevard to Hawken Road saying, "So what do you think?"

"About what?" his partner sullenly replied.

"About Gracie Griggs' car."

"I'd put money on her having been home, passed out in front of the TV. She would never have set foot in that church if she didn't have to be there. And she didn't have to be there Thursday night or Wednesday night, for that matter."

"Then who had her car and why did they have it?"

"Maybe Charlotte Pentecost's car really didn't work. Jerry from the Amoco station did stop by on Friday morning for a jump."

"Wouldn't Gracie have mentioned that she lent her car to Charlotte?"

"I suppose she might have forgotten."

"I think it's more likely that Charlotte—or someone—*borrowed* the car for cover."

"I suppose that wouldn't be difficult to do."

"No. Not at all..." Merton looked out the window at the familiar streets. Then he turned to his partner and said, "You know, I ran into Ms. Pentecost last night by accident at Lenny's. When I left she tried to follow me home."

"No shit," said Leona. "What did you do?"

"I pulled off the road. She didn't follow."

"What did she want?"

"I think she wanted to find out where I live."

"I wonder if she has a habit of following people."

He nodded. "She said something that made me wonder if she'd seen me Wednesday night."

"You should have asked her—it would give her an alibi."

"Not necessarilly. Cole was killed between ten and eleven o'clock. She might have had time..." His voice tapered off, unconvinced.

Leona cleared her throat. "So you're really getting to her?" she asked as she pulled into the driveway and braked noisily.

176

Holy Comfort

"I don't think it has anything really to do with me."

"What?" she said, unbuckling her seat belt. "What are you talking about?"

"No. It isn't personal—it's something else. Something to do with Page...what Page doesn't have."

"Christ," she said groaning. "When are you going to stop obsessing over that woman?"

"I'm not obsessing. I'm trying to understand Charlotte Pentecost. *She's* the one obsessing—"

"Yeah, over *you*."

"No!" he said, unbuckling his seat belt and throwing it aside. "Obsessing over Page. Don't you get it? She's got this sick thing about Page. She hates her, but she wants to be like her."

Leona chewed noisily on a piece of gum for a while, then stopped abruptly. "So you're saying Page Hawthorne turned down Miles Costello and Brad Cole...and Charlotte got 'em on the rebound..."

Roy nodded.

"And she's hoping to land *you* next?"

"I don't think she'll try too hard," he said. "But it's difficult for her to ignore me, because of this thing she's got going."

Vesba turned noisily in her seat. "Supposing you're right...where does Chester Hawthorne fit in?"

"Good question," he said. "I've been wondering about that myself." He looked at the station wagon in the driveway ahead of them and at the house which was a small, neat country cottage, brick with green shutters, built in an era when compactness was a virtue and not necessarilly a sign of poverty. There were three or four similar houses on the street, all no doubt candidates for tear-downs, eyed voraciously by developers. Perhaps Gracie Griggs had an ace up her sleeve yet.

Vesba opened her door and stepped out of her car. She adjusted her skirt and strolled over to Gracie Griggs' car and then motioned her partner to join her as she peered inside the dark blue Taurus wagon. "Will you look at that?" Vesba called. "The damn keys are still in the ignition."

Merton peeked inside prefunctorially. "Do you suppose she makes a habit of doing that?"

"I bet she does. That way she'd always know where they are."

Merton nodded and leaned against the car. "Do you think it'd be worth checking for finger prints?"

"No. All that'd prove, if Charlotte's were in there, would be that she'd driven the car sometime, but it wouldn't prove she'd driven it the Thursday night in question."

He nodded again, then turned and walked around behind the car. He opened the back and leaned inside. He called to her moments later. As she joined him, leaning inside, he brought his right hand up to her face. "Look. It looks like barbecue briquette dust. *That* might be worth checking."

She leaned over for a closer look at the dark blue carpet.

"Leona!"

Emmerging from the back of the wagon, Vesba followed her partner's pointing finger to the side of the garage to an old black Weber kettle. On the ground next to it sat a half-full bag of Kingsford barbecue briquettes.

Vesba shook her head. "Even if the lab can link the coal dust in Gracie's car to the coals on Costello's head and we have a witness acknowledging that this Taurus wagon was at the church Thursday night, we have no witness who saw who was driving the car Thursday night. It's all circumstantial evidence—"

"Pointing to Gracie Griggs."

"Do you think someone was trying to frame Griggs?"

"I think we need to talk to Gracie again."

"Talk to *me* again?" Gracie Griggs stood in the shadow of her house by the Weber kettle. She wore an old chenille robe and the hair around her face was wound up in bobby pins. She bent to pick up her newspaper and, upon straightening, said, "You *must* be desperate."

"No," said Merton, stepping forward. "Just interested in a few loose ends. May we come inside for a moment?"

"I suppose," she said grudgingly. "Follow me." She turned and led them in a side door. Once inside, she turned right and picked her way through a tangle of coats and boots and boxes to the kitchen. "Make yourself comfortable," she said indicating the kitchen table which was piled high with mail and newspapers and dirty dishes.

The detectives sat down and looked around. Gracie did not offer them coffee but poured herself a cup and leaned against the stove, lighting a cigarette. The detectives waited.

"So what do you need me for, all bright-eyed and bushy-tailed early on this Saturday morning?" she asked and drew deeply on her cigarette.

"Just a few questions, Ms. Griggs," said Vesba casually. "For starters where were you Thursday night, October eighth, the night before the murder of Miles Costello?"

"Haven't we been through this? I have better things to do than repeat myself, you know."

"Thursday night," repeated Vesba.

"*Thursday* night, October eighth. A week ago *last* Thursday..." she paused, evidently thinking. She sat down heavily and exhaled loudly. "I was home. No meetings. I probably made some calls and watched TV. Yes. I watched *E.R.* and fell asleep on the couch. You can ask my husband."

"We will. What about Wednesday night, October fourteenth?"

"Home again, home again, jiggety jig. All night meetings were cancelled this week. If it was Wednesday night I was watching *West Wing*."

"Did you know that your car was seen at Holy Comforter on both nights? It was parked out in front on the north side."

"That's impossible. I told you, I was home all night on both nights. The car was parked right outside, like it is now, on the driveway."

Holy Comfort

"Do you always leave your keys in the ignition?" asked Merton, trying to make eye contact with her through the haze of blue smoke.

Gracie coughed and waved her hand idly through the smoke. "I don't know...I suppose fairly often. No one's going to steal that piece of crap, not in this neighborhood."

"So it is possible that someone could have borrowed your car on those two nights? Has anyone ever done that before? Borrowed your car?"

Gracie looked puzzled, then her eyes opened a millimeter wider for a second only and she coughed. She stubbed out her cigarette in her saucer. "Well, I don't know. It's possible. But I really can't remember—"

"Please try," said Merton.

"I don't remember," she said curtly.

"Then we'll have to assume it was you who drove it over to Holy Comforter on the nights of October eighth and fourteenth," Vesba said amiably. She scribbled something in her notebook as Gracie looked on, concern wrinkling her forehead. She tapped her pack of Pall Malls against her hand and extracted another cigarette.

"Look," Gracie said, her cigarette bobbing between her lips as she spoke and simultaneously attempted to light it. "I was home Thursday night. I watched television. I fell asleep. Same for Wednesday. If someone borrowed my car, I didn't know anything about it. It could have been anyone. It could have been Page Hawthorne."

Vesba snorted and stood up. She faced Gracie with her hands on her hips, leaning forward slightly. "Oh bullshit, it was Page Hawthorne. You know damn well it wasn't Page Hawthorne and I for one am sick and tired of being sent on these wild goose chases after Page Hawthorne. You're the one who started us on the Page Hawthorne-had-the-hots-for-Costello snipe hunt in the first place. None of it was true. You and your pathetic cronies just thought it was funny, didn't you? Well, I don't give a rat's ass what you think is funny, Ms. Griggs. I just want to know who borrowed your car or you could find yourself locked up. Understand?"

Gracie stared, the cigarette momentarily forgotten and hanging limply from her parted lips, as Vesba leaned over the table, her pendulous breasts heaving. "Are you threatening me?" Gracie asked, her eyes narrowing.

"You're damn right," said Vesba more calmly. "All fingers point at you right now, so it's in your own personal interest to tell us what you know. If you can remember, that is."

"Go to hell, Detectives," she said as she looked straight at Vesba. "You're bluffing and you know it. You don't have a thing. If you did, you'd be reading me my rights."

Merton, who had watched his partner's explosive performance in silence, said, "I wouldn't be so sure, Ms. Griggs. Do you know what an accessory is?"

"Do I know..." she began and then faltered. She reached for the pack of cigarettes on the table, shook one out, then remembered that she had one in her mouth already. "I'm no accessory. *I don't know anything.* You're crazy as well as incompetent."

"It's just a matter of time, Ms. Griggs," said Merton calmly.

"If someone took my car, I had no idea..." she said, her voice rising.

"Then it would be a shame if you took the fall," said Vesba. "Maybe you better try and find out who took your car. Prison is no place for a lady like you."

Holy Comfort

Chapter Forty-Three

THERE WERE NEARLY four times as many people in attendance at the funeral of Bradford Cole than at the funeral of Miles Costello five days earlier. This was not because Brad Cole had been more popular than Miles—in fact, probably the opposite was true—but because of his social position in the community. The members of every board he had ever sat upon were there, the members of his clubs were there, fellow alumni of his schools were there, his business partners and employees were there. The entire vestry was there. His former wives were in attendance as were his children and stepchildren.

The two remaining priests from Holy Comforter officiated, supported by a former senator who was also an ordained Episcopal priest and a priest from Chicago who had flown in for the occasion. Three bagpipers preceded the empty coffin into the church, a fact which Page noted was probably a bad sign that the rector's power was slipping as he had formerly forbidden the presence of pipers in the sanctuary. Maybe it didn't mean anything—perhaps, she thought, he just didn't care anymore. The full choir sang during communion accompanied by a small chamber orchestra. The Bishop gave the homily.

Holy Comforter, it could be said, put on its finest show, and those in attendance, resplendent in fur and gold jewelry, were appreciative. Undoubtedly, a few potential members would show up on Sunday, having been moved deeply by the ritual, pomp and pageantry of Bradford Cole's funeral. There were plenty of people there, Page guessed, who were there to see who else was there. Morey Nieman, the local paper's gossip columnist, sat to the side, taking notes. It was a temptation to look around, but Page suppressed her own inclination and tried not to think of her neighbors being seduced in that way.

The two detectives, Vesba and Merton, stood in the back of the church on the opposite side. Page could see Detective Vesba because the purple dress she wore stood out like a Mardi Gras hat in a sea of black.

Page sat alone in the back row on the Gospel side. She stood up, sat down and knelt along with the rest of the congregation, but she did not participate in the service. She knew somehow that she would never worship in this church again. She prayed for the rector, hoping he would not stumble or misspeak during the service. He was not in top form and there were plenty of important people who would call him on it—the senior warden, for one. She looked up the long center aisle to Richardson Bell, tall and sleek and polished, sitting in a prominent place for all to see. He had arrived early, making a show of praying on his knees for fifteen minutes. *God have mercy on his soul*, thought Page. *God have mercy on all our souls.*

Less than a week had passed since Miles' funeral when she had been oppressed and weighed down by the sensate experience of evil in the sanctuary. Today she was not incapable of participating—she could produce a sound, she could move. She felt no nausea. What then was it? Was it the desire to flee, to escape? She had to stay this time; she could not run out with those detectives watching at the back of the sanctuary. *Teach us to sit still even among these rocks...Our peace in His will and even among these rocks...Suffer me not to be separated and let me cry Come unto Thee.* She recited the words of the half-remembered poem inwardly like a prayer. She calmed down. She sat. The service ended. She sat with her hands folded, waiting for everyone to leave. She had no desire to attend the reception, to be seen, to chat and reminisce; she felt no desire to move at all now. And so she sat for a long time. The green-jacketed ladies collected the funeral bulletins and straightened the pew cushions and turned out the lights. As she sat in the dark, she knew that someone was watching her. She turned around but no one was there.

Finally Page stood up, ready at last to leave the sactuary. She would walk through the reception. She would stop only if someone spoke to her. It was a fairly safe bet she could make it without being noticed.

She stood at the entrance to the Great Hall and, like a swimmer poised on the starting block, took a deep breath and dived in. Passing through the tightly packed bodies demanded some careful maneuvering, but the well-groomed, impeccably dressed people took little notice of Page. Snatches of conversation heard here and there as she moved silently through the animated crowd sounded like cocktail party chatter. Muffled laughter suggested that everyone was enjoying themselves, and indeed, it was an occasion for many people, who might not have seen each other, perhaps since the last large funeral, to become reacquainted.

"Oh my God, the addition is taking nine months to complete. I could have had a child in the time it's taken! But we just could not live with the house the way it was..."

"No, we're skipping Naples this year. We're going to Sea Island with the Haylocks...I know, aren't they? But their house is gorgeous..."

"Do you think? Honestly? I might have to try the lyposuction behind my knees, too. Weezie looks fabulous..."

"Oh, yes, fantastic. I always say Holy Comforter does a funeral like no other church in town...although I could do without communion. It just makes the whole thing go on forever..."

Page had almost made it to the other side of the room and the safety of the kitchen door, when she felt a hand on her arm and a shrill voice in her

Holy Comfort

ear. "Oh, here's Page Hawthorne! She can fill us in on what's going on!" It was Chelsea Milne, with whom she had graduated from high school, and two other classmates, Julie Dillard and Nancy Gray. "Page, you look fabulous! Do tell us what's going on here."

"Yes!" chimed Julie. "This is too creepy."

When Page did not immediately respond, Nancy reached out to touch her hand and say, "Page, this must be so hard on you," in a good immitation of a caring tone. "We're so sorry."

"Oh, yes, we're so sorry," agreed Chelsea and Julie, nodding.

"I remember how close you and Brad were for a while," said Nancy eyeing Page and mentally adding up how much her outfit cost.

"I really can't tell you much of anything," she muttered. "I'm sorry."

"But, Page, you *must* know something. You still work here, don't you?" whined Chelsea, showing a lot of bright, chemically-whitened teeth.

"I hear Pinkney's really taking it hard," said Julie too eagerly. "He sure messed up a few times today."

Chelsea and Nancy's heads bobbed in agreement. "You know, I just think he should be able to hold up better," commented Chelsea, flipping her hair in a much-practiced gesture. "*It's his job* after all. He's paid to perform just like anyone else. Just because he's a minister doesn't mean he can slack off."

Page crossed her arms defensively and shifted her weight.

"Clyde Cullen would have risen to the occasion," said Nancy. Julie and Chelsea nodded, concurring.

Page stared for a few seconds at their synchronized heads and then unloaded a dazzling smile on her former classmates. "Well, it was fabulous to see you girls, but I've got to dash off."

"But wait, Page," said Chelsea, a new light in her eyes. "Where's that detective? The one I've heard so much about. He's supposed to be real cute."

"Oh, yes," said Julie. "We want to look at him."

Page looked around the room quickly. "I don't see him."

"Oh, Page just wants to keep him all to herself!" laughed Julie. Chelsea nudged her.

Page froze. "Look, I've really…"

"What's the hurry, Page?" asked Nancy stepping forward. "Can't you spare a few minutes for your old friends? We never see you anymore since you moved away to…Rockville. We see Chester. He seems to be doing well. He was so broken up after you two split, but he's rallied. Don't you think?" Julie and Chelsea nodded.

"I'd love to talk," said Page, "but I've got to get back to work."

"Oh, yes, your *work*. In that case," Nancy said, touching her shoulder lightly and pointing to the table in the center of the room. "I think that cookie tray needs to be filled."

Julie and Chelsea blinked and exchanged glances.

"I'll be sure to check on that," replied Page, smiling again. "Goodbye now." She headed off toward the kitchen and disappeared.

The kitchen was warm and inviting, the pots and pans hanging from the ceiling and the trays, utensils, foil and food spread on the counter, all indicative of the good, nurturing work that went on there. Page poured herself a cup of coffee and leaned against the metal counter next to Demetrius Barton who was busily filling the dishwasher.

"Nice service?" he asked, glancing over at her.

"Very nice. Lots of people—the church was packed. I guess Bradford Cole would have liked that."

"Yes, indeed, I believe he would have," agreed the sexton. He paused in his work and looked at Page. "Mr. Cole was an old-fashioned kind of gentleman. The kind who treats the help well and says, 'Demetrius, my friend, how are you?' like I should be impressed that he remembered my name. But he'd say all manner of rude things to Mr. Pinkney and *curse* like it was real amusing to make him flinch. Man, how that man could curse." He turned back to the dishes. "But I guess he was a nice enough guy."

"Yes. He was nice enough," Page agreed, but she was thinking about something else.

Demetrius looked over his shoulder. "You finished with that cup? I got room for one more."

"Sure," she said, taking a last sip and placing it in the tray. She hesitated a moment. "Dee, did you happen to see my ex-husband in the Great Hall? I didn't, but I know he must be here."

"I seen him. Over in the corner with the senior warden and Charlotte Pentecost hanging on his arm." He pushed the tray into the stainless steel machine, closed the door and turned it on.

"In that case I think I'll exit stage left." She rolled her eyes toward the side door.

He smiled. "I guess I better go check on how those cookies are holding up. I've never seen people eat more cookies. This is one hungry crowd."

Page smiled at the sexton as he pushed into the Great Hall, then headed to the door that led to the Lodge Room where she hoped to bypass the reception and Chester. As she pushed open the swinging door she immediately regretted her choice. At a round table in the middle of the room sat the two detectives, the senior warden, and the rector. Merton sat facing her, his expression grim, and their eyes met. Immediately, Page lowered her eyes and backed quickly through the door, heading toward another exit which led out of the kitchen and into the alleyway behind the church. She lurched out the door and ran straight into Harry Rose who leaned against the building smoking an unfiltered cigarette.

"Sorry, Harry!" Page exclaimed. Her heart was pounding.

"Now where are you going in such a hurry?" He laughed.

"Oh. I'm just in search of some fresh air. There's a real shortage of it at that reception."

Holy Comfort

"Yeah. That's why I'm out here. If one more person comes through that door asking for something...I don't know what the attraction is, but people just can't stay out of the kitchen."

Page smiled. She could think of several witty comebacks, but she was weary of wit. Just being with "those people," just passing through, wore her out. She remembered when being clever and sophisticated had seemed important to her, but somewhere along the way she had realized that being witty frequently hinged on being hurtful. Being funny had been the basis of her popularity all through school. The ability to turn a comic phrase, to mimic, to tease, and ultimately demean had made her a force to be reckoned with. It had given her power in a community where gaiety and irony were valued above all else. It was easy, teasing Harry Rose, so she refrained and probably disappointed him in the process. "I've got to get back to my office," she explained, heading down the alley toward the church playground.

"He's an ex-Marine. Did you know that?" Harry called after her.

"What?" she asked, his non sequitor confusing her and causing her to stop in her tracks. "Who?"

"The detective. He's a Marine. In my book, that's something."

She stared at him, not sure how to reply.

"We've had a few talks. He's a nice boy," he said, stubbing out his cigarette on the ground. "Well, I like him. Give him time and he'll clear all this up," he said vaguely.

"I hope so," she said, wrapping her black cashmere sweater tightly around her.

"Turning cold," stated Harry as he looked up at the slate gray sky. As long as she had known him, Page had never seen him wear a coat, only a flannel shirt at the most. He was wearing a white t-shirt at the moment. "I guess I'll go in, too."

THE IMPROMPTU MEETING in the Lodge Room was not going well. The senior warden fumed as the rector sat dazed and unresponsive, seemingly oblivious to the bombastic threats of his warden and friend. The service had taken its toll on Charles Pinkney and he wished to be at home and in prayer. He needed desperately to be alone.

Vesba was also uncharacteristically quiet. Her silence reflected, more than anything, her boredom with the players in the game. She thought the senior warden was arrogant and opportunistic. Although he professed loyalty to the rector, she did not for one moment trust the man and she thought Charles Pinkney was a fool to do so. She considered the rector to be weak and secretly she thought his future in serious question. Richardson Bell was not about to go down in flames with anyone. He'd be the first rat to leave this sinking ship. And the ship *was* sinking. One murder, she knew, had been bad enough, but with time it might have been forgotten. The second murder, this time of a parishioner, signaled real trouble and doom, she was sure, for the rector. It was strange, she thought, but no one seemed to be really concerned with solving the actual crimes, only with maintaining equilibrium.

The appearance of Page Hawthorne had been jarring to all, but particularly unsettling to Merton who sank afterwards to a heretofore unknown level of verbal ineptitude. He remained sullenly silent and the surprise appearance of former warden, Mayor Willis McHugh, had further disrupted the meeting.

"Well, Gentlemen," the mayor said, ignoring the hard-to-ignore presence of Detective Vesba. "I've just had an interesting conversation with Morey Nieman about a tidbit of news he hoped to include in his next column." He waited before continuing. All eyes except Merton's were aimed at him. "It concerns you, Roy."

Merton slowly raised his eyes and looked McHugh squarely in the face, which was what the mayor wanted. "It concerns you and one of our own, a staff member, Page Hawthorne."

"What?" asked Richardson Bell. "Go on, Will. Go on. Don't draw this out."

"Well, Rich. It seems there's a rumor that our esteemed detective and Ms. Hawthorne have been hitting it off rather well, spending a lot of time together—even at night."

"Is that true, Detective?" asked Bell, turning his attention to Merton.

"We had dinner together Wednesday night. We talked about the case," Roy answered mildly.

Vesba watched her partner closely. The rector, who had been idly drawing on a pad of paper, straightened up and looked at the mayor.

"What's the matter, Charles?" snapped McHugh eyeing the rector critically. "I seem to have surprised you."

The rector said, "Yes. I am a bit surprised."

"*Will,*" interrupted Bell impatiently. "Did you get Nieman to promise not to print that? We can't have Holy Comforter's name associated with gossip of such a low type."

"Low type?" asked Vesba, breaking her silence. "Having dinner with a detective automatically puts you in the gutter?"

Bell ignored her question and continued distractedly, "Hawthorne always was a lightening rod. She does a good job but anyone could do what she does. It isn't rocket science…I'll have to talk to her…maybe get her to take a long vacation…"

"No. Don't talk to her," interjected the rector. "There's no reason to talk to her. She's done nothing wrong. Neither has Detective Merton. You're jumping to conclusions here. I'd like to know where Mr. Nieman heard this rumor. Who knew about this?"

"He wouldn't name his source," replied McHugh calmly. "But it seems to be circulating fast."

"I still think I should talk to Page," said Bell. "She'll listen to me."

Holy Comfort

"If you talk to her, she'll sue your ass," said Vesba, tired of being ignored. "I know I would."

Bell, McHugh and the rector all turned their heads in unison at the mention of the word "sue" in order to stare at Vesba who smirked brashly and folded her arms across her chest. They blinked. Then McHugh turned once again to Merton and said, "Well, it's all been taken care of anyway—Nieman's easy enough to deal with—I just hope you'll confine your investigations to the murder and concentrate on the case." He paused a moment to see if the rector would respond, but when Charles reverted to his pad, he said, "Roy? Do we understand each other?"

"I *was* concentrating on the case, Mr. Mayor," said Merton evenly. "And I know who started and spread the rumors. It's all coming together just as Leona and I planned."

"You want us to believe you planned this whole thing?" asked McHugh sarcastically, snorting loudly.

"Believe what you want," said the detective. He still had not moved and his eyes reflected a dead calm.

Vesba smirked, despite efforts to the contrary. The rector shook his head wearily and thought about Page, his mind spiraling back to his conversations with Merton and with Colin. Senior Warden Bell said, "Well, I for one am glad to hear someone has a plan. I just want to stress once again how we want to avoid adverse publicity. We can't afford any more publicity."

"And no more murders," said McHugh cheerfully. "How about no more murders?"

"CHARLOTTE!" HISSED GRACIE Griggs as she grabbed the younger woman's arm and pulled her back to face her. "I've got to talk to you!"

"Gracie, dear, you look a fright! Calm yourself!" Charlotte looked down on the other woman's upturned face. It was strained, the eyes wide. She could smell liquor on Gracie's breath. "*What is it?*"

"Come back here," Gracie whispered, pointing to the dark hallway which led from the kitchen to the sextons' office. Charlotte obeyed. They stood huddled, half in the china closet, out of the way of anyone who might enter the kitchen.

"Your friends paid me a little visit early this morning. I wasn't even dressed yet. I hadn't had my coffee...they were sniffing around in my driveway and in my yard. They were particularly fascinated by my car and my...my barbeque..."

"What? You're not making any sense, Gracie. Who came to see you?"

"*The detectives*—they asked me where I was on the night *before* Miles was killed. They said my car was seen at church that night—late after everyone else had left..."

"How would they..."

"Who cares *how* they know? They just know..."

"Bay..." whispered Charlotte to herself.

"*I was home.* That's the point. I was home. I never drove my car to church. I didn't have to be there...why would I be there?" Gracie was talking fast now, hardly stopping to breathe. She pressed closer to Charlotte and grabbed her hands. "*Charlotte.* Did you borrow my car? Did *you* take my car? You've done that before. *Tell me—*"

"Why on earth would I take your car, Grace dear?" Charlotte said slowly. She shook her hands free and jammed them into the pockets of her navy sweater. "You're not making any sense." She looked over Gracie's head into the china closet.

"You didn't come in Friday morning. You told Tammy you were having car problems."

"And I *was* having car trouble...on Friday morning. Not on Thursday night."

"But who had my car?" cried Gracie. "They say I'm an accessory. I could go to jail! I can't go to jail. Help me, Charlotte!"

"Stop it, Grace, you fool," snapped Charlotte. Her tone was brutal now, her eyes hard and unforgiving.

Gracie Griggs stopped abruptly, swallowing her words in mid-thought. She was looking straight at Charlottte when Charlotte slapped her hard across the face. Her hands flew to her face and she shrunk back against the door of the closet, rattling cups and saucers.

"If you're under suspicion, dear, you musn't fall to pieces. There, there, now," said Charlotte, changing her tone again and patting Gracie's shoulder fondly. "I'm sorry I struck you, but it was for your own good. You've got to control yourself, and you'd better stay off the sauce for a while. You don't want the police to see you like this. You look guilty...you look pathetic."

"Charlotte, what shall I do? What about my car?"

"What about it? All you know is that you parked it in the driveway, right? You were home—Morris has corroborated that, hasn't he? Just stick to the truth, dear. The truth."

"Yes. I don't know anything. I was home," Gracie murmured as she rubbed her cheek. "I don't know anything. I told them anyone could have taken my car—even Page Hawthorne."

"Dear God, Grace, you've got to stop making those wild references to Page Hawthorne. That won't win you any popularity contests around here."

Gracie wasn't listening. She continued to rub her face as if she couldn't remember whose face it was. "I think I'll go home now. I can make calls from home."

"Yes, dear, you do that," said Charlotte as she put her hands on Gracie's hunched shoulders and directed her back into the kitchen. "Have a nice rest at home. I'll call you later."

Holy Comfort

After they were both gone, the door to the office slowly opened and Demetrius Barton came out into the hall. He stood there for several minutes thinking before he closed the door, locked it and walked out of the kitchen.

"Detectives," said Willis McHugh sharply. Vesba and Merton stopped short as they hurried to the door and escape. When they turned to face him, he continued in a more amicable tone, "May I have a word with you?"

They waited. He approached them smiling. He touched Vesba's elbow in a friendly way, turning her into the center of their circle, and lowered his head to speak in a hushed voice, forcing Merton to lower his head in order to hear. "I hope you two weren't blowing smoke back there about having a plan, because we're drawing way too much fire over this second murder. I've got to say we have some mighty worried parishioners here."

"Why is anyone worried?" Vesba asked.

"Oh. Come now, Detective. First Costello. Then poor Cole. Both with mysterious burning body parts and sinister lectionary connections. Everyone's scurrying to their Bibles looking for clues to find out whose ass is next."

"Who else has a reason to be worried?" asked Merton. "Anyone in particular?" He studied McHugh from a height advantage of seven inches. The top of the mayor's bald head, he noted, was sweating.

The mayor looked up. "Oh, I was speaking generally, of course. How would I know anything in particular that you don't know?"

"How indeed," said Vesba, crossing her arms across her chest. She was aware that her armpits were sopping.

McHugh looked back and forth at both of them and, stepping forward so that his head nearly touched theirs as they bent to listen, he said, "A word to the wise, Detectives. Shift into overdrive and put an end to this investigation or your futures may be in serious question and we may be discussing your career options the next time we meet." He stepped back then and looked up. "Do we understand each other?"

The detectives nodded.

"Good afternoon, Detective Vesba," he said, dismissing her. "It's always a pleasure."

She glanced at her partner as she turned on her heel and left, wasting no time. Merton did not acknowledge her, but stared icily at the mayor.

When the door had closed behind Vesba, the mayor narrowed his eyes and said, "I thought you were smarter than this, Roy. I thought you knew your place."

"My place?"

"Everyone's got their place, Roy. Your boss, Falcon's, got his place. He's county executive because I said so. We play golf every Tuesday at the club I got him into. It's not my club, but it's the next best."

"I don't follow."

"Let's just say I wouldn't want to see another of my friends killed because of you. You screw Page Hawthorne on your own time."

Merton did not blink, but his jaw was working.

"And don't give me any more shit about a plan. You two don't have a plan. You never did."

"We do, sir. We have a plan."

"Don't fuck with me, Roy. I know bullshit when I hear it."

Merton suddenly put his hands in his pockets and smiled. He threw his head back and laughed.

"What's so funny, Detective?" the mayor asked cautiously.

"Oh, it's just a picture that came to me," Merton said.

"*What* picture?"

Merton stared at the mayor who stared back at him, brows knitted, unsmiling. Then the detective smiled again slowly and said, "Oh, it's a picture of you, sir, and your small group when you meet again, if you meet again. You're actually praying."

"Hey, Detective," called Tony Spitz, stopping Roy as he hastened to leave the building following his dismissal from the Lodge Room. "Might I have a word with you?"

"Yes?" said Merton noncommittally. He did not try to conceal the fact that he was annoyed at being caught inside the building. He was in no mood now to trade banter with vestry member Spitz. He desperately wanted to get out of there. He loosened his tie.

"Sorry to bother you when you're so busy, but I was wondering how things are going," said Spitz, full of concern. "You and your partner weren't exactly forthcoming last night. I hear Willis McHugh is fit to be tied. You think maybe he's worried about being next on the hit list?"

Merton considered the overly eager and inappropriately curious Spitz, waiting a moment before saying, "Or maybe you are."

"Me?" Spitz exclaimed, his hands slapping his chest. "No way. I was kidding about a hit list…unless you think…is there really some connection with the small group? Is that it?"

"Did the members of your small group do something that would make someone want to kill them?"

Spitz had blanched. "No," he stammered. "Absolutely not."

Merton gazed over Spitz's head and exhaled. "Then you have nothing to worry about. But all this conjecture by the parish isn't helping us solve the case."

"No, I suppose not," said Spitz defensively. "But, then, neither is your romancing Page Hawthorne. Everyone's heard about you two. It's all over the church."

"People will say anything."

Holy Comfort

"Oh no. I've heard it from more than one person. In fact, I just heard it in the Great Hall from Chester Hawthorne. He asked me if I knew anything about some Jeff-co cop who was hitting on his ex-wife."

"I'm not from Jefferson County."

"Well, that's beside the point."

Merton took a step toward Spitz. "The point being..."

Spitz inhaled and tipped his chin up. "The point being you're paying more attention to her than to the case. Of course, I'm not saying you've been successful," he said, stepping back as Roy stood up straight and unloaded his metallic stare on Tony's watery blue eyes.

"What *are* you saying?"

"Just that better men than you have tried and failed where Page Hawthorne is concerned. Everyone knows she's an ice queen." Spitz chuckled man-to-man. "Poor old Chester—he really had a time...some say she's a lesbian...some—" His next words were cut off as the detective grabbed his collar and shoved him hard into the tangle of hangers suspended from the built-in coat rack behind him.

"Get your hands off me!" Spitz squeeled, attempting to rally his nerves as he feebly endeavored to extricate himself from the hangers. "Who do you think you're trying to push around?"

"I'm not *trying* to push anyone around," he replied, giving Spitz a final shove. He stumbled into the hangers again. "You should try to be more careful," said Merton. "You could get hurt." He turned then and headed out the south exit, pausing to hold the door for a young woman grasping a red-haired toddler by the hand.

The cold air hit Merton hard in the face as he exited the building and hesitated at the top step. He searched the sky which was gray and ominous with low hanging rain clouds. The temperature had dropped considerably since his arrival at the church a few hours earlier. The weather was like that, changing rapidly and precipitously. Just like people.

Scanning the street for his partner's car, he realized that most of the funeral-goers had departed, leaving only a few groups of two to three people standing around. In one of the groups, at the point of the wedge of land where Holy Comforter was located, stood Page Hawthorne and a tall blond man he recognized as her ex-husband, Chester Hawthorne. The man was smoking a cigarette and gesticulating. Page was hugging herself as if she were cold and looking off in the opposite direction. The man was speaking loudly and even at a distance of one hundred yards, Merton could hear snatches of his diatribe. "What will people think, Page? I repeat, what...will...people...think? *Don't you care?* Don't you even care?"

"Oh, shit," sighed the detective, realizing that Vesba's car was parked on the far side of the gesticulating man. Inside the car his partner gazed into a compact mirror, oblivious to the drama unfolding in front of her. Merton was not about to head back inside or take the long way around, so he leapt down the stairs in two strides and loped off towards the car. As he approached it, thinking maybe he might actually make it unnoticed, Page turned around and saw him. She quickly turned back and interrupted Chester. "I'm freezing to death and I've got work to do—"

"I'm not finished—" cut in her ex-husband.

"I don't care. You haven't said one new thing since your last lecture. *So goodbye.*"

"Not so fast, Page, and look at me when I'm talking to you! I want you to tell me you won't see this asshole again."

"What concern is it of yours if I do or I don't?" she asked. Without waiting for a reply, she turned and took a step toward the church. He cut her off by standing in front of her, moving to within an inch of her body. He was tall and his chest met her at eye-level. It was an aggressive stance and when Page tried to move again, he moved with her, blocking her escape.

"Son of a bitch," whispered Merton, watching from behind the car.

"Get out of my way," Page said softly, reluctant to make a scene. "Please, Chester, just move." When he stood firm, Page tried again. "You can't tell me what to do anymore. Why can't you just mind your own business?"

"It is my business as long as you have custody of my sons," he said, taking a step closer and pushing her slightly with his body. "It's my business if you're making a laughing stock of yourself while you neglect them to sleep with some cop. Jesus, no one could talk about anything else in there. 'Did you hear about Page Hawthorne and some cowboy cop?' The absurdity of it astounds even the worst, most brain-dead idiots among them. It might even be funny if it weren't so humiliating. I mean if he's the same one who came to my office, you really must be desperate. Can't you do better than that, Page?"

Merton exhaled and realized he had been holding his breath. He began to move around the car, but stopped when he noticed Demetrius Barton laying down a rake in a pile of leaves, and beginning to move towards the couple.

Chester, taking another step and pushing Page again, did not notice Demetrius coming up behind him until he had a hand on his shoulder. "Excuse me," he said, moving Chester aside politely. "But Page, you have a phone call. Tammy said it was urgent."

"Oh," Page replied distractedly. "I better go."

As she turned and jogged off, Chester called after her, "We'll finish this conversation later. I'm not finished." Demetrius mumbled something, and Chester, reminded of his presence, swung around. "What?" he said.

"I said, she just a little bitty thing. You shouldn't be pushing her, man."

Chester looked myopically along his nose at the sexton. "What fucking business could it possibly be of yours? You're the fucking janitor, for God's sake."

Demetrius drew himself up and glared at the smirking man in front of him. "That's right, man," he replied. "You know me." He turned and strolled back to his pile of leaves.

Holy Comfort

"Hey, you wait," called Chester, his hands on his hips. "If you've been raking, how did you know Page had an urgent call?"

"Oh, I made that up," said Demetrius. He smiled innocently. "I figured that was better than kicking your butt."

Chester paused for a beat, started to make a mental note and then abandoned the idea. Then without a word or a change of expression, he turned and scanned the street for his car. His eyes took in the tall man staring in his direction over the top of an old Ford, but they continued to scan the street, paying him no attention. Where had he parked his damn Infiniti? Then, remembering that he had left it over on the other side of the church in front of Martha Van Patton's house, he started off in that direction. "Goddam waste of time," he muttered as he threw yet another cigarette onto the sidewalk.

Demetrius Barton watched Chester walk up the sidewalk until he was out of sight, and then, with a shrug, resumed his raking.

Merton opened the passenger door, but closed it again. He motioned to Vesba to stay put. He crossed the lawn and stopped in front of the man with the rake. "Can we talk?" the detective asked.

The sexton stopped raking and looked up. His eyes met the detective's. He did not smile. "What about?"

"You handled that well," said Merton, gesturing with his thumb in the direction Chester Hawthorne had taken.

"You were watching?" said Demetrius scanning the street.

"Yes."

"He's an asshole," he said with feeling.

The detective nodded. "And Page Hawthorne? What's she to you?"

"A real nice lady."

"You seem to be around a lot when she needs help," said the detective, folding his arms and resting his weight on one leg.

The sexton stared blankly at the detective, his chin raised, while his hands squeezed and released the rake handle, turning it slowly. Then he expelled air and resumed raking. "Page Hawthorne can take care of herself. She would of gotten rid of that bastard eventually. I just got sick of listening to his bullshit. I figured she was, too. Lately she's...she's a little fragile is all."

"Fragile," said Merton.

"That's right," the sexton said and stopped raking. "Fragile."

"Implying she might break?" said Merton. "I think I'd give her more credit than that."

"I'm not saying she's weak," he said. "It's just that she's a disappointed lady who works hard and goes home every night and cooks dinner for her two boys. And one morning she comes to work and finds a dead body stinking of death and scorched hair and skin and she gets sick and someone at the staff meeting makes a big joke of it and of her. And some big studly cop comes on the scene and listens to every eccentric idiot spouting their diseased babble. He acts real nice and interested and sniffs around and cozies up, but all he wants to really know is who killed the priest."

"Who do you think killed the priest, Demetrius?"

"How would I know?" He resumed raking.

The detective looked up at the overcast sky. The wind had picked up, making the sexton's job more of a challenge. "You don't like me."

"Do I got to like you?"

"No," he said quietly. "And no one's blaming you for keeping an eye on Page Hawthorne, especially since…did you know Miles Costello was bothering her? Maybe you didn't like that."

"He was an asshole, too," Demetrius said, throwing his rake down. "He had women coming and going. He had them *in his office*. But that wasn't enough. He wanted her…"

"Who did he have in his office, Demetrius? Who?"

The sexton placed his hands on his hips and looked off down the street. He breathed loudly. "That rich bitch with the fur coat. Ellen something and—"

"And who, Demetrius?"

"There were others. I tried to stay out of his way."

"Did Costello know that you'd seen him?"

"How could he not know? He *liked* people to know."

"Did the rector know?"

"He's too busy praying to look around and see what's going on at his church. He's looking the other way all the time."

"Intentionally?"

"No. He's a good man. Too good. His wife might of known."

"Adair Pinkney knew? How?"

Demetrius looked at the sky. "It's going to rain."

"How did Adair Pinkney know? Was she there?"

The sexton glared at the detective. "I might of told her. She wanted to know what he was up to. She was thinking about hiring a private investigator, you know, with hidden cameras and all, but she knew her husband would never go for any of that so—"

"*Who else*?" said Merton patiently. "If you know what other women he was with, it's time to tell. Two men are already dead and who knows who else might be in danger."

Demetrius sighed. "Charlotte. He had Charlotte Pentecost. They were loud."

"When? When did they do it?"

"At night. Usually Thursdays. After her meeting."

"Pretty regular?"

"For a while."

"What about that last Thursday—the night before the murder?"

"She was around. He wasn't. She was mighty sore." Demetrius bent to pick up the rake. "It's starting to rain. I've got to hurry."

"So it is," agreed the detective. "Thank you, Mr. Barton."

Holy Comfort

The sexton looked up. "You're welcome," he said. Then the rain began to pelt them and they parted.

"When the hell were you going to include me in your plans, partner?" asked Leona through clenched teeth. She scowled at the church through the windshield of the car.

"What was I supposed to say? That we have no plan? You know very well what I was talking about. Charlotte Pentecost has been spreading those rumors, probably with the aid of her two weird sisters, Griggs and Dunwoody."

"Gossip, Inc.," she said, smirking. "And you were implying that our plan was to set up Page Hawthorne to draw out Charlotte Pentecost so she'd show us her cards, i.e. the pattern you were talking about of her taking what Hawthorne rejects?"

He nodded. "Not in so many words, but that's what happened. Why not credit it a plan?"

"But we didn't..."

"No, it was a hunch. But there were too many coincidences not to notice a pattern."

"When did you put this all together—all these coincidences?"

"Thursday night. I talked to Page Hawthorne again on Thursday night. She—"

"Thursday night? When *the hell* were you going to get around to sharing this with me?"

"I'm sharing with you now."

"I am so pissed with you," she said, fumbling with a mystical array of cosmetics in her purse. "I have never been so fucking pissed with you as I am now. We've got McHugh on our backs because of you. We've got—"

"There's something else," he said. "Tony Spitz let something slip to me just now. He joked about a hit list and McHugh being worried he was next. When I said something about *him* being worried, he got really nervous and asked if there really is a connection with his small group. There *is* a connection."

"We talked to all those guys. There was nothing."

"Page hinted that Costello was a pimp of sorts—maybe he was pimping for the small group."

"But we've talked to every bastard in that small group. No one said a word about—"

"I know it seems pretty far-fetched," he said. "Barton just told me Thursdays were Costello and Charlotte Pentecost's special nights. He wasn't there that last Thursday night. She was mad. She probably paged him over and over—"

She zipped her bag conclusively. "How would they have kept anything like that quiet? Especially with Charlotte Pentecost involved?"

"Well, they didn't, in the end."

The two partners gazed out the windshield at the church. For Merton, the building he had once naively imagined to be a humble expression of devotion to God, he now considered an extravagant and pretentious exhibition of human pride. The place sickened him.

"It's got to come out sometime, doesn't it?" asked Vesba. "What they were doing, I mean. We're talking scandal, baby, big scandal."

"I think Mayor McHugh is confident that he can hush things up. Money talks, or conversely, shuts everybody up."

"In the meantime, who's next? Someone in the small group? Chester Hawthorne? *You*?"

He shook his head. "I don't know. I think we need to talk to someone in the small group again. Tony Spitz, for instance. He's the weakest unit on that list of losers. I say we lean hard."

"Now you're talking," said Vesba smiling. "The little bug should crack."

Holy Comfort

Chapter Forty-Four

THE ROOM IN the downtown office building was on the top floor and commanded a view of the riverfront. It was a dark room, paneled in walnut and decorated with murky oil paintings. In addition, all the wooden blinds were closed except for those on one window, which allowed the light from the late afternoon sun to fall on the man who sat at the head of the long mahogany conference table. The backlighting from the lone window cast the man in dark shadows, and as a result, his short, bullet-like stature took on an even more menacing character than usual.

The room and the building belonged to the man at the head of the table. It was his table. He did not use the building himself except to call occasional meetings like this one. The other offices in the building he leased at a very low rate to his A.A. buddies who needed a fresh start and a hand up. It was a very charitable thing to do. He was banking on it getting him into heaven...on the days when he believed in heaven.

"So what are we going to do about this problem?" asked Willis McHugh, directing his question to the seven men seated around the table. No one offered an answer, so he continued with more questions. "Do we leave the investigation to the police? Do we hire our own private detectives? Do we wait around for another one of us to get killed? Do we have any ideas about the identity of the murderer? Do we deal with the murderer ourselves? What?"

The seven men stole furtive glances at each other and at McHugh, then lowered their eyes. No one spoke.

"Oh, come on, men...we know someone has a vendetta against this group. I think we know who it is. We've all slept with her, except maybe Tully there," said McHugh, pointing to an older man dressed expensively in a gray suit and white starched shirt just like the other men in the room. "If Tully shows up dead, I'll revise my theory."

"Maybe..." began Tony Spitz before faltering and lowering his eyes.

"Maybe what?" barked McHugh.

"Maybe we should tell the detectives...about the group...what we know."

"Oh. Sure. Good idea, Tony. I can see the headlines: *Priest Pimps for Prayer Group Elite*. Are you crazy? We can take care of this ourselves."

"What if we're wrong?" asked Gordon Kelly. "What if she didn't do it?"

"Who else could it be? Do you have any bright ideas? Please...I want to hear," replied McHugh impatiently. His tone sent Kelly's eyes immediately toward the tabletop.

"It would be murder, Will. Murder, pure and simple," said Amos Peacock. "What happened to trial by jury?"

"This would be an eye for an eye. It would be self-defense. Who knows who's next...maybe you, Amos. Which of us can afford to wait and see?"

"I think Will is right. We have to act," suggested Alex Reardon. "We have to do something."

"We don't *have* to do anything," said Chester Hawthorne slowly. "It's not our job to *do* anything. We can protect ourselves now that we've been warned. We know who to look out for. We're not stupid."

"Neither were Miles and Bradford," put in Reardon.

"They were caught by surprise," answered Chester. "They didn't see her coming."

"Look," interrupted McHugh. "I'm tired of discussing this. We've brought down headmasters and sent rectors packing. We've fired foundation heads...we can take care of this problem. It's our duty. We'd be doing it for the good of Holy Comforter."

"We've never murdered anyone," shouted Tully suddenly, standing up.

"I'm not suggesting we do it ourselves," replied McHugh smoothly.

Tully, still standing, began to shake. "I'll be no party to murder. Leave me *out*," he said as he turned to leave.

McHugh shouted, "Tully!" stopping the older man in his tracks. McHugh quickly recovered his composure and lowered his voice. "By all means go, Tully. Leave with your conscience, but remember, if you're no party to this, you'll be out of the party entirely. Can you afford that? It would just take a word here and a word—"

"Shut up, Willis!" said Tully, throwing him a look of over-ripe contempt. He left the room then, followed by Gordon Kelly and Amos Peacock. The rest of the men seated around the table watched them go in silence.

"Now what, Will?" asked Chester. "You can't do anything now—if she shows up dead, you've got witnesses who'll say it was you."

"I can do plenty," McHugh stated calmly, only his narrowed brown eyes betraying his outrage. "Not to her maybe...but I can do plenty."

The remaining three men exchanged looks surreptitiously and Tony Spitz got nervously up to turn on the lights. While they argued, the sun had gone down and the room had grown dim and then suddenly dark. To sit in a dark room with Willis McHugh was impossible.

Holy Comfort

Chapter Forty-Five

THE RECTOR SAT by the fire and tried to read the book that he held loosely in his hands. He could not focus on the words; his mind wandered relentlessly, always returning to what Detective Merton had told him that afternoon about his conversation with Tony Spitz. He played it over and over, the hurtful words about the small group, Costello's small group, which had twisted the model he himself had introduced into an almost unrecognizable and unutterably vile and unholy version. *Horror has overwhelmed me...Oh, that I had the wings of a dove! I would fly away and be at rest...*Oh, fly away, fly away home. But there was no escape. He would have to face his congregation, his bishop.

He put the book down finally and closed his eyes. It was decent, anyway, of the detective to tell him. He didn't have to. He wondered when and how he had grown accustomed to being out of the loop. Why was he surprised when his authority was actually recognized? *Make me, O Lord, modest and humble, strong and constant, to observe the discipline of Christ...May I exalt you, O Lord, in the midst of your people...Grant that in all things I may serve without reproach.* He sighed. It was all a reproach to God. The entire parish was nothing but. He sighed again and opened his eyes.

Adair sat across from him now by the fire. Her cool blue eyes studied him. She smiled. "What are you thinking about, dear?"

"It's funny," he said. "I was thinking about Abraham and his bargaining with God, 'May the Lord not be angry, but let me speak just once more. What if only ten can be found there?'"

"Ten righteous men at Holy Comforter? Heavens, that might be a stretch."

"Exactly...*don't look back.*"

"You've done your best, Chick. That's all anyone can ask."

"I believe I was asked to do more than just my best at my ordination."

"Your best *is* good enough."

"I let what happened...happen. It all went on right under my nose!"

"How could you have known what was going on? You're overworked and understaffed, you're—"

"I was their shepherd! I left my sheep in the care of a wolf. I turned my back. I abandoned them."

"You did no such thing. You've done nothing wrong, Chick. Don't take on their guilt," said Adair, the color rising in her face.

"But their guilt *is* mine. I should have known. But I was always so offended by Charlotte—her vulgar tongue, her obnoxious personality. I turned away. I turned away from Miles."

"And no one can blame you."

"I can blame myself. I just didn't want to see what was going on."

"Page should have told you."

"Page had no idea of the extent of Miles' corruption and she was trying to protect me. Ironic, isn't it?"

"Yes," she said dully. "I suppose so. I knew myself, you know. Demetrius told me. I wanted to tell you, I wanted to *do* something, but I was afraid."

"Afraid of what?"

"Afraid of losing all this." She held out her hand and moved it in a wide arc. "Now *that's* ironic," she said. "Now you will be taken down with Miles, and there's nothing I can *do* anymore to stop it."

"And thank God for that."

"What do you mean?" she said. "You've committed no crime."

"But I have, don't you see? If there is no crime, there is no sin. The culture says what crime? There is no crime. We are all just victims. We all just make mistakes. The culture of carelessness, the culture of complaint—it is not *my* culture. *I have sinned*. I have offended against God's holy laws. I have left undone those things which I ought to have done; and I have done those things which I ought not to have done; and there is no health in *me*. I *am* a miserable offender. Perhaps the church sees its people as so virtuous these days, so spiritually healthy, that we don't need to be forgiven anymore—I say I need to take responsibility. *I need to be forgiven.*"

"Forgiven, yes. But we'll be turned out on the street. What about Colin and the staff? Miles will have won in the end, you know. He'll have wrecked the whole place and you with it. It's what he wanted. You can't let that happen."

"I'm going to talk to Hunt in the morning. I'll abide by whatever he says."

"Yes, but you've got to appear strong. Show him you've got everything under control."

"God chose the weak things of the world to shame the strong."

She looked at him and understood nothing. "You're not weak. You were never weak."

"God's grace is sufficient for me. For when I am weak, then I am strong."

"I don't understand," whispered Adair.

"It doesn't matter," he said, taking her hand and kneeling in front of her. "You'll understand later. You see, it's like the poet once said,

Holy Comfort

comfort is one and always the same for every human heart. We have no other comfort but the fear of God."

Chapter Forty-Six

"I'M NOT A fool, you know. I've watched enough police dramas on television—I know all about the good cop, bad cop routine. I know you think you'll be able to soften me up, lavishing those big bad eyes on me, and then you'll bring in fat ol' Detective Lesba to bring me to my knees. Don't try to deny it, Roy. That's the game plan."

Merton stretched out his long legs and crossed his arms. He stared at the tabletop, denying nothing.

"Is that a two-way mirror?" Charlotte asked gaily, pointing at a large rectangular mirror at the end of the room. "Do you really have one of those? Who's watching?" She waved at the mirror. "Hello! Why am I here? Isn't anyone going to talk to me?"

"Detective Vesba will be here any minute. We'll talk then."

"Well, *off the record*, Roy dear, can't we talk off the record?"

He looked directly at her for the first time. "I don't want to talk *off the record*."

She leaned forward. "Why do I repulse you so, Detective? I can hear your skin crawling."

He stared at her. "You don't repulse me."

"Spoken bravely," she said, settling back in her chair. "Like a man." She sighed and folded her hands. "All I have to do, you know, is call Clyde Cullen and he'll snap his fingers and one of Wilton Bartlett Burnbaum's best and brightest will race over here to hold my hand. Just one call. But I don't need to do that. I don't need anyone to hold *my* hand."

The detective smiled weakly.

"No, I'm not the hand-holding type. I can take care of myself."

The detective looked at the door and mirror and pictured his partner watching. She had not liked it that he wanted to try Pentecost alone. She had been very effective with Spitz. She was on a roll. She wanted a chance to break Charlotte. He stood up and drained his coffee cup and threw it in the wastebasket. He sat down.

"Tell me, Detective," said Charlotte opening her blue eyes a centimeter too wide. "Isn't Page Hawthorne the hand-holding type? I always

Holy Comfort

thought she would be, but I guess she didn't like it when you got a little rough. You shouldn't have bruised her. That was...careless."

The detective continued to stare.

"You won't catch this killer by being careless, Detective," she said as she leaned forward, her hands flat on the table. "You must be as careful as the killer." She straightened up and smiled. "Page Hawthorne is a very meticulous little lady, very careful about her appearance. So neat and scrubbed. So clean. Everything about her grooming perfect—except her nails. Have you ever noticed that, Detective?"

The detective did not answer.

"You must have—all those afternoons in her office. What were you looking at if not at her? What were you thinking about, if not about her?" Receiving no answer, Charlotte yawned. "Why don't you look at me," she said.

The detective blinked. "You just don't get enough attention, do you, Ms. Pentecost? You're like a little kid acting out constantly so that someone will at least yell at you, negative attention being better than no attention."

"I'm not a child."

"Well, then, like a teenage girl who sleeps around rather than not go out at all. Is that what you were like in high school? Were you the easy one, the one everybody on the football team passed around?"

"Do tell me about the football team, Detective," said Charlotte.

"We were talking about *you*, Ms. Pentecost," he said uneasily.

"Well, generalizations are never worth much," she said leaning back.

"I find that most people are pretty predictable. They make the same mistakes over and over."

"Oh really? What was your mistake, Detective Merton? Did you push too hard? Or not hard enough? You won't get a second chance with Page Hawthorne. She's famous for that, you know."

Merton sighed and folded his hands on the table. "I think that you and Costello must have been quite a pair, talking about everyone in the church, wishing you could be like them. You two weren't like *them*, but you were a lot alike, isn't that so?"

"I don't know where you got that idea. It's ridiculous," she said decisively. She turned away.

"Trouble is, you thought that meant more than he did. You thought *you* meant more...to him." He tried to pry her eyes away from the wall, but failed. "All those hours in his office, talking...then things got physical, didn't they, and you thought, *Oh, he's mine now*. You and Costello rutting like animals in the back of his crumby office up against the wall, the wall by Ms. Hawthorne's office. Do you think that excited him? Was he thinking of her when he was fucking you? Did he close his eyes and imagine it was her he was with? What was that like, I wonder, *for you?*"

Charlottte threw back her head and shrieked the forced laughter of a person well-practiced in simulated gaiety. "I don't know," she said as her elbows came out and her head came down. "You tell me!" She laughed again and reached forward to grasp his hands. Her nails, he noticed, were bitten to the quick. "*See*. I knew I could get you to talk! But you'll never get *me* to say anything, because I don't have anything to say! I told you that the first time we met. Remember, Detective? *Nothing's changed*."

"Something has changed, Charlotte," he said shaking free of her hands. He put his hands behind his head and stretched. "Someone has finally paid you the attention you deserve."

"You, Detective?" she asked sweetly.

He nodded. "You followed me the other night. Have you done that before?" He brought his hands down onto the table and folded them together. "Did you follow me Wednesday night? Were you watching outside her house? Did you check your watch and think, they're sitting down to drink tea now and talk. He's helping her off with her cowboy boots now, he's…"

She breathed in sharply and looked away. Her head bobbed a little. "Well, there you go, Detective. You're better than I thought. I didn't give you enough credit. What came off next? Her underwear or did you work it slowly?"

"You were watching," he said. She closed her eyes and sucked in her cheeks. "It's to your advantage to tell me, because if you were watching Page Hawthorne's house, you didn't kill Cole, did you?"

"I didn't kill Cole."

He sighed. "Who did, Charlotte?" She looked away. "We talked to Tony Spitz a little while ago, Charlotte," he said. She did not move. "He talked."

"The jig is up?" she said turning back to him. Her wide blue eyes narrowed. "I don't know what that means or what you're talking about. I hardly know Tony Spitz."

"He told us all about Costello's small group, Charlotte. He said they all know you—in the biblical sense."

"Oh, hah hah. Aren't you funny? Well, it's all nonsense, just a lot of crude little boys talking. But I suppose you believe him because it's convenient for you to do so, and you're one of them, after all." She crossed her arms and brooded for a while. He let her.

"She gets everything, you know," she said after a few minutes. Her voice was small and coming from somewhere far-away. "It isn't fair. She got Chester and she threw him over, just like that, like…she could have had Miles. He wanted her—and not just for sex—but she didn't want him. Or Cole either for that matter. She'll, no doubt, decide she doesn't want you, Mr. Brave Detective, if she hasn't already."

"What happened, Charlotte?"

"I would have taken any of them," she said. "But they didn't want me."

Holy Comfort

"What did you do, Charlotte? You can tell me."

"I didn't do anything, Detective Merton. You'll just have to keep looking, I guess."

"You paged Costello Thursdsay night from the church. You borrowed Griggs' car."

"So what? Everyone knew I was there Thursday night. What of it? And if I paged Miles, what of *that*?"

He stared at her. "You had a motive. They all—"

"Oh, please. So I slept around. So do lots of people, so do *you*." She brightened and her eyes focused. "I think I'd like to call Mr. Clyde Cullen right now. He'll send over an attorney, one well experienced in hand-holding. I deserve a hand to hold. I deserve that much."

Chapter Forty-Seven

She met him at the front door, swinging it open before he had a chance to knock. She slipped through it without looking at him. He followed her back down the front walk.

"The boys are finally in bed and I don't want to give them an excuse to get up," she said when she stopped. "It's a nice evening anyway, don't you think?"

She hadn't looked at him. Now she was sitting down on a step halfway to her driveway. He followed her, glancing once at the darkened second-story windows. He sat down next to her. She was wearing those faded jeans again and a pale pink sweater. Her hair hung down in straight shiny sheets just as it had the first time he saw her. He sighed and scratched his head. "We talked to Tony Spitz again. He opened up finally on the subject of the small group. You were right to be suspicious. Costello was a pimp. Charlotte got passed around. There were others."

She grunted softly in response. She laced her fingers together and contemplated them. The moon was nearly full and when he glanced sideways, he had a clear view of her profile which was upturned as if she could feel the moonlight on her skin and was enjoying its touch. Her eyes were closed and then they were open, staring at the dark street.

"We brought Charlotte in for questioning, but she denied everything," he said. "We couldn't hold her. She's got some attorney now that Clyde Cullen called in for her."

Page rested her chin on one hand. "Do you think she's the killer?" she asked. "I mean she's always worn her victimhood like a badge of honor, going to AL-ANON meetings for twenty years. She never seemed in any hurry to recover and get on with her life."

"So what turned her into an avenging angel, what pushed her over the edge?" asked Roy. He shook his head. "Miles Costello, I suppose. She'll tell us all about it someday. They all do."

Page appeared to reflect on that and said nothing for a while. She was intent again on her fingers and played with her rings. "And in the meantime?"

He turned and the moonglow was reflected in her hair. He cleared his throat. "We'll be careful," he said.

Holy Comfort

"There is something I wanted to tell you," she said. He leaned slightly in her direction in order to hear her. "Have you read the lectionary for next Friday by any chance?"

He exhaled loudly. "That's getting a bit ahead of ourselves, don't you think?"

She stood up abruptly to avoid his eyes. She turned her back to him and crossed her arms, pulling her sweater tightly around her in a now-familiar gesture.

He stood up also but did not approach her. "Tell me, Page. What did the scripture say?"

"Revelation 10:1-11," she said, pulling a piece of folded paper out of her jeans pocket. "Here." She handed him the paper over her shoulder.

Roy took the paper and walked with it over to the lamppost at the end of the walk by her driveway. He began to read aloud. "*Then I saw another mighty angel coming down from heaven. He was robed in a cloud, with a rainbow above his head; his face was like the sun, and his legs were like fiery pillars...*" He chuckled. "So? I'm afraid I don't get it."

"No. Only I would...Charlotte used those exact words to describe Chester to me. It was after Miles' funeral. She had been talking to him at the reception. He was going to call her about having lunch the following week. She was really excited—going on and on to me about how great he looked. I remember because I said something like 'That's a bit of an exaggeration, isn't it?'"

Roy studied the paper. "This could mean something else entirely...or nothing at all, Page."

"It could mean that Chester is next on her list." She took a step closer. "I couldn't believe it, you know, when I heard—from Charlotte—that Chester was in that small group. I had a really bad feeling, like I knew then that what I'd sometimes suspected was true—that it wasn't a real small group, it wasn't a Bible study group. They didn't *pray*...and I was right...*Chester was part of it.* He used Charlotte and now he's on her list."

"Page, you could be wrong."

"You know I'm not wrong," she said. "She went out of her way to throw it in my face that she knew more about Chester than I did. That he'd gone to St. John's, that he was in the small group. That he was calling her. You know...Page doesn't have him anymore, but I do."

"Just like she did with Brad Cole and Miles after he shrouded you?" asked Roy.

"I guess she did," said Page. "But it's not the same. They were never *mine* in the same way. I mean—"

"I know what you mean. In her mind, though..."

"God. *In her mind*...Chester's next, Detective." She turned away again. "You want to know the worst part?" she asked.

"What?" he said, staring at her narrow back, willing her to turn around.

Then she did turn around, still hugging herself, raising her peerless eyes. "The worst part is I almost didn't tell you. I actually thought about not telling you and waiting to see if she could do it. *God.* With Chester dead, my life would be...so simple." Page laughed and bent her head back. "I know that's terrible. I'm a terrible person."

"You told me, Page," he said. "You did the right thing. And now I have to do the right thing."

Page turned to him. His eyes were large and gray and unsmiling. "I already called Chester. I thought I'd warn him, you know. He told me to kiss his ass. He wasn't worried."

"Why the hell not? Tony Spitz is worried. Even Willis McHugh is worried. Why isn't Chester?"

"He said he isn't afraid of Charlotte, that he can take care of himself."

"He's an arrogant son of a bitch," said Roy. "Or maybe he *can* handle her."

She didn't respond, but turned away and sat down on a step.

"Does he frighten you, Page?" he asked as he folded up the piece of paper and put it in his jeans pocket.

"I'm not afraid of him."

"He was at Costello's funeral, wasn't he? Didn't you see him there? Is that what scared you?"

"No...I don't know. Charles said it was the presence of evil in the church."

Roy made fists of his hands and folded his arms. "I wouldn't want to contradict Charles, but the fact is Chester was there and then after Cole's funeral today he was there again, pushing you around..."

"I'm not afraid of him—not for me anyway. Sometimes I worry about Walter and Tal."

"Would he try to hurt them?"

"Oh, probably not—no. But I've seen him go right up to the edge of crazy and peer over the side. You don't forget that. The truth is he doesn't care enough to really do anything. He likes to threaten me about their custody, but what would he do with two little boys? It's much easier to let me take care of them and then harrass me about it. Sometimes I think he might hurt them to get back at me. But again, I don't think he ever cared enough about me to bother."

Merton, still standing, unfolded his arms and looked down the street.

"Have you ever been married, Roy?" she asked quietly.

He looked down at her and paused. "Yes," he finally replied.

"Divorced?" she asked.

He nodded. "It wasn't much of a marriage. In high school, my girlfriend got pregnant. We got married. She had a boy. We stayed together for a few years. Then I joined the Marines. She married a nice guy and they had three more kids. They raised Peter. They live near Owensville. After the

Holy Comfort

Marines, I came back, joined the county police department, took classes at the University at night."

"Did you see much of your son?"

"That's the only reason I moved back here."

"Oh," she said staring at her hands. "Why did you choose law enforcement?"

"I never liked bullies, I guess," he said stiffening. "Guys like Chester Hawthorne."

Page looked at his profile, but it was too dark to see his eyes.

The detective exhaled. "Today, after the funeral, I heard Chester tell you to promise not to see me again...that it was still his business if you were making a fool of yourself with a cop..." He paused, watching her, but she was looking at her hands again. "Earlier in the week he told Vesba and me that if Costello wanted to fuck his ex-wife, he was welcome to her. Two very different attitudes. Which one was genuine?"

"How lovely," said Page. She shrugged her shoulders wearily. "I don't know. He doesn't care, so fuck her. But he wants to control my business, so stop making a fool out of yourself, Page."

"No, I don't think so. He was acting the first go-round. I think the attitude yesterday was the real thing. Pure outrage that you might be seeing someone—*anyone*."

She was silent, refusing to look up.

"Page, did he confront you about Costello, about Brad Cole?" Still she would not look up, so he squatted in front of her, resting on the heels of his boots, and tried to search her face. "Did he threaten you? *Tell me*."

She raised her eyes. "No, he didn't, but I never went out with *them*."

His eyes remained on her face. "There *was* a difference then?"

"Yes," she whispered. "Today he was very angry. He hadn't even been drinking but he had that wild look in his eyes. It was like he didn't even know where he was anymore. Thank goodness for Demetrius."

"Yes. Thank goodness."

"What I don't know is how he knew in the first place."

"Charlotte started the rumor."

"*Charlotte*? But how did Charlotte know? I didn't tell her."

He stood up. "Charlotte follows people. She followed me. Who knows, she may have followed you. And Costello. She watches."

"But how did she get away with that without anyone noticing?"

"No one pays attention to her. She was written off as this loud-mouthed golddigger a long time ago. You did, I bet. You turned away."

"Yes. I suppose I did. Charles and Colin don't take her seriously. They put her in the same category with Diana and Gracie. You're right. They stopped paying attention."

"She's smart and she's manipulated everyone."

"Do you think Chester could be involved with her somehow? I mean involved beyond his having had sex with her? Maybe she thinks she's actually got a chance with him."

He leaned down and pulled her up. He caught her eye for a moment and dropped her hands. "I don't know." He smiled briefly at her. "We'll keep an eye on Chester. And you keep things locked up tight."

"Wait a minute," she said. "Wouldn't you like to come in for a drink? The boys are asleep by now."

"I would, but I'll take a raincheck."

"Why?" she said, taking a step closer.

"Why?" he repeated. He paused, forming an answer. "Let's just say it's time to hide my face among a crowd of stars."

She felt her skin flush, and she stepped forward again. "I like Yeats," she said. "I like you."

He reached down and pulled her right hand up to his lips and kissed her bruised wrist. He held it for a moment and she felt him exhale. He let go and started to turn away.

"You forgot your raincheck," she said, catching him up. She pulled his face down and kissed him. This time he closed his eyes and kissed her back. Then he put his arms around her and held her briefly before forcing himself to pull away. He said, "Goodnight," and stepped away. He looked up at the night sky. The moon was still there. It would be there tomorrow. There was comfort somewhere in that.

She turned and raced up the walk to her front door. She went inside, and the door closed. The lights went out. All was dark.

Holy Comfort

Chapter Forty-Eight

PAGE DID NOT remember sleeping. She had gone to bed thinking about Roy Merton, remembering the sad, doubting look in his eyes, feeling the touch of his lips. When she woke up it was very early; still dark and the streets perfectly quiet. She didn't know what had woken her up. Some smell? Smoke? She threw back the covers, jumped out of bed and pulled on her bathrobe over her pajama pants and tank top. She paused and listened. Silence. She crept into the hallway, one hand on the wall following the slight smell into the front hall and around the corner. She hesitated, seeing the tall figure sitting comfortably in front of her fireplace, his head enveloped by blue smoke, then walked into the room with all the confidence she could muster. "What are you doing here?" she asked carefully. "You have no business being here."

He looked up, unstartled, his dark eyes hooded. "I came to see you, Page." He snorted. "Do I really need a reason? I just want to talk."

"Put that cigarette out," she said pointing. "You scared me half to death. I don't want to talk now."

"Be nice, Page," he said, standing up and facing her. He stubbed out the cigarette obligingly on a saucer he had brought in from the kitchen. He looked her up and down and the corners of his mouth pulled back. "You never change, do you?"

Page forced herself to look at Chester. He wasn't drunk. He spoke precisely. He didn't stumble as he moved toward her, but there was definitely something wrong. He moved slowly as if through water. She pulled her robe together and tied it tightly at the waist.

"Where are the boys?" he asked, his dazed brown eyes almost black in his pale face. He was tanned, but his skin had a strange wrung-out quality. He had large dark circles under his eyes and his hair was ruffled.

"They're in bed, of course. It's four in the morning," she said glancing at the clock on the mantel. "What do you mean coming here in the middle of the night? How long have you been here?"

"Oh, not long. I just wanted to see my boys."

"Why?" she asked, genuinely alarmed now. "You're not scheduled for a visit for two weeks."

"I don't fucking care when I'm *scheduled* to see them. They're *my* boys. I want to see them now!" He shouted the last sentence. She winced and swallowed. She was in trouble now. Drunk or not, he was heading down that dark road, and she was in his way.

She looked bravely up into his face. "What's the matter, Chester? Why are you so upset?"

"Upset? Do I look upset?" he sneered. "Well, let's just say I don't appreciate being followed by the police and watched."

"Followed by the police? What are you talking about?"

"Please, Page. Don't play dumb with me. There's been a car outside my house ever since I got home."

She crossed her arms and tried to look relaxed. "I suppose they're trying to protect you."

"*Protect* me! But please explain to me, Page, what they are protecting me from?"

"From Charlotte Pentecost, like I told you. She killed Miles...and Brad. I was afraid you were next."

"Yes, yes, you explained all that in your sweet phone call. But did you share that theorey of yours with your new boyfriend?"

"I told Detective Merton what I thought. I suppose he ordered the—"

"When did you tell him?" He stepped closer.

"Tonight."

"*After* I told you not to see him again?" He was right up next to her now, towering over her. "Tell me, Page, how deep are you into it with that detective?" He put his hands on her shoulders and began to shake her. "Have you slept with him? Are the rumors true?"

"No," she screamed as she pushed against him with her forearms. "None of it's true."

He stopped shaking her, but he did not let go. "I didn't think so," he said mildly. His face softened a bit, but his fingers still dug into her arms. "Tony said your cop nearly went beserk when he suggested that you might be a lesbian," he said chuckling. "Now why do you think he would care so much what Tony said about you?"

Page mumbled something and gazed passed his shoulder at the oil painting over the mantel.

"Don't mumble, Page," he said catching her chin in his hand. "I can't hear you when you mumble. I'm not mumbling. You understand me, don't you?"

"I don't know, Chester," said Page turning away. "Why would the detective care?"

His fingers dug into her arms again. "Because he wants you and Tony's stupid comment insulted him."

Page rolled her eyes, and he slapped her hard across the face. She tried to pull away, but he held her with his other hand. "Don't you touch me, Chester," she said pulling harder. He let her go, and she fell onto the sofa. She stood up quickly and circled around the sofa, putting it between them.

He lit another cigarette and took a deep drag. He exhaled. "Why do you make me do that?" he asked waving his cigarette at her. "I was all set to be nice about this. I liked it that you called to warn me about Charlotte. It was almost like you cared again. But you shouldn't have put the police on my tail. That was wrong. All wrong. They had no business following me."

"That wasn't my idea."

"I know, Page, but you should have guessed. You used to be smarter than that."

Something metallic rumbled and Chester looked into the hallway. "What was that?"

"The furnace," said Page quickly. "Just the heat coming on."

"Oh," he said vaguely. He stubbed out his cigarette and headed for the hall. Page followed and he turned suddenly and caught her by the wrist. "You know, Page, I half expected to find your boyfriend here tonight. You are alone, aren't you?"

Before she could answer he turned again and pulled her into the hallway and then the bedroom. He scanned the empty room and her bed. "No," he said. "No action here." He shoved her forward onto the bed. "The way Charlotte made it sound you two couldn't make up your minds. Hot and cold, just like always, Page?"

She rolled onto her hip and looked at him. "Charlotte told you that? When did you become so chummy with Charlotte?"

Chester raised his eyebrows. "Didn't your boyfriend tell you?"

"Tell me what?"

"Tony spilled the beans about the small group. It's no secret anymore. The word is out. 'Priest Pimps for Prayer Group Elite'—to quote Willis McHugh. They'll have it on a billboard soon enough. Then it'll be bye-bye for your other boyfriend."

"What are you talking about, Chester?" said Page raising herself up on one elbow.

"Curtains," said Chester drawing his hand across his throat, "for the the Reverend Charles Pinkney. So sorry, really." He leaned down and pushed her back on the bed. "I told you I'd do it and as you know, I'm a man of my word."

"Chester, please," said Page, moving around him in order to sit up. "I'm not following."

He straightened and shrugged. "This is the first place the police will look, I suppose," he said turning halfway around.

Page licked her lips. "Why are the police looking for you? You're not making any sense, Chester."

"I am making perfect sense," he said, his voice rising. Then he paused as if to calm himself by counting. "And I didn't say the police are looking for me. Not yet anyway. They're a little slow that way—like you."

"Why *will* they be looking for you, Chester?"

He sighed. "When they find the body."

"Whose body?" she said calmly.

"Charlotte Pentecost's body," he said reaching inside his jacket. He pulled out a large, unfamiliar handgun and pointed it liesurely at Page. "Shot dead with this."

"Charlotte's dead?" she whispered, keeping her focus on his eyes and not the gun.

"Dead as the proverbial doornail." He smiled. "It was self-defense, killing Charlotte, pure and simple. I was next on her list—you said so yourself."

Page stared at him as her mind struggled to make sense of the conversation. "She thought you were going to marry her, didn't she? That you'd start a new family with her—"

"She thought what she wanted to think. I let her. That's no crime." He looked at Page fondly. He reached down with his left hand and grabbed her by the lapels of her robe and pulled her up. "I want a drink." He pushed her into the hallway and back to the kitchen where he waved the gun at her. "Come on, get me a drink. You must stock something for that cowboy."

"I have a bottle of sherry, that's all," she said, opening a cabinet.

"That'll have to do, then," he said, laying the gun on the island and leaning on his elbows. He ran his fingers through his already ruffled hair and yawned. "I can't picture that Marlboro Man drinking sherry. Don't you stock some Rolling Rock for him, Page?"

She poured the drink and handed it to him. "No," she said.

"But he has been over here." Chester tipped his head back and gulped the sherry. He pushed the glass toward Page. "Charlotte told me all about your big date. Dinner and dancing. He must have spent a pretty penny on you, Page. Don't tell me he didn't expect something in return."

She passed him his refill. "Chester, tell me, *who* killed Miles and Brad?"

Chester's eyebrows jumped and he smiled with mock abashment. He took a large swallow and then placed his hands on his chest. "Oh, I did, of course. Charlotte didn't do anything—except make herself look like a suspect."

"But Charlotte had a motive...and the calls she made to the pager and the car—"

"Oh, I know, Page. Costello was supposed to meet her Thursday night. They had a standing date. She even borrowed that drunk's car to get there. But he never showed. Just a lucky coincidence for me."

"I'm not sure I believe you. What reason could you possibly have for killing him?"

"You should understand, Page," Chester said with a great show of sincerity. "I was doing God's will."

"God's will?" she said.

"Yes. It came to me in that small group. It was written out as plain as day in Daniel, even those morons should have seen it. 'He shall come in

Holy Comfort

without warning,' it said, 'and obtain the kingdom by flatteries,' on and on. It said those who know their God shall stand firm and take action. Well, I was the only one with balls enough to take action. It was for the good of old Holy Comforter...for you, Page."

He shook another cigarette out of the pack and reached for it with his lips. He lit it and inhaled. "I mean, what's the point of reading the Bible if you're not going to take its direction when it's crystal clear like that? Those other men were such losers, looking for 'meaning.' They couldn't see it, the idiots, but I could. They wanted to take your typical ass-backward, round-about CEO way, but I saw The Way. Quick and easy."

"You're losing me, Chester. You went after Miles, why?"

"I never went after Miles," he said, finishing his sherry and handing her the glass to refill.

"But you just said—"

He sighed. "I killed Costello because he was a pig who needed killing. He was into everything and everybody. Even Martha Van Patton, Wesley's *mother*, for god's sake. She wouldn't listen to me. No. She thought she *knew* him...but she didn't, of course. He just told her what she wanted to hear—that she was beautiful and glamorous. Disgusting. It was the same with her friends. He knew what to say to get what he wanted. He even wanted to join the club, if you can believe that. But he went too far when he thought he could have you, as if he was as good as me, *my equal*!"

"What about Brad? He was your friend."

"Don't be dramatic. He wasn't my friend. He was about to figure out that it wasn't Charlotte after all. He would have blabbed. He was distraught. I put him out of his misery. They were both just a means to an end, anyway." He smiled, and remembering the gun, picked it up and waved it carelessly at her. "The gun belongs to Charlotte. She had it for *protection*."

"A means to what end, Chester? If you weren't after Miles, who were you after?"

"Don't you get it?" he said, raising his glass in an imaginary toast. "I said I'd torpedo Pinkney and I did. Now he's dead in the water. His career is over. He'll never work again."

Page winced and backed up to the drawer by the sink. She took a deep breath to quiet her pounding heart. "What did he ever do to you, but try to help?"

"Try to *help*," repeated Chester. "Try to help? Jesus Christ, he destroyed my life."

"*He* did," said Page.

"Yes, *he* did. He told you to get a divorce. He talked Newcomb into taking the case. He screwed me start to finish after he screwed my wife. He took everything I had and then threw it away."

"Where did you ever...who told you that?"

"Charlotte told me about you and Pinkney. She said you—"

"It's all a lie, a viscious lie!" she blurted. "Why in the world would you believe her?"

"Why wouldn't I? What did she have to gain by lying?"

"You," she said. "She had you to gain. She'd say anything to get you."

"Oh, come now," said Chester tapping the counter with his empty glass. "She was a *whore*. She never expected anything, not really."

"Oh no? Why did you go to Charlotte's tonight?" asked Page as she poured another drink.

"As a matter of fact, after you called me, I thought I better check on old Charlotte and make sure she was holding up all right...and have a farewell fuck as it turned out. Charlotte was okay in the sack—she'd do anything, very obliging—not like you at all. She was very supportive."

"And what happened?" asked Page. "What changed?"

He sighed and looked down at the gun in his hands. "Tonight she wanted me to promise her the moon, to sign on for the duration. She said if we were married, we couldn't testify against each other. She had a million reasons. Well, I told her to forget it, and she freaked out, screaming all sorts of bullshit, making a scene. I had to shut her up. I hate scenes. I don't want a scene now, Page."

"I've never been a big fan of scenes myself, Chester. You know that," she said evenly. "But you've run out of time. Detective Merton suspects that you were having a relationship with Charlotte. *He knows you're in this*. Why do you think he was having you watched? They must know you're here now."

"He knows nothing and they know even less." Chester's eyes were very large. He was very close now. The hand that did not hold the gun came up and caught her hair, pulling her head back. "I never deserved any of what happened to me. But now I'm going to give you what you deserve."

"Merton's figured everything out."

He twisted her hair and pulled her away from the drawer, pushing her against the island. "Bullshit."

"Go now, Chester, while you still can..."

"I've had enough bullshit," he said, leaning against her. Their eyes met and she thought she saw something behind the anger, some weakness, but he glanced away and pushed her out of the kitchen into the hall.

She hit the wall by the stairs and turned to face him. "Tell me, Chester. When did you get the idea to tie the murders to the lectionary?"

He gripped her by the wrist which was wedged between them. The gun he aimed casually at her throat. "Oh, you liked that? I thought you might." His breath was hot on her neck. "It was so easy, you know. Really, the whole thing. I knew that scripture would send them running in the opposite direction of me. No one would ever accuse me of being a Bible scholar. But they might think Pinkney...they might even think *you*. Or Charlotte, as it turned out...anyone but me."

216

Holy Comfort

His lips grazed her neck and she turned sideways sharply, throwing her back into his chest as hard as she could. She grabbed for the hand holding the gun, but he held tight to her wrist, yanking her left arm around behind her. As they struggled, he twisted it hard in an upward thrust. She screamed and went down on her knees. Suddenly, he dropped on top of her, pressing her to the floor, her twisted arm in between them.

"Get off of my mother!" shrieked Walter from the stairs. "I'll hit you again!" He grimaced and posed menacingly while brandishing a lacrosse stick above his head.

"You little bastard," growled Chester as he lifted himself with difficulty off Page. He put his free hand to his head, which was bleeding, and lurched to the front door where he turned towards his son on the stairs. He lifted the gun. "I'm your father, for God's sake."

"So what? I'm not afraid of you. Am I supposed to be afraid of you? Mom's not afraid of you. You're just a big dick-head."

"You can't talk to me like that," Chester whispered, his face red and mottled as he began to breathe in asthmatic gulps. He continued to aim the gun at his son. "See how you turned them against me, Page? This is your goddamn fault. I don't deserve this."

Page pushed herself up with her good arm into a sitting position. She couldn't stop a whimper from escaping as she dragged herself up on one knee. "Chester, don't," she said.

"Go on, Mom," said Walter who was flipping his stick aggressively. "Get out of here."

"I'm your goddam *father*!" said Chester.

"Go back upstairs please, Walter," said Page.

Chester blinked repeatedly as if it hurt him to look at his son. "Where did you get the goddam lacrosse stick anyway? I never said you could play goddam lacrosse—"

"Go back upstairs, Walter," repeated his mother.

A voice behind her said, "Do what your mother says, Walter."

"Jesus, it's the goddam calvary," said Chester as his son stepped backwards up the stairs.

"Put the gun down, Chester," said the voice behind Page. "It's over now."

"The Lord protects the simplehearted," said Page.

Chester made a noise with his tongue. "You've always got some bullshit handy, don't you, Page? That's from today's lectionary, isn't it? But, unfortunately, not entirely appropriate. You may be in great need, but no one's going to save you. This time there's no priest, no goddam janitor. The detective knows this. You should see the worried look on his face." He wiped his forehead with his gun hand. "Well, I'm done with that bullshit. It's served its purpose, but like our friend the detective says, it's over now."

"Put the gun down now, Chester," repeated the voice from behind Page.

Chester turned from the stairs and aimed the gun at the voice. "You can try to make me," he said.

"Fine," said another, shriller voice coming from the living room. "Make it easy for us."

"Make it easy?" said Chester. He looked at Page. He lowered the gun at her and fired.

Another gun went off and Chester crumpled. The child at the top of the stairs screamed. A pair of gentle hands took hold of Page and lifted her upper body off the floor. A familiar voice said, "Get an ambulance." Then the gentle hands smoothed her hair and the voice murmured something she couldn't understand.

"Mom," said Walter.

"Walter," said another voice. It sounded far away and muffled.

"They're safe," the familiar voice said. The hands still held her. There was pressure on her chest. "Don't worry."

"Run, Walter," she said. Then she sank and heard nothing more.

Holy Comfort

Chapter Forty-Nine

THIS ROOM WAS square and white with a slight greenish tinge. The light was soft in the late afternoon, slanting through a single window. She looked in its direction. The view was all gray sky.

Lyle Lovett sat in a chair by her bed and played softly on a guitar. His long denim legs were crossed and he leaned forward slightly, singing sweetly with his eyes closed. *Some questions beg for an answer/ Like a poet begs for a rhyme/ Somehow all I can remember/ Is holding your hand in mine.* He sang patiently hour following hour and on through the night, his wistful scarecrow's face in shadow. She heard every word of every song. Once he was interrupted and he left the room quietly on Texas boots while Patty Loveless, dressed in a white uniform, came in to ask Page kindly in a soft mountain drawl how she was feeling. She held her wrist in her cool hand and consulted her watch. She smoothed her hair and murmured something. After a while, Patty left and Lyle returned. He picked up his guitar and began to sing again, bathed in moonlight.

The sun woke her up and she opened her eyes. The room was less greenish and whiter. She blinked.

"You're not Lyle Lovett," Page said.

"No," said Roy Merton. "Were you expecting Lyle Lovett?"

"Well, sort of. He's been here for days playing and singing."

"I reckon you've been dreaming, ma'am."

"I reckon."

"I hope you're not disappointed."

"No," she said. "I'm glad to see you." Page allowed her right hand, which had been resting on her abdomen, to relax at her side, palm up, as if she wanted him to take it.

Roy stood up and walked to the side of her bed and took her hand. Then he sat down very carefully on the edge of the bed. "Is this okay?"

"Yes. Please...help me to sit up. Is there a button somewhere?" she asked, craning her neck and wincing with the effort.

They looked around together and finally Roy found the button and pushed it. The bed under her upper body rose forty-five degrees and she relaxed and closed her eyes for a moment. He looked at her small hand in his own and sighed deeply, causing her eyes to flicker open. She smiled and he smiled back.

She looked at her hand. "How am I, anyway? I guess I'll pull through?"

"Yes, you'll pull through, all right. You took a slug in the shoulder." He pointed with his free hand to her bandaged left shoulder. "And you have a broken arm. Does it hurt?"

"No. A little. I feel pretty woozy."

"The doctor says you'll be fine."

She smiled. "As good as new?"

"As good as new."

"Where are the boys?" she asked, reminded suddenly of their existence.

"They're with the Pinkneys. They've been there since last night."

"Last night," she said, trying to remember such a long time ago. "How did you know to come?"

"The surveillance team called me when Chester left his house. Tal called my cell phone, too, but I was almost there at that point."

"How did he do that?"

He smiled a sweet, wistful smile she did not remember. "This you may not believe. Walter woke up and heard you and Chester arguing. He knew it was serious, so he woke up Tal and lowered him by rope down the laundry chute to the basement."

She laughed and then cringed because it hurt. "They've been practicing that since we moved to our house. I grounded them for a week the first time I caught them."

"Walter told him to call me from the basement phone."

"How did he know the number?"

"Walter had seen it on my card on the bulletin board."

"He has a photographic memory like his father." Her eyes clouded over and darkened and she looked away.

He squeezed her hand. "He wrote the number down for Tal. He told Tal to unlock the door from the basement to the garage and then go out the side door to the driveway and wait. I came up through the basement."

"And Walter waited upstairs?"

"With a lacrosse stick. He'd filled his pockets with rocks."

"Is Chester dead?"

He nodded. "Leona shot him."

"Do they know about their father?"

"I don't know," he said shaking his head. "I've been here."

"*You've been here?*"

"Yes," he said matter-of-factly. "Where else would I be?"

"Roy," she said. She lifted her hand out of his and pointed to his bloody shirt. "Were you hurt?"

"No," he said, taking her hand back. "That's your blood."

Holy Comfort

She looked away at the window. "Did you know that Charlotte Pentecost is dead?"

He nodded. "Shot in the back at close range. We were wrong about Charlotte."

"It was all Chester all along. I think she knew he was doing it. She didn't try to stop him. He said he killed Miles because it was God's will."

"The quote from Daniel?" She nodded. "I knew that would figure in this somehow," he said.

"It had nothing to do with God's will. Daniel just gave him an idea. He killed Miles as a way to get to Charles. He was his real target. Chester blamed him for ruining our marriage. He thought we'd had an affair."

His gaze did not falter. "I made the same mistake."

"He wanted to make Charles suffer."

"So he killed Costello to humiliate Charles? And Brad Cole?"

"Brad was figuring things out. Two murders would do double harm to Charles. He killed Charlotte because she was trying to tie him down. I'm not sure why he came to my house after shooting her. I guess to kill me."

"I think he was going to kill himself, but as it turned out, he got Leona to do it for him."

She relaxed into her pillow and gazed at the detective with half-opened eyes. "I'm glad it wasn't you."

He put her hand to his lips and kissed it, then pressed it to his cheek, closing his eyes. A few minutes passed. He opened his eyes. She had fallen asleep. He put her hand down and stood up. Then he turned and walked out of the room.

Chapter Fifty

"Do you ever have doubts?" asked George Fontaine. He did not look at the other man when he asked the question.

"No," said Willis McHugh without inflection.

"Attendance on Sunday was way down—half what it is usually. There was no one at church."

"That's bullshit. *We* were there."

"You know what I mean."

"You know what *I* mean."

"If all those people actually transfer out, our pledge total will be cut in half."

"And a few of us will write a few checks to make up the difference. Big deal, George. We'll ride this out. Pinkney was nothing."

The two were silent for a while as they sat in George Fontaine's Mercedes and contemplated the stone church across the street. It was not an extraordinary church to look at. You could find plenty of similar structures throughout the country and across England. But the Episcopal Church of the Holy Comforter, sitting placidly on clipped lawns like a weathered garden ornament for eighty-five years, had always maintained its perfect decorum through good and bad years. It had stood sentinel on this wedge of pie-shaped land through many a storm and crisis. It was no cathedral; it boasted no towering spire, signaling its presence for miles around, trumpeting its importance. On the contrary, it was low and dark and fortress-like.

Willis McHugh looked at its battlements and smiled. "I was brought up to believe that the surface must always be kept pleasant. I believe that still. There's a certain comfort in that, don't you think?"

"Yes, Willis," agreed Fontaine. He turned on the ignition and shifted the car into drive.

Born out West, C.R. Compton has lived most of her life in book-filled houses in St. Louis, Missouri (with a few years spent back East in college and graduate school.) Writing stories since the third grade, she is an inveterate day-dreamer, agreeing whole-heartedly with writer Lew Wallace who maintained that "life is dreaming."

A graduate of Smith College, with a M.A. in history from the College of William and Mary, she has worked in Christian publishing, as an advertising copy chief and as the Communications Director of a large Episcopal Church. She currently works at Washington University. When not writing, she spends as much time as possible with her husband and three talented children.

Her hobbies include reading, pulling weeds, looking for old stuff on eBay, and watching movies. In answer to the question "If heaven exists, what would you like to hear God say when you arrive at the pearly gates?" she would have to reply, "Welcome, Pilgrim. Here's John Wayne to show you to your room."

Printed in the United States
50611LVS00003B/178-276